Tony Jones
smokeout@comcast.net
339-3202

Operation Smokeout

Operation Smokeout

Anthony P. Jones

Allen Publishing Company

Allen Publishing Company
P.O. Box 9759
Richmond, Virginia 23228

Library of Congress Cataloging-in-Publication Data
Jones, Anthony P., 1958-
Operation Smokeout / Anthony P. Jones.
p. cm.
ISBN 0-88053-951-8
1. Journalists—Fiction. 2. Washington > (D.C.)—Fiction. I. Title.

PS3610.O585O64 2005
813'.6—dc22
                        2005015938

Manufactured in the United States of America

For Mom, Sylvia, Sara Ann and Bill…my torch bearers.

This is the most important part of any book, because without these people there would be no story to read. I hope to include as many names as possible, but undoubtedly there are some names that I will miss. Please forgive me ahead of time.

I would first like to thank God for granting me the gift of a vivid, overactive imagination and for making me wait before sharing the story. To my mother, Edith D. Jones, who insisted I write this story and who never got to read one word of it. To my wife, Sylvia and kids, Nick, Morgan, Alex and Cassidy, who put up with my stressful tirades when I was questioning whether this book would ever happen. To my Dad, George F. Jones, he may not have understood my drive to get this done in spite of everything else, but he never passed judgment. Very special thanks to Bill Cox who patiently reassured me and made sure that I interacted with the right people so that success is possible. To Frank Underwood, you believed from the beginning. To Henry Rhone, who got the educational ball in motion. To Marita Golden, who began my formal education at Virginia Commonwealth University and who introduced me to the Hurston/Wright Foundation— now I can make a difference. To the James River Writers who made sure I had a "never say die" approach to writing and the intricacies of publishing.

Now for the second wave— you guys put the meat on the bones. No matter how good the imagination, a book would be ordinary without information. To the science department at Xavier University of Louisiana who taught me to research; it really does apply to everything. To all the writing instructors at the University of Virginia, who made me write everything one more time. To Che Che and Cynthia, you guys wouldn't say anything but you made sure I looked at the news and read the papers. To Mike, Marty, Frank, Kashawn and Tiger— you guys are some of this country's loyal and knowledgeable military muscle. To Ryan and Chris, who I turned to for information about the SEALs, at such a young age, your knowledge is overwhelming. To Kevin and Jerry Gaughran, who are both serving this country protecting others— I would have been lost without your input. To Alexis Herman, fellow Xavierite, Lori Perine and Jerry Gaughran who made sure I got to see the White House and helped to remove barriers in order to maintain some sibilance of accuracy within its walls. To Mathew who used to manage the Capitol Grill— thanks for the personal touch. To the many federal workers at places like the Lincoln Memorial, the National Medical Library and the seven foot linebacker-looking guard walking the bomb-sniffing bear (dog) in front of the White House, who all met my question with a question of their own— "why do you want to know?" I think the "bear" was trained to lick his lips during the stone cold silence as I waited for an answer. All of you guys, after my explanation, helped me keep it real. To Dr. Clarence Scranage, a good friend, doctor and among other things, local ME; thanks for making sure I eliminated people correctly. To Hilda Jones, Rob Buchanan and all the guys at Old Virginia Tobacco Company, Jim, David, Ned, Bob, Wren and Russ, who kept me supplied with cigars, especially when the funds were low, you guys are invaluable. To all the guys that regularly met for cigars at OVTC, you guys are my second family— if a writer can't find a story in a place like that he should choose a new line of work, the "bull" there is thicker there than the smoke when the fan is broken. To Dr. Kay Clanton, DeWayne Wickham, Auturo Sandoval, Tim Reid, Carlos Fuente, George Welsh and his family and to everyone I've interviewed concerning Cuba— your knowledge and experiences added flavor to the story. To Janie Tisdale and Frank Brogdon, who over the past ten years have read this story probably more than they care to. To Jennifer N. Cislo from Merriam-Webster, who found just the right word for the flap when I was totally stuck. Anyone not signed up for their on-line "word a day," should take a moment to do so, especially writers.

Now for the third and final wave— the industry folks who make things happen. To John Emory of Macoy Publishing, who was willing to take a chance on a new writer.

Back when David Baldacci came to Richmond to sign copies of *Absolute Power* he had the misfortune of having me to himself for nearly an hour and a half— I bugged that man to death and he still allowed me to stay in touch. He is a perfect example of what new writers hope to become. To Walter Mosley, who always treats me like and old friend the few times we have been together— I have learned a lot from Walter and David, you guys are always kind to the people around you. To Dave Robbins, fellow author and founder of the James River Writers Festival— I almost didn't come to the first annual festival, it would have been a mistake, it proved to be the glue I needed to pull everything in the right direction. To Dennis Danvers, one hell of a good writer, educator and friend— you're way too underrated. You understood the frustrations I felt along this path. To Michelle Bowen, fellow author and friend— you constantly reminded me to keep faith in His plan and things would come together. To Tim and Daphne Reid, who were a source of inspiration, and friendship— you guys really know what the struggle is all about. To Blair Underwood, Wynton Marsalis, Anna Marie Horsford, Michael Beach and Gregory Hines (God, I miss his talent) you guys let me subject you to copies of the manuscript early on and your feedback and encouragement kept the fire burning. To Ken Nolan, one hell of a great screenwriter, who has consistently subjected himself to my relentless e-mails— I can only hope that we get to work together one day. To George "Gar" Roberts, everyone should have a friend like you. To George Folsey, Jr., who probably wondered, "what did Gar get me into?" Your words of encouragement helped keep me on track. To Rita, Lorilyn, Henry, Janice and Jim, my readers— I could not have done it without your input. To Marilyn Wallace, my first editor— you're the best! You got the story on the right track. To Rob Isaacs, my agent, friend, and editor— you're destined to be one of the great ones. To Bill Craighead, life-long friend and web designer extraordinaire, you have helped me spread the word. To Lee Breauer, friend and fantastic photographer, you've made the years look kind. To Scott Sherman, who is responsible for such a fabulous cover. To Debra Williams and Sharon McCreary, you guys make the rubber hit the road and can make a lead penny shine like gold. To Jamie Fueglein, who came on board a week before we went to print; you did your best to correct the inaccuracies of a neophyte. You worked wonders with in such a limited time. Lastly, but most importantly, to each of you who were willing to spend your hard-earned cash to purchase a copy of this book; without you, this would have been an untold story.

"[Political reform] is the pretext that they use, and for many years they have used many different pretexts. At one time when we were in Africa, they used to say if the Cubans withdrew from Africa, then the relations would improve. That pretext was left behind. Later they said that when the links with the Soviet Union were cut off, then our relations would begin with the United States. Now the Soviet Union is not supporting us anymore, and nothing has changed. They keep on moving the goalposts back. Before it was Latin America subversion, the situation in Central America...and when they talk about reforms in Cuba, it is a precondition that we cannot accept because it has to do with independence and the sovereignty of our nation. It would be like if we were to give a precondition to the United States that it must change something in the Constitution in order for us to open up relations again. That's absurd."

-Fidel Castro;
Cigar Aficionado Magazine,
Summer 1994

Prologue

Schaffer O'Grady sat a bottle of Hendry Block 8 Cabernet Sauvignon on the counter and looked around for whoever was on duty.

Waiting for the clerk to arrive, he flipped through several of the photographs he'd taken of scantily clad prostitutes. Without moving an eye, he realized a presence. "If this were my old job," he said, "I'd have to run you in for sticking your nose where it doesn't belong."

"Whatever." Dismissing Schaffer with a flip of her hand, she walked behind the counter. "It's been three years and you still haven't stopped talking about that job. Maybe you should go back."

"No way. That job wouldn't allow me to come in here and get wine before going to work." Schaffer tapped the pictures against the counter to straighten them out and placed them under his arm.

"From the looks of those," she said, pointing at the photos, "work is the last thing you have on your mind. God help me, I can't understand why a man who looks as good as you would waste a forty dollar bottle of wine on women like that."

"Who says they're incapable of appreciating fine wine? You should stop being such a hard ass, Shelia." He held one of the pictures in front of her face. "Look at this girl, she's just what I'm looking for — tentative, fearful, and apprehensive. You can tell she's new to the streets. She'd be willing to take my money, and thank me for sparing her from having to bob her head up and down in some man's crotch, or bounce with him in the back seat of his car."

Sheila grasped the bottle of wine by the neck and waved it as if she planned to smash Schaffer over the head. "I always knew you were a kinky SOB."

Schaffer sucked in air, making a sizzling sound. ""Baby, I'm so freaky I hope I can save any one of these women from their destiny."

Sheila smiled and slid the wine into a bag. "How does a guy who's been shot at, been shot up, and seen some of the crap you've seen still have room for idealism?"

"S & M," Schaffer said, and instinctively rubbed the spot on his back where the bullet entered three years earlier. "That was the job at the time."

"Yeah, and you've never stopped talking about it."

"It's okay. I get to live vicariously through others. That's enough for me."

Sheila slid the bag toward him. "Is it really?"

Schaffer lifted the bag and cradled it like a newborn. "Fourteenth Street is waiting. I have a lot of hookers to interview to get this story finished. If they're not too busy, I should be able to complete the interviews by tonight."

"Good luck, honey. Remember, don't go wasting that wine on those girls."

He held the bag in the air. "I may have a swig or two with them. The rest I'll drink when I log the story on the computer."

¤¤¤¤

Schaffer sipped wine as he waited for the computer to display his e-mails. There was only one new message, from a longtime friend and former Recon commando, Tito Valencia. Tito's exit from the Marine Corps led him on a different path from Schaffer, straight to the CIA. The two of them often shared their exploits serving in different areas of government service. Although Schaffer had left the Secret Service, Tito still filled him in on the excitement in his life as directed by the CIA.

Schaffer knew that some may have considered their exchange questionable, but once someone reached a clearance level as high as his, he was never really out of service.

Reading Tito's message, Schaffer already couldn't wait for a follow-up:

> I am on my way to Cuba. It seems Castro has been sitting on a goldmine and is none the wiser. Our four man team is posing as a group investigating plausible ways to end the embargo. I'll be in touch soon.
> Tito

¤¤¤¤

Tito and his team had completed their dive of the ocean floor just off the coast of Havana. They huddled in the hotel suite, logging their findings with CIA headquarters. Tito used a military encryption garnered from his days in his Recon unit just in case his message was intercepted.

A forceful knock at the door threatened to dislodge it from the hinges, quickly followed by threatening shouts in Spanish. Before any of the team could respond, the Cuban military burst through the jamb, dislodging the wooden frame and thrusting their AK-47s towards the men in the room, halting all activity.

Tito looked up from the computer, but his fingers never stopped moving across the keys. The encrypted message disappeared from the screen, replaced by a blank e-mail screen.

The Cuban soldiers tossed the four men to the floor and continued shouting in Spanish.

Tito recently installed a Red Dragon talk-type program on his computer and Schaffer's e-mail address was the only one he'd set up. He spoke quickly: "Schaffer O, at *Washington Post* dot com enter. Diplomatic mission, enter. Here on diplomatic mission for United States government period. Why are you barging in our room waving guns yelling about spies period. It's a setup, if you don't find us, we're dead, send."

One of the Cuban soldiers noticed the computer. "Sir," he shouted in Spanish, "the machine is typing something out, in English."

The soldier leading the group spun, training his gun on Tito. In Spanish he shouted, "Turn it off! Unplug it! Stop the damned thing. He may be trying to send a message."

The underling yanked the cord from the wall, but the battery power kept it running. The soldier standing over the computer smashed the butt of his gun into the laptop, shutting it down forever.

The leader pressed his gun barrel into Tito's neck. "What were you doing just now? Sending a call for help?"

Tito took care not to move. "No," he responded. "I was saying to you that we are here on a diplomatic mission on behalf of the United States government. The treatment we're receiving isn't going to help your president get a treaty signed." Tito hoped the program had functioned properly, that the message had transmitted. He hoped Schaffer would rally the necessary help. A moment of panic overcame Tito. Had he correctly entered the bypass code? If he hadn't, the message would first pass through the computers at Langley and be 'cleaned' before reaching its destination. There was no telling what Schaffer would know if that happened.

The leader of the Cuban soldiers swung his gun, crashing the butt against Tito's head. His world went dark.

Chapter
1

Schaffer O'Grady left his house to complete research for his latest column for the paper.

A reporter for the *Washington Post* since leaving the Secret Service three years earlier, everyone from his hometown of Kenbridge, Virginia expected him to go to law school, since that was the only thing he ever talked about growing up. He wanted to save the world by affecting the laws that governed the land. Journalism had never entered his mind.

Darkness began to overtake what was left of a busy day. The cooling air chilled him. Spring fever was returning to peoples' faces day by day, as the sun managed to extend its stay in the western sky. March ides began to roll in, bringing with them warmer temperatures, gradually longer days, and the promise of new life.

This evening, however, the winds were restless. They danced across the Potomac River, moaning in a low tone when they whipped into the center of the city. The ides' prophecy of change proved true, especially at 1600 Pennsylvania Avenue, where conversation always stirred, just like the winds outside tonight.

Schaffer took an unusual route to Fourteenth Street tonight. He left Georgetown on M Street, jumped on G.W. Circle and ended up on Constitution Avenue. He often enjoyed taking different routes to his assignments, but he couldn't explain what made him want to circle the White House tonight. Through the trees, Schaffer noticed the lights on in the Oval Office. Even though the day was winding down for most people, President Nicholas was still hard at work.

An untrained eye would never have noticed the eight Secret Servicemen discreetly perched on top of the White House, watching the grounds, the streets, watching the sun duck beneath the horizon. Schaffer knew persistent terrorists' threats made their presence necessary, and watched as they slipped on jackets and ski masks to shield them from the cool night air.

During his mandatory four year military career, to earn his free college education, Schaffer had served with pleasure under General Alexander Nicholas. The Three Star General once paid an unannounced visit to Korea's demilitarized zone, where Schaffer served as a Recon officer. General Nicholas had barely stepped from his jeep when Schaffer saw a flash from the scope of a sniper's rifle. Seconds before the trigger collapsed to its firing position, Schaffer had tackled him.

After his initial shock, having watched the windshield of his jeep disintegrate, General Nicholas awarded Schaffer a battlefield promotion and a place by his side for the duration of his service. Alex, the only thing the general allowed Schaffer to call him, became the driving force behind Schaffer's decision to join the Secret Service. Ten years later, when Alex became Presidential Candidate Nicholas, Schaffer was not surprised that the general requested to have Schaffer as one of the Secret Service agents guarding him. The two men had remained fast friends over the years. Schaffer supported Alex, and felt proud to serve him once again.

With only one month to go before the election, Schaffer once again found himself tackling Alex to save him from an oncoming bullet, a bullet that this time struck not its intended victim, but Schaffer. The bullet lodged against his spine, and doctors concluded he would never walk again.

Schaffer's spirit sank lower than he could ever remember until befriended by a nurse who encouraged him to pray and to journal his thoughts about the event. Nina DeApuzzo, named for jazz singer Nina Simone, seemed to be an outwardly battle hardened nurse, but who possessed a soul of a saint. She bought him his first journal and submitted his writings for publication to her husband Joe, an editor at the *Washington Post*.

Schaffer smiled, thinking how hard Joe had worked to convince him to join the *Post*. Schaffer allowed his writing to be published, and was rewarded with tons of encouraging fan mail. After taking those first steps, Schaffer never looked back on his former life as a Secret Service agent. Joe's words rang true. *It's not as dangerous as stepping in front of bullets and the pay is better*. Receiving a Pulitzer for his first story about the ordeal sealed his decision.

A cool breeze shook Schaffer from his reverie. He took one last look at the men pacing the top of the White House, and eased the car forward towards his assignment.

¤¤¤¤

Just below the Secret Servicemen, in the Oval Office, President Alexander Nicholas held a private meeting with Secretary of State Ian Mackenzie and Chief of Staff Harold Cosby. Thirty minutes earlier, a liaison to Cuba's President Castro had called and informed the White House that they were holding four men suspected of being spies for the United States. Harold had taken the call and had confirmed the identities of the men. They were indeed members of the CIA posing as businessmen on a fact-finding mission for the president.

The message Cosby reread from Castro was short and to the point. "We have your spies. They will be tried and executed for the entire world to see. Cuba will not stand by and let the United States try to destroy our government."

President Nicholas nodded. "And what do you perceive the mood in Cuba to be?"

"Well, sir," Cosby explained, "they desperately need our help, but are unable to sidestep pride to ask for it. Taking our men was their way of crying out for aid."

Secretary Mackenzie waited impatiently for the Chief of Staff to finish speaking. At his first opportunity, he jumped in, blocking immediate discourse from Harold. "It's clear what we must do. Mr. President, we have got to hit these bastards with all our force and get our men out!"

"No." Cosby snapped to his feet. "We must attempt to negotiate with Castro first. Only if negotiations fail can we consider going in. Remember, those men weren't even supposed to be there in the first place, at least not in a secret capacity."

Mackenzie returned fire: "There is no need for negotiations. We simply can't do business with dictators, especially Castro!"

Cosby turned away from him, and looked at the president. "What about China, Mr. President? We've had great success there. Their record on human rights surely isn't any better." Cosby folded his arms in defiance and waited for Mackenzie's response.

Mackenzie jammed his finger in Cosby's direction. "You don't know what you're talking about, Harold. These are two completely different situations. China has things to offer in return for our support."

"Then why don't you call China and ask them to have Castro send our men home?"

President Nicholas listened to both sides as best he could, but soon lost patience. "Gentlemen," he said, "that's enough! I asked you both here because you are my trusted friends and I deeply value your opinions and insights. My greatest concern is to free our boys, not debate Cuba's credibility. I can see right now we're not going to make any progress."

Cosby and Mackenzie gave the president's statement little attention and returned to their argument.

The president watched the veins rise on their foreheads, their necks swell. He puffed his Opus X and threw up his hands in frustration. He'd always welcomed strenuous debate among his cabinet members, but this one was going nowhere fast.

Cosby pounded both fists in the air. "You can't just invade a country without giving the American people a good reason. We haven't even tried talks yet! Not to mention, how are you going to explain why our men were in Cuba in the first place?"

"They are soldiers, Harold, and just like all the other men I send out, death is part of their jobs."

"That's your problem, Ian. You place no value on human life. We have to start with talks!"

Mackenzie sat near the president's desk. "We don't have to ask permission from anyone to go in, surely not the fucking Communists. We can't alert the Commies that we're coming to get our men by telling the people of the U.S. that they're there. If we do that, then we'll really have a mess on our hands. We have to keep this mission quiet." He came to his feet, poking his finger again. "While we're in Cuba we should kill two birds with one stone, and get rid of Castro. It's past time for that bastard to go!"

"Forget it, Ian! I'm not going to stay here and listen to your McCarthyism!" Cosby turned and started to leave.

President Nicholas slammed his hands on his desk. "Alright, that's it!" He puffed on the cigar, hoping it would help him calm down. "Why don't we adjourn for the evening and continue this discussion in the morning, when cooler heads can prevail?"

Cosby strode towards the door, waving the president's memo. "Whatever you wish, sir."

"Sir?" Mackenzie said.

"Enough, Ian," Nicholas said, "Tomorrow."

"Mr. President …"

"Tomorrow." He pointed to the door.

Mackenzie hung his head, said, "Yes, sir," and left.

The president rose, puffed his cigar, and walked to the door to be sure he was alone. "Dee," he called.

General Deidre Roseboro, chairwoman of the Joint Chiefs of Staff, entered from her private room adjacent to the Oval Office.

"Did the headphones pick up all that yelling?" he asked.

"Yes, sir. You really jammed your stick in the hive this time. I don't think I've ever heard Harold that upset. He's usually a poster boy for the 'in control' society."

"Yeah, Dee. I didn't expect such a fight." The president sat down and picked up the memo. "I knew their approach would be in opposite directions, but Harold's reaction took me a little by surprise. I would like to have heard both sides present a logical approach, and then come down somewhere near the middle."

Dee stood in front of the president's desk. "Would you like me to have him watched for awhile, Mr. President?"

"No. Harold's just upset. He would never do anything to harm this office. By morning, it'll all blow over. I think I'll have you here in plain sight tomorrow. I may need your help keeping Ian corralled." He sat back in his chair, closed his eyes for a second, and exhaled.

"Just let me know what time, sir." Dee paused. "Sir, do you think we should tell them what our agents were doing in Cuba?"

Alex never opened his eyes. "No, not yet. They'll find out in time. Have we received any info about what they found?"

"Not yet, sir. There was one transmission. I'll have the transcripts later."

"God, I hate having to compromise those men like that. I hope letting Castro take them won't come back to bite me in the ass."

"They'll be fine. Castro won't blow it. He has too much to loose. I'll be in my office waiting to hear from you." Dee turned to leave.

"Thanks," Alex said. "And Dee?"

"Yes, sir?"

"Thanks for the advice. I'm glad I can depend on you."

"Yes, sir," she replied, and left the Oval Office.

¤¤¤¤

Secretary of State Mackenzie darted into his office and slammed the door. He reached for the cell phone on his desk and punched seven numbers.

"Cordell! Get your ass over here right now! Harold Cosby is about to leave the grounds. Follow him and report in with all information about his whereabouts. Be ready in case we have to take action." Mackenzie sat back smiled and thought *Cuba is just the opportunity I've been waiting for.*

ﾛﾛﾛﾛ

Harold wanted to build support for his position before morning. He decided to visit a long-time ally of President Nicholas, Florida Senator Hector Hernandez. Hernandez delivered the Hispanic vote to the president in the last election. In Florida, the Hispanic population was comprised of several Spanish-speaking communities including Mexican, Puerto Rican, and Honduran. But the Cuban exiles embodied the largest segment, concentrated especially in Miami.

Hernandez asserted that the Cuban exiles didn't want the United States to reenter Cuba by force. Internal unrest leading to civil war was the best scenario. Negotiations were fine, as long as the exiles were included in them, and resulted in Castro's removal from power. The exiles' vote was the key to any candidate winning Florida. Hernandez knew this, as did the president.

Harold walked into the senator's office and was immediately shown in. Hernandez ended a call after finalizing plans for lunch tomorrow. Harold strained to catch the name Hernandez spoke, but his attempt proved unsuccessful. He couldn't help but wonder if Ian had beaten him to the punch.

Hector cradled the phone and stood, taking Cosby's hand. "Harold, good to see you. How can I help you this evening?"

Harold was well aware of Hernandez's sympathetic position towards Brothers for Freedom, the group of Cuban exiles dedicated to returning to Cuba and repossessing property seized when Castro took power. Fulfillment of that pledge required Castro's overthrow by anyone other than the United States, even by means of civil war, allowing Brothers to reenter Cuba undetected. Harold knew all this. Once there, they would wield power in the form of more money than most of the mainland Cubans had seen in a lifetime. They felt the economic starvation suffered by the Cubans for so long would allow their dollars to buy all the power they desired.

Hernandez was up for re-election next year and for the first time facing stiff competition. His opposition, a Cuban-American businessman whose platform consisted of lifting the embargo against Cuba could be a threat. Harold counted on Ian's position infuriating Senator Hernandez. If successful, Hernandez would contact the president, buying Harold the needed time to implement a peaceful return of the agents.

Harold discussed the meeting he'd just left, concentrating on Secretary Mackenzie's approach to freeing the four CIA agents being held in Cuba.

"I can see we really have a problem here. Let me give it some thought and I'll call you in the morning, Harold." The senator stood and walked Harold to the door.

Less than fifteen minutes after entering the senator's office, Harold was on his way back to the White House. Another idea hit him and he signaled to his driver to pull over. "I need a little fresh air. I'll walk from here."

"Sir, I wouldn't recommend it."

"I will walk from here, driver," Cosby said again.

"Sir, this area of town can be a bit dangerous especially during this time of the evening."

"I've walked here a thousand times at night without incident. I'll be fine. See you tomorrow." Harold patted his driver on the shoulder and exited the car.

Chapter
2

Schaffer O'Grady's phone rang, threatening to pull him from his coma-like sleep.

From deep within the fog of his dream, he could see a faceless man telling him to answer the phone. "Not tonight!" Schaffer answered from within the dream. "Go away!" His mind rushed to the surface of consciousness. The evil beast continued to ring. Reluctantly, he opened one eye above the surface of his precious slumber. The clock blared back in bright red neon, like the eyes of a hungry dragon: 2:15.

At the sixth ring, he knew he would have to answer the phone or the ringing would never stop. He reached for it. "Schaffer O'Grady," he whispered, exhausted, trying to sound put off by the intrusion. On the other end, Schaffer could only hear heavy, panicked breathing. He started to hang up, but heard a grunt forming in the caller's voice. Schaffer sat up, wiped the sleep from his eyes, and turned on the lamp. Was this a family member? A friend? One of the prostitutes he'd befriended during the weeks of his investigation? Still too groggy to make out words, whoever it was sounded in trouble. Adrenaline pumped through Schaffer's veins, and suddenly he felt revived. Automatically he grabbed a pen and pad from his bedside table, covered with notes and scraps of paper he'd been scribbling and reading before falling asleep.

"This is Schaffer O'Grady," he repeated. "Are you in some type of trouble?"

"Yes," the caller's voice squeaked, one syllable of fear.

It was a male voice, almost inaudible, indistinguishable to Schaffer. He looked at the caller ID, and peered at what should have been the number. It read 'PAY PHONE', no number. He toggled the key on his caller ID box to get more info, but only a series of dashes ran across the window.

"I'm not sure that I'm doing the right thing," the voice trembled.

Schaffer readied his pen. He knew he had to keep the voice talking, get the name of the caller, the reason for the call. "Tell me what it is and maybe I can help you." He felt his breathing quicken as he anticipated the caller's response. Blood rushed through his ears, the rhythm marking time that seemed like hours passing. Impatient, Schaffer shouted, "Come on, man, give me something! You called me!"

"This is… Harold Cosby. We met during the president's campaign."

"Chief of Staff Cosby?" Schaffer clarified. He could hear what he thought was the metal coil of the payphone cord grating against the metal shelf of the phone booth. Why was Harold Cosby calling him at 2:15 in the morning?

"I have information about four Americans being held in Cuba that the people of the United States need to know about," Cosby said, breathlessly. "If I don't do something, we could start a war. You were the only person that I could think of that I can trust. You proved that during the election."

"Why are they being held?" Schaffer nearly shouted. He rose from his bed, cradling the portable phone, pen and paper in hand. He moved toward his dressing room.

"Ian must have found out about it. I'm afraid the president will agree with Ian. Secretary of State Ian Mackenzie, that is… We'll invade Cuba needlessly."

"Invade Cuba?" Schaffer stopped in his tracks.

"We already have a SEAL team ready to go in to get them," Cosby explained. "Xavier Benderis, also called Ciefuentes, is leading the team. They could be into Cuba as early as tomorrow. People are going to die because we want what they have. What makes this even more deplorable is the Cubans aren't even aware of it."

Schaffer's mind reeled. "Is Castro holding these men because he knows of the invasion?"

"I told you they don't have a clue about anything," Cosby shouted, the fear in his voice transforming to impatience. "Innocent lives will be lost, don't you understand?"

"I do," Shaffer said coolly. "I understand."

"I'm sorry. The innocent lives that will be lost is where we need to focus. We've got to stop Ian Mackenzie before a lot of innocent Cubans are killed!" Cosby grunted.

Schaffer calculated. "Beginning a war over four CIA agents won't help our standing with the rest of the world." He felt his eyebrows rise thinking over this. "I guess we've started wars with less solid reasoning."

"Look, we can't talk about it on the phone, it's too dangerous." He sounded faint now, as if he were about to hyperventilate. After several sharp gasps of air, he continued. "Meet me at the Lincoln Memorial in one hour. I'll fill you in at that time. Don't be late. I can't wait." The line went dead.

Schaffer tossed the phone back to the bed. He looked at his clothes, all evenly spaced, and arranged by color. His shoes were on shelves, and each pair contained shoetrees to keep them fresh. An old girlfriend once said he could dress in the dark. He slipped on a pair of jeans and a sweatshirt before leaving the dressing room.

Chapter
3

Harold Cosby hung up the phone, rested his head against the receiver, and sighed.

He hadn't noticed the BMW motorcycle that followed him now and pulled behind a beat up Ford Taurus across from the old post office where he stood.

Inside the car, a homeless man couched down to escape the night's chill. The homeless man jumped when the door of the car opened, but before he could protest the intrusion two bullets silently hit him, one exploding in his chest and the other in his forehead. Without a second thought for the homeless man, the motorcycle rider pulled the dead man from the car, dumped him under it, and jumped in the front seat. While Harold made the call, the motorcycle rider raised a radar-like device to listen to the chief of staff's conversation.

He retrieved a small keypad from his jacket, punched the numbers and positioned the mouthpiece on the side of his helmet directly in front of his mouth. Inside the helmet, he could hear the line ring.

"Yes," Ian Mackenzie's voice came from the earpiece.

"He just made a call from a pay phone. It sounds like he's setting up a meeting at the Lincoln Memorial. What do you want me to do?"

"Just baby sit him for a while. If he doesn't head back to the White House, call me immediately."

"Sure thing." He pressed a button, disconnecting the phone call. He watched Harold walk down Constitution Avenue, and climbed back on his motorcycle.

Harold reached the fence in front of the White House. He stopped and grabbed the iron bars with both hands, which made him look as if he was peering from a jail cell. For a long time, he just stood there glassy eyed. Then he turned and started walking in the direction of the Washington Monument. He cut across the Mall, heading in the direction of the Lincoln Memorial.

Cordell pulled the keypad from his jacket and pressed re-dial. "He's heading in the direction of the Lincoln Memorial. That's where he said they should meet."

"Fool! Who did he arrange the meeting with?" Ian taped a pen on his desk.

"I didn't hear him call anyone's name."

"Do you see anyone else in the area?"

Cordell looked around at the empty streets. "Negative."

"Get to the memorial first. Make sure you don't tip him off that you followed him. I don't want him spooked. We need to see who he's meeting."

"Wrong agency for that." Cordell joked at Mackenzie's unintended reference to the CIA's nickname, 'spooks.'

"Cut the shit and stay focused." Ian stood and walked over to his window and peered out. "There's got to be somewhere you can hide without him seeing you. Find a secluded spot. Then if someone else arrives, take Cosby out. We can't let him talk."

"Yes, sir." Cordell sped towards the Lincoln Memorial. "What do you want me to do with whomever arrives?"

"Just see who it is." Ian let the curtain covering the window in his White House office fall. "They could prove to be of some use later."

Chapter
4

Schaffer got dressed.

He patted the breast pocket of his jacket to see if his tape recorder was there. He hadn't been able to think straight since Harold Cosby's call. He felt anxious to find the reason for the president's chief of staff calling him so early in the morning to tell him about going to Cuba to free four men. Schaffer had always been a highly vocal supporter of President Nicholas. In the three years since the inauguration, Schaffer had only spoken to Cosby at a couple of White House functions. The much more intriguing question was what's the truth behind the 'it' Harold had referred to and why the U.S. felt the need to acquire *it* by force? Harold was willing to circumvent the president to make whatever *it* was publicly known, so Schaffer knew there was more to the situation than what was being said.

The streets outside Schaffer's Georgetown brownstone were unusually quiet. No matter what time he walked this stretch, he'd ordinarily see someone walking a dog, or making out on the corner. There would be some other life on the street. Tonight, the streets held less life than a graveyard. An eerie feeling overtook his initial excitement of the call. He stood for a long moment as if he expected to see someone appear from the shadows, leftover baggage from his days with the Secret Service. The cool air was heavy with humidity. The vapor of his breath blended with the fog that rolled in from the Potomac.

Schaffer turned the ignition of his 1965 Corvette, but to no avail. Over the past two weeks, he'd noticed more problems with the car. He'd planned to take it in for a tune up, but the convenience of the Metro system aided his procrastination. At this hour, as the Metro wasn't available, and as waiting for a cab would cause him to miss his meeting with Cosby, driving was his only option.

Schaffer had thought ahead, leaving the car parked on an incline to assist it in starting. He released the hand brake and pressed the clutch. The car began to roll downhill. Placing it in gear, he jerked his foot from the clutch. The car sputtered and coughed yet managed to crank alive.

Schaffer's car was the complete opposite of what people expected of him. The Corvette, which sputtered its way to the Lincoln Memorial, was his first car out of college. The car was an old friend. It was time for a complete restoration if he would continue to drive it full time — one more thing on his ever-growing to do list. "Baby, I'll fix you up good," he told the car, patting her dash. "Just get me to the memorial in time."

He jerked the car into third gear and sped from Georgetown. The loud rumbling and occasional backfire made it painfully obvious to his neighbors that his muffler also needed replacing.

Schaffer used the time to dig deep into the coils of his gray matter to retrieve his knowledge of Harold Cosby. A man of medium height, nondescript, balding, Harold had married for the second time the year before the election. At the time, he had two children in high school, but one of them was about to graduate and go off to college. The kids were from his first marriage. He and his second wife, fifteen years his junior, were working on child number three. Other than the president, Harold talked incessantly about being a father. The times he'd met Schaffer, he appeared to be the perfect father. Every spare moment he had, it seemed — and there weren't many — he vacationed with the wife and kids, whether skiing in Aspen, trout fishing in Montana, or trekking around Orlando.

Schaffer couldn't imagine anyone not liking Harold. He always greeted people with a genuine smile and a handshake that made Schaffer feel he was glad to see him. At one time, Schaffer thought Harold would make a better priest than a politician. He was too good a person to be in such a dirty business. Schaffer reflected that maybe Harold should have gotten out of politics before it destroyed him. From the sound of his voice on the phone, tonight could be the beginning of his downfall.

Chapter
5

Harold Cosby paced nervously in front of the seated massive stone figure of the sixteenth President of the United States.

Occasionally, Harold felt his head twitch involuntarily. He hoped to God that he'd done the right thing. He knew leaking this story meant the end of his career as a politician. At this point, he didn't care.

He peered out from the monument. Leaving the White House meeting earlier that evening, he tried to assure himself no one had followed his car. As far as he could tell, there had been no one in sight. He wiped the sweat from his brow, watched the vapors of hurried breath escape him.

He pulled out the Cohiba Esplendido Cuban cigar the president had given him at the meeting earlier that evening. The Cohiba, designed for Castro and once only given as gifts by him, was now more widely available everywhere except in the United States, where it was a coveted prize. So many thoughts babbled through his head, some mocking the president: *This is what it's really all about, isn't it Mr. President, your goddamned Cuban cigars? One of Castro's finest. It surely can't be about four men being held captive. Four men you would deny existed if someone asked you about them. The same four men you sent to Cuba and have less passion for than you do one of these damned cigars! What a fucking mess.*

He wanted to know how in the hell anyone else knew those men were CIA. Only three members of the cabinet were aware that they'd been sent into Cuba. No one else was supposed to know what their real mission was. Castro himself knew that the president was considering lifting the embargo, and taking those men hostage could only hurt his chances to normalize relationships with the U.S. It didn't make any sense. Harold made a million dollar bet to one of these cigars that Ian had a hand in their capture. He'd always talked of overthrowing Cuba, of ridding the world of another Communist country. This could be his way of forcing the president's hand to get what he wants. He simply had to stop Ian.

Harold walked back and forth like a tin solider, tapping a manila envelope against his leg. He planned to give all the information about the operation in Cuba as well as a dossier on Ian to Schaffer after their conversation. If he couldn't prevent war, at least he knew the dossier would topple the secretary of state and save the president.

He lit the cigar. Stepping from the cloud of blue smoke, he carefully hopped over the chains guarding Mr. Lincoln and began reading the inscription over his head: *IN THIS TEMPLE, AS IN THE HEART OF THE PEOPLE FOR WHOM HE SAVED THE UNION, THE MEMORY OF ABRAHAM LINCOLN IS ENSHRINED FOREVER.*

Harold's life and rise to political power flashed before him as he glared at Lincoln's boots. He had been a good friend to President Nicholas since Alex was a young politician running for and winning a hotly contested Virginia senate seat. The two of them had been inseparable ever since.

Harold now felt betrayed by the president. If Alex listened to the secretary of state, he ran the risk of collapsing his political career, dragging everyone down with him. Calling Schaffer O'Grady was a last ditch effort to bring the president to his senses, even if it meant ending his own career.

Harold was aware of Schaffer's connection to the president. Before taking a bullet for Alex, Schaffer's name had been mentioned, more than once, for a secondary cabinet position. Alex trusted Schaffer and he owed his life to him twice over. It was a debt Harold hoped Schaffer would use to have the president reconsider overthrowing Cuba. If Alex didn't listen, armed with the information about the takeover plans and on Ian, Harold knew Schaffer had the power of the *Washington Post* backing him to persuade Alex.

It was a gamble, albeit one Harold felt he had to take. He'd prided himself on being the dutiful servant. In the sixteen years that they'd known each other, this was the first time he and Alex ever disagreed.

Harold heard what sounded like a tank approaching. He sighed heavily, placed the cigar back into his mouth and turned to see if Schaffer had arrived.

¤¤¤¤

Cosby still failed to realize that he was not alone. As he paced, the dark figure hidden in shadow attempted to eavesdrop. To him, everything Cosby had said this evening and their context were meaningless. Cordell was only told that Cosby was a class-three security risk, the highest level of threat issued against any person by the Secret Service. If someone else arrived, Mackenzie had instructed him to terminate Cosby with extreme prejudice.

Behind the ranger's station, in the only unlit corner of the Lincoln Memorial, Cordell waited for just the right angle. He eased a M40A rifle used by snipers in the Marine Corps, with a silencer attached, from his side to his shoulder. He watched Cosby pan left to right, attempting to see out into the darkness. The spotlights shining on Mr. Lincoln blinded him during the three seconds it took his head to turn. Cordell waved the rifle to gain the perfect aim. The tendons in his trigger finger tightened and clicked as Cosby moved his head. When it came to rest, a red laser dot from the rifle's guidance system lay between his unsuspecting eyes.

Cosby gazed right at the dark figure and squinted, quite possibly trying to make out where the beam of red light originated. Cordell laughed, assuming Cosby wondered why an inferred sensor would guard a monument that never closed. Cordell completed the flexing of his finger, launching the projectile along the deadly red beam to its ultimate target.

The fiery flare from the end of the silenced muzzle was the last thing Harold Cosby saw. The bullet hit him with such force that his eyes did not close, nor did the cigar leave his lips. He seemed frozen in time as most of his brain splashed onto the boots of the former president.

Slowly, the body released its grip on gravity and plopped to the floor. The blood, escaping his body, pulsed from what appeared to be a third eye in the middle of his head as the heart beat six final times. Cordell counted. He knew it took mere seconds for the brain to relay the news to the heart that it was no longer needed.

And within those few seconds, Cordell jumped up, ran over to Cosby and removed an envelope from his hand. To make the scene appear to be a robbery, he threw back Cosby's coat, removed his wallet, watch and keys, and then vanished into the night.

Chapter
6

Schaffer's tires skidded to a stop on the damp pavement.

Realizing that he was not parked on an incline, aware he had no way to restart the car, he left her running and got out. Pulling out the extra key stashed in his wallet, he locked the door and jogged towards the Lincoln Memorial.

Schaffer saw a figure, dressed in black from head to toe, dash across the front of the memorial. The red beam from the darting figure's rifle sliced the night sky, bouncing off the fog that hung low around the memorial. From his Recon training, Schaffer knew danger awaited him at the top of the stairs, and that he should look for cover. But the Secret Service had reprogrammed some of his inclinations, and his feet kept moving forward. His heart stopped when the dark figure paused in mid stride and pulled the rifle to his shoulder. The red beam centered between Schaffer's eyes. Schaffer's pace slowed and he reached for his gun that was no longer there. Angry, he picked up his pace, knowing Chief of Staff Cosby needed his help. He ran and leapt.

The figure continued running and jumped from the side of the memorial, disappearing into a clump of bushes.

Schaffer moved fluidly and his senses heightened. He knew he had to be on guard. He heard the sound of a motorcycle cranking, then speeding off into the darkness. His adrenaline pumped so hard he started to sprint, bounding the stairs of the Lincoln Memorial two and three at a time.

Schaffer's foot made a slight splashing sound when he stepped in a puddle that waited for him as he reached Cosby. Immediately he realized that he had arrived too late.

He looked at Harold Cosby's body lying in a pool of blood before Lincoln. Schaffer stood, dumbfounded, watching blood pool around the chief of staff's head. It would be useless to check for signs of life, since the back of Cosby's head was blown away, and his brain splattered across Mr. Lincoln.

Schaffer tightened his fists and shouted, "Shit, shit, shit, shit!" Helplessly, he squatted in front of the dead chief of staff. Schaffer had seen many disturbing things during his former and current careers, yet this lifeless shell of a man staring at him filled him with questions. "What did you have to tell me? What was it? If I'd gotten here a few seconds sooner would this have happened?" Schaffer closed Harold's eyes, and realized that he'd be dead, too. A cold chill ran over his body remembering the bullet he took for Alex.

He remembered how Harold had gained his respect during the election when he told a group of reporters he didn't believe in hiding faults. Harold thought it was better to admit your shortcomings and then deal from a position of strength. What foresight! His philosophy got Alexander Nicholas elected. For Harold to be ready to divulge what appeared to be classified information, something must have been extremely wrong at the White House. Schaffer knew that he had to find out the truth behind Harold's phone call and this violent death.

"What a waste." Schaffer sat next to Harold, pulled out his cell phone. He dialed 911 and then the Secret Service. Even though he knew the police would have more questions than he wanted to answer, or could answer, he stayed with Harold and waited for them to arrive.

Schaffer knew Harold's death represented a sad reality of life. No one is safe anywhere, not even the president's goddamn chief of staff. He heard the approaching sirens.

Schaffer was even more exhausted than before he'd left the house. He wanted to get back to bed, but his day had already begun. He spent the next five hours answering questions for the D.C. police, the FBI and the Secret Service. He wished they would have all come in the room at the same time. At least then, he could have told his story once. But getting different law enforcement agencies to cooperate in this town was like asking for a glass of water in Hell, especially when someone this close to the president had been killed. He knew this technique was designed to see if he would change his story in any way. He wasn't even given the benefit of the doubt as a ten-year veteran of the Secret Service. Schaffer told each of the detectives what time Harold called him and that he'd requested a meeting at the memorial. He purposefully didn't mention Harold's reference to four men being held in Cuba, or the impending mission to free them. Schaffer wanted to see how that information would eventually bubble to the surface, and he'd be damned if he was going to give it to anyone else. He didn't care who was asking, or how many times they asked. That information was at the root of Harold's death and could be the only thing that prevented his. He considered calling the president after the police dismissed him, but decided against it. If Alex needed him, he'd call.

Walking back to his car, Schaffer tried to piece together everything that had happened despite his fatigue. So caught up in the goings on, he'd forgotten Harold wasn't the first person to mention Cuba in the past twenty four hours — Tito was most likely one of the captured men.

Chapter
7

Secretary of State Ian Mackenzie sat in the Capitol Grill anxiously awaiting his guest, Senator Hector Hernandez.

Ian loved the Capitol Grill. It was a unique place to eat around The Hill. Steaks the size of roasts hung in the front windows, dry aging to perfection. The Grill's green and gold china made him feel regal, and menus the size of newspapers added to the larger than life character of the restaurant and its patrons.

Immediately after arriving, Ian went to inspect his personal wine locker. The engraved brass nameplate served as a badge of distinction. Anyone who saw him using his key to open the locker would know that he was powerful, even if he didn't recognize his face.

The manager of the Grill seated Ian in the back of the restaurant. Surrounded by mahogany, brass, and dimly lit chandeliers, his was the only table inside a booth in a section of the restaurant that was reserved for senators, congressmen, and members of the president's cabinet. The booth was a perfect haven for privacy. Glass panels sat over the top of both the elevated sides, and were lit from the bottom by an eerie pink light.

The Grill's manager arrived at Ian's booth with Senator Hernandez. "Excuse me, Mr. Secretary. Senator Hernandez."

"Have a seat, Hector." Ian turned his attention to the manager. "Give us a few minutes."

"Yes, sir." The manager nodded. "Just call if you need anything."

Ian waited for the manager to leave before turning his attention to Hernandez. "Hector, this is the last face-to-face we can have until our little problem blows over."

"What problem is that?" Hernandez asked coyly.

"You know damn well what I'm talking about!" Ian snapped and shot him an icy stare.

"Let's assume for the moment that I do." Hernandez's eyes drifted to see who might be near. He leaned close to Ian. "Let's further assume that your aspirations haven't waned in the least. Then how could you implement them unless you were willing to take some action? Anything that has happened has happened for the best."

Ian took a moment to consider what Hernandez said. He looked into the senator's eyes. "That said, I'm sure there'll be no problem with your silence?"

"There's no reason for you to build a body count on your quest," Hernandez said, and sat back in his seat. "My silence assures my position in your future power structure. What could I possibly gain by talking?"

"Keep it that way." Ian jammed his finger in Hernandez's face. "No one else needs to know what happened last night."

Hernandez laughed and hardened his expression. "Calling you last night after that sniffling fool left my office was done out of a sense of duty to my country. Just make sure that you see to it that President Nicholas brings Castro down. Then give me credit publicly for helping the cause. My re-election and your aspirations depend on it."

"You'll get what's coming to you," Ian said. "You don't have to worry." He stood and walked from the table.

Hernandez called after him. "What, no lunch?"

Ian ignored him, but stopped by the manager's post. "Give him whatever he wants. Bill it to me."

He exited without further acknowledgement.

¤¤¤¤

Seated on a bench directly across from the restaurant, Gato Canoso watched the secretary of state leave the Grill. When he was clearly out of sight, Gato stood and approached the Grill. Once inside, he waited to for the manager to show him to Senator Hernandez's table.

Hernandez, a rotund man, with hands as thick as the steak he was cutting, took a moment between bites to offer Gato a seat. "Gato Canoso, in your pinstriped suit and fedora… You look more like a mafia Don than Chairman of Brothers for Freedom."

"Why waste my time?" Gato asked.

"Take off those dark glasses," Hernandez said, pointing his fork. "You look like someone who is trying to not look suspicious.

Gato kept his sunglasses on.

"I've got good news, Gato. Within the next forty eight hours, we will have begun Operation Smokeout." He lifted his glass to take a drink, swishing around the bits of food that remained in his mouth. "Shortly thereafter, Cuba should once again be a democracy."

"The arrogance of you Americans kills me," Gato said. "Cuba has never been a democracy. However, it is about time you all did something! My people have suffered long enough." Gato watched Hernandez shovel food into his mouth. "Why isn't this information public already? Surely, it will help the current administration in the upcoming election."

"That may be true, but they have chosen to keep it quiet." Hernandez stopped cutting his steak and looked at Gato. "I suggest you do the same."

Gato leaned towards Hernandez. "Should I take that as a threat, Senator?"

"Take it any way you want to." Hernandez tossed more food into his mouth. "But if you go out blabbing this information to the public none of us will win. Not to mention, your cause will loose any support from the U.S. government. Your dreams of returning to Cuba to reclaim your assets will become a pile of shit."

"Yes, well, remind your connection that his boss has an election coming up, as do you. The president needs Florida to win this time. And you need me." Gato played with the salt and pepper shakers as if they were chess pieces. "It would be wise for you both to keep in mind our interests in Cuba. We haven't waited this long just to have the president pull the rug out from under us. Castro must go!" Gato tipped the peppershaker on its side, as if capturing the king in a chess match.

"Of course he must." Hernandez picked up the shaker and put it back in place. He knitted his fingers and peered at Gato. "Just don't fuck everything up by muddying the waters. You have a tendency to be very impatient. Sit back and let us do our work. You'll be pleased with the results."

"We just want what's due us," Gato snapped. "We've waited much too long for the United States to act. If you want to see muddy waters, just look into the pool of government incompetence and inactivity."

Hernandez picked up his fork and looked down at his plate. "You talk about getting what's coming to you. You bastards are the ones who have kept us out of Cuba for so long. We probably could have negotiated something long ago, but you won't let well enough alone. You all want to antagonize the fuck out of Castro. I'm sure you're aware of what William F. Buckley said during the Helms-Burton debates concerning rightful ownership of Cuban property?"

"Why don't you refresh my memory?" Gato said with disgust.

"He said that if we begin demanding that property be given back to the rightful owners, the Native Americans would own the hemisphere. It may have been a cold war with a few hot moments, but it was war nonetheless." Hernandez pointed his knife at Gato. "And you side lost. Listen to me. If this mission can be pulled off quietly and efficiently, there's a ninety percent chance you all can get what you want. So I say again, don't fuck it up!"

Gato's face was red with anger for being chastised, even though he knew Hernandez was right. "Just get it done. And be quick about it. We won't wait forever." Gato stormed from the table.

Hernandez never bothered to lift his head from his steak.

Chapter
8

The sun had barely peeked from behind the horizon.

The stale air already held the promise of a sweltering day. Rays from the morning sun playfully danced across the Constantia wire that snarled its way around the refugee camp, thrusting razor blades over its entire three hundred and sixty degree perimeter.

The American Naval base at Guantanamo Bay, Cuba, in the southeast province, called Gitmo by the soldiers, housed two camps, the largest being Camp Buckley, which was home to nearly thirty thousand Cuban refugees crowded in tents across the base, all waiting to go to the United States.

Most of the arriving Cubans appeared malnourished, fatigued, yet happy to be with the Americans. Once in the States, it would be easier to make the money needed to provide for their families.

The boats they arrived in did not earn the description seaworthy. Many were built from empty oil drums tied together with rope. Wooden planks were stretched across the drums for token reinforcement, as well as some place to sit. Pieces of planks and rags were sewn together to create makeshift sails. The Cubans arrived along the rocky cliffs of Gitmo all hours of the day and night, yelling and cheering to the waiting American soldiers.

Boat People, as they were known, were seldom up so early in the morning. But this morning by 6:00 a.m., many people moved from their tent city to the yard near the camp's front gates. The soldiers restricted the refugees' movement around the camp. They were not allowed in the shopping area of Gitmo that housed McDonald's, a Wachovia bank, and other luxuries for Americans. They were also separated from the Haitians to help cut down on conflicts. Nevertheless, many fights still broke out among the Cubans, though they were not as intense as if the Cubans and Haitians intermingled. These fights, prompted by an obvious disparity in treatment by the soldiers, seldom ended before bloodshed. The limited mobility closed in on the Cubans like the walls of a small, overloaded elevator.

A man spoke to the gathered crowd. His movements and mannerisms, carried out with such precision, appeared well rehearsed. "Are we prisoners of these American oppressors?" he shouted. "Should we remain here and live like cattle? We are not allowed to walk anywhere here except inside the confines of this razor wire." His words burst into their ears, stinging their hearts, rousing their emotions.

The crowd was mesmerized by his deep baritone voice. At just over six feet, his strong muscled body was that of a professional boxer, rather than of a man who'd fled his country because of oppression and economic hardship. Over the past few weeks, Xavier moved throughout the camp with the grace and silence of a tiger. And like a tiger, no one knew he was ready to strike.

"This is our homeland!" Xavier pumped his fists in the air. "No one has the right to control our destiny!" Pounding his chest with each successive word, he continued. "We, my brothers, must take control." The crowd jumped to their feet as Xavier Ciefuentes spoke these words.

Noticing uneasiness in some of their faces, Xavier addressed what he perceived to be their concerns. "The power over our destiny is in our hands because we have chosen it to be so. It is true that we face soldiers here and at home who wield greater firepower than our hands possess. And yet their weapons are no match against the desire in our hearts."

Again, the rumbling grew loud. Remaining undaunted, Xavier yelled above them. "If the Americans will not help us," he stopped to observe the crowd, "we shall help ourselves. Life here in Cuba has been difficult, but we can make it better. We shall return home and build a new Cuba."

Emotion ran high through the crowd as he sang La Bayamesa, the Cuban national anthem. Tears streamed down the faces of many in the gathering. They missed their homes and their families. They wanted a better life, even though it seemed impossible at this moment. The realization of the challenge that lay before them left a bittersweet taste in their downtrodden hearts and hope in their eyes.

¤¤¤¤

From an observation tower, the American soldiers grew uneasy with the mounting tension. The rising temperatures and humidity pressed their already frayed nerves.

"Get me fifty men in riot gear out here!" Sergeant Wilson barked at the private. "Don't stand there looking at me! Do it now! Then get in contact with General Michaels' office. Double time, soldier!"

The lieutenant in charge answered the call. He sat hunched over his desk, straining to hear the private. "Slow down, slow down. What?" The young private, not yet accustomed to military crisis, gasped to catch his breath as he tried to relay the situation. The lieutenant listened to the description of the chaos. "I'll contact General Michaels right away."

The lieutenant disconnected the phone with one push of his finger. Jotting a few notes to make sure the facts were straight, he called the general's quarters.

General Michaels' aide, Captain Jenkins, answered and carefully listened as the lieutenant described the unfolding events. Realizing the seriousness of the call, he stopped the lieutenant so that he could speak directly to General Michaels. Jenkins knocked on the general's bathroom door. "It's the ops lieutenant. I think you should hear this, sir."

Michaels furrowed his brow. He put his razor down, leaving his face half shaven, opened the door and reached for the phone. "Okay, lieutenant, what have you got?"

"Sir, there seems to be a major problem brewing at the front gate of the main camp." The lieutenant tried to remain calm as he gave the general a first hand account of the developments.

"Well, son, get your ass in gear and pick me up right away!" Michaels barked. He handed the phone back to Jenkins, waiting just outside the door, and continued to shave. He took long slow strokes with his straight razor, stopping only to sip coffee. He did not feel overly excited. He would assess the situation and call General Walker at the Pentagon, in accord with General Roseboro's instructions.

"Jenkins!" he snapped. "Don't just sit there looking nervous, boy! Get me General Walker." As he waited for the phone call to go through, he flipped through his calendar to review the detailed notes he taken while talking with the Chairman of the Joint Chiefs.

He considered all probable catalysts for the disturbance. The only possible explanation, especially since he was required to contact the Pentagon, pointed to a coordinated effort. The uprising, rather than happenstance, was scripted. Most likely, the CIA had interacted with the men in the camp. He believed General Roseboro sat waiting for its inevitability.

Chapter
9

President Alexander Nicholas rose from his hand carved mahogany desk and walked over to his humidor.

Ritualistically, he opened it and selected his favorite cigar. Holding the Opus X before his eyes, he gently inhaled its fragrance. From his left pants pocket he retrieved a small pocketknife and cut the tip. Using an antique brass Zippo lighter, a gift from his wife, he lit the end. Once a red glow completely encircled the cigar, he put it to his lips and took a draw.

Alex left his office for the two minute trip to his study in the middle of the White House. After three years in office, he could tell anyone exactly how many steps it took to get there. He loved to smoke a cigar and survey his kingdom through the wavy glass that distorted his view of reality.

Rubbing the lighter between his fingers, he raised it to once again read the engraving. *Mr. President, you are the light of my life.* He loved his wife with all his heart. In large part, Jennifer was responsible for his success. He remembered the walks they used to take together on the farm in Virginia. Jenny always said it was her retreat, the one place that could bring them both back to more humble beginnings. She had been Alex's stabilizing force, a yin for his yang.

Jenny left him during the second year of his Presidency. Following a five month battle, breast cancer took her. He remembered how she used to say, *you love those damned cigars more than you do me.* His response was always the same. *I did have them before I had you, and besides they never let me down.* She had never let him down either. Her death left a massive void in his life. He tried to overcome the pain by working twenty hour days, but her memory proved too formidable.

Stepping out onto the Truman Balcony, he noticed the cherry trees were beginning to bud. It was March, and his quest for re-election was only eight months away. In the chilly air, away from the protection of the wavy glass, reality rushed forth. He remembered walking across the very lawn below the balcony as a young boy. Lyndon Johnson had been standing on the Truman balcony. Johnson had waved to his group, which was summer camp. In retrospect, he figured the president came to this spot for a moment of escape from the difficulties of the Vietnam war.

The image of Johnson had left such an indelible impression in Alex's mind that it led to an eventual political career. As a young Marine Corps lieutenant, Alex had received the nickname 'Earp' because people said he looked more like a cowboy than a solider.

A black and white photograph of him that had graced the cover of *Time* magazine some twenty years earlier, a photo shown often on television and printed in papers, taken while he stood on a hill with his back to the setting sun, reminded everyone of a statuesque man, larger than life, more deity than mere mortal. His thick mustache, strong chin, and cigar smoking added to the image. His kind eyes, mousy gray-brown, were covered by bushy arched eyebrows, and proved to be deceptive to his enemies. Wisdom and laughter created lines on his face. One of his opponents in the first election used the picture in attack ads, calling Alex an unpredictable cowboy. The ploy backfired, building Alex's base of support.

With the exception of his salt and pepper hair, more lines in his face and a few extra pounds, he looked the same. Alex stayed in excellent physical condition by lifting weights and swimming. He was frequently considered a role model that everyone should imitate.

Alex had earned his men's respect, and they never hesitated to follow him into battle. He ended his twenty-five year military career once he'd attained the rank of four-star general. He kept his mind sharp by lecturing at colleges throughout the United States on service to country and government responsibility. At every address, he encouraged debates and intense questioning among his students. He always responded to the media that picking the brains of the young keeps us in touch with the future.

Service to country served as Alex's rallying call. It also represented his life – an exceptional military career, the Virginia Senate and ultimately, President of the United States of America.

Despite overwhelming support during his first campaign for the presidency, unforeseen natural disasters and fears of runaway inflation caused by rising oil prices threatened to unseat the first Independent elected to the country's highest office in the upcoming election. Cuba could change that. This incident presented him with the opportunity to rally the people to his side. Toppling the hemisphere's last Communist dictator and bringing his men back to the U.S. would win him support and the next election. Success of the mission was more important to Alex than the election. The CIA agents' findings, if positive, could, almost immediately, ease the over-stressed economy.

"Excuse me, Mr. President," said Annie, Alex's executive assistant, "they're here."

"Thank you Annie." He patted her hand. "Give me about two minutes and show them to my office." He closed his eyes, bringing Jenny back to his thoughts. In his mind, he held her close and kissed her. Then he focused his attention back to matters of state.

Alex stepped back through the glass doors and eased them shut. Cigar protruding from his lips, he took a long, slow draw. He pulled the cigar down and blew several smoke rings into the air. He turned to the four Secret Servicemen waiting just behind him. "Okay, boys. Let's put on our game faces."

The agents assumed their positions around Alex, and the five men left for the Oval Office. When they arrived, Alex handed what was left of his cigar to one of the agents, and slipped through the back door of his private office.

Assembled in the War Room was the cabinet.

Alex waited thirty seconds longer than his projected return time before joining his cabinet in the War Room. One of the agents opened the door and Alex stepped through. Two agents followed him, carrying a sheaf of memos, which they dispersed to each of the cabinet members. Alex briefly discussed strategies that would enable him and his cabinet to maintain the White House for another four years. "Take a look, please, at the memos in your hands."

They all looked at the memo.

10 March communication from Cuban government:

The government of Cuba, in particular President Castro, has detained four men sent here by the United States as spies. Under the guise of lifting of the embargo, Cuba openly welcomed America's ambassadors. According to the United States, these men were businessmen sent here to Cuba to examine trade possibilities after the embargo is lifted. Their actions while visiting proved that they were here conducting an investigation related to our military bases as well as the size of our Navy. These men were arrested while trying to gain illegal entry to a naval base in Havana.

The spies will be tried and executed by this government. The United States has seventy two hours to respond to these charges of espionage against us. If you do not respond, they will be hanged in the center of Havana with the world watching. Cuba will selfishly guard her sovereignty, as would the United States.

When everyone finished reading, Alex spoke: "As if you couldn't tell by that memo, we've got one hell of a mess on our hands."

Dee Roseboro stood. "If we are not able to correct this problem soon," she said, "we can all look for a new line of work."

The secretary of defense spoke up. "Mr. President, these men were sent to Cuba on a diplomatic mission. Who gave the order for them to enter a military installation?"

"They were not trying to enter the base," Alex responded. "They were visiting a shipping port that is sometimes used by Cuba's Navy. It's also not important. What is important is getting these men out of Castro's hands."

"These men are CIA," the secretary of defense stated. "If Castro finds that out, we're really going to have problems and not just with Cuba. Our allies won't like the fact that these men were sent under false pretenses. Sir, our allies won't stand up for us, and I'm not sure the people of the United States will be willing to send their sons to Cuba to fight to get men out of Cuba who shouldn't have been where they were captured."

"Ask their mothers if we should get them out," Alex retorted.

"Sir, that's not fair," the secretary of defense shot back. "Of course I think we should bring those men home. I'm just having a hard time understanding firstly why they were at a military base and secondly how they were identified as spies. The CIA is very careful when it comes to espionage. For them to have been captured suggests the Cubans knew something ahead of time."

"That aside," Alex said, "we still have to get them out. They have sensitive information that we can't let fall into the hands of the Cubans, even if it takes a full scale invasion."

"Mr. President," the secretary of defense responded, "that seems to be a bit drastic."

Dee Roseboro walked over to Alex and touched his shoulder. "What the president is saying, gentlemen, is that these men are our excuse for entering Cuba. A smokescreen, if you will. We want these men and their information safe at home, but that's only half the story. Normalizing our relationships with the Cubans allows us access to the entire land. We can help them rebuild their country, which will elevate our standing with other Latin American countries." She turned to the defense secretary. "We don't have to worry about any large-scale invasion, as you will soon witness. We are only sending in two men and one is already in place posing as an intelligence specialist with the Cuban military. The citizens of this country will never know we're there. They will just see the doors open to Cuba, nothing more."

"How in the hell are two men going to pull that off?" the secretary spat.

"Check your tone, Mr. Secretary," Alex warned. "I may be easy to get along with, but the last time I checked I was still president."

"No offense, sir. Sorry."

"Let's get back to the point at hand." The president's intercom interrupted the flow of conversation. "Yes, Annie."

"Mr. President, I have General Michaels and General Samuels on the line for General Roseboro."

"Thank you. Put them through." Alex looked around the room. "It seems as though everything has gone as planned."

Everyone except Ian Mackenzie and Dee looked puzzled.

"General Roseboro," General Michaels' voice called out over the intercom, "all hell has broken loose here in Gitmo."

"Walter, this is the president."

"I'm sorry, sir."

"No problem. General Roseboro is here along with my staff. I'll let her fill you all in."

Dee moved towards a screen, which automatically lowered to project the unfolding events. "Gentlemen, what you are seeing is a well rehearsed sequence of events. Xavier Ciefuentes is actually Commander Xavier Benderis, United States Navy SEAL. Gentlemen, Commander Benderis is to receive your full cooperation."

"But General Roseboro," General Michaels interrupted, "we've had no contact with him."

"Exactly, nor will you unless it's absolutely necessary," Dee responded. "Two years ago, we sent the Benderis to live in Cuba. A priest who is also a CIA operative arranged the commander's transition to Cuban citizenship. There is another operative who will provide the Benderis with the necessary alibi in the event it is needed. He has so far earned the trust of the refugees at Gitmo. His mission now is to lead a group of loyal men back to mainland Cuba, where he will gain the trust of — and eliminate — Castro. If he is in need of your assistance, he will contact you."

General Michaels gasped.

Everyone in the room held their breath, waiting to see what was next.

"Walter," Alex broke the silence, "you make sure that nothing happens to him. Our Country cannot replace this man. It took us a year to train and coach him here, two years in Cuba, and millions of dollars for this mission. I'm sure all of this is still a bit unclear to you."

"I assure you," Michaels said slowly, "it most definitely is."

Alex rose from his chair and straightened his tie. "I don't have to tell you what a great opportunity this is. Other than China and Korea, Cuba is the only Communist country left that concerns us. Of course, the Chinese and Koreans pose no immediate threat to us. They have become Capitalists-Communists, so trade is too important to them. But Cuba, who poses no threat to us at all, has been a thorn in our side for years, simply because they had the balls to point missiles at us forty years ago. They need us now. There's no one else left that can give them the aid they need."

"Excuse me," Vice President Gillespie interjected, "but this is the same strategy Bush tried to employ unsuccessfully with Iraq in 1990."

"Exactly," Alex said, "but he forgot to get Saddam out before leaving. We won't make that mistake with Castro. We can go in and play the role of savior. The Cuban economy is in shambles and their former savior the USSR no longer exists. If we are successful in eliminating Castro and establishing a favorable government, our problems basically go away. Instant reelection. The Cuban people will be so happy to get financial relief that they won't miss Castro and they will welcome whatever government we choose to establish." Alex sat back and smiled.

Ian Mackenzie scanned the faces in the room. "Has anyone given any thought to how an attempt to take over Cuba, not to mention eliminating Castro, will affect our relations with the rest of the world? How can we justify an invasion of Cuba? They have done nothing to provoke such drastic measures."

Alex felt his smile drop. He inched forward. Mackenzie's wrinkled expression and his use of the same phrases his former Chief of Staff Harold Cosby used just two nights ago stunned Alex, especially after they argued so fiercely. "Ian, didn't you just hear what General Roseboro said? I'm not suggesting any type of large-scale invasion. Of course, we can't begin any type of negotiations with the Cubans. It's a matter of pride. America has carried this chip on her shoulders for over four decades."

Alex stood and walked around his cabinet. "The conservatives are not yet ready to forgive Castro for pointing missiles at our shores, and of course, embarrassing us at the Bay of Pigs. Even as difficult a time as the Cubans are having financially, you can bet they'll not request our help as long as Castro is in power. Therefore, this will have to be a one team operation, at least in the beginning. Once Castro is out, we can send in peacekeeping forces. They will be there to help guard against civil war. Of course, we will offer economic stability to help further curb any unrest, allowing us to influence the selection of their new leader. Immediately, we will begin to move into Cuba and regain our stronghold."

"Excuse me, Mr. President," General Michaels jumped in, "but shouldn't this operation involve many more people? I don't see how one or two men can carry this off unless it's a suicide mission."

Alex turned to the speaker phone. "It's hardly a suicide mission, General Michaels. What it is, is a finely tuned and planned mission that will strategically enable us to walk back into Cuba and establish us as the country that saved them. It will also help us to ease relationships with other Latin American governments. And if it fails, we have only three men at risk, thereby limiting our exposure to global scrutiny. However, keep in mind what really started this is my men being taken hostage. I'm a Marine and I'll leave no man behind!"

Looking at Alex with a puzzled expression, Press Secretary Tynes asked, "Sir, have we investigated asking the Cubans to release the men as a goodwill gesture?"

Ian didn't give Alex time to respond. "We don't have to ask Communists for anything. Taking over Cuba is long overdue."

"Thank you, Ian," Alex said. "I think I can handle it." Alex turned to Tynes. "I have already answered your concerns. This is the only way unless we want to send in a full-scale invasion. In which case, too much blood will be shed. This way, casualties will be kept to a minimum, if there are any at all."

"Generals Michaels, General Walker," Alex said, "if there are no other pressing concerns?"

"No, sir," Michaels said.

"No, sir," Walker said.

"Then I bid you good bye."

"May God be with these men," General Michaels mumbled. The line went dead.

Alex sat. "Ladies and Gentlemen, pulling this off is exactly what we need to erase the problems we have faced during our first term in office. Creating a democracy in socialist Cuba will be the final coup de grace we need to assure our return to the White House. Now, if you will turn your attention back to the viewing screen, modern technology will allow us to witness progress as it unfolds. General Roseboro, the floor is yours."

Alex sat back and lit a new cigar, this time a Cohiba Esplendido, while General Roseboro described in detail how Xavier would proceed from Gitmo into the Cuban mainland. Alex paid half attention. He knew the plan, and he couldn't stop thinking about Harold Cosby.

The cabinet thanked her at the presentation's end.

"Ah, yes," Alex said. "Thank you, General. May I see you outside?"

They stepped out of the War Room.

"Get in touch with our contact in Havana," Alex told her. "Let our contact know that Xavier is on his way. We don't want any mistakes."

"I'll call him right away," Dee said. Do you need me to do anything else?" She glanced at her watch and waited for further instructions.

"Thanks Dee, no. I have to contact Schaffer O'Grady. I've waited long enough to talk to him. By now, I'm sure he's seen Mr. Valencia's transmission." Alex looked over his shoulder at the closed door. "He may already know more that anyone else that's in this room. It's already public knowledge that he was going to see Harold. I'll need him to focus things in a different direction. We don't want the world investigating our intentions in Cuba."

"Let's hope it's not too late, sir. If they got wind of our ultimate goal, it would be impossible to prevent the onslaught of potential would be saviors rushing in to offer their aid."

"That secret rests with the men Castro is holding. Even Castro knows that they are a decoy. They won't talk and that only leaves you and me." Alex watched Dee's face and stuck the cigar between his teeth. "In time, we'll inform whoever needs to know, there's no need for unnecessary complications."

Chapter
10

Aided by staggering heat and the impatience of poverty and oppression, Xavier whipped the detained Cubans into a froth of screaming, cheering people begging for more.

For weeks, Xavier had met with small groups of the Cuban men at Camp Buckley. He took time with each group to detail his plans for a safe return home. Once there, he explained how they could aid him in bringing prosperity back to Cuba. Xavier's discussions lead many to believe that his ideas would work. He furthered his standing with these believers by assuring them that the funds needed to rebuild their country were waiting for them. When asked, he would only say that private bankers had put up the money. The night before he planned to leave Gitmo for Cuba, Xavier gathered his men and handed each of them a new one hundred dollar bill. Though they were amazed, no one asked or cared where he got the money.

The time had come for them to return home. Everyone stood, throwing their hands in the air, shouting praises to their newfound leader. The U.S. squad sent out to control the situation, which had grown increasingly uneasy, moved into place. Seeing Xavier's strong determined face and fire in his eyes, they knew that it was useless to try to deter him from his course. Secretly, he had their admiration. None of them wanted to confront him face to face, nor did they want to cut him off from his followers.

Sergeant Wilson watched the situation get out of hand. He lifted his walky-talky. "Lock and load! Put a bead on that son of a bitch."

The men in riot gear immediately obeyed. They slid their bolts backwards then forward, lodging the first round into their M-16s. The familiar sound of the sliding metal chambering deterred no one in the rioting group.

Private 1st Class Smith, one of the two men in the tower, held Xavier in the cross hairs of his riflescope. Corporal Willow stood silently observing the ordeal at the front gate. Drops of sweat traced the lines from Smith's head to his chin, dripping into a small pool beneath the stock of his rifle.

His palms and fingers were also covered with sweat. He wiped his hand repeatedly on his pants to keep his trigger hand dry. Smith became a sniper after consistently scoring bull's eyes during training, but this was the first time he'd been called on to kill a man. He had not yet developed the aloofness to easily carry out the deed.

Corporal Willow never moved from his position. Although subjected to the same scorching heat, he didn't break a sweat. His indifference to the orders made Private Smith even more nervous.

In an attempt to ease his anguish, Private Smith questioned the corporal. "You ever have to kill anybody, Willow?"

Corporal Willow waited a long time before answering. Then, nearly to himself he responded. "No one you would know."

"Hell, I don't know any of those bastards down there. I guess that makes it easier?"

Willow didn't answer, but continued to monitor the men below. For nearly three minutes, he let Smith stew with the question. In a whisper, as if an afterthought he answered, "It's never easy." As he spoke, his eyes never left the men below.

Xavier moved his men to the front gate. "Today we take control of our destiny. Open the gate," he shouted, and in a mock gesture, he grabbed the chains and shook them as if he could rip them from their post.

"How will we make it through the mine fields?" one of his men asked.

The crowd quieted for the first time, anticipating Xavier's response.

Xavier retrieved a helmet from the burlap sack at his feet and thrust it into the air. The helmet was black with white skull and crossbones on the sides that appeared to be shredded by claws. Across the front was scrawled 'Saber Tooth.' Several men burst into cheers, even though they did not comprehend the significance of the helmet. Xavier put it on and lowered a dark colored shield down to cover his face.

Inside the helmet, the shield lit up. Xavier scanned the gate and the mine field that lay on the other side. He inched closer to the gate and thrust his thumb into the air to signal he was ready. His men attacked the gates, ignoring the Constantia wire, determined to tear them from the walls.

Sergeant Wilson yelled. "That's enough!" He put the radio to his mouth. He screamed, "Take that bastard out!"

Private Smith began to squeeze the trigger, made slick by the sweat. As the muscles in his finger tightened, his heart pounded so furiously he had to fight to keep his target in sight. Finally, the trigger squeezed back.

Anticipating the completion of Smith's shot, Corporal Willow lurched forward, with catlike quickness, and thrust his hand under the gun barrel, raising it into the air, pulling it from Smith's grasp. Willow's breathing never changed and his heart rate never rose. The shot rang out, sending the men below looking for cover.

"Have you lost your fucking mind?" Smith was livid. "Sarge will have your ass for this." Willow had just deprived Smith of his first kill, something the private desperately wanted to accomplish.

Willow's expression remained stone like. Without a word, he returned the binoculars to his steel blue eyes to examine the crowd, which was quietly hovering close to the gate and looking in their direction.

Smith stared at Willow with contempt, yet made no move to retrieve his rifle and complete the job.

General Michaels' jeep slid in the loose dirt, creating a cloud of dust. "Who in the hell gave that order to shoot?" Michaels' feet hit the ground before the jeep came to a complete stop. The momentum threw him forward, almost tossing him to the ground. Regaining his balance, Michaels moved between Xavier and Sergeant Wilson.

Sergeant Wilson stepped forward, his shoulders hunched forward. He looked like a scolded dog. "Yes, sir. I did, sir. This situation was getting out of hand, sir."

General Michaels cut him off, raising his hand. "Sergeant, you have never been authorized to order someone killed unless we were at war. Use that goddamned head for more than a place to park that cover!" Michaels' face flushed red with anger. He realized just how close he'd come to losing the man the president told him to protect. Unbeknownst to the General, the president and his staff witnessed the entire event, thanks to Willow's transmission through his binoculars and a satellite passing overhead.

"General Michaels, sir, I thought…"

"No Sergeant you didn't think!" He moved face to face with Xavier and then turned back to the Sergeant. "What is it these people want?"

The Sergeant pointed to the gates. "They want us to open them so that they can leave, sir."

General stared down the self-righteous sergeant.

Xavier used the absence of attention on him to retrieve a key from his pocket and quietly unlock the gates.

"If they wish to die, it is not our concern," Michaels said. "Their blood will not be shed by our hands." Looking directly into Xavier's eyes, he rubbed his palms together, as if washing them. He turned back to the sergeant.

"Yes, sir." The sergeant snapped a salute.

Xavier let the chains fall to the ground and pushed the gates open. The men with him ran past him into the mine field.

General Michaels watched as the Cubans charged the gates. Instantly, two mines exploded, hurling several people into the air. The general's heart skipped a beat. "How did he get...?"

"Stop!" Xavier yelled. His men froze with fear and he walked ahead of them. "If we are to make it to our homeland you must follow in my exact footsteps." Xavier looked at the screen inside his helmet. Scanners tweaked, revealing the probable makeup of everything he viewed. Satisfied that there were no other immediate dangers where they stood, Xavier, carefully placing each step toward the front of the group, to begin their journey home.

Chapter
11

The Cuban soldiers observed the commotion from a distance of less than a quarter mile across the mine field.

Nervous laughter escaped from some of the soldiers as the mines exploded, sending bodies flying high in the air. "That's what they get for deserting their country," one of them said.

General Raul Santiago entered the observation post, grabbed a pair of binoculars from one of his men, and watched with more than idle curiosity. Santiago, now sixty-three, had been by Castro's side since he took over Cuba four decades earlier. His loyalty and cunning, not to mention the fact that he was Castro's half brother, gained him his current position of second in command of Cuba's army. Not quite as tall as his reputation, he measured only five feet four inches. His hair was still coal black, despite his years. He wore a beard to help hide a scar that ran from his hairline to the bottom of his cheek, which he received after making unwanted advances to a woman who'd been betrothed to another.

"What is he using to navigate the mine fields?" General Santiago asked himself aloud. "Does he think that helmet will protect him from flying debris?" Several soldiers laughed again.

He watched the helmeted man scan the mine field, combing every square inch. Some of his men seemed shaken watching their fellow Cubans' arms and legless torsos twitch in the dirt.

Those Cubans in the field looked hesitant to move, with no clear path back to the safety of the camp. The helmeted man gestured for them to form a single line behind him. They followed him, footstep for footstep.

Major Manuel Lopez approached Santiago. "General, should I notify President Castro on the most recent events, in case he wishes to come to the camp?"

"Not yet, Major Lopez," he answered, unconcerned. "See to it that we are in top form in case we need to contact him. Prepare to retrieve their bodies and place them into the proper storage area before he arrives."

"Yes, sir." Major Lopez scurried off to comply with his orders.

General Santiago entered the communications room using a card key that he ran through sensors. This was one of the remaining traces of Soviet technology. The room housed the intelligence division of the base. Computer screens lit up the room. Some clicked, others chirped, as they spat out data concerning their American opposition. Much of what they received was deliberately relayed by the U.S. troops. Santiago retrieved the name and background of the man leading their countrymen across the mine fields. The right side of the room, a broadcast station, displayed live shots of the men moving through the fields. On the left side, radios maintained communications with Havana. Due to the sensitive nature of the information gathered in this room, Santiago allowed no one in this room without his permission.

"We have a new member on the team." General Santiago moved closer to inspect the man. "What is your name?"

The young man stood. "I am Lieutenant DeCana, sir."

The senior intelligence officer approached Santiago. "General, Lieutenant DeCana was hand picked by President Castro and placed here," the officer explained.

"I see." Santiago eyed him. "What type of transmissions have you been receiving, Lieutenant DeCana?"

"So far, General Santiago, we have found out that the leader's name is Xavier Ciefuentes. After running his name through the computer, we know that he is from a small village near Manzanillo."

The senior intelligence officer spoke up: "I have dispatched a team of men near the area to investigate."

Santiago's eyes never left DeCana, who showed no fear. "Very good work, son," Santiago said. "Let me know the minute you hear anything." He watched as DeCana took his seat.

Major Lopez entered the room. "General Santiago," he said. "The men have just entered our mine fields."

For a moment, everyone in the room stood still.

Santiago broke the silence. "It will not be long now. Major, is the recovery team in place?"

Chapter 12

"They might make it through the American fields, but, ours are quite another story."

The intelligence room was kept cool because of the large number of computers it housed. Despite this, the chill the men felt in the room was induced by Santiago's presence.

General Santiago had been instrumental in developing the design for the Cuban mine fields. Confident no one could safely navigate such well-placed mines, at this moment he wished he could superimpose himself at the beginning of his fields, taunting the men to move forward.

Tension grew high throughout the Cuban camp, contrasting with their laughter just a few moments earlier. Some of the men crossing the mine fields could have been their brothers, cousins, or possibly even fathers or sons.

Most of the Cuban soldiers moved to the front gates to watch the men weave the hazardous fields. They wanted to cheer them on as they progressed inch by painful inch. Their success through the treacherous fields converted the Cuban solider to supporters of their countrymen, despite their earlier feelings of treason.

Only a few of Santiago's men knew how the mine fields were arranged. Assured that no one could get through them alive, they nonetheless felt strangely drawn to watch them try, and silently prayed they would make it. The Cuban soldiers paid no attention to the Americans at Gitmo, still dressed in riot gear, lining the walls watching the men in the mine field side by side with the Cubans who stayed behind. It was seldom the two sides agreed on anything. The sight of a few brave men risking it all to get home momentarily united these adversaries in support of what seemed to be a hopeless cause.

Xavier stopped as he reached the edge of the Cuban fields. His men felt their assurance wane. Both the American and Cuban soldiers collectively held their breath waiting for the next move.

"Why has he stopped?" one of Xavier's men asked. They quibbled among themselves. Many wanted to turn back, to run to the safety of the American camp. Several large banana rats ran onto the field to feast on the flesh already decaying in the hot sun. Two more mines exploded under the weight of the fat rats, serving to unnerve the men precariously stuck in the middle of the two mine fields with no idea of how to escape.

"Quiet," Xavier snapped. "I need to examine this entire field before we move. It's quite a maze." Xavier smiled, finally seeing the solution to a safe passage to mainland Cuba. He maneuvered the men through the path between mines. The train of men moved at a painstakingly slow pace in order to stay safely on course.

"How could this be?" General Santiago asked. "No one has the plans to that field." Furious, Santiago turned to Major Lopez. "If the traitors make it through, bring them to the interrogation area. Make sure you separate them immediately!" He turned to leave, knowing that if they made it, he would have to answer to Castro as to why a group of unskilled men were successful and why he had failed.

¤¤¤¤

In Castro's Havana mansion, Castro's niece Demetria lifted the receiver of her phone before it completed a full ring.

"The eagle has flown."

Before she could respond, or ask any questions, the line went dead. Momentarily paralyzed by the comment, she stared into space and her arm fell from its bent position. The receiver dangled from her hand. She had expected this transmission for three years, yet hearing it made her feel outside of herself, outside of anything she had ever known, in a place where she felt unaware how to act.

She looked at the clock. She had to go rouse her uncle. Castro needed to be prepared, for the man foretold in her vision was about to arrive.

Chapter
13

The invasion had happened less than one hour ago.

Everything had fallen properly into place, and the mission progressed as planed. Regardless, there was one outstanding wild card — Schaffer. Inserting him into the proper slot elevated Alex's likelihood of total success. He was, after all, not accustomed to losing. Positioning Schaffer was mastering the hand he had been dealt. Before returning to his office, Alex determined just how he would involve Schaffer: he would head the investigation into Harold's death.

Alex leaned forward, rested his elbows on his desk, and pulled the cigar from his mouth. "Well, it seems our guy made it in." He looked to Dee. "General Roseboro, how long do you expect it will take before he completes phase two?"

"Mr. President, Commander Benderis will be through the Cuban mine fields shortly. Then he can begin to gain the confidence of Castro and his staff. Our contact in Cuba will attempt to help ease Xavier into a position of comfort. From what we know of him, I believe the most difficult person to convince will be General Raul Santiago. He's very paranoid and he also has good instincts."

The intercom buzzed again. Everyone waited for Annie's voice. "Mr. President, Admiral Gregory is here for briefing."

"Very well Annie, have him take a seat. We will be with him momentarily." He turned to Dee. "What does the Admiral know about the mission so far?"

"So far, Mr. President, he only knows that three of his SEALs have been sent on a highly sensitive mission. No one outside this room has any information on this operation."

"Good." Alex buzzed Annie. "All right. We're ready for Admiral Gregory."

The door opened and Alex stood. "Come in, Donavan. I'm sure you're full of questions right now."

"Yes, sir, I am."

"Have a seat. We waited before giving you more information because we wanted to make sure this mission could precede. Because of the need to remain enigmatic, I personally selected the men for this mission. General Roseboro, would you be so kind to brief the Admiral?" Alex puffed on his cigar and turned his attention to the screen.

Admiral Gregory sat back to listen. Arms folded defensively across his chest, he fidgeted his fingers and tried to imagine why the president had summoned him to a top-secret meeting, and late, at that. It spoke of President Nicholas' betrayal and apparent oversight. Keenly aware of the tension between Cuba and the U.S., he found his uneasiness replaced by pride. As General Roseboro described the top-secret device known as Clear Vision, he had to interrupt. "The possibilities of such an invention are unlimited. Has it been tested?"

"It has," Dee responded. "One of our men successfully used it to navigate these mine fields at Gitmo." She stood and pointed to a wall map. "Your fleet will be responsible for the extraction of our men. On your way back to the ship, you will make a short stop by Gitmo. There, Chief Warrant Officer John Willow, one of the SEAL team will join you. For the past few weeks he has posed as a corporal in the Marine Corps." The Admiral couldn't prevent a frown from spreading across his face, considering the ongoing competition between the two branches of the military.

General Roseboro continued: "He will brief you further about your mission. You should also know that a sub will accompany your ship. Its use will be revealed at the prescribed time. All other information will arrive as needed."

"Let me be the first to wish you Godspeed, Admiral." President Nicholas quietly looked around the room. "I won't leave anything to chance this time. Not a word of this meeting is to leave this room. There will be no mistakes! No leaks! Do I make myself clear?" The president stared deeply into the Admiral Gregory's eyes. Gregory raised his brow, feeling the coldness of Nicholas' stern look.

"Or you'll end up like Harold Cosby," Secretary Mackenzie muttered under his breath.

Alex ignored Ian's rudeness. "Okay ladies and gentlemen, let's get to work." He sat back with his cigar as his cabinet left.

Harold was still on Alex's mind. So far, the police had no leads, and no terrorist organizations had claimed responsibility for the shooting.

The most powerful man in the world with the most commanding intelligence agencies on earth could only think of one person to help him solve the dilemma of Harold's death. His intelligence agencies had to follow far too much protocol to be as effective as a single person with the same skills. And Schaffer could work with complete autonomy under the protection of Alex's extensive power.

Alex's frustration compelled him to lift the phone receiver and punch in the same seven numbers that Harold called his last night on earth.

The ringing stopped just after it started. After a short pause for a response, Alex spoke. "Schaffer, we need to talk."

Chapter
14

The Cuban soldiers perched just ten feet from the border of their mines.

Abruptly, they drew their weapons and ran the few steps to meet the men coming out of the mine fields. As they arrived, the soldiers threw each one to the ground, and ordered them to place their hands behind their heads. They aimed their rifles at areas they knew would mortally wound the prone men.

General Raul Santiago walked up and removed Xavier's helmet. He placed it on his own head and lowered the shield down. Violently, two of his men jerked Xavier to his feet. Santiago looked through the shield with no apparent results. "What is this thing? How does it work? It seems only to be a simple pilot's helmet."

"So it seems," Xavier answered curtly.

Angered by Xavier's response, one of Santiago's men struck him in the stomach. He doubled over in pain.

Anticipating his reception, Xavier had removed the tiny activation chip from the helmet and tossed it into the mine field. Even though he knew the soldiers would thoroughly examine the men, no one would look in the mine fields for anything the men had left behind. Unless the soldiers completely destroyed the helmet, they would not locate the backup chip secretly stashed in the helmet.

"Bring him to the interrogation room," Santiago said, a cruel smile twisting across his lips.

They stripped Xavier to examine his clothing. Santiago's men ripped the sleeves from his shirt, and shredded his pants. They tore the soles from his shoes, and pulled off the heels. Between questions, two of the men took turns battering Xavier. One punched him in the kidneys, the other in the diaphragm. To each question asked, Xavier responded only, "I wish to see President Castro."

¤¤¤¤

Demetria sprinted to Castro's room and knocked anxiously against his closed door. To her surprise, her uncle opened it immediately.

He observed the look of near panic on her face and beckoned her in. "What is the matter? You look pale."

Demetria warily entered the room, unsure of how to begin. "It's the vision, uncle. He is on his way."

Castro frowned and stroked his beard. "Why are you so upset? You said this day would come, and that I should treat this man like a lost son. Have you seen something to contradict your earlier vision?"

Demetria shook her head. "No. I just wonder if everything I've seen is correct."

"Why should you question yourself? You are a seer. Everything you've seen in the past has proven itself true. Why would this be any different?"

Demetria knew she was indeed clairvoyant about many issues. But knowing Xavier and knowing about his arrival was contrived clairvoyance. The planners had promised a comfortable retirement for her uncle. So many times he'd expressed to her a desire to step down if only he could find the right replacement. His persistence about retirement made it easy to sell her the plan, and her psychic ability made it an easy sell to her uncle.

She stalled, guilty, nervous. "I've had a vision," she remembered telling him. "A man will return to Cuba after being held by the Americans. He is the one that you've waited for, and will lead the country forward in a manner that will give you great pride." Now that Xavier had come through the mine fields, Demetria knew she had to move quickly to save him from Santiago.

"Uncle," she said. "We must hurry. He is coming through the mine fields of Guantanamo. Santiago will have him soon."

"Then I should leave immediately," her uncle responded. "Have my aid inform Raul of my intentions. I will meet with the young man as soon as I arrive."

"I will see to it," she said, and turned away from him, feeling a sense of betrayal for perpetuating the lie, but ultimately understanding it was the only way to save her uncle.

¤¤¤¤

Xavier spent several hours in the interrogation room when Castro arrived at the compound. All of the men jumped to attention. Xavier winced with pain and barely managed to stand. General Santiago ordered Xavier to clothe himself, and held out the helmet to Castro as if it were a prized possession.

Castro's hands remained behind his back. "What have you found out so far?"

Santiago pointed to Xavier with his ridding crop. "All he would say, sir, is that he wanted to see you."

Castro turned to Xavier. "You wanted to see me. Now I am here. Tell me what's on your mind." Castro ordered his men to bring two chairs. The two men sat, and Castro asked the first question. "How is it you managed to get through my mine fields?"

Xavier used a piece of his torn shirt to wipe blood from his mouth. "It was simple, sir. I stole this helmet from the Americans. I observed them using it in a training exercise. One of their men became careless during the night, and he never saw me before I slit his throat. No one will ever find his body." Xavier reached for the helmet. "Shall I show you how it works?"

"In time," Castro continued, nodding his head, occasionally glancing at the helmet. "In time."

Chapter
15

"Schaffer, we need to talk."

Alex's call came the night before Harold Cosby's funeral.

For the past two days, Schaffer had been looking for clues relating to Harold's death, pouring through police records, conducting interviews with anyone associated with Chief of Staff Cosby outside the White House. So far, all his leads had dead-ended.

Schaffer agreed to meet with Alex after Harold's funeral. He felt it was the least he could do. After all, he did have the last known conversation with him on this earth. Curiously, it seemed to Schaffer that no one at the White House cared what he knew. They appeared to take comfort in the fact, that at least in their minds, what happened to Harold Cosby was a random act of violence, as stated by the D.C. police.

Schaffer knew better. He couldn't forget that dark figure running across the front of the memorial with his infrared laser shaving the low hung clouds. The lack of knowledge surrounding him smelled like a cover up to Schaffer. If the White House was hiding information, he knew it would be nearly impossible to discover it. He planned to try.

As Harold's casket was lowered to its final resting place, Schaffer watched Alex. He lifted his head, looking from the casket directly into Schaffer's eyes. Most of the people attending the funeral were led back to their cars, but Alex and Schaffer remained in place.

Alex kissed Harold's wife on the cheek. This was most likely the last time he would see her, unless she attended further White House functions. However, this was highly improbable considering she was originally from the "Ink Well" at Martha's Vineyard and planned to return in the coming days. Her distain for politics assured she would avoid the D.C. scene.

Alex left the widow's side and strolled directly to Schaffer. "Let's take a walk." Schaffer looked out across the headstones and held out his hand so Alex could choose the direction of their stroll. Everywhere he looked stood headstones in perfect rows. It lay quiet except for an occasional robin chirping to let them know spring was almost here.

Schaffer didn't know whether he should fear for his life. Nothing was clear about this situation. Even though he used to be one of them, it unsettled him to know that the six men behind them, as well as the numerous invisible sniper agents stationed around the cemetery, were heavily armed. He took comfort that there lay no freshly dug graves in the direction Alex and he headed.

After fifty paces in silence, Alex turned in Schaffer's direction. "Schaffer, I need your help. Harold's death has really upset me." He looked down and put his hands in his coat pockets. "I know he called you and requested a meeting. What did he tell you he wanted to talk about?"

Schaffer looked at the side of Alex's head, wishing to see inside to his inner thoughts. "He only requested that I meet him. I've told the investigators this repeatedly."

"Come on, Schaffer." Alex took an Opus X from his inner breast pocket. "Are you sure that's all?"

The Secret Service agents moved in a little closer before he could answer, "Yes, Mr. President." They seemed to be reinforcing the president's apparent doubt, or hoped to impart subtle intimidation. Schaffer once taught this technique to young agents, so it had no effect.

"Can that, would you?" Alex said. "It's me, Alex. Just because you may be pissed I'm asking you the same question as the investigators doesn't mean you need to adopt a formal tone."

"Okay," Schaffer said. "Alex."

"Thank you. Now, we were working on some rather sensitive material that night. Harold left my office very upset." Alex stopped and lit the cigar.

"What type of material?" Schaffer asked bluntly.

Alex laughed. "You haven't changed a bit. Dive right in and get your story. Well, Schaffer. I could tell you, but then they'd have to kill you." Alex thumbed over his shoulder. He turned towards Schaffer, letting the cigar smoke escape his lips, and looked down at his feet. "Schaffer, I really need to know what happened to Harold."

Schaffer held his gaze. "That's a question I've been trying to answer for days. I can damn sure tell you it wasn't a random act of violence." Schaffer felt his face tighten. He felt angry. "Whoever was involved hired a professional to protect their identity."

Alex blew a cloud of smoke in the air. "How do you know it was a professional hit?"

"How often do people who commit random crimes carry a laser-guided rifle and dress like a Ninja?" Schaffer let his question linger a few seconds. "When the perp was dashing from the scene, he left the laser on. It was clearly meant to deter me. I told your investigators about this, which is why I was dumbfounded when they concluded it was a random act of violence."

"My men have been instructed to remain discreet." Alex peered at Schaffer. "Do you understand?"

"I think so," Schaffer replied. "You want to know, but you don't want anyone else to find out."

"I think you're on the right track." Alex pulled the cigar from his mouth. "I don't mind if everyone else knows, just not right now. There's no need to risk tarnishing the memory of a man."

Schaffer pointed his finger at himself. "So you want me, a reporter for the *Washington Post*, to keep a potential blockbuster story quiet while I solve this mystery?"

Alex returned the cigar to his lips. "Just until I have a chance to deal with the situation and whoever is involved. I want the truth to come out, after all, and not what people suppose is the truth."

"Okay, Alex." Schaffer nodded. "Now tell me how this is going to advance my career."

"I don't guess telling you it's a matter of national security is good enough?" He could see Schaffer trying to gauge his reaction.

If anyone other than Alex was asking Schaffer this question, he would have laughed or made a sarcastic remark. But that response seemed a little out of place. So he tried to maintain some decorum, and instead said, "You've got to give me something more to go on. I've supported you in the past and I will in the future. But you can't be so vague about this mystery if you want the truth."

Alex sat on a stone bench and blew smoke in the air. "You've put me in an awkward position here. Things would be much easier if you still worked for me."

"You act as if I've changed sides. I left the Secret Service and not once have I betrayed your trust. Friendship is still sacred to me."

Alex arched one eyebrow and looked up at Schaffer. "Yes, but now you're in the business of disseminating information, not keeping things to yourself."

Schaffer sat next to Alex. "I took an oath that binds me till death. I've never taken that lightly or considered breaking it for the sake of a story. We've been through a lot together, and you know there are things in my head that would've made great newsprint, yet you've never read one word of it in the press." He held up an index finger. "I sure think I've earned your trust."

"Is this where you pull out the 'I've saved your life twice' speech to attempt to get the information you want?"

Schaffer shook his head. "That was my duty, not something I did to build up favors. However, it should speak to the depth of my loyalty. You don't believe for a second that Harold's death was random, but you're very concerned about whatever information he passed on. Since we both know he was killed for this information, I have to assume that it's powerful. So powerful it could cause harm if it became public. Let's further assume that it could harm you more than others by becoming public." Schaffer turned to face Alex's unwavering profile. "How am I doing so far?"

Alex brushed an ash from the sleeve of his coat. "You should have stayed with the Service." Despite trying to maintain a neutral facial expression, Alex's brow wrinkled. "This information in the wrong hands could cause all sorts of complications. Leaks occur all the time at the White House. Hell, sometimes we even cause them on purpose. I don't know if that's what Harold planned when he called you. The result, as we both know, is deadly."

Schaffer held his breath. He felt for a second hesitant to speak. "You've got to admit that this doesn't look good for your office. If it becomes public knowledge that Harold called me and requested a meeting just before he was killed, there's going to be a firestorm in the media."

"I'm trying to avoid that. Even so, I'm more concerned about you. If the killer thinks that Harold talked to you first, they might want you next."

"I don't think so. The shooter knows who I am. He had ample time and the perfect opportunity to blow my head off. He even took the time to make sure he saw who I was."

Alex scowled. "Why didn't you tell the investigators that?"

Schaffer shrugged. "I didn't really see it as important."

"Listen," Alex said, peering intently at Schaffer. "Be honest, now. Do you think I had something to do with Harold's death?"

Schaffer turned away. "Stranger things have happened. You never know what can change a guy. Even after saving his life and all."

Alex's face relaxed into a slight smile. "You're a real son of a bitch, you know that?"

"I do my best." Schaffer's shoulders relaxed as he felt a burden lifted from them. "How can we help each other?"

Alex blew several smoke rings in the air. "I need someone who's not bound by government constrictions. Someone who can get in and extract the truth without having to worry who's looking over his shoulders. At the same time, I need someone who knows what he's doing and someone that's not afraid of the truth."

Schaffer looked out over the cemetery. "There's got to be thousands of operatives you can turn to who fall directly under your control. Why me?"

"Because I know that I can trust you," Alex replied. "Besides, you are only guided by the truth, not by perceived loyalties to this office."

Schaffer watched the smoke rising from Alex's cigar. "I think you enjoy placing me in impossible situations."

"So, you're in?"

Schaffer nodded. "I'm your guy as long as there's quid pro quo. How do you suggest we get started?"

Alex blew a long stream of smoke from his mouth, laced with a heavy dose of relieved sigh. "I'll be reinstating your top-secret SCI clearance, just as if you were still in the Secret Service, and I'll grant you full access to my resources. The problem is I'm not sure whom I can trust right now except for you and Dee Roseboro. Therefore, she'll become your only contact with this office. When you two need to meet, do it away from the Hill and never, and I mean never, never call her at the White House. I'll have her fill you in on everything that we know of so far."

"Everything like what?"

Alex shook his head. "At least you're consistent."

Schaffer saw this as his chance to find out about Tito. Alex was bound to know something about his capture. "How about Tito Valencia. I have no doubt you know he's one of the men Castro is holding, and is a good friend of mine."

Alex pulled the cigar from his lips. "Valencia's a soldier, just like the other three. They are there to gather information for me. This isn't public knowledge, and I'd like to keep it that way."

Schaffer felt his spine stiffen. "It seems to me you may already have the truth you seek."

Alex took several long puffs from his cigar, put on a pensive expression. "Yes, I know that Valencia is a friend of yours. I guess in some way I thought that it would increase your interest in this case. I didn't expect Harold would involve you in what was going on."

Schaffer jumped at the comment. "So you put one of my best friends at risk. This same situation gets your chief of staff killed, and now you want me to clean up the mess and keep your office uninvolved?"

"Yes," Alex said. "Look. We both realize Cuba is desperate for help. They need economic stimulus, and we're in a position to help each other. Nevertheless, the major political parties in this country are not ready to forgive Cuba for kicking our asses at the Bay of Pigs or for pointing missiles at us during the late, great John Fitzgerald Kennedy administration. If Jack were alive today, he'd lead the charge to lift the embargo. Especially, I might add, if he ran out of his prized Cuban cigars. As it stands, we hold onto the embargo as a way of holding onto Kennedy. Hell, the people holding tightest would oppose him were he alive today and campaigning to lift the embargo against the wishes of either political party."

Schaffer relaxed. "That still doesn't explain who you think is involved in Harold's death, or why Tito is being held. Just what the hell are you saying about Cuba?"

"I don't know who would possibly be involved in Harold's death. Only three people other than me knew we were investigating ways to convert Cuba's government." Alex puffed his cigar. "Valencia was there to gather information, as I've already said. Getting our men freed is just our excuse to go in."

"Convert? Why don't we call it what it really is. An overthrow."

"I would like to see a favorable government in Cuba." Alex remained calm and candid, which surprised Schaffer. "Then we could resume normal trade relations without pissing off my constituents."

"What about pissing off the world community by..." Schaffer looked to Alex before concluding, "Oh, I don't know, by having Tito assassinate Castro?"

Alex pulled his cigar away and blew smoke into the air. "I'm not going to have my men kill anyone. Castro's an old man. We won't have to kill him. Nature will take care of that for us."

"I see. You won't kill him, but you'll have no problem helping out nature."

Alex's face distorted and reddened. He looked down a path indicating that he was ready to walk again. "Damn it, Schaffer, some things take care of themselves."

They stood and walked, and for a few moments, both remained silent. Schaffer looked out over the headstones. "Who is looking into the other people present in your office the night in question?"

"I have no reason to suspect them. And yes, I have talked with them personally. Dee was with me for some time after the meeting. There wouldn't have been enough time for her to orchestrate anything like a hit on Harold. Besides, I would have to have given my okay. We both know that's absurd." Alex puffed harder and smoke surrounded them. "None of this makes any sense."

"I know one thing for certain. Someone wanted Harold dead." Schaffer slammed his fist into his hand. "I've replayed that scene over and over in my head since it happened. I know what I saw and it was no random act, it was a professional hit."

Schaffer's anger silenced him as they turned in the direction of the president's waiting limo.

Alex glanced at Schaffer and then down towards the path before resuming his discussion. "There was a group of men that left Gitmo the other day. Two of them were part of a SEAL team that I sent in."

"Are they going in to get Tito and his men out?"

Alex hesitated. "Among other things."

Schaffer's voice strained against the tension in his vocal cords. "I don't like the sound of that. What else are you up to?"

Alex tried to smile. "Their mission is to infiltrate Castro's political structure." One of his agents opened the limo door for him. "I got it," Alex said, waving the agent away. He sat in the car and rolled down the window. "Even though I would like to keep this under wraps, it's too big for the press not to find out about. Thirty or so men left Gitmo."

"You're right. It is too big for the press to not know about." Schaffer ran his hand over his head, taking it all in.

Alex leaned out of the window to get closer to Schaffer. "The details of this mission must remain quiet. The lives at stake depend on it."

Schaffer raised his eyebrows. He said, "Sir, you realize that I may have to be a bit hard on you in public?"

"Do what you need to do." Alex looked in Schaffer's eyes and put the cigar between his lips. "I've taken more intense heat than yours before."

Schaffer leaned on the side of Alex's limousine. "You also realize I will need full, unencumbered access to your office? I want to know what's happening before it happens or at the very least as soon as it happens."

"That's why I told you to stay in touch with Dee Roseboro. She'll fill you in this evening. Expect a call from her later. She'll be the least of your problems." Alex held out his hand. "I'm counting on you Schaffer."

"I'll do my best, sir."

Schaffer watched the limo leave the cemetery with full pomp and circumstance. When he got to his car, he wrote a note to himself: 'Harold-invasion-Cuba-murder.'

The information he'd withheld from the police about what Harold said made more sense after speaking with Alex. While the U.S. conducted hundreds of secret ops a year, the very knowledge of this one cost a man his life. Schaffer assumed his conversation with Alex supplied him the information Harold had wanted him to have, and he'd agreed not to make it public. However, he considered, he might just need it to save Tito.

Chapter 16

Schaffer knew the meeting with Alex would prevent him from butting his head against the wall while looking for information.

Alex offered all the resources of his office to help solve Harold's murder. Schaffer hoped it would be enough to get past the bubbling bureaucratic bullshit that flowed more generously through Washington than did water in the Potomac.

Experience around Washington taught him it was best to try to find out as much information as possible on the outside of the political structure if he wanted the truth, or at least, what passed as acceptable fact. He placed a call to lobbyists and to his longtime friend Ralph. Schaffer knew if he didn't have any relevant information, none probably existed. Ralph had a knack for having information the Hill considered classified. Those who were lucky enough to have Ralph as an ally assumed he possessed the power of invisibility to have such intimate knowledge. For all Schaffer knew, his real name wasn't Ralph: he'd been dubbed that after Ralph Ellison, author of the *Invisible Man*. Ralph was skilled at working the system by including on his payroll those often beheld as insignificant — cooks, janitors, busboys and the like. Most of their employers never gave them a second thought. Who better to slip a micro transmitter beneath a plate or on the stall in the bathroom? Even better, they knew when any room or office would be swept for bugs, allowing them to remove the bugs before they could be detected. Ralph could even tell you whose name got called in the bedroom at night, especially if it was an illicit liaison.

Schaffer arrived at Etta's House of Chicken in southeast D.C. and ordered the Mother and Child Reunion, fried chicken and eggs, with a side hash browns and a thick dark brew of coffee and chicory. Two biscuits came with every meal to help sop the grease and gravy that Etta so liberally spread across breakfast.

Ralph slipped discreetly into the booth as if he had been waiting for Schaffer under the table. "Now, that's a meal that can keep a man going for a while. Don't nobody fix it like Etta."

"It's a good thing I don't need information from you too often," Schaffer said, taking a bite of biscuit. "I don't think my arteries could take it."

Ralph laughed and shifted into a comfortable position. "Some folks appreciate a good meal. When Clinton was in office, he used to come by fairly regularly."

"Was he one of your clients too?"

Ralph's face tightened into a smirk. "You know that information's classified." He brushed his hand across his head. "Presidents need information just like everybody else. Being elected to the nation's highest office doesn't come with a set of super powers, so they come to see what I know."

Schaffer blew across his coffee and took a sip. "I don't put anything past you. What have you got for me?"

Ralph sat up and leaned on both elbows, frowning at Schaffer's plate. "What have you gotten involved with? This damn thing is locked up tighter than an old man's bowels after swallowing a pound of bubblegum. Nobody's saying a thing about this, and I can tell you that's beyond unusual on the Hill."

¤¤¤¤

Secretary of State Ian Mackenzie sat in his Watergate apartment contemplating his next move. He knew the press would not sit still on the White House's official reason for Harold's death, especially since President Nicholas' meeting with Schaffer O'Grady. O'Grady was famous for digging up things others felt should be left alone. Mackenzie felt the best way to throw off a bloodhound was to plant a new set of tracks. Before leaving for the White House, he lifted his cell phone and punched in Cordell's number. "I've got another assignment for you."

"Will this seal my directorship when you become president, or are you just holding the carrot further in front of my face?" Cordell challenged Mackenzie.

"You should stick to your assignment and forget about becoming director. Until we complete our mission there's nothing to discuss. Besides, you're in no position to negotiate." Mackenzie pushed his finger forward in the air as if Cordell were sitting across from him. "Your ass belongs to me."

"Fuck you, Mackenzie!" Cordell shouted fearlessly. "If I decide to get a conscience and expose you, we'll see who your ass belongs to. There are some nasty boys in these federal pens. So, until you grow the balls to do your own dirty work, don't threaten me again!"

Mackenzie felt his face knot with anger. "I think you need to get more fiber in your diet," he said calmly. "I hear a backup of your system can make you testy. I had to disembowel the last motherfucker who had the unmitigated gall to offer to fuck me over."

"Whatever you say." Contempt was thick in Cordell's voice. "What do you want?"

"Nicholas has dedicated a lot of manpower to finding out what really happened to Harold."

"Why don't you let me take O'Grady out?" Cordell said anxiously. "He was the only one who saw anything. You said Nicholas is talking to him. And that makes him a liability."

"The time isn't right just yet. It'll come soon enough. What we need to do right now is to throw off suspicion that could possibly lead anyone in our direction."

"What do you have in mind?" Cordell asked.

"I think O'Grady should begin to look a bit shady." Mackenzie hatched a brilliant idea.

"Easier said than done."

"Not really. I'll let you in on a small secret. Last week USA Tobacco negotiated to purchase the U.S. rights to most of the old Cuban cigar labels. They will make this information public in a few days. We're going to have Mr. O'Grady begin to purchase large quantities of the stock."

"I'm not clear on what you mean," Cordell said.

"You are a slow ass," Mackenzie said. "Shut up and listen. I want you to call Humphries Brokerage Firm and open an account using O'Grady's name. I'll wire you the funds once you're ready. Start buying USA Tobacco's stock. Before long, we'll have the SEC breathing down his neck on insider trading charges. As a former federal agent, they won't show him any mercy."

"What about the paperwork?" Cordell asked, obviously warming to the idea.

"Get a post office box near O'Grady's home. Have everything sent there. You won't need to go in personally."

"That sounds as if it might work," Cordell said.

Mackenzie put on his suit coat and looked in the mirror to make sure everything was in perfect place. "Of course it will work. After you have put three hundred thousand dollars into USA Tobacco's stock, you're going to leak news of the Cuban invasion to the press. In addition to redirecting the focus of Harold's murder investigation in O'Grady's direction, we will make a boatload from the stock."

"How much of this boatload do I get to keep?" Cordell asked, by this point perceptibly salivating at the idea.

"I don't see why we couldn't split the profit down the middle." Mackenzie said. "That should take some of the sting out of this task."

"I'm going to need some information, social security number, birth date, salary, address and anything else you can dig up on O'Grady."

Mackenzie jotted down notes. "You'll have it before noon today."

"What time do you expect that USA Tobacco will inform Wall Street of their purchase?"

Mackenzie leaned back and put his feet on his table. "The CEO is scheduled to be on CNBC tomorrow morning at 9 a.m. I think he will do it then. Make sure you're watching. If he makes the announcement, leak the story tomorrow afternoon. Make your calls from a pay phone."

"No shit, huh," Cordell laughed. "I think I'll drive up to Pennsylvania. There's a little area I know that will be the perfect spot."

ᗅᗅᗅᗅ

By 1:00 p.m., Schaffer O'Grady had a new brokerage account opened at Humphries Investment Firm. Everything was handled like clockwork. By 1:30 p.m., thanks to a downturn in the stock price, and due to speculation about rumors of tomorrow's CNBC visit, Schaffer owned fifteen thousand shares of USA Tobacco, with money left over.

Gus, the broker at Humphries, questioned such a large purchase of a tobacco stock, given the climate surrounding current tobacco company litigation. Cordell, posing as Schaffer O'Grady, insisted on the purchase.

At 3:30 p.m., Cordell called Humphries for a second time.

"This is Gus." The broker said answering his phone.

Cordell tapped a new pack of cigarettes against the side of his hand. "Hi, Gus, Schaffer O'Grady here. Where's USA Tobacco now?"

"It's down another half a point to nine and a half."

"Great." He popped a fresh cigarette into his mouth. "Pick me up another fifteen thousand shares."

"Mr. O'Grady," Gus said, concern in his voice. "This is highly unusual. You aren't trading on any inside information are you?"

"It's just a hunch, but I think the news tomorrow will be good." Cordell lit the cigarette. "The damned analysts on Wall Street never get the story right. So, I'm countering the prevailing expert position. If the stock price returns to where it started out today, I'll make over thirty thousand dollars."

"I hope you know what you're doing."

"Don't worry about me. Just get the order in before the market closes." Cordell demanded leaving little room for doubt.

"For the record," Gus informed him, trying still to discourage the trade, "I have to inform my manager about two such large trades in one stock. I will also let him know that I advised against it."

"You do that, Gus," Cordell said. "You do that. And for the record, buy the damn stock now before it goes up."

"Let me do it now while you're still on the phone," Gus yielded.

"No problem, Gus," said Cordell, lightening his tone. "I'll wait."

A few moments later Gus returned to the line. "You're executed at nine and three eights."

"You should follow my lead, Gus," Cordell offered. "I'll have made a lot of money by tomorrow this time."

"No thanks. I'd just as soon not."

"Suit yourself." Cordell threw his cigarette out the window. "At least you'll make some commission money."

¤¤¤¤

When Schaffer's cell phone rang he immediately recognized the number as Ralph's. "What did you find out about Harold Cosby?"

"You've got to be kidding. I'm not going to discuss anything like this on the phone. By the way, did you hear that Duke was kicking it over on 'U' Street?"

Schaffer knew Ralph's code. He asked, "What time is that happening?"

"I don't know exactly, but I bet it'll be in the afternoon."

Schaffer looked at his watch. It was already early in the afternoon. "I may have to check that out. I appreciate the information. However, the question still remains, when will you give me the other info?"

"Man, I think you best let things cool down a while, we'll talk later."
Ralph hung up.

¤¤¤¤

Schaffer arrived nearly thirty minutes later. He spent several minutes observing the Duke Ellington mural and the surrounding area with genuine interest.

Ralph casually approached Schaffer from behind. "Hey mister, I got one area walking tour map left. It's yours for five bucks."

Schaffer never turned around. Instead, he began walking down the sidewalk. When no other people were around he asked, "Does it contain any useful information about anyone I might be interested in?"

"Mostly just general info. I found it interesting that President Nicholas put two such polar opposites on his staff. Cosby and Mackenzie used to fight all the time, according to my sources. It's even whispered they've nearly come to blows on more than one occasion."

Schaffer nodded. "Alex wanted to maintain some semblance of balance on his team. I think that's smart. Both Cosby and Mackenzie are very passionate people, so I'm not shocked by their reactions. Is that all you were able to come up with?"

"In a way, yes," Ralph said.

"What does that mean?" Schaffer asked.

Cautiously, Ralph continued. "Well, whoever wanted Cosby dead has dug in so deep that looking for him is like looking for Frosty the Snowman in a Miami July. I even checked with a certain Italian fraternity connection I know and they would like to find the bastard who killed him as well. Some of Cosby's stands on issues would have benefited them in Cuba if we return. They planned to resume Cuba's casino trade. Peaceful talks would have saved them millions of dollars of payola."

"Why would you have even suspected the mob to be involved?"

"Hey, when you got no leads, you go to any source you can think of, that's all," Ralph answered frankly. "Often you'd be surprised at the knowledge they have, no matter who's involved."

Schaffer looked at his notes. "At this point, nothing would surprise me."

Ralph tossed out more ideas. "How about President Nicholas himself? Have you considered him as a suspect?"

"The thought originally crossed my mind, but I've since reconsidered." Schaffer thought back on their meeting. "He had no reason to want Harold dead."

"Not that you know of, anyway. Stranger things have happened." Schaffer laughed. That was exactly what he'd said to Alex.

"What's so funny? Nobody else's got the power to keep something like this quiet. Hell, if I were you, man, I'd be watching my back. You are the only witness to the murder the cops said was a random act of violence. By the way, why didn't you tell them the killer was wielding a laser-guided rifle?"

Schaffer froze hearing the question. "How did you know about that? No one released that information."

"See, I'm better than you think," Ralph gloated. "Obviously, I can't reveal my sources."

They walked deeper into a southeast neighborhood, making it easier to spot any possible outsiders. The shirt and tie crew seldom came so far into this area, especially if they were white.

"Is that so?" Schaffer raised an eyebrow. "Well, tell me what you have on Secretary of State Mackenzie."

Ralph's tongue was suddenly too large for his mouth. It was several seconds before he could speak. "You suspect his involvement?"

"I know Harold didn't trust him and wanted to prevent his solution concerning Cuba." Schaffer sensed Ralph's hesitation, but waited for him to respond.

"Look, Schaffer, we go way back and you know I wouldn't bullshit you. Mackenzie's nothing but bad news. He's into some real deep shit."

"Like what?"

"Man, this motherfucker's hobby is studying torture techniques. He enjoys practical application, too." Ralph ran his hand over his head and face. "I had someone on the inside once. She called Etta's to fill me in on something she'd overheard. Mackenzie cut her fucking tongue out."

Schaffer's eyes grew wide. "Why didn't she go to the police?"

"They went to her, so to speak. They found her body in a crack house in southeast with her tongue missing." Ralph had to gasp to catch his breath. "All the bones in her fingers had been crushed. The police said someone did it with pliers before she died."

"What makes you think it was Mackenzie?"

Ralph's face was covered in sweat. "He had the tongue delivered to Etta's with a copy of a tape, which contained our conversation. Thank God, I use a modulator to disguise my voice. There was also a note. All it said was, 'be careful who you let use your phone.'"

Schaffer felt clammy. "Why didn't you ever tell anyone?"

"Because, I like my feet on the ground, not under it."

Schaffer felt uneasy with the information. "Is there anything else I should know?"

"Yeah, watch your damn back!" Ralph warned Schaffer.

"Thanks, I will. Call me if you find out anything else."

"Make sure you keep your phone on. You never know when something else may turn up and I may need to reach you quickly. I have another client meeting later today. I've got a sneaky feeling it may be related to this issue."

Schaffer took the map and headed in a different direction from Ralph.

Broken fingers, missing tongues and taped conversations. Schaffer questioned the wisdom of leaving his cell phone on.

ロロロロ

The next morning at 9 a.m., Cordell was at home watching CNBC. The CEO of USA Tobacco was being interviewed on *Squawk Box*. He informed his interviewers that they purchased the American rights to ninety percent of all the old Cuban cigar labels. Then the questioning really started.

"Why would your company spend money on a worthless asset?" the commentator asked.

"We don't view ownership of the labels as worthless," the CEO responded, maintaining his poker face.

The commentator pointed out the obvious: "Okay then, you have just acquired an asset that will have no value unless the embargo is lifted against Cuba. And of course these rights are owned by others in the rest of the world…"

"Precisely." The CEO smiled. "It is our belief that the embargo will be lifted soon. And as you suggested, we will only control the American distribution of these cigars. Americans will do just about anything to get their hands on Cuban cigars. It's a supply and demand issue. They are in demand, and we'll control the supply."

The commentator's face twisted. "What makes you think the embargo will be lifted after forty years?"

The CEO explained. "Two things. First, the embargo has long outlived its usefulness. We are a compassionate country, while the people of Cuba are suffering and the majority of our citizens want to help. Second, if we are still reluctant to enter Cuba because of one man, our worries will soon be over. Even Castro can't live forever."

"We'll have to take your word for it," the commentator said, looking into the camera. "That's all the time we have."

Cordell wasted no time getting to his car. An hour later, he was in York, Pennsylvania, dialing CNBC from a pay phone. "Hi. I need to speak to that Faber guy that was on with the CEO of USA Tobacco earlier."

"May I ask what this is in reference to?" the assistant asked.

"I have information that will make him look like a genius," Cordell said, attempting to control the direction of the conversation. "It concerns the interview with USA Tobacco, but I will only give it to him."

"He's still on the air," the assistant said. "Have you tried to e-mail him? He reads them while he's working."

"Why don't you e-mail him and tell him you have someone on the phone who could help his career?" Cordell's anger rose in tandem with his voice. "He's the first person I've called. If he's not interested, I'll call someone else. Tell him it ties into why the President of the Untied States' chief of staff was killed."

"Hold on a second, let me see what I can do."

A few moments later, a different voice came to the phone. "This is David Faber."

"I wanted to let you know the guest you had on at nine is a genius."

"What makes you say that?" Faber asked.

"Because, the United States is secretly invading Cuba as we speak." Cordell said with pride.

"That's ridiculous —"

"You think so? Why don't you look into why there was an uprising at Camp Buckley at Guantanamo Bay, Cuba?" Cordell laughed. "It surely wasn't because of overcrowding."

"How do you know this?" Faber continued to probe.

"Because I was the last person to see Chief of Staff Cosby alive." Cordell abruptly hung up the phone.

Chapter
17

Driving home, Schaffer listened to an all-news radio station when at noon the story about Cuba broke.

It didn't take much imagination to realize that the White House switchboard was jammed with incoming calls. Schaffer spun his car around and headed towards the White House. President Nicholas would hold a press conference this afternoon, and Schaffer wanted to be there early.

Allied nations called the White House and wanted to know if President Nicholas had indeed sent in forces to overthrow Castro. News networks, national papers, and everything from weekly-published small town papers to the tabloids, flooded the White House with calls. Nicholas was furious. His phone had not stopped ringing since the news story broke on the floor of the New York Stock Exchange after CNBC mentioned it on air.

Stomping around his office and drawing heavily on his cigar, Alex looked like an oncoming freight train. All the major networks were calling the White House to ask about the Cuban invasion.

"Annie," Alex yelled. "Get everybody in here now! Make sure we have a representative from the SEC. Goddamnit, I'll fry the bastard who leaked this information. How in the hell did this happen?" The president spun, throwing ashes in the direction of Secretary of State Mackenzie, who shrugged his shoulders with his hands spread out to each side.

"Mr. President, should I assemble the press?" Annie's voice helped to soften Alex's facial expression.

He quieted his tone. "Give them a meeting time of 3 p.m., Annie."

"Yes, sir," Annie responded as she set out to carry out his orders.

The cabinet and staff were assembled. They were joined by Zachary Dillon, head of the SEC, Chris Daly, Director of the FBI, Anthony Caprelotti, Director of the CIA, and General Pete Rogers, the Director of the National Security Agency.

"Ladies and gentlemen, we have a hell of a mess on our hands." The president paused and looked each person directly. "I want to find the source of this leak and plug his ass up so tight he won't shit for a week." He stopped, and turned towards his window. This time, the wavy glass did not change his perception. His view of the current crisis was crystal clear. "Let's hear your suggestions."

No one spoke up fast enough, so Alex interrupted the silence. "Don't everyone speak at once. Zach, what the hell have your people found out?"

Zachary was caught off guard, and was not accustomed to seeing the president so angry. "Sir, we know that between 10:15 and 10:25 this morning all the major New York brokerage firms received a call from an unknown man telling them that the U.S. was invading Cuba. This of course, happened after he called CNBC to break the story. The call originated from a pay phone in Pennsylvania. He claimed to be the last person to see Chief of Staff Cosby alive. Wasn't that O'Grady?"

Alex abruptly cut him off. "Chris, you get with Zach and make sure you have all the tapes from the firms as well as CNBC. See if there is any type of voice match. If it's O'Grady, I want to know right away. I don't have to tell you how to do your job. Anthony, have we received any reports that suggest the Cubans suspect anything, or that they may have started this rumor?"

"So far we don't have anything, sir." He looked in the direction of the Director Rogers of the NSA. "We haven't yet determined whether the Cubans have even heard this news."

"Good." The president shifted directions. "General Roseboro, what is being done to insure the safety of my SEALs?"

"Mr. President, I've been thinking about that the past couple of minutes." She handed him her notes. "I think it would be best if Press Secretary Tynes addressed the press as soon as we are out of this meeting. I think we should tell them that some of the Cubans held at Gitmo decided they would rather be at home than guests of the United States. So we helped them return safely to their homeland. As far as the SEALs, to our knowledge no one has suspected anything. Of course, we have not yet been in contact with Commander Benderis. If there was a problem, DeCana would have informed us."

"Finally, someone who's thinking. That's an excellent idea. However, I want to handle this press conference myself. I think it will make a more definitive statement to the world." The president pressed the intercom, "Annie! Get the press here for 2 p.m." He lifted his finger from the intercom. "For now, that is all we will say. Oh, and of course, someone apparently mistook this for an invasion. Pete, do you have any updates on the men?"

"Not as of yet, sir. Commander Benderis has not begun his voice transmissions. It shouldn't be too long before he begins."

The intercom buzzed. "Mr. President, the East Room is ready for your press conference."

"Thanks Annie. Pete, I'll get back with you before you return to headquarters. From here on, the NSA will maintain the only contact with the SEALs." Alex slammed his desk as if banging a gavel.

Director Caprelotti suddenly felt there was something he was not being told. "Annie buzzing the president didn't seem like an accident to me." He whispered to Director Daly. Caprelotti walked over to General Rogers. "Pete, what were you about to say about Commander Benderis?"

Just then, the president put his arm around General Rogers, saying, "Pete, why don't you come with me for a little moral support during the press conference?"

Rogers looked at Caprelotti. "Duty calls."

"I'll want to speak with you a little later," Caprelotti reminded him. The competition between the two agencies was as fierce as ever.

Rogers waved his acknowledgment. Alex leaned over to Dee. "Keep Caprelotti away from Pete. He knows as much as he needs to, given the fact that we haven't found the leak yet. Tell Caprelotti to stick to the orders I gave him, and make sure he knows I want him to personally monitor the wires, just in case there's something of great importance that he needs to tell me."

The president began the conference by denying involvement in everything that Press Secretary Tynes covered earlier.

Chapter
18

Outside the selected meeting room, General Santiago paced uneasily in front of the door, talking to himself.

"Why would Castro not invite me into this meeting? I am the Minister of Revolutionary Armed Forces in charge of his army in Cuba, and I have been loyal to him for over forty years. Something here doesn't smell right to me. I'll personally interrogate this prisoner to get to the truth."

Santiago was forced to move as the door opened and the two men emerged from the room. Castro looked at Santiago. "We're flying back to Havana now."

"But, sir," Santiago protested. "What do you know of this man?"

Castro turned to Santiago, "General, this is a very brave man. He risked his life to return to his homeland to bring us new technology. And so far, you have not yet been able to operate it. He is the only one who knows how to, proving him to be invaluable. Your man gave me his background. Did he leave anything out anything that I should know?"

"No!" Santiago said, and held Castro's gaze with contempt.

"Then, who are you to question me?" Castro shot back.

"With all due respect, sir, this man could be a spy sent by the United States. Just like the others we have in custody. How can you take such a risk?" Even though Santiago seemed to be pleading, his anger was still evident.

"I suggest you find out if he is a spy," Castro snapped, then turned to Xavier. "Let's go, it's a long trip back to Havana."

They entered the helicopter and flew off toward the setting sun. The orange and gold rays playfully tickled the water, flashing and sparkling until the sun ducked below the ocean. Watching the sun proved hypnotic to Xavier. Soon he drifted into a deep sleep.

Santiago swore as the men flew away. "DeCana, get on the computers and find me everything you can on this man." Under his breath, he cursed. "My brother is a fool! I will expose this peasant, prove Castro incompetent, and then Cuba will be mine!"

Santiago set out to devise a plan to rally his men. Taking Cuba from Castro would not be easy, but it could be done just as his brother took her from Batista.

Chapter
19

Reporters crammed the East Room of the White House.

Seated in the front row, Schaffer O'Grady waited for the president to enter the room. Everyone knew that Schaffer was well liked by President Nicholas. They'd remained friends even after the election. Even though he was no longer the White House reporter for the *Post,* their friendship usually allowed him preferential treatment during press conferences he attended. That, of course, pissed off many of his colleagues. Nevertheless, it allowed Schaffer to be comfortable in asking the questions no one else dared ask, which usually pissed off the president.

President Nicholas was the most honest man to have the presidency since Carter. Luckily, he was also a war hero like Eisenhower, which allowed him to please both sides of the aisle on the opposite side of Pennsylvania Avenue. But if word of the captured CIA agents leaked — not to mention their mission — it could give the most popular president ever elected loads of trouble. Especially since he neglected to inform the people who elected him of their capture.

The noise rising from the group of reporters sounded like a hive of bees waiting to pounce on the last flower in the field. Schaffer tried to relax his mind so that he would be able to think clearly when Alex arrived. But it was not to be. Harold Cosby, or at least the image of him, burned in Schaffer's brain. He could still see the blood pooling around Harold's head as he lay lifeless on the cold granite. The image haunted Schaffer, begging him to find the truth so that Harold could rest in peace. Schaffer didn't think Alex was involved, but he decided to turn up the heat today to see who else might squirm.

The president walked through the East Room doors wearing a huge smile. He didn't look like a man about to tell the United States that they were currently invading Cuba. He was so popular with the people of the U.S. that members of the Senate and House walked on eggshells when they publicly attacked him. For the past three and a half years, the Republican

Speaker of the House Davis had been looking, to no avail, for something to detract from the president's popularity to further his own political ambitions. But recently, an inordinate number of natural disasters, the growing oil shortage and rising inflation left Nicholas vulnerable to attacks. If the invasion of Cuba were indeed true, the Speaker could use the secrecy surrounding the event to further his political gain.

Watching the press conference from a private office, the Speaker leaned forward and quietly spoke to several other members of his party seated near him. "Does the president realize he can't declare war on any country without the approval from both Houses? Has he already forgotten his agreement? I knew he would renege before his term was over. Damned Marines are always looking for a fight."

The president took the podium. With a look of dead seriousness, he raised his head, and exhaled. "Ladies and Gentlemen, Mrs. Nicholas once told me that my golf game could cost me the next election. Yes, it's true. I hit another Secret Service agent two days ago. At the rate I'm going I could shut down government faster than Congress."

The crowd erupted in laughter. Disarming the press corps, the president went into the topic of the conference. "It seems that a vicious rumor has been circulating that the United States is invading Cuba. Let me say first and unequivocally that this rumor is false. The day before yesterday a group of Cuban refugees relayed to General Michaels, Commander of Forces at Guantanamo Bay, Cuba, that they intended to return home. One of these men, it seems, stirred a group into frenzy, and efforts to reason with the refugees failed. To prevent a riot, which could have resulted in many deaths, General Michaels yielded to the wishes of twenty to thirty men, avoiding major conflict. The men were allowed to leave. Any questions?"

Alex recognized Schaffer. "Yes, Mr. O'Grady."

He stood. "Schaffer O'Grady, the *Washington Post*." Once again, he was allowed to question Alex first. Under normal circumstances, he would ask a question designed to help Alex make a point. This, however, was not a normal circumstance. "Mr. President, I have a two-part question. First, were any of these men injured?"

"It is my understanding that three or four of them were killed. However, it was not by our hands."

"Part two, sir. I understand these men left via our mine fields. How did they successfully navigate the fields without the help of the Marines?"

The president raised his hands to his sides, shrugged, and offered, "Blind luck?" Again, the reporters laughed. "Actually Schaffer, those details have not yet been made available."

CNBC wanted to know what type of gear this group had. They spoke of reports that the leader of the group was wearing some type of advanced radar system that allowed him to see through the earth to the planted mines.

"Scott, you watch too much television." The president turned to call for his next question.

A *Washington Times* reporter stood. "Mr. President, if it comes to the surface that you have ordered an invasion of Cuba, won't that further Speaker of the House Davis' chances to move ahead of you in the polls?"

"Apparently you have not been paying attention today or in the past. First of all, and let this again be completely clear. I have not ordered an invasion of Cuba. Secondly, everyone is aware of the Speaker's presidential aspirations. Of course, you made a point of emphasizing 'Republican.' For the past few years I have stressed it's not the party, it's the people. As long as you do what's right for the people, your party affiliation, or lack thereof, does not matter. We are doing our jobs by informing the world the truth, not trying to keep ourselves in office by offering some candy coated explanation we think you all want to hear."

Schaffer jumped to his feet, even though Alex had not called on him. "Mr. President, one more question. Was there any connection between the news of this invasion and the untimely death of Chief of Staff Harold Cosby?"

Schaffer's question silenced the audience. The icy stare he received from Alex chilled the entire room. Schaffer couldn't tell if the president was pissed or hurt that he'd asked that question. If Alex's face looked any colder, Schaffer thought, everyone would be able to see his breath rolling from his mouth and nose.

Speaker of the House Davis sat up, giving his full attention to the exchange developing between Schaffer and the president. He looked as if he wanted to say, *Well, Mr. President, what do you have to say for yourself?* Then he leaned close to one of his colleagues, trying to whisper directly to him. Despite his effort, one word happened to make its way above the whisper, "investigation." He wanted those seated in the room with him to hear that one word loud and clear. It took no imagination to decipher what he was talking about. The Speaker wanted to launch an investigation into Cosby's death to see if there was presidential involvement.

Tension engulfed the entire room as everyone waited for a response.

The president paused several seconds. "Mr. O'Grady, it has been reported that Harold's murder was a random act of violence. Don't you read your own paper? If you did, you would already have the answer to that question. To make such an accusation is not only irresponsible, it's dangerous."

The president's anger was painfully obvious. All of the reporters in the room turned their attention from the president to Schaffer, who remained standing. Alex and Schaffer were locked in what one reporter later termed "a death gaze." Schaffer's fellow reporters dared not look at the president. Instead, they focused their attention solely on Schaffer. He was not uncomfortable having their eyes on him; he realized that he'd just struck a nerve. Alex didn't seem to be nervous, just pissed. Regardless, Schaffer had to do it. He and Alex were working for the same goal. If someone close to the president was involved in Harold's murder, Schaffer didn't want that person thinking Schaffer wanted to help the president cover anything up. And if it appeared that the president was his chief suspect, hopefully the real perpetrator would relax. Over-confidence always breeds mistakes, Schaffer knew, and his job right now was to make the murderer as over-confident as possible. His comment was akin to lobbing a smoke grenade in a foxhole: it was designed to flush the killer out into the open.

Chapter 20

On the way back to the Oval Office, the president lost all patience.

"Ian, find out where O'Grady is getting his information and plug it fast! All we need is an over-zealous reporter blowing the lid off this operation and getting a lot of good men killed. I thought you'd taken care of this." The president stopped walking and stood motionless for a second. He held an uncut, unlit cigar inches from his lips. Slowly, his hand dropped to his side. All the color left his face as reality struck him hard, like a blow to the gut. Then the thought pulsed through his brain. *Taken care of— Oh God, Ian, tell me you didn't have anything to do with Harold's death.*

Alex worked to maintain his composure. The thought made him nauseous. He was still pissed, and did not want to seem surprised when he turned to Mackenzie.

"You were about to say something, Mr. President? Sir, we have a lot to do in the upcoming days. We'd best prepare to avoid any mistakes."

The president placed the cigar in his mouth. Offended by the thought that Mackenzie could have been involved with his friend's death, he quickly dispensed his final orders of the day. "Make sure you stay away from O'Grady and his editor. On second thought, just stay away from the whole damned paper. Do I make myself clear?"

"Yes, sir." Ian was secretly pleased with the current outcome. Fingers were pointing in several directions, but none of them pointed at him.

"We don't want to arouse any suspicion," Alex said. "There's no need to pique their curiosity. Now, get with Dee and make sure she is ready for Gumbel in the morning. On second thought, we'll have a strategy session in my office at 5:30 a.m. Take care of it!"

Alex stepped into his private office and slammed the door behind him. He felt suddenly guilty for suspecting Ian. All three of them were good friends, even though Ian constantly got under Harold's skin.

ⰔⰔⰔⰔ

Schaffer's cell phone rang and he knew immediately who it was.

"Sorry, Alex. I had to do it that way."

"I'm sending a driver for you," Alex told him. "Where the hell are you?"

"I haven't even left the press parking area yet."

"Good." The president turned to his director of security. "Radio for two of your men to get O'Grady from the press parking area." Alex yelled into the phone. "Two Secret Service agents are on their way to get you from the lot. Get your ass in my office and don't even think about stopping to take a piss." He turned to another agent. "Get me a Johnnie Blue."

The two agents escorted Schaffer to the Oval Office. The door had barely closed before Alex started in on him. "What the fuck did you hope to accomplish asking me some shit like that?" Alex's voice was high pitched with anger. "Now everyone in the country is thinking I had something to do with Harold's death. Goddamnit, Schaffer, I'm trying to keep the peace. I don't need people thinking that I could be a killer, because I'm not!"

Schaffer tried to defuse the situation. "Believe it or not, putting you in the fire is the perfect way to show that you will not be burned. You know what they say about gold tested in fire. However, if there's a rat nestled close to you, the fire may run them out."

"Why are you always talking like Jesus, like Confucius... what the hell are you trying to say?" Alex drained the glass of scotch.

"Book of Wisdom," Schaffer said.

"What?"

"Never mind. Let's just see if anyone starts running for cover. By the way, I need to get to Gitmo. Will you take care of it for me?"

"Why in the hell would you possibly need to go there?"

Schaffer didn't flinch. "As strange as it may seem, I think there may be some answers to the question of why Harold was killed."

"You're a real piece of work. One minute you're screwing me in public, and the next you want a favor." Alex shook his head. "I'll have Dee take care of it. She'll be in touch. But first, let me give you some advice. Avoid stepping in any shit at Gitmo. It will make you stink and there may be nothing I can do to help you get rid of the smell."

¤¤¤¤

The evening came quickly. Schaffer looked up from the desk in his study and noticed the sky had turned black. A quick glance over at the clock, coupled with the grumble in his stomach, let him know it was time for dinner. He took another second to go over his notes. Alex told him about the thought he'd had about Ian, and that he'd dismissed it. It was easy to become paranoid with so many daggers coming at you. Even still, Schaffer placed an asterisk beside Ian's name on his list of suspects, especially after what Ralph had told him. He tapped his pen against the list of three names. According to the president, none of these names belonged here: Alex, Dee, *Ian. For the moment, Schaffer didn't know where to start.

The other unsettling tie to the whole Cuban mess was Tito. Since Harold had told him about the captured CIA agents, Schaffer had tried to make contact with Tito. Although he felt the act was futile, he checked his e-mails. The computer screen quickly splattered a horde of new e-mails for his supposed viewing pleasure. His initial reaction was to forward all the junk e-mails to every member of congress. It would serve them right for taking so long to pass an anti-spam bill. His anger sublimated when he saw the message from Tito planted among the trash.

Schaffer quickly moved the pointer over the subject line and clicked. The message came onto the screen, but had been transformed into a binary code that seemed to spin like a slot machine, constantly changing the code. The numbers stopped spinning and two words flashed on the screen — *we're dead*. He lifted the phone to call Alex but remembered he'd told Schaffer not to contact him there.

Schaffer sat looking at the numbers on the screen. Tito and Harold had contacted him just hours apart, both talking about Cuba. Harold was dead; Tito might be. And then there was Alex. He was left to discern the tangled truths and lies. Conflict over loyalties could have been a question, except, as always, Schaffer's loyalty was to the truth.

He pushed himself away from the desk. Just as he stood, the doorbell rang. He hadn't invited anyone over. He looked through the peephole and standing in jeans, a sweatshirt and a driving cap worn backwards like Michael Jordan was Dee Roseboro. He tried to see if anyone else was with her.

She sensed his apprehension and whispered through the door, "It's okay, I'm alone."

Schaffer opened the door and still looked around, just in case. "Come in," he said. "I wasn't expecting to see you tonight."

"I know you weren't, sugar." Dee pulled her hands from her back pockets and walked in. "We have a few things we need to take care of. I won't be in your hair long."

She walked to his sofa and sat down. Then she patted the spot next to her, and beckoned him to fill the empty seat.

It was a very odd moment, but for now, Schaffer obliged. "What brings you to Georgetown tonight?"

"I told you. We have some business to take care of." She sat back and crossed her legs.

She bent over and reached into the purse that was sitting next to her feet. As she pulled her hand from her purse, Schaffer instinctively grabbed her wrist. He could tell her hand was grasping something that wouldn't allow her palm to close all the way. "Dee, what are you doing?"

She didn't try to fight his grasp, but simply turned her head to face him. Trying to fight back her smile, she asked, "Do you think I came here to kill you, Schaffer?"

He didn't try to hide his nervousness. "I don't know what to think right now, or who to trust."

"Ouch. That hurt. I'll tell you what. Since you have such a firm grip on my wrist let's pull our hands out together." Dee waited for him to move first.

"Good idea. I'll lead." Their hands moved slowly in unison. At the other end of her hand was a small device that looked like a cell phone.

"Why don't you take it, then I can tell you how it works." Dee handed it to him.

Schaffer looked at her sheepishly. "Sorry, Dee. I guess I overreacted."

"I understand. Everybody's a bit jumpy right now." Reaching over, she took the device and flipped the cover panel open. "Here, take a look. It looks like a mini laptop, but it's much more. When it's open like this, you will be able to send and receive messages several ways. Slide your pen out."

He took it. "That's a pen?"

"Don't you use a PDA by now?" Dee asked with disbelief.

"I've been meaning to get one." He shrugged. "I just haven't had the time."

"Well, this pen, or stylus, is similar to theirs. You can use it to write messages and send them or you can turn the green side of the pen towards you and reinsert it. When you do that, I can hear anything you say. And when I talk into mine you can hear me." Dee repeated her action. "If you take the pen out and use the point to push this circle, your earpiece will pop out." She demonstrated and handed the earpiece to him. "Put it in your ear and slide the pen back out, red side facing you, and you can hear me directly in your ear. I like to call that silent mode, since your speaker is off." She handed it to him.

"How did you happen upon this little jewel and how does it involve me?" He pulled the pen out and replaced it as Dee had done.

"The NSA is good for something." She winked at him. "This is how you will stay in touch with the White House. It was the president's idea."

"If the NSA is involved I don't want any part of it." Schaffer handed it back to her. "I can see it now. They'll use some type of homing device planted inside here to find me and blow my head off."

"Take it easy, Schaffer." Dee patted his leg. "These two only have ten channels and can only send messages between one another. If you flip it over you'll notice this smoky colored plate." She turned it. "That's your solar cell. You don't even need wires to charge it, just put it in a little light once in a while. The president wants you to know everything that's going on in the White House and with our operatives. He also thinks it best that you stay away from the White House for a while, so I've been assigned to keep you abreast."

"How thoughtful." He took the device back. "But why can't we just use conventional means?"

"Because these two units are controlled by our military satellites. The signal is broadcast digitally and scrambled one hundred times every five seconds so the code is constantly changing. As long as you're not speaking around someone else, I'm the only one who can hear you when the green side of the pen is facing you. And don't worry, because the NSA will not be able to monitor you."

"Pretty damned impressive, if you ask me." Schaffer warmed to the idea of the device. "What's this button here for?"

"You know what they say, curiosity killed the cat." She smiled. "Of course he already used up eight lives before he became curious."

"You expect me to push a button that you've not explained?"

"You damned Secret Service types are always so suspicious. It simply changes modes so that you can hear the operatives involved with the mission in Cuba."

"Ain't technology grand?" Before Schaffer had the chance to get out another word, his stomach growled as loudly as it possibly could.

"Am I keeping you from anything right now?" Dee asked.

"To tell the truth, I was about to go out for a bite. Would you like to join me?" His offer was genuine. "I know a place just down the street. It doesn't look like much, but the food is great."

"I'd love to." She stood and tugged at her hat. "I don't think anyone will recognize me looking like this. We should be okay."

"Where are your Secret Service agents tonight?" Schaffer looked out the window.

"I told you, the president wants to be discreet about this. No one knows I'm here." Dee wedged her hands into her back pockets.

He turned to face her. "How'd you swing that? I don't recall ever allowing a cabinet member to go out alone."

Dee tilted her head. "The president gets whatever he wants. Moreover, you know the service only protects the president and vice president. Since Clinton, we're left to supply our own security force."

"Well, I'm sure as hell not going to tell anyone." Schaffer put his hand on her back. "Let's go get something to eat. They can come too if they want." Schaffer pointed over his shoulder, referring to the agents he knew were there somewhere.

¤¤¤¤

After finishing their meal, Schaffer walked Dee to her car and watched her pull off. Inside the house, he pulled out the device and looked it over. Schaffer activated the earpiece and placed it in his ear. Much to his surprise, he heard his favorite jazz station playing. A couple of seconds later he heard a voice.

"See Schaffer, it works," Dee said

He reversed the pen so that she could hear him. "I'll be damned, it does."

"Sweet dreams, sugar. Call me soon." Dee's laugh was deep and throaty.

Schaffer looked all around the device. "If you keep calling me sugar, I'm going to have to start following you around."

Dee laughed wholeheartedly. "I'll be in touch." She paused a second. "Sugar."

Signing off, Schaffer walked over to get a glass of Hendry cab. He turned the stereo on and popped in *The Essential Charlie Parker* CD, then sat in his grandmother's antique hand carved recliner, humming to *Bird Gets the Worm*. He laughed to himself, considering the relevance of the song, and examined the device Dee gave him. He looked at the button he'd asked about earlier. Schaffer took a gulp of wine and pressed the button. He heard voices in his earpiece. This time however, they were in Spanish. He understood the conversation, but was at a loss who was speaking until he heard two words: "Presidente Castro."

Chapter
21

Cordell lifted the phone and called Gus at Humphrey's.

He wanted to find out how the stock was performing since the president publicly denied the United States was invading Cuba.

"This is Gus," he answered, looking at the caller ID for a hint as to the identity of the caller.

"Hi, Gus. Schaffer O'Grady. How's USA Tobacco doing since the commotion?" Cordell took a drag from a cigarette that seemed instantly to turn to ash.

Gus typed in the symbol. "Of course, it ran up to fifteen after the announcement on CNBC. But since the president denied that we were invading Cuba, it's back down to twelve."

"Good. According to FedEx, you received my margin papers this morning. Use the margin value to pick up another fifteen thousand shares." Cordell couldn't wait to hear Gus' reaction.

"Mr. O'Grady, I know you don't like being told what to do, but as your broker, I must let you know the risk. If this stock goes against you, all your profit will go with it." Gus offered his expert advice. "I think it's a better idea to sell what you already have, not add to your position."

"Thanks for your advice, Gus. Now buy me fifteen thousand more shares. Make sure you tell your manager that I made you do it," Cordell said with some sarcasm.

Gus placed the order and immediately went to consult with his manager, who already had someone in his office. As Gus turned to leave, his manager called out. "Gus, I was just about to call you. Come in. This is Zachary Dillon."

Gus' throat went dry. For a moment, he couldn't catch his breath. It seemed like an eternity before he could put out his hand. "Pleased to meet you." He felt his face blanch as he wondered *what's the head of the Securities and Exchange Commission doing here? And what does he want with me?*

Dillon anticipated Gus' question and responded before Gus could ask. "I'd like to ask you a couple of questions about your interest in USA Tobacco."

Gus' felt his own hand go clammy. He knew his eyes were full of fear. He knew this Dillon guy enjoyed exercising his power over those he considered mere mortals, that he'd mastered the art of thrusting fear into the hearts of those he questioned. After all, Gus knew his job was to enforce one of this country's most complex and elusive laws, the tangled web of insider trading.

Gus' shaking knees were beginning to fail him, so much so that he actually felt relief when Dillon asked him to take a seat. After that, he did not hear another word of the conversation. His lips moved, forming the words. *What have I let O'Grady get me into?* But no sound came from him.

Chapter
22

"Sandoval, ready our pilots. We fly to Cuba in the morning!"

At Brothers for Freedom headquarters in Miami, the buzz grew even louder as Gato Canoso told of the impending invasion. People were still flooding the room to hear him speak about the mission. "We must prepare our people to return to power. Cuba shall be returned to her former glory!

"Liberate Cuba! Long live Cuba!" The crowd shouted louder with each successive chant. Their yells became a frenzied roar, crying for freedom and long life. Extended fists moved forward and back, pumping in unison with their demands.

Gato raised his hands and patted the air.

Before he could speak, Juan Pablo, nicknamed The Weasel because of his appearance and mannerisms, shouted, "Gato, when will this invasion take place?"

Gato looked at Juan Pablo. "It will be soon. The U.S. has already begun to launch their plans."

Searching for more detail, Juan Pablo continued. "Will they go in from Guantanamo or do they plan to hit Havana directly from aircraft carriers?"

"They have not said. However, a direct attack on Havana is more practical. The best way to kill your enemy is to cut out his heart." Gato held up his hand, closing his fingers as if crushing a heart with his hands.

Juan Pablo persisted in his questioning. "Where have you gotten this information? It would seem to me that it could only have come from a very high source."

"Juan Pablo, your questions seem to be filled with doubt. Have I ever told you anything but the truth regarding the matters of our country?" Gato challenged, and shifted his feet.

The gathering no longer cheered. No one spoke. Their attention was given to the exchange between the two men.

Juan Pablo realized he needed to divert attention from himself. He raised his fist in the air, and shouted, "Cuba libre, desea Cuba viva."

Again, shouts rose from the membership, this time even louder than before. Gato knew it was senseless to try to quiet them, so he didn't even try. After what seemed an eternity, Gato raised both hands. The room quieted and he spoke. "We have much work to do if we are to be prepared for our flights. Our friend here from the Cuban Intelligence Agency will detail our flight plans."

Quiet laughter rumbled through the group at Gato's joke. Sandoval was an aviation specialist for paramilitary groups supported by the United States CIA. Everyone present knew his background, though they never spoke the initials 'CIA' aloud, for doing so would somehow taint their mission.

As Sandoval began to speak, a pestilent seriousness shrouded the room. "This time we will not enjoy the protection of clouds to assist in our cover. Furthermore, the Cuban Government has said that any planes crossing into Cuban airspace will be destroyed. It is imperative that we stay in international airspace. Stay out of Cuba's territory. If you drift over their line, get the hell out as quickly as possible. They cannot shoot us down if we're over international airspace." He spoke with complete confidence and concern.

"The leaflets will be packaged in these pouches. Mini-parachutes are attached." He held up one of the packs. "The winds are blowing directly to the Cuban shoreline, so the packages will be carried directly to the Havana area. Attached to each leaflet is a voucher for five-hundred dollars in goods and services from our friends in the U.S. They can be redeemed as soon as Castro is gone and Cuba embraces democracy."

"What will keep people from hording all of the leaflets for themselves?"

Sandoval smiled. "Of course we will honor only one per person. See here, it also says the voucher is only good until next New Year's Day, which should serve as incentive. Now let's get a good night's sleep. We will leave tomorrow at 1 p.m. sharp."

The crowd again began to roar. The excitement diverted everyone's attention, which allowed Juan Pablo time to weasel from the room unnoticed.

Chapter 23

Gus Stewart felt as though he'd barely escaped the jaws of death.

His body's flight or fight syndrome took over, causing his breathing and heart rate to increase, while the sympathetic nervous system reaction caused his skin to redden and warm. His first instinct was to call Schaffer O'Grady.

Lifting the receiver, he heard two clicks before hearing a dial tone. He raised the phone receiver to his computer screen, which caused the items pictured to contort towards the receiver. Gus once heard that a phone receiver that seemed to magnetically attract a computer screen indicated that a bug had been placed in the phone. He looked over his shoulder, but saw only people he knew. The new trainee, furiously dialing for dollars, looked overly clean cut to Gus. *Maybe he's FBI*, Gus thought as he peered suspiciously at him.

Paranoia was beginning to take over Gus' usually clear head. He felt the walls of his office closing in on him. His collar suddenly became too small, cutting off his breath. He had to get away. He stood, put on his jacket, and called to Shelly, his assistant, "I'm going out for a drink. I won't be back today."

She walked closer to him. "Gus, you don't look so good. Are you feeling all right?"

"Yeah, sure, I...I'm fine. See you tomorrow." Gus stopped as he stepped out of the office. Looking cautiously to both sides, he walked erratically, stopping and starting in weird shaky motions. He stopped to tie his shoe, only to find that he was wearing loafers. Satisfied that he was not being followed, Gus entered Union Station near Capitol Hill. It was filled with people, and Gus was suspicious of all of them.

Even with all of the precautions taken and attempts to be observant, Gus missed the FBI agents stationed on the tops of buildings, in cabs, and posing as D.C.'s homeless. As his path was already determined by his usual habits, by now even the FBI knew Gus had a drink in the afternoon while waiting for traffic to die down. They also knew his favorite bar. An agent was stationed at B. Smith's posing as a bartender. As anticipated, Gus went right to the bar. Before sitting down, he walked from one end of the bar to the other. "Can I help you find someone?" the bartender asked.

Gus looked at the man. He had a beard, scraggly hair, four earrings in his left ear, and a cross with the inscription 'In God We Trust' tattooed on the back of his right hand. Feeling a bit more relaxed, Gus took a seat. "You must be new. I thought there might be a friend here waiting for me." Gus was wet with perspiration, and his movements were still a bit jerky. "Give me a double Johnnie Walker, neat."

The bartender poured.

Gus threw the amber liquid to the back of his throat, swallowing as he slammed the empty glass on the bar.

"Would you like another Scotch?" The bartender had the bottle ready.

"Absolutely!" Gus' drinking slowed a bit as he felt himself beginning to relax. The alcohol was warming his veins, washing away his problems. "You know," he said to the bartender, "it's a damn shame that we don't stop our friends when they go too far." Gus grunted sarcastically. "The problem is, by the time you realize it, you're the one in trouble." Gus' fear retreated with every swallow of scotch.

"I know what you mean," the bartender said. "This friend of yours has given you quite a thirst." He poured another glass. "This one's on the house."

"Ah! Wonderful!" Gus said. "Hey, listen. I need to call a client. Can I use your phone?"

The bartender handed Gus a cell phone. "You guys have gone hi-tech. When did you switch to cellular?"

The bartender never missed a beat. "Actually, it's digital. The boss owns the booth out there. She thought it would be good for business when customers see how clear they are. Besides, we get a commission if you buy one as a result of our referral." He handed Gus a card.

"Good thinking."

The phone rang and Cordell, posing as Schaffer, answered.

"Schaffer, you fucking bastard," Gus started in.

The bartender went to the side of the bar, lifted his drink and spoke into the straw. "Broadcasting live. Do I have a copy?"

The agent on the other end responded. "Loud and clear. The tape tracks are rolling. Give our friend another drink so his tongue will loosen a bit more. Alcohol is the ultimate truth serum."

Gus was almost drunk on three drinks and slurred his words. "You coulda costed me my fuckin' job!"

"What the hell are you talking about?" Cordell retorted.

"The fucking head of the fuckin' SEC was in my office today asking me questions about your lousy fuckin' dream stock, USA Tobacco. He wanted to know why you were buying so damn much of it, and if you had inside information about the company."

"What did you tell them?" Cordell asked.

"Only that you thought it was a good investment after doing some work for the company." Gus took another drink.

"Shit, Gus, have you lost your mind?" Cordell laid the groundwork to implicate Schaffer. "They might think I have some type of secret information."

"Do you, dumb ass?" Gus swayed on the barstool.

"None that I would admit to." He paused. "Gus, where are you calling me from?"

"From fuckin' FBI Headquarters, where do you think, you stupid. I'm telling them all about you." Gus laughed and raised his glass.

"Are you drunk?" Cordell asked.

Gus laughed again. "I'm so fucked up!"

"It doesn't take a genius to figure that out. Gus! Where are you calling me from? Stop bullshitting!" Cordell conveyed his irritation to further implicate Schaffer, since he was certain others were listening.

"I'm at my usual bar in Union Station, B. Smith's. Where else could I be getting drunk? This nice bartender even gave me two drinks." Gus drained the glass. "Of course he lemme buy a coupla ones first. He even let me borrow this great phone. What a great phone! If I don't go to jail, I might even buy one of these fuckin' things. I can hear you good as shit."

Cordell needed to sound more panicked. He started breathing heavily. "He let you borrow the phone? Do you know this guy? I mean, have you ever seen him there before?"

"No, Schaffer, why are you so worried? It's my ass that's on the line, not yours. No pun intended." Gus held his glass up for another drink. "You get it? I'm on the phone, my ass is on the line. Ah, never mind." Gus chuckled, amused by his own sense of humor.

Cordell wanted to keep Gus paranoid. "No one gives free drinks in Union Station! Hang up the phone, Gus, the bartender's probably a cop."

"Why, Schaffer?" He took a drink. "We're just having a friendly chat."

Cordell started to lay it on thick. "Gus, will you hang up the goddamned phone! They're probably tapping this call. Now Gus, hang it up!" Cordell knew his fellow FBI agents were there, that they'd tighten the screws on Gus and Schaffer. He needed to call Mackenzie. Finally, he punched the disconnect button.

Gus looked confused as the phone went dead. "Humph. Can you believe it, this little fucker acted as if you were the fuckin' FBI or something?"

The bartender smiled.

Chapter 24

Schaffer admired the anatomy of the young lady as he jogged past her.

He recalled his favorite line: "Women are a testament that God exists, until you're in a relationship with one, that is. Then you realize that He has a wily sense of humor. It kind of reminds me of a moth and a flame, you can't stop moving closer even though you know that you're going to get burned."

The woman kept walking.

He'd sworn off serious relationships after his last singeing ten years earlier. They'd met three years prior, when Doran insulted him on the steps of her dorm. Schaffer had just started grad school and was meeting with some of his fraternity brothers. Apparently, these same guys played a trick on her earlier in the week and anyone wearing their colors became fair game. Schaffer just happened to be in the way.

Within a month, he knew he wanted to marry her and for three years, she turned him down. For some reason, she thought she could never make him happy. Then, without any warning, she disappeared. He tried to find her, but it was as if she vanished from the face of the earth.

A few years later Schaffer ran into a friend of Doran's. She told him that a pregnancy resulted from his last visit. She went on to say that Doran knew he would use the pregnancy as an excuse for them to get married. Because she didn't want him to feel trapped, she broke off all contact.

Schaffer never loved anyone as much as he did her. For that reason, he remained a confirmed bachelor, catching fish and throwing them back into the sea.

Thinking of Doran, Schaffer didn't see Dee Roseboro descending his front steps. During the last three blocks of his run, Schaffer'd picked up his speed. As he reached his steps, he lifted his head and flew into Dee. The two Secret Servicemen on either side of her grabbed Schaffer to prevent him from knocking the chairwoman of the Joint Chiefs of Staff to the ground. Schaffer was startled by the men but knew by the tightness of their grasp that it would be useless to attempt to free himself.

With their faces just inches apart, Dee spoke. "Mine looks better than hers."

Schaffer initially looked confused. "Huh?"

Dee patted her rear.

"Oh, I see what you mean. I guess you busted me. Hers was exceptional. I can't say that I've seen yours."

She didn't turn around, keeping him in suspense. "Trust me, it's extraordinary, sugar."

Schaffer, released from the agents grip, put his hands on his hips. "I guess I'll have to take your word for it."

"Let's get down to business. The president sent me over with the equipment you wanted. By the way, I've been trying to get in touch with you. Since you're not using what I gave you to stay in touch, I've taken the liberty to include an answering machine along with the rest of your equipment."

Schaffer poked out his tongue. "I detest those damn things! Is that absolutely necessary?"

"It is, at least until you start carrying my other toy." Dee patted her bag. "I need to be able to reach you at all times."

Sorry, Dee." Schaffer wiped sweat from his head. "I'll probably forget to turn the answering machine on, though."

"Not to worry. It turns itself on after five rings." She took his arm and led him to the house. "You see, I've thought of everything."

"I see you have."

"Let's go inside. My men will get started while you shower." Dee raised her eyebrows. "Then we can go to grab some breakfast."

"Yes, ma'am." He saluted. "You're the boss."

"Who says men can't be trained?" Dee laughed.

¤¤¤¤

Twenty minutes after going into the house, Schaffer emerged from the shower. He found Dee and her men standing in and around the coat closet at the entrance of his home.

As he approached, Dee turned in his direction. "That's an improvement. You smell a lot better than the last time you were in my arms. Other than that, there isn't much to improve on."

"My dear General, you are a tremendous flirt." He turned to her Secret Servicemen. "Is she always like this?"

They didn't answer, but deferred to the general. The look on her face spoke more than words ever could.

"Okay…moving on." Schaffer continued to dry his hair with a towel and looked into his closet. "When will it be functional?"

Dee stepped away from the closet and walked over to Schaffer's computer. "It's functional now. All we have left to do is seal up your wall and make it look as if no one was ever here." She handed him a slip of paper. "Here is the current code. It's a series of letters and numbers ten digits long. The first time you pull it up, it will ask you to change the code. You can use any of the characters on the keyboard, including the spacebar. Just make it something you can remember and don't use your birth date. That's too easy. If you don't use your correct code, the entire system will lock down. Only the correct code will restore it, and you get that only after you've called me for the instructions contained in an unopened capsule at the White House."

"Can I get information from a remote location?"

Dee smiled. "I'm so glad you asked that. Maybe I will finally be able to get you using the communications tool. I had NSA include a chip that allows you to link up remotely. Yours is the only one that will do it, so I won't be able to listen to the recordings. That privilege is reserved for you alone."

"That sounds like just the precaution I was looking for." He looked at the coded number. "So, are all the taps in place?"

"Yes." She walked toward the door. "There's one that's going to piss you off. Let's get to breakfast and I'll tell you about it."

¤¤¤¤

At breakfast, Schaffer and Dee sat at different tables than her agents. Schaffer waited for breakfast to be served. Then he went straight to the point. "Okay, so what's going to piss me off?"

"Actually, it's more than one thing." Dee took a sip of coffee. "First, there's a tap on your phone."

This did anger Schaffer. "By whose authority?"

"Dillon, over at the SEC. It seems you, or someone pretending to be you, is buying large quantities of USA Tobacco stock." She looked in his eyes. "We believe this same person leaked the news about a Cuban invasion."

Schaffer leaned forward on his elbows and cocked his head. "You can't seriously think I had anything to do with that?"

"No, we don't. Dillon spoke with the broker over at Humphries and he has never met the person saying he's you. Everything has been conducted over the phone and by FedEx. Before you ask, no one at FedEx has seen him either. He used drop off boxes and he never repeated drop off locations." She sat her cup down. "He's being very careful pointing the finger at you. About the only thing he hasn't done is to make a call from your house."

"When you find out who the son of a bitch is, I want to personally kick his ass."

Dee twisted the coffee cup in her hands. "I've got something that may be a start. You and I are the only people aside from the NSA agent I had working the detail that knows this information. I didn't even share this with the president. I was concerned after Harold was killed, with Secretary of State Mackenzie in particular, especially since they argued so fiercely just hours before. I assigned an agent to keep an eye on him. Mackenzie was seen the next day meeting with Senator Hector Hernandez, which was not a concern until Gato Canoso showed up."

"Canoso?" Schaffer recalled the man. "I did a story on Canoso a couple of years ago. Why was the head of Brothers for Freedom doing meeting with Mackenzie and Senator Hernandez?" Schaffer eased back in his chair.

Dee rubbed her finger around the rim of her coffee cup. "He only met with Hernandez. Mackenzie had already left when Canoso showed up. There was no time to get any type of listening device in place before the meetings took place, so we don't know why they met. I took the liberty of adding their names to your list of taps."

"Thanks." Schaffer smiled, sat back, and looked at people passing by. "It shouldn't take long now before we know something. An operation like Harold's murder involves more than one person. Someone's bound to become jumpy."

"In the mean time, the president thinks it would be good if you ran an article in the *Post* about the 'so called' invasion." Dee made a quotation mark gesture in the air. "Mention both Canoso and Hernandez. Let's see if it makes either of them nervous. Maybe then we can find out who's at the root of this problem."

"Can the president stand the heat that may come with this commentary? He was a little upset when I surprised him at the press conference." Schaffer smiled.

"Do what you need to do. He'll be okay." Dee reached out and touched his hand.

"In that case, it would be my pleasure." Schaffer looked down at her hand on his. "I have another question. Is the argument the only reason you had Mackenzie followed? I mean, how well do you really know him?"

Dee looked away. She didn't want her personal feelings about the man to have any influence on Schaffer. "He's good at what he does. Very capable."

"That's obvious. Now give me what your gut tells you." Schaffer noticed her facial expression dim.

"Let's just say that he's never made me feel warm and fuzzy. Although I don't always agree with him, he does get things done." She frowned and looked a bit unsettled. "This is going to sound weird, but when he doesn't agree with you about an issue, it seems to me that he enjoys inflicting any verbal pain he can on his opponent. And let me tell you, he's damn good at that."

Chapter 25

The next morning in Schaffer's op-ed piece in the *Washington Post*, likenesses of Presidents Nicholas and Castro appeared on opposite sides of a commentary which read:

Cuban Invasion?

An unnamed source informed the *Post* of a conversation in which they overheard a senior government official tell a member of Brothers for Freedom that the United States was about to begin an invasion of Cuba.

Gato Canoso, the leader of Brothers for Freedom, pressured President Nicholas to aid in removing Castro from Cuba without force. Stating that he wants to spare the innocent people, he urged the president to 'turn up the heat' on our trading partners and force them to stop doing business in Cuba. Now, however, it has been said that he would like to see Castro permanently eliminated.

In recent months, Brothers for Freedom has stepped up its activities in Cuba. Leaflets denouncing Castro and his "evil" government have been dropped to the mainland on numerous occasions. Just a few days ago, a flotilla of boats left Miami and attempted to enter Cuban waters. The Cubans, in much larger boats, rammed into several American boats in turn, injuring several American citizens.

Day after day, these men place their lives in jeopardy to end oppression by the last dictator in our hemisphere. How long will our government continue to stand by and watch this injustice? Or is there something more sinister at work here?

In the past, President Nicholas agreed with his predecessors and said that the United States would normalize its relationship with Cuba if they met the following demands:

- Remove all troops from Africa
- Halt support for revolutionaries in Central America
- Reduce military ties to the Soviet Union

All of these demands have been met, and yet no talks have begun; thus making it impossible to restore a relationship with Cuba.

The United States seems content to let groups such as Brothers for Freedom attempt to overthrow the Cuban Government by causing **her** people to revolt. Could it be that the wait is over?

The leadership of this country is keenly aware that our government is not ready to drop the torch of disdain it has carried against Cuba for over forty years. A "hostile take-over," on the other hand, allows the government to save face, and it can be carried out in the name of justice. The Cuban people are suffering at the hands of a dictator who, due to the worldwide fall of Communism, can no longer offer simple comforts to his people.

"Big Brother" to the world just can't sit by and allow this type of injustice to continue. Therefore, the only humane thing to do is a selfless takeover and rebuilding of this fallen country to its former greatness. Of course, this would allow the U.S. to return countless assets, allegedly illegally taken, to their former owners, now living in the United States.

Such a humanitarian task can only be applauded.

So, Mr. President, why the secrecy? Would negotiations, which have not been attempted, be more effective?

Chapter
26

Schaffer finished packing for his trip to the Marine base at Guantanamo and looked around the room taking mental inventory.

He'd left Dee Roseboro's little toy in the windowsill to make sure it was charged up before his trip. He popped in the earpiece and pressed what he now thought of as the Cuban mystery button. All seemed to be quiet for the moment, except for a little background noise. He sat device back on the windowsill and waited for a cab.

¤¤¤¤

In Miami, three Cessna 337 Skymasters sat on the tarmac, fueled and ready for takeoff. The cargo was loaded, and all the last minute checks were completed.

In the briefing room, Sandoval rehearsed the exact details of the flight with the crews who would fly the mission. The atmosphere in the room was more of a military mission than one of mercy, as purported by Brothers for Freedom. Sandoval moved a pointer over numerous charts, showing the routes they would fly. A last minute check of the national weather service confirmed the winds were indeed blowing in the direction of Havana. Soon, hundreds of parachuted packs would descend on the unsuspecting city.

"I would like to remind you that Cuban officials have warned that any plane crossing into Cuban air space will be shot down. Our intention is not to test the resolve of their Air Force. No one will be injured as long as all my rules are followed." Sandoval tapped a satellite photo. "Remember that we do not have cloud cover at the level that we will be flying. However, I am told that there will be cover of another kind in the air."

The men flying the mission understood that to mean the U.S. would have fighters in the area.

"Are there any questions?"

"Has anyone seen Juan Pablo? He was scheduled to fly with me today," one of the pilots explained.

"No one has seen Juan Pablo since yesterday," another pilot answered.

"Then I'll fly with you," Sandoval answered, happy to get a piece of the action. On several occasions to the flight crews he'd expressed his boredom with the mundane task of planning the flights. Finally, he could stretch his wings again. "We should go. Father Sanchez is standing by to bless our mission."

The six men left the room. They stood by their planes as Father Sanchez bestowed God's blessing upon them. Finally, they started their engines. The planes taxied in single file from tarmac to runway. The growl of the engines lifted each Cessna into the air one at a time.

The three planes were airborne. They pulled into formation and flew over their headquarters to view their motto painted on the roof, Cuba Libere. Cheers and well wishes pushed the planes closer to the heavens. In a little over an hour, they would begin another mission designed for the people of Cuba to reach freedom.

¤¤¤¤

Juan Pablo had slipped away from Brothers for Freedom's headquarters undetected the afternoon before. At a small private pier just outside Miami, his Sea Ray 260 Sundancer sat fully fueled and ready for the short trip to Havana. By early afternoon, his journey began. Seven hours after leaving, Juan Pablo would be back in his homeland with the details of Brother for Freedom's mission, as well as plans to block its success.

He arrived in Havana and immediately boarded a military flight en route to the Cuban base opposite the American base at Guantanamo. By the time the plane landed in Guantanamo, he had been in Cuba for twelve hours and his information had been dispatched to General Santiago.

As soon as Juan landed, he went directly to the General's office for their meeting. "General Santiago, Brothers for Freedom will come to Cuba tomorrow. They plan to fly directly to the Havana area to drop their propaganda." He handed General Santiago a copy of a pamphlet. "The CIA has suggested to the pilots to remain clear of Cuban air space, but qualified the statement saying they should test the resolve of our Air Force. He also suggested that they would not be flying alone."

Santiago took the literature. He paced as he read. "If they come," he said, "we will leave none of them in the air. It is time for the Americans to pay for their insolence! We will destroy their military planes as well. Castro is content to let the Americans fly into downtown Havana, and still he will not engage them. They will see that I am a man of action, and Cuba will not be trifled with on my watch."

¤¤¤¤

Schaffer's cab arrived and he was ready to depart. Leaving his living room, he heard a lot of activity through the earpiece. He grabbed the device from the windowsill just as his cab honked its horn. What he heard next confirmed that the Spanish was coming from Cuba.

DeCana transmitted the unfolding standoff. "This is Havana control. Please identify yourselves and your intentions."

"Havana control, we are a party of three planes from the United States," Sandoval looked over at his co-pilot, and released the plunger of the mike. "That'll get us a little respect." Again he depressed the plunger. "We have no intention to cross into Cuban air-space. International law protects our right to freely fly anywhere around your border."

Tower control in Havana radioed back. "Be warned, entering Cuban air space could result in military action against you and your party. A zero tolerance stand is in effect. This is your only and final warning." The operator covered his mouthpiece, and spoke to one of his men: "General Santiago has required us to notify him if any American planes come within fifty miles of our airspace. You had better call him now. He'd want to know right away."

He contacted Santiago as ordered. "Sir, we are receiving a transmission from Havana control. It seems three American planes are headed to our borders. We have been following the transmissions. They are less than fifty miles out."

Through his earpiece, Schaffer heard the entire exchange, which caused him to hold his breath and listen more intently.

"Are they military aircraft?" Santiago asked.

"No General. They are civilian planes. If our intelligence is correct, they are carrying men from the rebel group, Brothers for Freedom. President Castro has declared any action by them an act of war."

"So, the insolent bastards refuse to heed my warnings? This time we shall teach them a lesson. Send two MiGs to intercept these Americans," he said venomously. "When they get within one mile of our air space, blow them from the sky! It's time we show the Americans we mean business."

"Sir," DeCana sputtered, "should we notify President Castro?"

"No!" Santiago shouted. "Castro promised to destroy any planes from the U.S. that crossed Cuban airspace during his last visit to the United Nations, and he still allows them to caress our borders without recourse. Today shall be different."

Schaffer continued listening, but wasn't sure what was happening right now. Whatever it was, he knew it couldn't be good.

"But, sir." DeCana protested. "We have an obligation —"

"No! He is too busy with his new friend. Furthermore, he has grown soft when it comes to the Americans. It's time we take a stand and do what is right. We shall be commended for our efforts. Where are the American planes now?"

"They are just south of the 24th parallel." DeCana's voice was taut.

Confidently, Sandoval said to his co-pilot. "Let's move in a bit closer, if the others see us on the edge of Cuba's air-space unharmed their faith will be enhanced." Sandoval spoke to the other pilots and reassured them that they would remain safe as long as they did not cross the invisible line demarcating Cuba's protected borders.

Sandoval tilted the wing of his aircraft towards the ground. Just above the ocean avoiding detection flew four F-18 Hornets. He reached into his jacket to retrieve a second mike. "Zulu leader, this is Big Brother. We're about to begin our drop."

"You're all clear Big Brother. There are no signs of bogies in the air."

Concentrating on the conversation and position of his escorts, Sandoval was not paying attention to his gauges. His plane drifted into the buffer zone between Cuban and international airspace. Seconds later, the MiGs appeared behind them and locked on the Cessna. Realizing his mistake, he turned the plane north and edged the throttle forward to increase air speed, but not before crossing the line that denoted Cuban air space.

Sandoval again reached for the second mike. "Zulu leader, I've picked up bugs on my ass. Bring out the fly swatters."

"Negative Big Brother. You've crossed into Cuban air space. We can't engage as long as you are there."

The MiG pilot moved in closer to the Cessna.

"Shit!" Sandoval yelled. "Havana tower, we momentarily lost control of our rudder. We have now returned to international airspace." He waited for a response. Total silence persisted. "Oh God, we're in trouble."

"Eagle's Nest, this is Zulu leader. Permission to splash the bogies. They're in international air space threatening our planes."

"Negative, Zulu leader. We have just received word from the brass to let things play out."

"But sir, we could lose these men. One of the MiGs is closing fast."

"Repeat, negative! Return to the nest."

The silence was broken when the captain of the first MiG requested permission to splash the American planes.

"It's time to take some evasive action. For God's sake, Zulu, get these guys off us!" Sandoval nosed the plane toward the water hoping to see the Hornets. He saw them climbing west. Just as it seemed the plane would crash into the Atlantic, Sandoval pushed the stick forward flipping his plane upside down just a few feet above the ocean. The MiG stayed right on his rudder. Again Sandoval pushed the stick forward, the Cessna went skyward and flipped from its upside down position. The Cessna lurched upward into a wide loop, hopelessly attempting to shake the MiG.

The radio cracked with static. "Splash them all!" Santiago pounded his fists on the console.

A missile burst from under the wing of the MiG in pursuit of the Cessna.

Now speaking directly to the MiG pilots, Sandoval yelled, "Go to hell!"

"You first!" The MiG pilot returned.

The missile ripped through the plane. What had been a Cessna 337 Skymaster was now a ball of flame, smoke, and bits of burning metal falling into the ocean.

Seeing the blip disappear from the screen, the Zulu leader cringed. "They fucking blew one of our planes from the sky. Now they are after the other two. Sir! Request permission to rescue the other two planes."

Disgusted, the admiral hung his head and depressed the plunger of his mike. "You have your orders, Captain."

The other two American planes were flying northwest and climbing into the clouds. "Climb, climb, climb!" one of the pilots yelled.

The second MiG released a missile and the second Cessna exploded into a fireball of debris. Leaflets escaping the fire trickled through the air like leaves from a tree, littering the ocean with their unread message.

After the second blip disappeared from his screen, the Zulu leader pulled out of formation and slammed his throttle increasing his speed.

The pilot of the last Cessna looked down. "Shit, we're sixteen miles north of their air-space and they just blew the plane out of the air!" He began to hyperventilate. "Oh God, oh God, we've got to get the hell out of here!" He prayed.

"We cut off their balls," one of the MiG pilots laughed. "Their prayers can't help them now."

"Yeah, they won't be messing around tonight," the other uttered. Both pilots laughed.

Santiago laughed with them. "Good work men! That will teach the Americans to go against the will of Cuba! Where is the third aircraft now?"

"We have been unable to locate it." The MiG pilot answered.

A lone F-18 blew in front of the MiGs at Mach-1.

"What the...? An American F-18 just flew in front of us! Should we engage?"

General Santiago jumped to his feet. "Just as I thought, this is a military mission. Now let them taste our resolve. Blow him from the air!"

The MiGs increased their speed to catch up to the F-18 and attempted to lock on.

A sonic boom exploded, shaking everything within a mile of the noise. Seconds later, there were F-18s behind and on each side of the two MiGs. The Zulu leader lifted his mike. "Do you wish to engage?" He looped his Hornet skyward and took his place with the other F-18s.

The MiGs pulled down, followed by the F-18s. Outgunned, and unable to outmaneuver the F-18s, the MiGs signaled their desire to retreat. Accordingly, they set a course for home escorted by the superior F-18s with their missiles locked and thumbs poised to fire should the MiGs change course.

One of the F-18 pilots spoke into his radio. "Crap Shoot, you are one crazy bastard."

"That's how I got the name, boys. This was my fight. You didn't have to show up." He watched the MiGs cruise towards Cuba. "I'll take the heat when we hit deck. I just couldn't let those fuckers kill any more of our people."

"Why should we let you have all the fun? I could swear I heard the admiral say to prevent them from shooting down any more planes."

"That's what I heard."

"Yeah, me too."

"Thanks guys. I'll still take the heat." The Zulu leader led the attack group back to the ship.

"What the hell is going on? Why are you coming home?" Santiago sounded furious.

"Sir," the pilot responded, "we were outgunned and couldn't get them all. We had to save our planes. It is almost impossible to replace them."

Santiago's reddened face appeared ready to explode. He took several seconds to exhale before speaking. "You're correct. We'll have our day soon. Return to base."

Private DeCana took a few deep breaths and dropped his head. He wanted to tear Santiago's throat from his body and watch him slowly die. He swallowed the feeling and tentatively spoke. "Sir, should we alert President Castro now?"

"No!" The general waved his hand dismissing DeCana. "I want to tell him myself."

DeCana's transmission ended.

Schaffer felt as if his legs were made of lead. He found it difficult to step from the cab. The Cuban's act had the potential to send the United States in for a full-scale military attack.

Chapter
27

The steel gray darkness retreated as the sun edged above the horizon.

The sun's golden fingers danced around the room, gently caressing Xavier's face. Slowly, his eyes panned the vaguely familiar suite. Last night he had been practically carried to his room, exhausted by his ordeal with Santiago.

Xavier sat up, wincing in pain. The beating he took at the hands of Santiago and his men came rushing to the forefront of his mind as he grabbed his ribs. His eyes drifted to a love seat against the wall opposite the bed. On it were clean clothes that someone had placed there sometime during the night.

Placing his feet to the floor, his hands instinctively reached to massage his bruised, aching muscles. He looked around again. So far, he liked what he saw.

Pain or no pain, Xavier knew that he must stay in top physical form. He dropped to the floor to exercise, but the pain sent him directly to the shower.

It had not occurred to him to examine the door to see if it had been locked from the outside. If he were a prisoner, his surroundings were different from anything he'd seen in training. He took the time to savor the shower in case things took a turn for the worse.

He stepped from the shower, taking in his room, which was as nice as any hotel he'd ever stayed in. Laid out on the sink were toiletries for his comfort.

After shaving half of his face, he heard a quiet knock on the door. He stepped into the sitting room, with a towel around his waist. "Come in." The knob turned without the sound of a key unlocking it first and the door slowly opened. Xavier didn't know what to expect, but felt relaxed by the condition of his room. Involuntarily, his mouth opened as he glimpsed the most beautiful woman he'd ever seen.

She gracefully entered the room, carrying a tray with coffee, fruit, and croissants. She placed them on a table next to the helmet that had safely brought him across the mine fields. Xavier stood transfixed.

"I trust you slept well?" Trying not to stare, her eyes coursed over the bruises that covered his muscular frame and softened to mild amusement as she glanced at the dumbfounded look on his face.

Not speaking, Xavier shook his head to affirm her question, his jaw still slack.

Her lips parted, revealing a smile. She was accustomed to the effect she had on men, but Xavier held her interest. His gawking held an innocent quality. He seemed almost embarrassed that he could not stop looking at her so intently.

Liquid brown eyes, full lips, and jet-black hair that cradled her head and neck complemented her golden brown skin. Her gauze dress draped her full, proud breasts, narrow waist, and round hips, stopping just above the knee, revealing her strong legs. Noticing everything about a person was a necessity in Xavier's line of work. But viewing the woman in front of him was far from a call to duty.

She backed up a few steps before turning to leave. "Breakfast is at nine."

"Gracias." Xavier's heart filled with anticipation, but his response came out as if he were in a trance.

"De nada," she answered and walked to the door. "I was beginning to wonder if you could speak. You should not be concerned here, you're in good hands." As quietly as she came, she left the room without another word.

Xavier watched her leave, then took a seat at the table. He poured a cup of the thick dark coffee and took a sip. Already, he found himself haunted by her lingering scent. Xavier finished his shave, dressed, and prepared for breakfast.

Years of training had prepared him for all types of combat situations. A SEAL's job was to go in and hit a target hard, using enough fire power to blow away a small country if need be. For this mission, another type of training had been included. Now he understood why. Many a mission had been compromised at the hands of a beautiful woman. Demetria was hard to ignore. But the mission was foremost in his mind. Nevertheless, he hoped to see her again.

Chapter 28

"Mayday, mayday, mayday! Someone please answer! We are under attack by the Cuban Air Force! Does anyone copy, mayday!"

The last remaining pilot, now fifty miles from Cuban air space, frantically radioed for help, unaware that the F-18s sent the MiGs running for cover.

"This is Miami control. Identify yourself and repeat your message."

"Tango-Zulu-Foxtrot 454, American plane from Miami. We are under attack by the Cuban Air Force!"

"Under attack? We have you on radar Tango-Zulu-Foxtrot 454. There are no other planes in your area. Calm down." The control tower waited for the pilot's breathing to slow. "Now tell me what happened."

"They shot two of our planes right out of the air! We were not even in Cuban airspace. There was no warning. They just killed our men!"

"We have to alert the proper authorities. Come to runway number 10. You'll be met there."

NSA Headquarters monitored the downing of the two planes, and the escape of the third. Within thirty minutes after the explosions, a debriefing team was waiting at Miami International for the pilot's arrival. The tower had been instructed to keep the men in their plane until met by the NSA team.

After dispatching the debriefing team, NSA placed a call to Secretary of State Mackenzie. He hesitated to speak when he received the news. He gave the order to Admiral Gregory to have the F-18s return to the ship. He knew his instructions would result in disaster, which he hoped would allow for an escalation in actions against Cuba. Regardless of what anyone else thought, he had his martyrs and an additional reason for direct action against acts of war. "Thank you for calling," was his only response. He stood firm on his belief that the United States now had substantial provocation to enter Cuba.

Mackenzie called to his assistant. "Get me the president." Then very quietly, with a smirk on his face, he whispered, "We have an emergency on our hands."

¤¤¤¤

Bryant Gumbel invited President Nicholas to Orlando for a private round of golf prior to his annual United Negro College Fund Golf Tournament at Disney World. It was a perfect day for golf. The sky was blue, there was no hint of wind, and a seventy-four degree temperature surrounded the course all morning. Gazing about, the players surveyed perfectly manicured greens lying between sand traps and water hazards. Nature provided them with no excuses as they attempted to guide the dimpled ball onto the green and eventually into the hole.

Bryant waited for the president to tee off. He hoped to get some further insight on the so-called invasion that had been part of their news all week. "Great shot, Mr. President!"

"Bryant, I've told you, it's Alex out here." He attempted to be modest after driving the ball two hundred and seventy-five yards, which after rolling, rested in the middle of the fairway.

"Fine, Alex. It was still a great shot. I think you've been holding out on us. Publicly, you always downplay your skill. You're quite good."

"You're too kind, Bryant. The truth is this is the best game I have ever played. I don't think anything could ruin this day." After teeing off on the 9th hole, Alex lit his second Opus X.

Bryant watched, admiring the precision and dedication the president gave to cutting and lighting his cigar. Alex followed his regimen to the letter until he puffed and released a cloud of blue smoke. This was a love affair, not a habit. "Would you like one?"

Bryant looked over. "How can I refuse? You seem to enjoy them so much."

"Bryant, I enjoy golf." He held up the cigar. "I am passionate about my cigars."

"Excuse me, Mr. President. There is an emergency call for you." A Secret Service agent handed him the phone.

The president stepped away from his foursome and held out his hand. Answering the phone, Alex did not attempt to take the cigar from his mouth. After almost thirty years of practice, he could talk yet not muffle his words.

"Mr. President, it's Ian Mackenzie. We've gotten a call from NSA. The Cubans just shot down two planes belonging to Brothers for Freedom. So far, we have determined one of the planes momentarily drifted into their air space. The pilot immediately retreated to international air space. Five miles into international air space, the first plane was shot down. The second one was destroyed sixteen miles out. Oh, and sir, I've just gotten word one of the planes that was shot down had one of the CIA's most experienced Latin agents at the helm."

"Didn't we provide them with escorts?" The president blew forth a cloud of smoke with his words.

"Yes, sir. When the first plane drifted into Cuban air space, they were told to return to the ship."

"By whom?"

"By me, sir."

Alex took a moment to think. "What the hell did you think we sent an escort for?" He didn't wait for Mackenzie to respond. "Goddamnit Ian, you're getting close to not having a fucking job. In case you forgot, it's the president's job to make those types of decisions. Did Castro give the order to shoot the planes down?"

"NSA didn't match his voice with anything on their records. They're reviewing the tapes again just in case. We believe his brother, General Santiago, gave the order."

The president let out a sigh of relief. "Ian, why did you have the F-18s return?"

"The Cessnas accidentally crossed into Cuban air space, so I told Admiral Gregory to pull them back. I didn't want an international incident on our hands with what's going on." He paused and the silence begged him to continue. "I'm sure General Santiago gave the order to the MiG pilots. Our planes never stood a chance. Sir, I feel bad about our loss. But it can't hurt our cause."

Ignoring Mackenzie's last comment, Alex insisted, "Get Director Caprelotti on the phone, see what he knows. I'll have to get on the airwaves as soon as possible to denounce this action. Have Annie set everything up here at the Disney Club House in thirty minutes."

He handed the phone back to the agent and walked back to his group. "Gentlemen, let's finish this hole. I'm afraid duty calls, and I will not be able to complete our round. Mr. Gumbel, you may have an interest in the press conference I'm about to give, that is if you still have an interest in Cuba. They just shot down two American planes."

Bryant rested his club on his shoulder. "I'll be there, sir."

They finished the hole and returned to the clubhouse.

Only forty minutes had elapsed since the downing of the planes and already the media was buzzing with activity. One of the dining halls was quickly converted to a pressroom. Rumors began to flood the press corps. The reporters became restless awaiting the news.

Without one hair straying out of place on his head, wearing an exact replica of his purple polo, with the Presidential Seal over his heart, President Nicholas took center stage. The portable Presidential Seal covered the Mickey Mouse ears on the podium. Still, the edges peeked slightly out from the perimeter, giving it a comical look. Extra Presidential Seals were always carried for just such emergencies. Nothing, however, could be done about the peeping ears.

"Ladies and gentlemen," the president began, "around 3:25 p.m., two private American planes were shot down by the Cuban Government. These planes were unarmed, and therefore posed no threat to the Cubans. Furthermore, it is our belief that these planes were shot down over international waters. This is an illegal and unforgivable offense. I have dispatched the Coast Guard to search for survivors. I assure you that we will deal swiftly and harshly with the Cubans. No one has the right to harm our citizens in international airspace. We will not sit by idly and accept such a repugnant act, for to do so is equivalent to condoning their unprovoked attack. At this time I will attempt to answer a limited number of questions."

Chapter
29

Schaffer was on his way to the Orlando Naval base to catch a military hop to Cuba.

Just after he reached the luggage area, his cell phone started to ring. Looking down at the incoming number, he saw it was Joe DeApuzzo, his editor at the *Post*, trying to get in touch. Schaffer punched the button and answered the call. "What's up, Joe?"

"Schaffer. Glad I caught you." He breathed a sigh of relief. "The president will be starting a press conference in half an hour. The Cubans shot down two of our planes about an hour ago."

"You gotta be shitting me." Despite hearing DeCana's transmission earlier, Schaffer tried to sound surprised.

"I wish I were. I've arranged for a car to take you to the Disney complex. Some poor sap should be standing around with your name on a card. You should be able to get there in time."

"Thanks Joe. I'll call you as soon as it's over." After a twenty-eight-minute cab ride, Schaffer arrived at the Disney complex. He passed through the security post by using his press credentials and slipped into the conference practically unnoticed. The president was speaking when Schaffer entered the room. As soon as he finished, Schaffer stepped forward with a question.

Alex was surprised and seemed shaken to see him in the audience. Wounded at the completion of his last press conference, Schaffer knew he shouldn't expect Alex would ever call on him again. Reluctantly, he pointed towards Schaffer for the first question and then held his breath.

"Mr. President, is this incident in any way linked to, or caused by the rumors of a Cuban invasion?" After asking the question he thought, *that wasn't so bad, was it, Mr. President? You had to anticipate that question.*

"Schaffer, you know very well that those are only rumors, so how could they be linked? As to their state of mind concerning such rumors, one can only speculate. I prefer to deal with the facts." The president's response hinted of anger, but he remained in complete control. "This was an act of cowardice on the part of the Cubans. The planes were unarmed. If I were to send planes to Cuba, they would certainly be equipped for any possible conflict."

Schaffer probed further. "Were any of the passengers on the plane from the military, or the government?"

"As I just told you, the United States government didn't send in these planes. If I were to send in planes, they would be well equipped for battle. We were told these men were from a group known as Brothers for Freedom. As you well know, the government has no type of direct involvement with them. They are a private organization."

Schaffer's eyebrows rose. He wanted to add, *if you say so,* but instead he retreated to the back of the room. Schaffer's questions had not caused the president too much damage, although they may have started people thinking about the real possibility of an invasion.

The president answered questions for five more minutes. Reporters scurried to the phones to report to their respective news agencies. Alex retreated to a private area in the Disney clubhouse, passing right by Schaffer, but refusing to make eye contact. Schaffer punched redial on his phone and called Joe DeApuzzo at the *Post*.

Chapter
30

"Get me a double Johnnie Blue, would you?" the president said.

He pointed to one of his agents. "Why is Schaffer constantly trying to bust my balls? How the hell did he even get here? Get Ian Mackenzie in here now. Tell him to contact Director Daly. I want to know what Schaffer O'Grady thinks he knows. Make sure Mackenzie doesn't mess with O'Grady, though, and I also want the FBI to get me some answers right away. There's a file on him, have them look into it." Alex dropped into a chair. "This son of a bitch saved my life during the election. Find out if he's had ulterior motives all along. Goddamnit, I don't need this shit!"

Secretary of State Mackenzie received his instructions and then placed a call to Director Daly while the president continued to rant. "Schaffer O'Grady has shoved a stick up the president's ass. He wants you to find out everything O'Grady knows. Oh, and Daly, your ass is on the line so you'd better hurry." As soon as Mackenzie hung up, he walked to a quiet corner of the suite in the Disney complex. After making sure that he was alone, he placed a second call.

"Cordell, O'Grady's time has come. Get rid of him. He's causing the president too much grief. He's on his way to Gitmo to interview some people about the Cubans who left. Make it look like an accident. Now would also be a good time to cash in our stock. Once our fall guy is out of the picture, it'll be too dangerous to try selling the stock. We want all suspicion to die with him."

Cordell got up and closed his office door. "How in the hell am I gonna get on a military base without raising suspicion?"

"I'll take care of that." Mackenzie looked out the window of the suite. "I'll call the C.O. and tell him that you are to act as O'Grady's guide. As a matter of national security, of course."

"You should have let me take that bastard out when I did Cosby, two for the price of one."

"It would have brought up too many questions at that time. Just get it done, and don't fuck it up!" Mackenzie hung up the phone and muttered to himself. "I'll get your pest taken care of, Mr. President, and then I'll be the fucking hero, one step closer to my goal." Ian walked into the bathroom and ran his fingers through his hair. He stared in the mirror, admiring himself.

Alex sat drinking his scotch in the comfort of the Disney complex, contemplating his next move. He turned to an agent. "Go out there and find O'Grady and bring him in here. We need to talk."

Schaffer entered the room, escorted by an agent. Alex sat between two other Secret Service agents. Schaffer sat down across from the president. Mackenzie walked in. For the moment, there was total silence except for footsteps as Mackenzie returned to listen to the president.

Alex took a sip of scotch and placed the glass on the table. "All right Schaffer, it's time you know what's going on."

Mackenzie glared at the president with a look of utter disbelief. A short sound escaped his lips but before he had a chance to complete a word, the president's stare silenced him.

"The invasion you continue to ask about is a team of three men. I sent them there to assess our standing with the Cuban people." Alex was saying this for Ian's benefit since he already told Schaffer at the cemetery.

Schaffer played along in case this exchange held more significance. "Three men are hardly an invasion. What else is going on, Mr. President? This can't be all there is to it."

"You're right." Alex played with the ice in his glass. "Castro is holding four CIA agents prisoner in Havana. The SEAL team's mission is to free these men before Castro has them executed. You can appreciate the need to keep my men safe. Castro's already getting jumpy. I believe that's why the planes were shot down. If the media continues to fuel the rumor of an invasion, we may not be able to get the men out safely. Surely you can understand why we've remained silent?"

"For the time being." Schaffer sat forward in his chair. "However, I need a little more to go on. I also want to know the truth. Did you have Harold Cosby killed to protect your silence?"

"Hell no!" The president held his glass up for a refill. "I can't believe you even asked me that."

"How about anyone on your staff?" Schaffer persisted, clearly overstepping any sense of decorum.

"Schaffer, why would I allow someone to kill such a close friend?" Alex took his glass from the agent and sipped.

"Because he had too much information about the CIA agents being held and your planned invasion to free them." Schaffer sat back. "You haven't told the American people about the hostages. Could it be that you have other plans? Say, overthrowing Cuba's government while you're there."

"I've got a team looking into Harold's death. When I find out who killed him, I'll personally make them pay!" Alex lowered his head. "And I told you, there's no invasion. What then could I possibly gain by overthrowing Cuba?"

"How about gaining an island that once was known as a playground for the rich? With the proper figurehead in place, the United States could control everything. I would have said cigars, but you already have an unlimited supply of your favorite Cubans — the White House humidor is full of them. Then, of course, there's your re-election. Overthrowing the last bastion of Communism in this hemisphere surely wouldn't hurt you."

Everyone except the president focused on Schaffer. Still standing, Mackenzie took a step in his direction. "I think it's time for you to leave now." He leaned close to make sure Schaffer was the only one to hear his next statement. "We'll be watching so you'd better keep your damn mouth shut."

Schaffer ignored his comment and continued sitting. A Secret Service agent tugged at his coat. Before he stood, he looked towards Alex. "Mr. President, if there is any thing I can do to help please let me know. No one wants to see anyone die needlessly."

The president looked up. "If I think of anything I'll be in touch.

¤¤¤¤

Before Schaffer could get out of the conference hall and into his taxicab, the palm transmitter Dee had given him started buzzing. He popped in the earpiece. "I wondered how long it would take you to call."

"Do you always piss off so many people at one time?" Dee's voice was calm, given the exchange between Alex and Schaffer.

"I do my best. How was our little performance?"

"Judging how pissed off the room is, you're lucky you're still standing. We're very protective of the president, you know."

"Some are a little too protective." Schaffer looked out the taxi window. "Just ask Harold."

"So you think it was someone in the room?"

"Who else would have a reason to want to see him dead? I'm sure it's some perverted sense of loyalty, or self-righteousness. Regardless, it sucks." Schaffer's voice dropped off, completely disgusted. "Hopefully, this interview will help to flush them out."

"Schaffer, why did you decide to make yourself bait? I know you suspect Ian. If he is responsible he will not just let you walk in and point him out."

Schaffer ran his hand across his head and grabbed the back of his neck. "I made a promise to Harold and I intend to fulfill it. Somebody has to stop the sick bastard. Hopefully, I'll catch him before he catches me."

"Good luck, sugar."

"Thank Dee." He released his neck and sat up. "Hey, what the hell really just happened in the air over Cuba?"

She asked softly, "Did you have your earpiece in?"

"Yeah."

"You were listening to the Cuban side, right?"

"Right again." Schaffer still looked puzzled. "So how is it that I'm listening to a Cuban control room?"

"DeCana is one of ours. He's been in place for a while. You heard the same thing that I did. There was nothing else."

Still trying to piece things together in his head, he asked, "What the hell were F-18s doing flying with Brothers for Freedom?"

"We had a CIA op in the group. The F-18s were supposed to provide protection." She paused. "The president put them there, and Ian Mackenzie called them back when the citizen planes crossed into Cuban airspace. There was nothing else we could do. They broke the rules."

Schaffer shook his head. "Why send them up if they're not going to provide complete protection?"

"The president asked the same question. Nevertheless, he realizes that we have to respect international law. At least one of the planes did cross into Cuban airspace. Our ability to protect that one ended at that moment."

"You realize this incident just added fuel to the fire of a full scale invasion." Schaffer crossed his legs. "Every press agency in the world will start probing this issue. I hope your men in Cuba are safely placed."

"Don't worry about them. Maintain your monitoring of Cuba. It should start to get interesting. If I need you to listen in on our side, I'll send a text message. The president wants you to know what goes on here as well. Enjoy your trip to Gitmo. I'll talk to you when you return home, sugar."

Chapter 31

Xavier left his room, hopeful he would soon see the woman who had visited him earlier.

He walked down a long hallway in search of the dining room and the possibility of a large breakfast. He descended a short flight of stairs. The aroma of breakfast met him at the bottom step. Xavier entered the dining room where he found a buffet of delights and Castro awaiting his arrival.

The table was laden with fruits, breads, nuts, fish, juices, and coffee.

Castro beckoned Xavier to take a seat. "Please. Here in Havana, we like to take our time when eating. In Manzanillo, you all are too eager to get to your sugar cane fields to enjoy this time of the morning. We find it is a good way for us to begin discussions for the day." Yet Castro wasted no time making his point. "I was impressed by you crossing the mine fields yesterday. Perhaps your bravery can be used to help your country."

Xavier bowed. "I am willing to help any way you see fit."

Castro nearly smiled. "It was not me who saw fit, but my niece. She has the gift of foresight. She has never been wrong with her visions. Based on what she has seen, I have big plans for you."

Xavier felt a chill course through his body. If what Castro said was true, his cover could be blown. "Your niece has an amazing gift. I hope I'm able to live up to the expectations congruent with her vision."

Castro laced his fingers in front of his face and held them there a few seconds. "Cuba needs you. Since the fall of the Soviet Union, our country has been beset by the lack of funds to properly motivate production at our factories, farms and warehouses. The passage of the Helms-Burton Act by the United States has put a halt to any discussions we began in an attempt to end the embargo. We came close to an agreement earlier this year. It's a shame our talks failed. The lack of motivation is beginning to show in our people and our economy. Your actions were the centerpiece of conversation as soon as the news hit Havana. We can use your success to stimulate our people while we search out alternatives for our country."

Xavier focused on his plate as he listened to Castro. He ate from the bountiful table. He hadn't eaten in over twenty-four hours, and he shoveled food in like a starving man. The earlier snack in his room only whetted his appetite for real food. Still, he was careful to use some manners while eating, just in case *she* showed up.

Breakfast came to an end, but Xavier's goddess had not appeared again. He was not comfortable enough with his host to inquire about her, at least not yet.

Castro sensed Xavier's distraction. After a short pause he continued, "I would like a demonstration of the helmet you were wearing when you crossed the mine fields." Xavier snapped back to reality. "I'll go get it. I think you'll enjoy experiencing the helmet. I've never witnessed anything like it before."

Xavier reached his room and carefully combed every inch looking for any signs of recording or transmitting devices. Finding none, he felt that his safety was assured. Then he turned the helmet upside down. Inside the helmet, towards the front, was a small, smoky colored plate about three centimeters wide and thirteen centimeters long. Xavier raised the lining over the plate and placed his right thumb across it. Scanners flowed over his thumb, reading the print. When the scanners completed their trek, the plate opened. Xavier took a small object the size of a pencil eraser from the compartment, and placed it into his ear. The compartment also contained a pen, which he placed in the pocket of his new shirt. He depressed the plunger of the pen and gave it a quarter turn counter clockwise. He smiled and said, "Wake up everybody, we're live and in living color."

This was the sign NSA headquarters was waiting for. Those monitoring him blew a collective sigh of relief. Xavier was broadcasting live from Castro's house. Every step of his progress could now be monitored and plans adjusted accordingly.

Finally, he retrieved the extra microchip and replaced it in the helmet, instantly bringing it to life. Returning to the courtyard, where Castro eagerly awaited him, Xavier fit the helmet onto Castro's head and moved the shield down. Instantaneously, the inside of the shield lit up showing grids, distances, and possible compositions of the items within view.

Xavier proudly explained. "What you are seeing are thermo-radiation patterns. Everything is made up of atoms, which are in a constant state of motion. Thus, they give off heat waves. Look over to your right. Notice the palm trees appear to be a greenish brown. The rock next to it is a bluish-gray color. If I walk into your area of view, I appear red in the core and slightly lighter colors, such as orange or yellow, as you look to the outer edges of my body."

"I see a blue line just over your heart, what is that?" Castro asked.

"Now you are getting the feel of it. That is my pen. Metal appears blue." Moving from Castro's field of view, he walked over to the edge of the courtyard and buried his pen in five inches of dirt.

"What the hell is he doing?" a voice yelled through the receiver lodged in Xavier's ear. He smiled, knowing this would rouse the guys at NSA.

Castro walked to the edge of the courtyard and looked down as Xavier instructed. "I see another small blue line surrounded by brownish green and small bluish pieces."

"That's my pen again. This time, however, it is buried in five inches of dirt and rocks."

"Amazing!" Castro laughed. "I can see how this could be very helpful."

Xavier uncovered the pen and blew on it to clean it off.

One of the men listening at NSA headquarters jerked the earphones from his ears.

"I'm going to get you when you get back, you son of a bitch!" John Willow yelled from the SEAL Team's listening post. Knowing Xavier was in no immediate danger, the NSA team relaxed their guard, taking time to get coffee and cigarettes.

Castro removed the helmet. "I want you to go into the city to pick up suitable clothes for dinner tomorrow. We shall hold a reception to introduce you to my people. My niece, Demetria, will take you. I believe you two have met."

Demetria walked towards them. She looked over with a smile on her face. Seeing her a second time, Xavier felt even more captivated by her beauty. His eyes never left her as he answered, "We have."

She took her uncle's arm. Holding him securely, she smiled warmly at Xavier.

He returned her smile, and forced himself to consider the possibility that she could be Castro's version of "the woman in red," there for the sole purpose of undoing the mission he was sent to complete.

Chapter 32

The other reporters were scrambling to get their calls placed to their news desks.

Schaffer took out his cell phone on the way to catch a cab and called the naval base at Orlando to confirm the departing time of the C-130 to Guantanamo.

Before the phone rang, he decided to delay his flight in order to go to Miami. He knew Brothers for Freedom's headquarters would be abuzz with activity, and that uncensored information would flow freely.

"Hi, Sergeant, this is Schaffer O'Grady. I need to delay my flight plans for a day."

"Mr. O'Grady, I was just about to contact you. That flight has been canceled because of a problem with the plane's hydraulics. It will leave tomorrow at 0900 hours." In reality, Secretary of State Ian Mackenzie had arranged the delay to give Cordell enough time to get in place as Schaffer's military guide in Gitmo.

"I'll see you tomorrow." Schaffer hung up the phone and instructed his taxi driver make a U-turn after passing the turn for the municipal airport. He arrived just in time to catch the 2:45 p.m. plane to Miami.

Less than an hour later, at 3:30 p.m., the plane touched down. Joe DeApuzzo arranged to have a driver meet him. As soon as Schaffer exited the plane in Miami, he saw the driver waiting for him in the airport lobby.

¤¤¤¤¤

Schaffer looked out the window. "How long will it take to get to Brothers for Freedom headquarters?"

"About twenty minutes," the driver quoted with a heavy Spanish accent. He offered no further comment.

During the ride, Schaffer took in everything. The waterways, filled with boats, lapped the land at every turn. Even the downtown area had a marina. He imagined people taking their boats into work to avoid the traffic jams on the highways. Watching the people come and go, he began to get a feel for the area. The closer they came to Brothers' headquarters, the more heavily Latin the area became. Schaffer's ability to speak Spanish should help to buy him a little tolerance as an outsider.

As promised, they arrived within twenty minutes. Schaffer found himself swimming in the emotions of his hosts in the large meeting room at their headquarters. Many were still in tears at the loss of their brothers. The entire conference room was whirring with discussion of the day's events. People clutched pictures of the loved ones killed by the Cuban MiGs. Others brought flowers in memory of their lost friends.

A man at the front of the room addressed the gathering. "The United States surely will seek retribution for such a brutal crime, especially the murder of a CIA agent."

Schaffer eased closer. He turned his recorder up to catch the conversations around him. His pulse raced when he heard the speaker's last statement. He was surprised that the CIA agent was known to Brothers' membership. That fact would make the president's denial of U.S. involved in Cuba more difficult. If others in the press found out, it would be hard to protect Alex on that point, not to mention the fuel that would stoke the fire surrounding the invasion.

A middle-aged man addressed the crowd. "Castro will stop at nothing to prevent us from spreading our message of truth to our homeland. We will not let a tragic setback stop us. We will bring freedom to our native soil, and Castro will then receive the justice he deserves." The man stepped from the podium, while some in the gathering cheered through their pain.

Schaffer walked to the front of the room, catching the speaker before he disappeared among the people. He recognized him as Gato Canoso, head of Brothers for Freedom. "You said a CIA agent was one of those killed. How can you be sure?"

"His identity was not hidden from us," Canoso said impatiently. "We were made aware of his identity from the start. Of course, that is not the type of thing we broadcast to the masses, although now that Cuba has killed a government employee, everyone will find out shortly when they seek to avenge his death."

"Who was he?" Schaffer asked. "And how long was he with your group?"

"His name was Sandoval. He was with us for two or three years now, I can't remember. He was responsible for planning our flights. Strategic implementation, he called it."

Schaffer looked at the flight plans still posted in the background. "How did you know he was CIA?"

"I have friends in high places," Canoso said, smiling. His involvement was no mistake." The man turned and looked at the flight plans that held Schaffer's attention. "The U.S. wants to get back to Cuba as badly as we do."

"Why do you think they want Cuba?" Schaffer hoped to find new information that could prove beneficial.

"Have you ever seen the island?" The man's eyes glowed with excitement. "It is the most beautiful in the Caribbean. The U.S. can return, implementing a new government and control tourism netting billions of dollars a year in revenue. Isn't money always the real issue?"

Schaffer voiced his surprise. "You don't find this objectionable?"

"Not in the least," Gato said. He paused. "As long as we get back what is ours."

"Then why did you fly into Cuba after Castro said that he would shoot down any unauthorized planes flying into Cuban airspace? What made you take such a risk? Did you think this would help U.S.-Cuban relationships?"

"Mr. umm…"

"O'Grady. Schaffer O'Grady, of the *Washington Post*."

Gato folded his arms across his chest. "O'Grady. I think I know your name. Well, Mr. O'Grady, in war we must all make sacrifices. Some are just greater than others. Don't be fooled by the lack of military intervention. We're at war."

Schaffer felt taken aback by his words. Sandoval and the other dead men seemed to be pawns in the Brothers' game, necessarily dispensable for their cause. As Gato Canoso continued to speak, Schaffer quickly realized that Sandoval's sacrificial mission was really one of insurance. This mission helped to legitimize President Nicholas' need for an invasion. It guaranteed the president would not be able to negotiate with a hostile land. Blood had already been shed; no doubt more would be before this was over.

Schaffer wondered about his involvement with this entire fiasco. At this point, no suspect was out of the question, not even Alex. The deeper Schaffer dug the more confused everything became. His feeling of trust towards Alex waned, leaving him unsure of his next move.

He remained for the next hour gathering information from the membership. Once he had what he needed, he returned to the airport. Walking around various shops, he began to feel even more uneasy and decided it would be better if his notes were not in his possession, especially since he would be a guest of the United States Navy for the next few days. If the U.S. government was involved, and it sure seemed they were, his safety could depend on the possession of these notes. Schaffer purchased a mail pouch, addressed it to Joe DeApuzzo at the *Post* and enclosed a note: "Joe, keep these for me until I return. I can't risk any prying eyes at Gitmo."

Schaffer arrived back in Orlando at 9:00 p.m., too tired to eat, or, as it happened, take off his clothes. He fell asleep watching CNN with the remote still in his hand.

¤¤¤¤

The next morning Schaffer was up at 8:00 a.m. He laced his Nike cross trainers and headed for the jogging track in the Disney complex. He knew too many people his age destroyed by years of inactivity. He was determined not to let his thirty-seven years take over his body, reducing it to flab. Jogging helped him to relax and sort out all that he had absorbed during such a short time. It also kept him leaner than so many of his other friends. He ran harder than usual, attempting to piece together this puzzle, which was still as fragmented as a shattered glass.

Cosby had called him to discuss an invasion, but was killed before they had the chance to talk. Tito went to Cuba on a mission and was taken into custody. Alex swore he was not involved in any type of invasion, so far, Schaffer thought he believed him. But if he didn't have Harold killed who did and why? Finally, why would a group of refugees decide to return to a land they'd just left?

The president admitted to sending in three men, but thirty left Gitmo. They had to know that there was no chance of surprise, so why risk being jailed or killed? It just didn't make sense. Then, just a few days after these men return to Cuba, Brothers for Freedom decides to fly another mission to Havana, in the face of Castro's warnings. Their trips are not unusual, but their timing stinks, and they're blown from the sky. Maybe Castro had been expecting an invasion and was edgy, refusing to allow unauthorized aircraft entry to his country. One thing was for sure, this situation reminded him of an iceberg, the bulk of the truth resting below the surface. Schaffer felt

Gitmo should help him to put a bit more of the puzzle together. There had to be refugees there who knew why thirty men decided to return to their homeland.

By the time he'd returned from his run, he was soaked. Schaffer hoped no one was in the lobby of the hotel waiting to take the elevator up. He didn't want to offend anyone who'd have to stand within a few feet of him. He settled to the back of the elevator and watched the doors close. Just before coming together, an arm shot between the closing doors.

Disguised, John Cordell stepped on the elevator and quickly offered Schaffer his back.

Schaffer ran off the elevator and made a beeline to the shower. The hot water pelted his body. It was the perfect ending to an exhilarating run. For five minutes, he let the water wash off the sweat and salt covering his skin. He used the next thirty minutes to plan his next move. First on his list was to get something to eat.

John Cordell waited outside Schaffer's door until he was sure Schaffer had time to enter the shower. He slipped in the room and briefly looked through Schaffer's things. Nothing in the room held Cordell's attention. With only one bag to work with, Cordell planted multiple tracking devices in Schaffer's luggage and left the room.

¤¤¤¤

Schaffer finished breakfast and checked out of the hotel by 7:15 a.m. He wanted to get an early start to the naval base. Hopefully it would give him the extra time to talk with the Commanding Officer at the base before leaving. The missing pieces Schaffer did not get from the president or Dee he hoped would be waiting in Cuba. He felt as if he were living in the middle of a dream. And not a good one.

Schaffer's escort pulled in front of the command office. The driver stayed in the jeep. Schaffer walked in and went to the desk sergeant. "I'm Schaffer O'Grady. I believe this is where I'm supposed to meet with Lieutenant Francis."

"I'm sorry, Mr. O'Grady, Lieutenant Francis is unable to accompany you on this trip. He asked that I send his regrets, and to inform you that he didn't have a chance to call before he left. Lieutenant Cordell has been sent as his replacement."

Schaffer felt a little reluctant at first, something just didn't feel right. He'd spoken with Lieutenant Francis the day before, and was assured everything was in order. The desk sergeant's inability to focus directly on Schaffer, when he spoke about Francis, was his second clue that something wasn't right.

"Thank you." Schaffer could see something wasn't quite right with the man, who quickly looked Schaffer in the eye, then offered him a seat. Schaffer sat across from the sergeant's desk and waited for Lieutenant Cordell. The young Marine couldn't take his eyes off Schaffer. When he was sure that he had Schaffer's attention, he flipped a small American flag upside-down. Escape plans instantly entered Schaffer's mind in the event things went awry: the flag was a coded message. Just in case, Schaffer reached in his jacket pocket, pulled out his cell phone, and dialed Joe DeApuzzo's number.

After the first ring, Joe answered.

"Hi Joe. I just arrived at the Orlando Naval base. Everything seems to be going okay, except they had to replace Lieutenant Frances with someone named Cordell. The desk sergeant doesn't think much of him, he just flashed a distress message." Schaffer glanced over at the sergeant who was looking past him as if he wasn't there, but Schaffer knew the sergeant heard his entire phone conversation. "Something's not right here. I wanted you to know, just in case."

One man who had knowledge of the alleged invasion was already dead. Harold Cosby remained fresh in Schaffer's mind. Schaffer had no intention of being the second. He was alone with the sergeant in his office, but just outside the doorway were dozens of people. Schaffer listened intently for any unusual sounds. He would not let anyone catch him off guard. He watched the Sergeant for additional clues. Everything surrounding this case made him uneasy, the closer he came to the truth, the stranger things became and he had just begun to scratch the surface.

He wanted to contact Dee about the changes, but there wasn't time. At zero eight forty five hundred hours, Lieutenant Cordell came out to greet him. Schaffer's first impression of Cordell was that he seemed to be a bit too old to just have made the rank of lieutenant. Either he was a perpetual fuck-up, or he was too stupid to pass the rank advancement test, neither of which the Marines would accept in any officer. Every officer had to be outstanding, both physically and mentally. They had to stand out as shinning examples for the men they commanded. Cordell's face was weathered and wrinkled, and his physique was not as refined as a Marine's. Though he was not fat, he lacked the spit and polish for which the Marines are famous.

His hair was a bit too long, and his uniform looked as if he borrowed it from his younger, leaner brother.

The hairs on the back of Schaffer's neck stood at attention. He stood and sized up the lieutenant. From the moment Schaffer saw Cordell's eyes, he knew confrontation between them was inevitable.

After an extended pause, Schaffer extended his hand. "Pleased to meet you."

"Likewise," Cordell offered coldly. "Let's get moving. We don't want to keep the plane waiting."

The ride to the plane was short, but it was long enough for Cordell to ask a few questions to break the ice. "So Schaffer, how long have you been a reporter?"

"Three years." Schaffer anticipated his next question before Cordell had the chance to speak. From his previous military training, he began to think of what they were told to say if captured by the enemy: name, rank, and serial number.

"Where did you go to school?" Cordell asked.

"Xavier University."

"In Ohio?"

"No, in New Orleans."

Cordell was a typical government type: plow in and get the information. There was no time for niceties. Schaffer wanted to see what Cordell would come up with when he asked questions. Before Cordell had a chance to fire off another Schaffer asked. "And you? Where is your alma mater?"

"Oh, I just went to a hick school in the mountains of Virginia, U.Va. Class of... a long time ago."

Schaffer chuckled politely, because the lieutenant couldn't think fast enough to come up with a suitable date. "Why did you join the Navy?"

"I got tired of the rat race. Here I receive a steady pay check and I get to wear these neat uniforms."

The charade was completely transparent. Cordell failed the test. No Marine would admit to joining the Navy, even though the Marines are technically part of the Navy. It's a matter of pride.

Schaffer knew, whoever he was, he was about as military as a tutu. He had not called 'sir' one time during their entire conversation. The Marines were big on respect, especially when someone is their guest. Not only was Schaffer a guest, he was a former Marine who'd attained the rank of major before leaving. Who Cordell was, Schaffer didn't know. He could only assume he was from one of the government agencies, probably the CIA. Schaffer knew his background had been investigated, so Cordell should have known he had been in the Marines and the Secret Service. That was standard operating procedure before allowing a civilian to catch a military hop. He expected at least one Semper Fi, or an Ooh-Ra to put him at ease, but neither came. He knew it was time to keep his senses sharp. Cordell wanted something and he wouldn't have been there if he wasn't good at getting it.

They entered the C-130 transport plane bound for Guantanamo Bay. Schaffer could instantly tell he was in for an uncomfortable flight. The canvas jump seats looked to be about twelve inches wide and only six inches long. He sat down and strapped in. This was a long way from the business class flying he'd grown accustomed to.

Schaffer noticed several large boxes and crates. He desperately wanted to know what was in them, but he didn't want to ask Cordell. There was no reason to start him talking again. But his reporter's curiosity finally got the best of him. "What do all of these boxes contain?"

"Supplies to replenish Gitmo. They can't buy anything from the locals, you know, because of the embargo."

Schaffer wondered. *They? Who are 'they?' Shouldn't he have said we?* Cordell wasn't even aware of his slip-up. Schaffer sat back and waited to see what Cordell would come up with next.

"Where're you from, O'Grady?" he continued with questions designed to put Schaffer at ease.

Schaffer unfortunately reopened their conversation, so he carried it forward. "I'm from a small town in Virginia, a town where there were more tobacco fields than people. Kenbridge."

Cordell nodded. "So, how does someone from a one horse town end up in the nation's capital, writing for one of its largest papers, and winning Pulitzers?"

The hair on the back of Schaffer's neck stood up for the second time. "Hard work, I suppose. I see you've been checking up on me."

Cordell shook his head. "I wouldn't say that. I think it's polite to know something about my guest."

"It's a long story, Lieutenant Cordell. Maybe one day I'll have time to tell you." Schaffer eased his head to the side of the plane and closed his eyes. For the next forty-five minutes, they flew in silence until Schaffer noticed a .10 caliber Glock sidearm bulging from Cordell's jacket.

Schaffer noticed the Lieutenant opened one eye. He used the opportunity to ask about the gun. "When did the Marines start carrying .10 calibers? And when did they start letting you carry hog legs? We always had to carry .45 calibers on our sides."

Cordell looked reflectively at him searching for the right words. "Now we're allowed to carry them either place, our sides or in hog legs."

Schaffer knew it was an obvious lie and wondered if Cordell realized he had just been caught for the second time. "Two hundred years of tradition unmarred by change." Schaffer knew every Marine would recognize this credo. Cordell's face reddened and Schaffer let out a short laugh. "I'll be damned! Something at the Marines has changed."

Above the roar of the engine, the pilot yelled, "We're about to land, make sure you're secure." The plane began its descent to Cuba.

Chapter 33

The Cuban mine fields were abuzz with activity since dawn.

General Santiago was determined that no one else would cross them and live. He instructed his men to set up the mines to force a series of explosions if just one mine was activated. He vowed never to be embarrassed again.

Santiago's anger surrounding the recent events prevented him from considering the ramifications of speaking against Castro. He gathered his most loyal men in an attempt to convince them his time to lead had come. "I think it is time for a drastic change in our government! Castro no longer thinks clearly when it comes to dealing with the Americans. One would think he has joined forces with them." He paused briefly, only to read the emotion on their faces. "There are rumors that the American military is preparing for an invasion of Cuba. Castro has heard these rumors, yet he does nothing to prepare for a possible invasion. If they come and are successful, there will be nothing left for us, my friends. We have worked too hard just to give our land away."

Beads of sweat ran down the side of his face, and drenched his collar as he slammed his fist into his hand. "Do you think the Americans will take care of us? I think not."

All his men fixed their eyes on him, nodding their heads in affirmation. Santiago placed enough faith in his men to trust them with anything. Now he counted on them to revolt with him.

Lieutenant DeCana, concerned about the direction of the dialogue, parted his way through the group of men. He acted befuddled. "General, sir, with all due respect, we are just a handful of loyal men here. We are going to have to get a lot more people on board to pull this off. Not to mention, what President Castro will do if he even expects what we're planning."

A sly expression crossed Santiago's face. He said, "I'll be leaving for Havana this afternoon. Several of our higher-ranking officers have expressed allegiance to our cause. With their help, we will build the allegiance needed to complete our cause. By the time we strike, it will be too late for any competitive reaction."

"What of the Americans?" DeCana continued. "If they are indeed planning to invade our country, how could we prevent them?"

"You underestimate the power of perception. If the Americans choose to come here, they will be difficult to stop. However, if our group has begun their work by eliminating my brother, we gain the upper hand. They will be forced to negotiate with us because we have eliminated their obstacle and we will grant them access.

Santiago continued talking to his men. His statements were a rally for Communism and allegiance to him as their leader. DeCana shouted and cheered with the other men. He knew he would have to do something about Santiago soon, before the general became too powerful to stop.

¤¤¤¤

DeCana left the installation and headed in the direction of a small cafe where he could buy a drink. If he informed Havana, it might cast suspicion on many innocent men, causing them certain death. Castro never tolerated even the hint of insurrection. Santiago, on the other hand was stirring up his men, surely in an effort to plan a coup d'etat. Although it would complete the SEALs' primary mission, it threatened the subsequent mission of bringing democracy to Cuba. DeCana abruptly jumped up from his table at the bar.

He headed for an isolated path that led him back to his barracks. He veered off the main path and sat on a large rock surrounded by palm trees. Looking around in every direction to insure he was alone, DeCana slipped off his combat boot and raised the inner sole, exposing a small charcoal colored Lucite plate. Placing his right thumb over the plate, infrared scanners read his thumbprint. Seconds later, the plate opened revealing a small chip, similar to a hearing aid, which he placed into his ear. He also retrieved a small telescopic pen that he pulled to full size, gave it a half turn locking it in place, and clicked it, activating the speaker in the top of the pen. "Commander Benderis," he said, "this is DeCana, acknowledge if you copy." He waited, but there was no response. Impatiently, he repeated in a slightly raised voice, "Commander Benderis, this is DeCana, acknowledge."

An eternity seemed to pass. Finally, there was a slight crackle in his ear. The third member of the SEAL team and second in command answered after Xavier didn't. "DeCana, this is Guzman. Is there a problem?"

"Yeah, you might say that. General Santiago is attempting to gather a faction of men to rise up against Castro. He wants to remove him from power."

"Sounds like he wants to do our work for us, if you ask me."

"Sir, he plans to appear friendly to the Americans only until he has power. Then we can expect quite another person to emerge. Santiago's power hungry, and will stop at nothing to get what he wants. He's a ruthless bastard. If Castro had not arrived when he did, Commander Benderis would have been killed."

"Do you have any reason to believe that Santiago questions your loyalty?"

"No sir, I don't." DeCana paused to look around, to be sure no one watched him.

"Good. Then for now play along. Make him feel comfortable. We don't want him to think that you're not in agreement with his plans. I'll contact Commander Benderis. He'll make the decision on how to handle Santiago. Await further instructions."

Xavier heard the entire conversation during his meeting with Castro but was unable to respond. All he could do now was to wait for Ensign Guzman to arrive. By then, he would have mapped out a course of action.

Castro mentioned that Santiago would be attending the party tomorrow in the Presidential Ballroom. This would be Xavier's most opportune moment to draw the general into a trap.

¤¤¤¤

Xavier and Demetria went into town to shop for clothes. The only clothing he had was the military fatigues Castro had provided.

Demetria decided that they should make a day of it. She wanted to show off her new prize. "Why don't we pick out a few guayabera shirts? They will be much cooler than what you are wearing now."

Xavier remembered the loose fitting cotton guayabera shirts, so thin they reminded him of gauze. The shirts were pleated in front with big pockets and splits on the sides. He bought several from Superior Industries in Miami before coming to Cuba, to blend in with the people.

Demetria glanced at the sun overhead. "Why don't you change in the store, then we can continue our day and you will be more comfortable."

Xavier enjoyed the attention, even though his mind was occupied by the more dismal thoughts of his mission. "Thank you. You are most kind to think of my comfort. I'm a bit apprehensive, however. I have no way to pay for these items."

"My uncle has taken care of everything. You are to get all the clothing that you will need." She pulled his arm, dragging him towards the store. "We need to get items for the formal party in your honor tomorrow evening. Uncle wants to introduce you to his staff and party members. Then you will accompany him on a tour of the country. He wants you to deliver words of encouragement to our people. He has seen the effect that word of your escape from the Americans has had on the people."

"Your uncle is too kind." He put his hand over his heart. "I am only a commoner. I know nothing about the ways of a man such as your uncle. Why would he want me to meet these people?"

"You will be fine. Just let your charm shine through." Demetria reached over and stroked his hand. "Don't worry. I will be right there to help you." She could not hide the smile on her face. It was a warm, sincere smile, one Xavier prayed he would see more of.

"Am I to be your escort?" Xavier asked, with hope in his eyes.

"No."

Xavier's heart dropped.

"I am to be yours," she said.

Xavier smiled and could feel the blush that instantly came to his face. "I'm pleased that you think enough of me to sacrifice your time to be my escort. You will be my rock."

Demetria took his hand in hers. He held her gently, yet tentatively. She continued looking forward, and gently slipped her hand free. Holding on too long could give the appearance she was moving too quickly.

Since becoming a SEAL, Xavier had not let himself get seriously involved with anyone. It didn't fit in with a SEAL's lifestyle. Rationally, he had it all worked out. His heart was already at the edge of the waterfalls, ready to tip over and crash to the bottom with a loud splash.

An unexpected visitor passed them on their way in the store. General Santiago was in town secretly meeting with his loyal officers, trying to gain further support for his cause. His eyes met Demetria's as they walked.

"Miss Demetria, you look lovely today, as always." Santiago cut his eyes in Xavier's direction. "I see you've been put in charge of baby-sitting this rebel."

"I am not baby-sitting anyone, General," she replied. "Surely not a rebel, as you suggest." She turned to Xavier. "I suppose you have already met General Raul Santiago."

Xavier slowly nodded his head. "He and his men warmly welcomed me when I got back." The memory of the beating he received at the hands of Santiago was still fresh. Something about the way Demetria said Santiago's full name caused Xavier to frown, and he replayed Demetria's inflections over and over in his mind. Even though he heard the general's name in briefings before coming to Cuba, the way Demetria had said his name was laced with contempt and distrust.

Demetria noticed the frown on Xavier's face and the absent look in his eyes. She turned back to Santiago. "I am surprised to see you, Raul. You were not expected until tomorrow, when we will host a party in honor of Xavier." She took Xavier's arm.

"I decided to get a head start and arrived last night. I needed to find a few things. Before I bid you good day, might I caution you, this man is not what he seems. Please be careful, I wouldn't want to see my niece hurt." Santiago looked to Xavier when he spoke.

Demetria abruptly turned away, and tugged Xavier into the clothing store. Inside, she began to pick out things for Xavier to try on. She herded him into a dressing room with an arm full of clothes.

"I think these are perfect! Try them on and let me see you." Demetria handed Xavier six guayabera shirts and four pairs of pants. She was as lighthearted as a high school girl living out her fantasy.

Obediently, he accepted and proceeded to the dressing area. Xavier emerged a minute later in a new outfit. "This is my favorite."

"Mine, too. Let's take all of them." She handed them to the shopkeeper and proceeded to more formal attire. "Since you are not a soldier we'll select something more in the line of a suit." The store's tailor fitted the suit to Xavier's muscular body. "We will return in three hours, will you be able to finish the job by then?" She never wanted to take her people for granted, even though she was Castro's niece.

The people appreciated her politeness and tried to reciprocate whenever possible. "Yes, Senorita. We shall begin right away."

"Let's go and eat lunch, then we'll have time to see some things in town."

Xavier didn't know quite how to handle the situation. But it seemed the only appropriate response was acquiescence. Accompanied by their driver and guard, they walked to a small café for lunch. A lone lady worked in the front of the café. She escorted them to a booth away from the general traffic of the restaurant. The driver and guard sat close by where they could see everyone coming to and going from the restaurant. Even though she was closely guarded, Xavier was impressed by the freedom Demetria enjoyed in her country.

The area of town where the café stood reminded Xavier of a small European village. He assumed Demetria selected it for its quaint feel, which made her guard's job easier. The other parts of the city he'd seen were as bustling as D.C. or New York. He liked this spot much better.

Demetria requested a bottle of wine for the table. For the next few moments, they gazed into each other's eyes. Their menus lay untouched on the table. No words left their mouths.

Xavier was the first to speak. "Forgive me, I didn't mean to stare. I'm just touched by your kindness. It has been my pleasure to behold someone so beautiful. I've been very blessed to meet you."

Blushing, she tilted her head down. "Thank you. I too was staring. I've only known you for a short time and already I feel your goodness. You carry yourself as a king, yet you posses the humility of a monk. Only a special man could have these qualities. What is it that you did in Manzanillo?"

"I worked in the sugar cane fields," Xavier responded.

Demetria took his hand and turned the palm upwards. She made small circles with her fingers on his palm. "These are the hands of one who has worked hard, which explains how you have developed such a remarkable character. My uncle has greater plans for you. He feels that you would be a great leader of men. He wants you to join with him to rebuild Cuba."

"It would be an honor to serve your uncle in any way that I can. My only hope is that I am able to live up to the expectations that you and your uncle have for me. Leadership sometimes calls for tough decisions. I would hate to disappoint either of you."

Demetria's smile dropped. She looked at him with complete seriousness. "We will not be disappointed."

"I have to ask you a question." Xavier knitted his fingers in front of his face and rested against his chair. "How has your uncle decided so quickly that I am the right man for the job? He has only known me a day and a half."

"News of your escape through the mine fields reached Havana before you were even out of them. My uncle has ears everywhere. He heard what the townspeople were saying before he left to meet you. He decided before leaving that you would help him." Demetria looked into his eyes and spoke more slowly. "When he saw you, he knew that you were perfect for his cause." Her eyes drifted to the table. "He said that even faced with a brutal beating, you refused to bow."

"You knew about that?" Xavier seemed surprised at first, but swiftly nodded in understanding. "Of course you did, your uncle told me about your gift."

"Yes." Her eyes climbed to meet his. "After you were brought here last night, we talked about his plans. He wants you to be an example of loyalty and determination for our people. The fact that you survived what has been called impossible has already given you a god-like quality among our people."

The aroma of Cuban cuisine arriving at their table allowed for a change in the direction of their conversation. Demetria was grateful he did not question her about her visions. She wasn't prepared to explain the truth about her vision of him. They ate and made small talk, getting to know each other. This was the first time in years that Xavier could remember not having to rush through a meal. He was relaxed, enjoying this change of pace.

Abruptly, Xavier's ears perked. He set down his fork and listened intently, yet could not make out the exact words he heard. He brushed at the hair on his arm, which was standing straight. Lifting his head, he scanned the room. Other than their guards, the only other person Xavier saw was the lady who brought them to the table. What he heard came from behind him, yet he did not see anyone there. Standing up to investigate would most likely have frightened Demetria, so he kept his seat. His muscles tightened and all of his senses became acute. Keenly aware of his surroundings, he was ready to act at the first sign of danger.

Demetria noticed the change in his expression. "Is there something wrong?"

"No, I just thought I heard something," Xavier explained, still scanning the room.

Demetria strained to look over his shoulder in the direction of the kitchen. She did not see anything and her guard had not moved. She assumed it was probably just one of the kitchen staff.

Behind them, in the kitchen, General Santiago pointed Demetria out to several men sympathetic to his cause. "Remember her face. She will be an integral part of our success." They continued to watch the couple as they ate.

Santiago instructed the kitchen staff to go about their normal routine. He assured them that he and his men were only there to provide Demetria with extra security and it would be better if she didn't know.

"When we finish eating, we can go to hear the music in the square," Demetria suggested, hoping this would relax him. "If you are up to it, maybe we can even dance."

Xavier smiled. "I would like that. However, with these sore ribs I must warn you, I will not be the greatest dancer in the world."

Demetria winced. "That's all right. I had forgotten about that."

"I'm willing to give it a try if you would like to."

"Are you sure you're up for it?"

Xavier smiled. "It'll be fun."

They finished and asked the driver to return to gather the clothing purchased earlier in the day. Followed by the guard, they set off to hear the music of the late afternoon.

The Salsa band, Los Van Van exploded with rhythmic sounds at Plaza De Arms on Onobispo Street. Demetria wasted no time hoisting Xavier to the dance floor. Loosely grabbing her waist, Xavier extended his left thumb towards the air. Demetria took hold. Their hips and feet moved with the music. Xavier moved through the pain and soon forgot about it altogether. Neither the music nor their dancing ceased for fifteen minutes.

Break time for the band came at the end of their second dance. Before leaving, the lead singer put on a tape so that the people would not have to stop dancing. The mood of the music was quite different as Ibrahim Ferrer's soulful voice slowed the pace, giving the energetic Cubans a chance to catch their breath as well as move closer to their partners.

Demetria and Xavier now held each other closer. She looked up to his face. "Have you ever listened carefully to the words of this song?"

"This is the first time that I have heard it. What's it about?" Xavier paid closer attention to the words of the song since it was his first time hearing it.

"It is about two people who met under unusual circumstances. They were both involved with the same cause, but in different ways. In a very short period of time, they fell in love. He had to leave her to serve his country." Demetria looked into his eyes. "She walked at night, on the beach, where they met, crying as she waited, longing for his return."

Xavier returned her gaze. "Does he ever come back?"

"That question was never answered in the song." Demetria placed her head on Xavier's shoulder. They swayed with the music. She wondered whether her fate was that of the girl in the song, waiting, longing, and never knowing if they would be together.

Xavier rested his chin in the crown of her head. He wanted to hold on forever, but knew that was impossible. Once he finished his mission, he would return home. He looked into the distance, lost in the moment. "I think he comes back," Xavier whispered.

Tears eased from Demetria's eyes, sliding down her face, only to be dried by Xavier's new shirt. She clutched him a little tighter, gripping helplessly onto him. "I hope so."

Chapter
34

Schaffer exited the C-130, shadowed by Lieutenant Cordell, only inches from his heels.

The creepy feeling Schaffer had about Cordell persistently nagged him. It was obvious that Cordell stuck to every move he made, so he came up with an alternative game plan in order to lose the pseudo lieutenant.

"We have to stop by General Michaels' office first," Lieutenant Cordell insisted.

"Yeah, that's what's on the agenda." Schaffer waved a copy of the schedule he'd received in Orlando and mumbled under his breath. "Your ability to observe the obvious is truly outstanding." The last thing needed on this trip was some baby-sitter telling him what he already knew.

When Cordell and Schaffer arrived at Michaels' office, he strolled out to greet them at a leisurely pace. Lieutenant Cordell loosely and half-heartily saluted. It was apparent that he was out of practice with the Marine regimen, or he didn't give a damn.

"Good to see you again, Lieutenant Cordell," General Michaels said, as if delivering a line in a well rehearsed play. Turning his attention to Schaffer, he continued, "Mr. O'Grady, welcome to Gitmo. I understand that you are eager to get started."

Schaffer nodded in agreement. "If you will let my aide, Captain Jenkins, know who you would like to interview first, we'll have them brought in."

Surrounded by the military, Schaffer was reminded of their protocol. But since he was no longer active, he fought the urge to salute Michaels. "I would appreciate it if you would let me speak with the men at their posts, sir. I like to get a feel of their surroundings when I conduct interviews. Being called to the principal's office tends to modify their account of the events."

"Very well. The captain will provide you with transportation. Of course, Lieutenant Cordell will accompany you since he knows his way around. By the way, I understand you were in the Corps."

Schaffer belted out the traditional Marine Corps cheer, "Ooh-Rah, yes, sir. I went in to the Marine reserves right out of high school. It helped me get my college education; I spent a couple of years in Recon." Schaffer noticed a gleam in General Michaels' eye, signaling his pride at hearing his recantation. "Sir, do you mind if I ask you a couple of questions?"

"Fire away, Marine," Michaels said with delight.

Schaffer's face was much more solemn. "How did a group of approximately thirty men make it through two sets of mine fields without your help?"

General Michaels' pleasure dissolved to disillusion. His mouth hung open, impeding his ability to formulate a quick response. Instead, he held his hand out. "Why don't we go to my office? We can discuss it there."

Schaffer looked around. "Before I get too comfortable, sir, where's the head? I could use a break."

"Great idea," Lieutenant Cordell agreed. "I really could use the break too."

Captain Jenkins directed them to the rest room. Schaffer took a stall closest to the door. Cordell went two stalls down. When Schaffer heard Lieutenant Cordell sit, he cautiously eased open the door and tiptoed out.

"Where's a phone I can use?"

Captain Jenkins pointed him to an empty desk in the corner of his office. On the desk was a single phone. Schaffer hoped it was a secure line. He didn't want anyone intruding on his call. His first thought was to contact Dee, but he couldn't risk anyone hearing him speak with her or discover the device that she had given him. Instead, Schaffer decided to call Joe DeApuzzo. He lifted the receiver and listened for unusual sounds that might indicate someone was listening in on his line. He didn't hear any clicks, outside noise, nothing out of the ordinary, so he placed his call.

"Hi Joe. It's Schaffer. I need you to call the University of Virginia Alumni relations office, see if they had a John Cordell attend sometime in the early to mid-seventies." He watched to see if Cordell had returned. "I'll call back as soon as I can. Be on the lookout for any text messages. I may need a lifesaver."

Joe didn't know what was going on, but he understood Schaffer's coded message. Schaffer obviously meant he felt he could be in danger, and that Joe should send someone to pick him up immediately if he got a text message. Just like before, Schaffer would be sending a message instead of talking directly to him.

Schaffer hung up the phone, typed 'lifesaver' into his text quick list, and hurried back to General Michaels' office before Cordell had a chance to come out of the bathroom.

General Michaels attempted to explain the departure of the Cubans from the camp. "Somehow their leader managed to obtain a highly sensitive piece of equipment being tested exclusively here at the base." Feeling that it was just a matter of time before Schaffer found out the truth from the Cubans still in the camp or from one of his men, Michaels decided it was best to tell the truth as he saw it. "As a former Marine I'm sure that you can appreciate our need to keep this information quiet. I also noticed your SCI clearance was reinstated by the president, so I can trust you with this information. Any adversary who finds out about Clear Vision will attempt to copy it, or develop a counter device. Hell, we're not even letting our allies know about this, at least not yet."

"I understand." Schaffer knew not to delve any further into the issue. He waited to see what else the Michaels would offer on his own.

Michaels obliged. "Clear Vision is something like a radar device, only it scans temperatures of objects. For instance, the ground gives off a different temperature than a piece of metal buried in the ground. With Clear Vision, you can see the metal under the dirt." Michaels gazed at Schaffer to see if he understood.

"So, what you're saying is, their leader was able to see where the mines were planted in the ground?"

"Precisely." Michaels looked in Schaffer's eyes for his reaction.

Schaffer suddenly felt puzzled. "General, one more question. How did this man come into possession of this device?"

"That, Mr. O'Grady, is still under investigation. Off the record, I can't imagine how it was possible." He looked out his window. "Only a few of our men knew anything about it. They're not the type to kiss and tell."

Schaffer thanked Michaels and left to meet with the soldiers. The military was treating this as an everyday occurrence, routine for Gitmo. Soon it became apparent to Schaffer that the soldiers had been told to act as if everything was status quo. But he could see tension on their faces and hear it in their voices. It was clear that they had been given orders to perpetuate the military's version of the truth. Since it was apparent that he would not get the information he needed from the soldiers, he quickly moved to the Cuban refugees.

There he found things to be quite different. The refugees were filled with admiration for the man who left the camp to return to their homeland. They held Xavier in high esteem. Though they too left Cuba by their own free will in search of a better life, the truth was between the camps and home, they preferred home. Over the past month, Xavier had preached to his fellow refugees about returning to Cuba. His plans included finding a new trading partner that could fill the void left by the USSR. Then he did something that no one else had done: Xavier left the refugee camp across the mine fields and survived the journey. He went home to make things better for his people.

Schaffer wanted to understand what drove him to leave his home to begin with, only to risk his life by returning. The Cubans spoke of his words that still rang powerfully in their ears and hearts. They believed that one day soon they would return home to a new and better Cuba, a free Cuba.

Schaffer wondered how a person could arouse such feelings of hope in a downtrodden people in such a short time. Then he remembered how Martin Luther King's words made him feel when he'd studied and later taught his speeches in college classrooms. This was his moment of revelation and decision. He knew that he had to get to Cuba, he had to meet Xavier. Schaffer wanted to understand Xavier's plan. Once in Havana, Schaffer had a series of agendas to complete. He would look for a tie-in to Harold's death, as there hadn't been anything concrete in the States, but he knew there was a connection to Cuba. He would locate Tito. And he'd get out hopefully in one piece.

For two days, the computers installed in his home had been collecting data, but nothing had turned up before he left. He felt the answer, or at least part of it, had to be in Cuba, but not at Gitmo.

Schaffer heard all he needed to from the people at Guantanamo. He turned to Cordell. "Lieutenant, I need to get back to Michaels' office."

"Sure thing, O'Grady." Cordell walked towards the jeep.

Once they arrived, Schaffer rushed in. "Sergeant, what time does the C-130 head back to Orlando?"

"It just left, Mr. O'Grady. But I think there will be another one here in twenty minutes." He looked up at Schaffer. "It should leave about two hours later."

Schaffer's curiosity piqued. "How many do you have coming in today?"

"At last count, five."

"Do you always bring in that many supplies daily?" Schaffer waited for his response, suspecting it would be different form Cordell's.

"No, sir. The last four are bringing in men."

"Sergeant, I will need to be on the next plane leaving, if possible." Schaffer realized he'd found his breaking story, and it wasn't a man leaving this camp for home. Instead, it was the man himself, Xavier Ciefuentes and his plans for Cuba. In addition to that, it was the buildup of troops here at Gitmo that he assumed would help Ciefuentes bring down Cuba. The president neglected to include that fact in his briefing to Schaffer. Something big was about to go down and Schaffer wanted to know exactly what it was.

"I'll see to it, sir," the sergeant assured him, glad to have things returning to normal.

Schaffer left the sergeant's office, went outside, and sat on a bench near a landing strip to watch for the arrival of the plane. Just over the mountains, he could see a plane approaching. The engines growled and became louder as the C-130 got closer to the runway ahead of schedule. Another plane circled the airport waiting its turn to land. They certainly weren't wasting any time.

Schaffer found it disconcerting that Alex hadn't mentioned this to him. This was huge. He couldn't wait to hear Dee's take on the troop buildup. Once again, Schaffer suspected Alex's involvement in Harold's death. Schaffer thought Alex could be using him to facilitate his cover-up. The mere thought made him angry.

What did not make sense to him was why Alex would attack from Gitmo. Doing that prevented any possibility of surprise on Havana, unless he hit both locations at the same time. Schaffer's head began to ache considering the different options.

He had not spoken with Lieutenant Cordell in over an hour. Cordell was sitting less than five feet across from him on an identical bench. Breaking the silence, Schaffer asked. "Lieutenant Cordell, why are so many men coming in this afternoon?"

Cordell anticipated the question. He attempted to sound official. "These men are replacements for some of the men here now."

"That's strange." Schaffer pointed to the men passing by them. "I haven't seen any men packing to leave or out here waiting for planes. What do you make of that?"

"Well, O'Grady, the older men have to train the replacements." Cordell said matter-of-factly. But he hadn't finished his statement before he realized his mistake. Schaffer had been in the Marines, and they both knew quite well that the men were trained before they arrived. Only a few would be needed for transition. Cordell's face reddened and he seethed with anger at his own stupid mistake.

"Each C-130 holds about ninety-two combat troops," Schaffer said. "That's about three hundred and sixty eight troops and a hell of a lot of training." Schaffer quietly chuckled, turned his back to Cordell. *Checkmate, Cordell.*

Chapter
35

On the C-130, Schaffer could see that Lieutenant Cordell was still fuming.

For his part, Cordell wondered what he would do now. Ian Mackenzie had been clear about this assignment from the start. Cordell flipped open his note pad and read Mackenzie's words. "Escort O'Grady to Gitmo. Eliminate him there. Make it look like an accident." It was evident that his assignment could not be carried out exactly as planned. If he were to carry it out at all, he would have to do something soon.

As the flight progressed, the pressure to do something grew in Cordell's mind. His muscles tightened and twitched from the stress he was feeling. He appeared ready to pounce at any second, but the presence of witnesses everywhere prevented any rash action on his part. Cordell knew that O'Grady could be a serious threat to his freedom if he were allowed to live. It was a chance he was not willing to take. For the moment he was helpless to do anything except look at the man across from him and decide how he would kill him once they got back to the States.

The other thought that was clear in Cordell's mind was how quickly Mackenzie would turn on him if he didn't complete his assigned mission. Cordell once told him he thought Mackenzie would sell his own mother if it got him what he wanted. The comment didn't sit well with Mackenzie. Cordell acknowledged his feelings, but told Secretary Mackenzie that the only reason his comment upset him was because it was true.

The two loathed each other, but their futures were bound together.

¤¤¤¤

After two hours in the air, the plane slowed and the cabin pressure changed, which confirmed the C-130 was on approach and would be landing at any moment. After fumbling around in his jacket pocket a few moments, Schaffer located his phone, found the switch and turned it on before taking it from his pocket. He hoped Joe was at his desk or had his phone handy. Schaffer quickly retrieved the text message for Joe and sent it. He put the phone back in his pocket and turned to Lieutenant Cordell. "I appreciate your hospitality, but I've arranged to be picked up once we land."

"Oh, don't worry about that." Cordell smiled. "I can give you a ride anywhere you need to go."

"Thanks anyway. My boss likes to know that I am in good hands after such an informative trip." Schaffer kept his eyes locked on the plane's ceiling the entire time they talked. He looked as if he was pleading for an answer to a silent prayer. Schaffer used this method of communication many times before, and more than once it saved his life. As uneasy as he'd become with Cordell, this could very well be one of those times. Cordell was starting to smell like last week's garbage.

It was his habit to type a text message and call Joe before leaving for any important interviews. Schaffer learned this lesson all too well when he was interviewing several gang members in Washington. When the session started to go sour, he used a text message to summon Joe, who called the police. Another time a group of American-based Iranian terrorists suggested he would be a better hostage than a conduit for their message, because of his notoriety. That time, Joe immediately contacted the FBI. Within moments, the FBI had tracked his phone's signal. They broke into the meeting, rescuing Schaffer and arresting the terrorist. Both of those times, just as in this one, he knew early on that things weren't going well.

For a few minutes, Cordell's attention had been on the small note pad in his hand. He flipped the cover open with a quick jerk of his wrist, read his notes, and then he jerked the cover closed. He repeated this motion over and over, ignoring everything around him, including anything Schaffer had to say. Several times the pen in his left hand moved to the page as if he would write additional notes, but he never added a single word.

The plane's engines whined, slowing rotation as it quickly descended to meet the runway. Before they touched down, Cordell flipped the note pad open again. This time he wrote feverishly. Schaffer strained to see, but to no avail. Seeming pleased by what he wrote, Cordell tapped the pen against the note pad. Then, as if struck by a moment of brilliance he hurriedly jotted down something else.

The wheels of the plane screeched as the rubber grabbed the tarmac. Cordell replaced the pad in his pocket, and laughed. When the plane stopped, they stood to leave. Just outside the open door, two Marines stood by a waiting jeep.

Schaffer felt like the lump in his throat would have been obvious to anyone who saw him. He anxiously approached the Marines at the jeep. "I'm ready, gentlemen."

"Where would you like the Navy to drop you off today, O'Grady?" Lieutenant Cordell asked.

Schaffer directed his answer towards the Marines. "Back at the Disney complex would be just fine."

Cordell pushed his way in front of the Marine sentries. "That's okay, boys. I'll take Mr. O'Grady to his destination."

The jeep pulled out, heading for the front gate of the naval base. When they arrived, a Marine guard stepped forward, halting the jeep.

Schaffer moved as if he was about to stand, and Cordell pushed him back in his seat. Schaffer sighed with relief when he saw a limo a block away, moving rapidly towards the front gate, with the lights flashing and the horn blowing.

Schaffer hopped out of the jeep, knowing his best chance was to run like hell. "Thanks gentlemen. It seems my ride has arrived." He grabbed his bags and headed for the approaching limo without looking back. He hoped the sentries had his back.

"Where the hell do you think you're going?" Cordell screamed, and then reached under his jacket pulling out his .10 caliber. Barely taking time to aim, he squeezed off a shot.

The bullet zipped by Schaffer's right ear, nicking it and striking the top of the limo door. The Marine guards interceded by firing a warning shot and knocking Cordell to the ground. They pointed the M-16s at the back of Cordell's head. "Don't make me kill you, sir," one of them shouted as the other cuffed his hands.

Cordell squirmed viciously, attempting to grab his fallen gun. "Get the fuck off me. You don't know who you're fucking with!"

He was slammed to the ground. His note pad flew out of his pocket and landed near Schaffer's feet. Schaffer flung open the door of the limo, scooped up the note pad and dove inside the car. Blood dripped from the nick in his ear, staining his shirt and pants. "Man, am I glad to see you. Lose those assholes." The limo sped rapidly away. Schaffer continued to look back to see if they were being followed. His heart pounded in his throat. Finally, he sat back, relaxing just a little. Putting his finger to his ear, Schaffer felt the warm blood still dripping from the wound. He pulled his hand down and looked at his fingers, red with his blood. Suddenly he realized that he'd come within inches of having his head blown off. All his past training was geared to preparing him to deal with these types of stressful situations, but the bullet he'd taken four years earlier gave him a new appreciation for its seriousness. Schaffer breathed deeply to help regain his composure. Again, he looked behind the speeding limo. Confident that they were not followed, or that the jeep was too slow to catch up to them, he turned to the driver. "Get me to Orlando International." He reached into his bag and pulled out a clean shirt. His blood stained pants had to wait until he reached the airport. The driver was careful not to question him. However, after looking in the rear view mirror he suggested Schaffer grab some gauze from the first aid kit next to the bar glasses.

Schaffer applied pressure to the wound to stop the bleeding and then put the band-aid on his ear. He opened Cordell's notebook, what he read made him angry and relieved that Cordell's shot had been off.

Kill the bastard!!! NO Mistakes!!! Do it NOW!!!

Speeding down the highway, Schaffer could wait no longer. He retrieved the device from his bag and pressed Dee's contact button.

"Hey, sugar. How's the trip going?" she asked light heartealy.

"Cut the shit, Dee, and tell me what the fuck is going on!" Schaffer screemed.

Her demanor changed immediately. "What are you talking about?"

His voice was high-pitched with agitation. "Some asshole pretending to be a Marine leiutenant just tried to put a hole in my head. I don't appreciate it one goddamned bit! If you or the president wants me dead, at least have the balls to do it face to face and stop sending your goons to do your dirty work."

"Calm down, Schaffer! If I wanted you dead it would have happened when I came to your house. The president doesn't want you dead either. You're the only hope he has at finding out who killed Chief of Staff Cosby."

"He has a funny way of showing it. Who else has the power to order a hit? Shit, he even had the officers at Gitmo playing along. At the last minute my military escort gets changed to some goofy-assed jerk, if he's military then I'm the king of D.C." Schaffer looked out the back window again.

"I specifically requested Leiutenant Francis as your escort. I personally took care of your arrangements for Gitmo," Dee answered, sounding both surprised and incensed.

"Then maybe I shouldn't be having this conversation with you." Schaffer started to disconnect the device.

"Hold on just a minute!" Dee pleaded. "I already told you if I wanted you dead you wouldn't even have gotten to Gitmo. I've been with the president around the clock for the past two days. His mind has only been on his SEAL team's mission."

"When did the mission change?" Schaffer asked.

"I'm afraid I don't understand." Dee sounded completely serious.

"How do you explain the four C-130s full of troops arriving at Gitmo?" Schaffer's tone was condecending.

"There's not much to explain. We have to be ready in case plan A doesn't work."

"So, you are planning an invasion? Good luck keeping it quiet."

"Not a full scale invasion unless we have to."

Schaffer was even more upset. "You people really are pieces of work."

"Schaffer, when do you get back to D.C.?" she asked.

"You want to meet me at the airport?" Schaffer shook his head. "Or will someone else be there to finish the job?"

Dee yelled, "Can't you get it through your thick skull that I'm trying to help?"

"Sorry, but the hole in my ear and my blood-covered shirt have made me a bit jumpy. I'm not sure I want any help right now. I can't trust anyone, least of all anyone involved with the White House. People around you are dying too fast for me. I'm not sure what I'm going to do." Schaffer slipped his clean shirt on.

"At least keep your lines of communication open so I can contact you if I have anything."

Schaffer laughed sarcastically. "You mean, keep them open so you can track me. I —"

"Goddamnit Schaffer, enough already! I told you I have the only mate to your transmitter. I'm not tracking you. I'm trying to help, so give me a fucking break." Dee's exasperation was clear.

Schaffer didn't really know why, but listening to her, he felt as if he could still trust her. The device did give him a bit of an edge since he could monitor her, as well as Cuba. "Okay, Dee. But, I don't like it when people try to kill me." He paused to let his point sink in, but then he wanted to let her know that he would trust her a while longer. "So, are you still calling me sugar?"

She sighed heavily. "I'll fill the president in on what happened. If I'm uncomfortable after that, I'll help you disappear until we can figure out what's going on together. Better still, I'll back your story up and you can use the paper to blow the lid off the entire operation."

Schaffer quickly added, "Be careful what you say. You may have to make good on your promise. I'll talk to you later."

"I won't let you down."

"You'd better not, or you can't call me 'sugar' again." Schaffer ended the transmission and decided to get ahead of the competition. Dee wasn't going to have to help him disappear. He planned to do that on his own. The Secret Service had taught him that when he needed information people were willing to kill for, the best thing he could do was to become invisable.

Chapter 36

Schaffer stood in front of an older woman at the United Airlines ticket counter, thumbing through several one-hundred dollar bills.

He used cash to purchase an airline ticket to Mexico City. He didn't want to leave a trail that would be easy to follow even though he knew his identity was on a tape behind the counter.

To derail any possible followers, he stopped off at *The Sky's the Limit* gift shop and bought a Panama hat, a pair of inexpensive sunglasses, and a floral print shirt. On his way out of the gift shop, he picked up an English-to-Spanish dictionary. Even though proficient in Spanish, he reasoned that the dictionary could come in handy if there were slang terms he didn't recognize once in mainland Cuba.

At the departure gate, Schaffer walked behind the counter and stood in front of the window to watch for arriving planes. He took the opportunity to check in with Joe.

"Thanks for the life saver," Schaffer said, feeling relieved for the first time since the incident back on the base. "These guys certainly don't want to be identified."

"What the hell is going on, Schaffer?" Joe sat forward at his desk. "You sounded as if things were about to get nasty."

"They already did. Remember, one man with this information is already dead. They almost made it two. I nearly lost my head to a bullet back on the base." Schaffer touched his ear, which still throbbed with pain. "That bastard managed to take a plug out of my ear." He didn't want to spend too much time on what happened; Joe might think he was whining. He abruptly changed the subject. "So, what did you find out on John Cordell? Was he ever at U.Va.?"

"There is no record of any one with that name attending U.Va. during that time period. I even had them look from 1960 to 1990. I put in a call to a contact with the Feds. All she would say is she couldn't talk about anything

John Cordell was involved with." Joe paused and his voice became stressed. "I talked to her again when she got home. She said Cordell is bad news. He acts as a clean-up man for the FBI. If an agent botches a job, he can make it look like it never happened. The FBI started using cleaners after Waco. You really kicked somebody in the balls this time and they're pissed."

"The sons of bitches had it coming." Schaffer sighed and looked out the window at an arriving plane. "Why would the FBI be interested in my story? They're not usually involved in military operations. I have never heard of the FBI being used to assassinate anyone either. It's usually the CIA." He thought about Joe's comments on Cordell. "Random act of violence my ass. You'd better believe Harold Cosby's death was a hit." Schaffer rested his hand against the glass. "Sounds like your FBI friend knows something. But the FBI still doesn't make any sense. Since Harold tried to contact me, I guess my name popped up as hit number two. You know the old saying, no loose ends. But if they wanted me dead why didn't they do it the night they killed Harold?"

"Maybe," Joe said, "they wanted to know what information you had and they figured seeing what they'd done to Harold would help rattle it out of you. Renita did some digging at the Bureau, there's not even a hint of an operation there. If the president wanted to keep a military matter quiet, he'd use the CIA."

"It's not the president," Schaffer insisted, trying to convince himself.

"Who else would be going around killing people to keep a military operation quiet?" Joe asked.

"I'm beginning to think the so-called invasion is a smokescreen for the real agenda. I don't like anyone target practicing when my head is the target, so I plan to find out what's really involved as soon as I can catch Alex. Until then, I guess I best tell you what I'm up to." Schaffer could hear Joe stop breathing on the other end. "I'm headed to Mexico City. I need you to use whatever pull you have to get me a contact in Cuba so that when I get there no questions will be asked. That's where the real story lies. I'll contact you again when I can."

After a long pause and a brief rummage through his Rolodex, Joe lifted a card from the file. "Okay. When you get to Mexico look up Minister of Tourism Alejandro Javier. He'll have what you need. Schaffer, watch your back. You're making someone very nervous. If it's any consolation, I smell Pulitzer on this one."

Schaffer laughed. Joe always maintained his sense of humor no matter what the situation. "We'll see." The fact was that Joe had never been wrong when he sensed a Pulitzer.

¤¤¤¤

Schaffer exited the plane to the world's third largest city, Mexico City. The airport terminal was as busy as any he had seen in the United States. On his way to a pay phone to call Minister of Tourism Javier, he saw a man approaching him. Maybe Cordell wasn't the idiot Schaffer thought he was. Schaffer turned to escape, but a large group of people heading in his direction made it impossible. He hoped Minister Javier would find him before he ended up in a body bag.

The stranger's hand landed on his shoulder and Schaffer spun around as if he was under attack. Dodging bullets still had him jumpy. His eyes fell on Alejandro Javier, a thin, golden-brown man about five feet ten, with dark wavy hair graying on the sides, and the most meticulously groomed mustache he had ever seen. Javier had been waiting for Schaffer to arrive. As promised, Joe had worked out all the details.

"I believe you will need these, Senor O'Grady." Javier handed him several papers in an envelope. "We will need to have your picture made for your passport. I'm afraid the faxed picture we received did not do you justice. If you will, come with me we'll have coffee while we wait. Your plane will leave in one hour."

"Gracias." Schaffer smiled, pleased with Javier's efficiency, relieved that he was not one of Cordell's goons. "Sorry for being so jumpy. I'm dealing with a very sensitive case. I only hope the rest of my trip will go this smoothly."

Javier waved his hand, dismissing Schaffer's concern. "A friend of mine, Flavio Ortaga, was appointed by Castro as a liaison for Mexican tourists. He has reserved you a suite at Hotel Sevilla, in old Havana. He's also assured me that your stay in Cuba will be most comfortable."

"Gracias."

¤¤¤¤

Javier's conversation relaxed Schaffer, allowing him to recoup from a stressful day. All too quickly, his relaxation ended, and he was on another plane. Within two hours, he would be in Cuba, America's forbidden land.

Before leaving Mexico City, he converted fifteen hundred dollars to Mexican pesos for appearance, even though greenbacks would go further. In Cuba, the U.S. dollar was king. Its black market value far exceeded the Cuban or Mexican peso's value. Considering the average Cuban made the equivalent of twelve hundred dollars a year, the two thousand American dollars Schaffer carried in his pocket was plenty. As a Mexican tourist, he knew he would be allowed to move around freely to ask questions and take notes. He dressed casually to blend in and not arouse suspicion.

This was his first trip to Havana. Landing in the area, he noticed Havana's cityscape appeared like that of any large city. On the ground, things were quite different. Very few cars occupied the streets. Most, in fact, were leftover American cars or an occasional Russian model with one or two Mercedes thrown in. All of the American cars were from the fifties. Most people got around on buses, bicycles, or on foot.

Much of the architecture was grand and bold, ranging from Moorish stone to modern multi-colored buildings that would convince anyone they were in Miami. In general, Cubans wore colorful, festive clothing. The women wore brightly colored dresses, or skirts and tops. Many of the men wore tank tops and shorts, although an occasional floral shirt could be seen. The textured fabric was designed to keep them cool.

Many stores, even some larger department stores, lined the downtown area of Havana. Schaffer's cab driver occasionally pointed out parts of the city. "These stores are here for your shopping pleasure," he informed Schaffer. "Inside them you will not have to wait in any long lines. The native people tend to use other stores."

"Why don't the Cubans shop in these stores?" Schaffer asked out of curiosity.

"Most don't earn enough money to buy these goods. The stores cater to the needs of tourists. My people shop elsewhere."

Schaffer grunted at the ignorant policy. During the remainder of the trip, they rode in silence.

Most of the housing units in the downtown area were not in the best condition, although the city was neat and clean. Not one piece of trash littered any street. Schaffer's cab reached the hotel. Though old, it was beautiful. The Moorish building rose triumphantly into the air, setting itself above the natives' dwellings. He looked through the front doors and took note of the Asian rugs, crystal chandeliers, and polished brass, quite similar to the Four Seasons in Washington D.C. The grandeur of the building was a testament to their former wealth. Turning his attention to his driver, he said, "I hope the price tag doesn't match the interior." The driver shrugged his shoulders and Schaffer realized his attempt at humor had been wasted.

"Would you carry these bags to the front desk?" Schaffer politely asked the young driver.

"No, senor, I'm not allowed in this building. They'll handle it for you." He pointed to a bag boy, who was rushing from the lobby to fetch Schaffer's bags, while attempting to shoo the driver away.

Schaffer frowned and sighed loudly, aggravated by the bag boy's actions. When the bag boy walked around to speak with the driver, Schaffer asked, "Why can't you go inside?"

"They only allow my kind to drive. Hopefully, one day I will be promoted to an inside job." He longingly looked at the interior of the hotel.

Schaffer reached in his shirt pocket and pulled out a fifty-dollar American bill. It was one of the newer ones with the large picture of Grant on it, and it was still crisp. He unfolded it by grabbing opposite ends and snapping it before the driver's eyes. Then he re-folded it and placed it in the driver's hand. "Thanks for all your help." Tears filled the driver's eyes as he turned to leave. The bag boy flashed a big smile as though he too had found good fortune.

At the check-in desk, a clerk handed Schaffer a note from Flavio Ortaga. It read:

> I have arranged for a guide to meet you upon your request. He will be able to assist you during your stay. If you should need anything else, notify the desk clerk, and I will see to it that you are taken care of.
> Please enjoy your stay on the Island.
>
> Flavio

Schaffer folded the note and placed it into his shirt pocket.

"This way," the bag boy said, and led him to the elevators. When they arrived at his room, the bag boy asked. "Would you like me to hang your things?"

"No. That will be all," Schaffer said coldly.

The bag boy had seen the generous tip that Schaffer gave the cab driver. Now he grinned with anticipation as he waited for his tip.

Schaffer walked to him, handed him five pesos, and closed the door. Schaffer said, "That will teach him to be rude with the less fortunate." He sat on the edge of his bed still taking in what he had been through the past few days. Unloading his pockets, Schaffer looked at the transmitter that he'd received from Dee. Being out of the country helped him feel safer, at least for the moment, even though he knew Cuba was at the root of his distress.

After his shower, he hurried to the lobby to contact his guide. Once the guide arrived, they could venture into the streets. Schaffer wanted to go out among the people to see what, if anything, they knew about Xavier. He approached the desk clerk. "Senor Ortaga arranged a guide for me. Would you contact him and let him know that I'm ready to begin my tour?"

Her head quickly turned in the direction of a man standing in the lobby, looking out into the street. Even through the loose fitting clothing it was obvious how well defined his body was. His broad shoulders formed a V as they reached his waist and veins bulged from his thick forearms. He appeared to be standing at parade rest as he waited patiently for Schaffer to arrive. Upon hearing Ortaga's name, Guillermo Leon strolled across the hotel lobby to meet Schaffer.

"That's who you are waiting for, sir," the desk clerk said, pointing in Guillermo's direction.

Schaffer turned and offered his hand. "What do you do when you're not escorting tourist around?"

"I box," Guillermo answered.

"I guess I should have known. Are you a professional?"

"I'm an Olympian." He smiled as if Schaffer should have known who he was.

"That's fantastic. Shall we get started?"

"After you, sir." He held out his hand.

Guillermo had an intimate knowledge of Cuba and its people. To be designated as a guide, Guillermo had to profess his loyalty to the ruling party. Schaffer wondered if he was also classified as a citizen spy. He heard from Minister Javier that guides were expected to gather any information that could prove useful to Castro as the leader of the party. Schaffer knew that he would have to choose his remarks carefully, even as a tourist. "How long have you been a guide?"

"All of my life, senor. Tourism is as important as sugar or tobacco here. We are trained from an early age." His answers were succinct, with a sharp edge.

"Guillermo, is that correct?"

"Si."

"Guillermo, what is the most interesting talk around town these days?" Schaffer asked hoping to break the ice.

"There are many things to see and do —"

Schaffer cut him off. "No, no, what is the local talk? You know, the hot topic of conversation?"

"We should go to the market place. There's a bar there and you can hear the hot topics for yourself." Guillermo led the way.

"Tell me about the people here. This is my first trip to your country. What is life like here in Cuba?"

"Since the Soviet Union collapsed things have been very difficult. Everything is rationed to us. Meat, gasoline, everything. Only the tourists can get anything they want. Too many of my people have left the country in search of a better life. This is the only life I need to know. Castro has promised a better day for our beloved Cuba. I know that day will come soon. I believe in President Castro."

"There's a lot of talk in Mexico that the United States plans to invade Cuba." Schaffer looked for a reaction. "Have you heard this?"

Guillermo instantly became enraged. "No one would give much consideration to such talk. Castro has provided for us and protected us. He would not let that happen. Maybe you remember what happened to the U.S. at the Bay of Pigs." Guillermo's face reddened as he answered curtly.

"I didn't mean to offend you. I guess I wanted your reaction."

"And now you have it." Guillermo spat on the ground expressing his contempt for the U.S. "The U.S. assumes it holds the cure for all the world's ills. They stand ready to force feed anyone who doesn't like things just as they do, when what they should do is offer their humanity first. Wouldn't you consider that leadership by example?"

Schaffer raised his eyebrows as they entered a small bar on one of Havana's side streets. The building appeared to be a large hut without doors that allowed patrons to enter from all sides. Once inside, Schaffer could see the enclosed portion of the bar. The outer area was full of people talking and smoking cigars. He listened carefully to the conversation in order to gather information. It wasn't long before he heard what he'd hoped for, people talking about the men from Gitmo.

"I heard he walked across the mine fields as if he were daring a mine to blow up."

"Yeah, I talked with one of the men who returned with him. He said Ciefuentes showed no fear, not even to Castro's brother when he was taken into custody. Castro would be a smart man to use him as an advisor. He must have secret information or supernatural powers."

The men laughed at the last comment. Xavier had the people talking; a single daring act had rejuvenated their hope. If a man were willing to risk his life to bring his people home, there must be something worth returning to. Xavier had filled his follower's ears with potential and pride. And hope spread throughout Havana.

One of Santiago's loyal following, who was gathering information, decided to challenge what he'd heard in an attempt to determine empathy for Santiago and discredit Xavier. He quickly stood, knocking his chair to the floor. His erratic actions hushed everyone in the bar. Looking around the perimeter of the bar, he noted his strategically placed comrades.

Forcefully, he jetted his finger in the direction of the last person who spoke. "I hear this man was sent by the Americans. Anyone who can't see this as an attempt by the Americans to takeover our country is a fool! General Santiago will find out the truth. Then Cuba can be ruled properly!"

"Sir, your passionate soliloquy is quite ill advised," another man said. "Talk such as yours could land you in prison, or sign your death warrant, depending on whose listening. Why would you think the president's brother is more qualified than Castro himself?"

"Look at the state of our economy. When is the last time you've had meat more than twice a week or gas for your vehicle, or paper products in your home? And you still consider this man a great leader? He was a great leader in the past. Now things have changed. It's time we changed with them."

There was dead silence in the bar. People physically moved away from the man speaking. They were all aware of the penalty for anyone who criticized the president — death, if you were lucky, or you would be left to slowly rot in prison, where your flesh was rat food.

The next sound heard was clicking made by shoes striking the floor as Guillermo approached. He broke the silence. "Tu? eres el muerto andar!"

Schaffer was stunned by what he'd just heard. He considered Guillermo's words: *you are the walking dead.* He wondered if that was a threat or a promise.

Guillermo spat at the man's feet and turned to leave the bar. With a jerk of his head, he signaled to Schaffer it was time to leave.

Chapter
37

Director Daly repeatedly slammed a tennis ball, tightly gripped in his hand, against the top of his desk.

"How in the hell can a man walk right out from under your nose? This is the most incompetent action I have seen in my thirty-five years with the bureau. What do you think I should tell Secretary Mackenzie? Oh, I'm sorry, sir, I realize this was a matter of national security, but we fucked up." He continued spewing insults at Cordell for the next three minutes. He never once alluded to the fact that O'Grady was wanted on insider trading charges, which hardly posed a threat to homeland security.

"All you had to do was follow the man. You were assigned as his escort, how hard could it have been? It's not like you had to tail him unseen. I'd hate to see how badly you would have botched that assignment."

Cordell's head never bowed. Only he and Mackenzie knew that the real plan was O'Grady's execution. "I think I should tell you that I was able to get a tracking device planted in his luggage. At least we'll be able to tell where he is."

"Well, that's just brilliant, isn't it? So Agent Cordell, where does this little device tell you he is?"

Cordell hesitated. A shit-eating grin was plastered across his face as he enjoyed the moment. "The tracking satellite puts him in Cuba. Havana."

"Oh shit!" With his brow furrowed and after a long pause, Daly's words came out. "Havana? How did he get there?"

"We're not sure just yet." Cordell stood up. "I wasn't able to monitor right away."

"Now you're really pissing me off." Daly threw the tennis ball. "Did your tracking device just start working? Or were you too stupid to follow sooner?"

"I was detained, sir."

"Detained?"

"Yes, sir." Cordell scratched his head. "A couple of Marines didn't like the treatment O'Grady received. It took a little time to square things with the C.O."

"Why didn't you identify yourself?"

"I wasn't supposed to implicate the FBI at any time." He paused. "Your words, sir."

"Get the hell out of my office!" Daly picked up the tennis ball from the floor. He sat down and stared at the wall. He'd have to tell Secretary Mackenzie soon, which he was not looking forward to. The FBI failed to get the job done. Mackenzie warned that he would ask the president to turn things over to the CIA if they weren't up to the job. This was one more black eye for his directorship. He lifted the phone and punched the numbers. Mackenzie's assistant answered the phone.

"I need to speak with Ian Mackenzie please." Daly squeezed down hard on the ball.

"He's meeting with the president and Director Caprelotti. Is this an emergency?"

"Shit! Yes. Go get him. Now."

Moments later, Mackenzie answered. "Give me some good news, Daly."

"The good news, sir, is that we were able to find the source of your leak. The bad news is we were not able to complete our mission as it relates to O'Grady. We did, however, place a tracking device on O'Grady's belongings before..."

"Before what, Daly?" Mackenzie snapped.

"Before he left the country." Daly tapped the ball against the side of his head. "He has managed to get to Havana."

"Havana? *Cuba?*" Ian toyed with the director. "Maybe he should be working for us instead of against us. Where is he getting his information?"

"We're not sure that it's a direct source, but your leak is Senator Hernandez." Daly leaned his head against the tennis ball in his hand. "He told Canoso about an invasion. My guess is most of Brothers for Freedom know by now."

"God, I hope they don't all know." Mackenzie's demeanor returned to a more calm, even tone. "Keep me informed."

Director Daly slid open his middle desk drawer. Without looking down, he reached in and took out a pack of Marlboros. He stood and tapped the pack, freeing a cigarette. Putting the cigarette to his lips, Daly reached for his lighter. Twice more he pulled the cigarette from his mouth only to put it right back in before finally lighting it. Daly drew on the cigarette deeply, as if it were his last breath. The smoke made him choke and he coughed violently. It took him several seconds to catch his breath. Daly fell back in his chair and reached for the glass of water on his desk. He drank from it and wiped the sweat from his brow. This was his third cigarette in two years. He was not accustomed to the smoke, even though he previously smoked three packs a day. "These damn things must be too old. I'd better quit before they get the best of me."

¤¤¤¤

While Mackenzie was talking with Director Daly, Dee walked to a corner and pressed Schaffer's contact button.

"Yeah, Dee. Que pasa?" Schaffer asked jovially.

"Something is coming in from Director Daly's office. I know it concerns you. You might want to hear the exchange going on in the room right now. Don't try to respond right now, I'll call you later."

Mackenzie's voice was the first Schaffer heard. He was sharing his findings about O'Grady with the president, Director Caprelotti, and Dee, who were all neatly assembled in Alex's office. He neglected to share the bungled attempt on O'Grady's life, especially since only Cordell knew who ordered it.

Director Caprelotti jumped at the first mention of the FBI's misfortune in detaining Schaffer. "As I told you Mr. President, this is a job for a more experienced branch of government. O'Grady's in Cuba. I've got men there. The CIA can handle the situation."

Caprelotti's words made Schaffer's skin crawl. He reminded Schaffer of the surgeon's motto: if it ain't right, cut it out. Caprelotti was trigger-happy, but he was straight-laced and would only follow Alex's orders. Schaffer hoped he didn't have to worry.

"The last time I checked, Anthony, it was not your job to *tell* me anything unless I requested it. You are, nevertheless, supposed to keep me informed. So let's analyze the current situation. O'Grady has made it to Cuba. You have a few men in place there. I want you to follow, just follow him. Try to find out what he is up to. I repeat, don't do anything until you talk to me personally. Is that understood?"

"Yes, sir." Caprelotti held his lips together so tightly they formed a single white line across his face. He was a man of action and wouldn't understand the president's inaction.

Alex escorted him to the door. "Thanks for coming." He stepped through the door, watching as the Director walked down the hall.

Alex went back into his office and grabbed an Opus X. Mackenzie was looking over some papers on the president's desk as he waited for him to take his seat. Alex sat at his desk with his head tilted back, reflectively blowing smoke rings in the air. Secretary Mackenzie had seen him do this a hundred times and he knew that whatever he was about to say would be well thought out.

"Have a seat, Ian." He blew a few more rings into the air, buying him extra time to think. "We have to do something about O'Grady. He has made it to Cuba. I can only assume that he is snooping around trying to find out what is going on. I can't risk him exposing my men."

Hearing the president's words, Schaffer felt like a hunted animal. In this case, the hunter had gotten too close and Schaffer was ready to dash if he came close again. The only problem was there was nowhere to run. Everywhere he went, they seemed to have a bead on him. He made a note to look for the tracking devices in his luggage when he returned to the hotel, and to flush them.

¤¤¤¤

"What would you like to do?" Mackenzie asked. "One phone call and I can make your problem disappear." He snapped his fingers.

Before the president could answer, Dee spoke up. "Mr. President, I believe eliminating O'Grady is a much too drastic course of action."

"Why?" Mackenzie stood. "He's caused enough problems. It's time to cut your losses."

Alex raised his hand, shutting down the debate. "I've been thinking." He paused, twirling the cigar in his mouth. "I need to replace Harold Cosby. I could move Press Secretary Tynes to Harold's old position and offer his position to O'Grady. God knows I would rather have him on our team than bashing us at every opportunity."

Dee said, "That sounds like a feasible solution, sir. He certainly is well respected by his peers, thinks well on his feet, and he's a Pulitzer winner. He would make an excellent addition to the team."

Mackenzie raised his eyebrows. "I should have known you'd stick up for him."

"What's that supposed to mean?" Dee bristled.

"Don't you think he's too idealistic? I'm not sure he would even take the job." Mackenzie rubbed his fingers together. "He may consider it a payoff to keep him quiet."

Alex pulled the cigar from his mouth. "In a way, I guess it is. We need to keep our image as pure as possible. Idealism may be just the ticket. The last two articles Schaffer wrote in the *Post* caused us to drop by ten points in the polls." He looked at Mackenzie and Dee. "Who else knows the details of the Cuban plan?"

Mackenzie fielded the question. "Only you, General Roseboro, Commander Benderis — to a lesser extent — and me, of course. Harold proved there was too much risk in telling anyone else. That's why I was surprised you ever involved O'Grady."

Alex sat strait up in his chair. "What the hell do you mean, too much risk telling Harold? He was a part of the team just like you two. If someone hadn't killed him, I could've made him see that what we are doing in Cuba is necessary. Is there something you know that I don't?"

Mackenzie waved his hand, blowing off the president's concerns. "I don't think we should get into that right now. The less you know, the better."

"Ian, I'm the goddamned President of the United States." Alex slammed his fist down to his desk. "I should know everything that's going on. Harold was my friend! He was your friend, for God's sake! Did you have him killed?"

"Mr. President, Secretary Mackenzie's a loose cannon." Dee stood. "His indiscriminate, unauthorized actions could bring all of us down. I won't let this excuse of a man ruin the career I fought so hard to build!"

Ian looked at her with contempt. "Both of you are being shortsighted. I know what will work, Mr. President. There's no way for it to fail. I have considered every possible outcome. What could I possibly have forgotten?"

"Your brain," Dee offered.

"I think you're jumping to conclusions about this killing Harold business," Mackenzie said. "I haven't done anything but look out for your best interest. No one has suffered because of that, including Harold Cosby. I haven't killed anyone."

The president still looked at him with disbelief. "I've had a nagging feeling about where this mission is taking my team for some time now. Disgrace is not an option for us. Ian, from now on, everything, and I do mean *every*thing you do is to go through me. Is that clear?"

Mackenzie nodded as if he had been publicly shamed.

Alex stood and walked the two members of his cabinet to the door.

He approached Annie. "I don't want to be disturbed for the next hour." Alex walked back to his desk, sat in his chair, and laid his head back, closing his eyes. Several puffs of smoke left his lips as he spoke. "I'm sorry, Harold. I am so, so sorry. Just what I need, one more fucking mess to clean up." The throbbing in his head grew stronger as the guilt he felt about Harold's death swept over him.

◘◘◘◘

Dee beeped Schaffer again. "Schaffer, did you hear all of that conversation?"

"Yeah."

"Did it do anything to bolster your confidence in the president?" she asked.

"It helped. But anyone can see Mackenzie is trying to hide something. I think we both realize who's behind the triggerman." Schaffer touched the scab on his ear. Although he'd learned from Joe that Cordell was FBI, he asked Dee, "Have you found out anything about Cordell?"

"He's not CIA. He hasn't even appeared on any of the other agencies records." Dee looked at her notes. "If he works for us, he's in deep."

"He didn't just appear out of thin air. How did he get away from the Marine sentry in Orlando?" Schaffer remembered seeing them holding him on the ground.

"I'm working on that. Touch base again soon." Dee disconnected.

Schaffer clicked the Cuban mystery button to monitor any changes there. He would have to deal with his suspicions about Mackenzie once he returned home.

It wasn't long before Schaffer heard conversations resuming in Cuba. There were at least two people coming through his transmitter. Adjusting a wheel on the side of the device allowed him to zero in on one transmission at a time. In the short time he'd listened, he could already distinguish between voices. Xavier became his current target of interest.

Chapter 38

Xavier sat enjoying lunch at the gazebo.

Resting his fork on the edge of his plate, he closed his eyes and deeply inhaled the fresh sea air. Paradise could cause anyone to want never to return to a real job. After a few moments, he opened his eyes and wiped the corners of his mouth, acknowledging that he had finished lunch with Demetria and Castro. He excused himself, noting how awful it was to go inside on such a beautiful afternoon, and he stood to leave. So much had happened in such a short period of time that he went back to his room to think over the events.

Xavier realized that his relationship with Demetria was moving at a pace that he couldn't control. The last thing that he wanted to do was to end up in a situation that he might regret later, especially as he was not directly responsible for his actions due to the nature of his assignment. Currently, he reminded himself, he served President Nicholas.

Castro knocked lightly and entered. "May I accompany you on a walk?"

"Of course. I was just preparing for tonight."

Demetria sat in the hallway and watched Xavier and her uncle approaching. She rose to join them.

Castro waved her off, which caused her to look like a defeated little girl who just lost her favorite toy to a competitor. Castro clasped Xavier's arm as they walked. "I've noticed the way my niece looks at you. I've never seen that look in her eyes before. It's as if she's found something that was lost and she doesn't want to let it go for fear that it may leave again. Look at her now. She's accepted the fact that this is our walk, although she's not happy about it."

Xavier looked over at Demetria and smiled.

"Many men have tried to become a part of her life, all have failed. It's just as well. None of them have ever met with my approval."

Xavier placed his hand over his heart. "I assure you I haven't tried to gain her attention."

"You'd be a fool if you didn't try," Castro laughed. "For years, any idiot who considered himself in my favor has tried. Countless officers in my military, party officials, many of our premiere athletes. I don't know why any of them thought themselves qualified. And now there's you. I'm not upset. I think you're a very respectable young man. I'd like you to know more about her before you go any further, however."

Castro turned and watched the waves rolling to the beach. "She came to live with me when she was six years old," he told Xavier. "Her father, Carlos Castellano, a former Olympic boxer, was an officer in my armed forces. Tragically, he died during a military training mission in Angola. He and his best friend, Demetri Markev, were flying low-level practice missions when a ground-to-air missile struck their MiG. Demetria was born the next day. Carlos insisted that the baby be named after his best friend. That's how she ended up with a Russian name. Tragically, her mother never recovered from the loss of her husband. She started hanging out in the streets, drinking heavily, finally becoming a whore to support her lifestyle. For long periods of time, she would leave Demetria with her grandmother, my sister. When Juanita left for the United States, I insisted she leave Demetria here. Since then, Demetria has taken my last name and lived with me. Her mother is now quarantined on our island for those with AIDS. I've tried to make life for Demetria as pleasant as possible. I would never let anything hurt her. She has already suffered more than anyone her age should have to."

Xavier understood the weight placed on Demetria by life. Demetria was the most giving, pleasant person he had ever met. He never imagined that she had suffered so much. "You've done a wonderful job raising her," he said. "I'm amazed at how well she carries her burden. How did you manage raising such a wonderful person with all of your responsibilities?" Xavier smiled warmly at Castro.

"Love. I love her because she and I are one." Castro paused looking at Xavier. "Look at the expression on your face. You think I know nothing of love? Although I have little time for outside activities, I have always made Demetria a priority. I take her with me almost everywhere I go. We have never been separated for very long. I set aside time for her everyday, even if it's only by telephone. Since Demetria is all I have left in this world, she gets my free time. That's a lesson I learned from the nuns in school when I was growing up. It's too bad I didn't pay closer attention to it before my own daughter left for America."

The two men continued walking towards the patio, passing a series of guards along their path.

Xavier asked, "Don't you find it a bit strange that you have drawn from your religious education since you abolished all forms of religious schools? Everyone must attend government schools now, and religion surely is not encouraged."

Castro stopped and wagged his finger in Xavier's face, a move that usually signaled he was upset.

Xavier crossed his arms and waited.

Sounding angry and defensive, Castro answered. "Part of what you say is true. However, I've not abolished organized religion. It flourishes here. As with most Spanish speaking countries, it is overwhelmingly Catholic. The members of my party are like me. We have no need for religion. Maybe somewhere within me I've remembered some of the church's teaching. If I didn't love this country, I couldn't have stayed in power so long. All the people of Cuba are my children. As their father, I have love for each of my children. And like children, they need a father to teach them. That's what I've tried to accomplish these past forty years."

Castro put his hands behind his back as he walked. A frown crossed his face and he continued to talk. "As long as I was able to provide for them, things were fine. Of course, now that the Soviets have fallen there's much less money available for everyday comforts. So, my children have started to leave my beloved Cuba. They can't see all that they have here any longer. I've built the top medical community in the world, and it's available to everyone regardless of social status. Our doctors are highly respected worldwide. Anyone can see evidence of this by simply looking at the number of speaking engagements they have worldwide. Everyone in Cuba must get an education. This opportunity is available to every citizen, and no forms of discrimination are tolerated here. When I received my law degree, this was not the case. Batista required citizens to pay for their education. Under his system, only the wealthy could afford to be educated. Many Cubans of African decent, such as Demetria's father, had no chance under such a system. Here in Cuba everyone is treated the same and we don't have such petty problems much of the world faces. Nowhere else has a country given so much to her children, yet my children continue to leave. I don't understand why they can't see that suffering is necessary for growth."

Xavier uncrossed his arms and turned towards Castro. He meant the gesture to suggest he'd warmed to Castro's remarks. "Could it be that your children have matured? Like most children when it is time to leave the nest they may seem ungrateful for all that they've been given. Only later do they find out how good it really was at home." Xavier attempted to express empathy and explain his return.

Castro dismissed Xavier's comment. "Maybe the time has come for Cuba to have a new leader." He looked at Xavier and let his eyes drift back to the ocean. "I've grown tired of the daily demands that are placed on me. When I was younger, Cuba was like a little child. When a little child cries, a mother attends to its needs. This was the case with the Soviet Union, as they were the only ones to hear our cries. Now there is no one to listen. I'm in my seventies, and my hearing is not so good any more. The Soviets have ceased to exist, and the United States doesn't wish to listen as long as I'm in power. Time and time again, I've expressed a willingness to begin talks. Still they are deaf to our request. Life isn't mine forever, consequently, I've found someone who can quiet my people's cries and lead my country to new beginnings."

Xavier stopped cold. Castro looked at him, as if peering into his soul.

Reluctantly Xavier asked, "Who's the person that you've found to lead in your place?" He held his breath, already surmising his answer.

"You." Castro watched shock spread over Xavier's face. "You'll be the one to lead this country forward. There's no sense arguing. Demetria has seen it. This brings me back to my original point. You'll need someone by your side, someone who is strong, who can help you, and who understands you. Someone you trust. Demetria shall be that person. The love between you two is apparent to all. I plan to announce your engagement tonight at the party."

Xavier couldn't speak. He smiled at the mention of Demetria but immediately frowned again contemplating what Castro just said. His primary mission remained to remove from power the very man who trusted him with his niece. Replacing Castro as President of Cuba was not part of his stated mission. It was one more obstacle he had to overcome.

"Thank you for your blessing," Xavier said. "I don't, however, know anything about running a country. On the other hand, I'd be most pleased to marry your niece." His words didn't coincide with the look on his face. His expression held confusion and trepidation and his focus was distorted by the turn of events.

Sensing his discomfort, Castro offered encouragement. "Don't worry about running this country. Knowing my niece, I'm sure you'll have plenty of help." Castro smiled. "Then it's all settled. You should go back and get changed, and get Demetria. Let her know I plan to announce your engagement so that it'll not come as a total surprise tonight."

"I guess you're right." Xavier still carried a look of disbelief and wondered how President Nicholas would respond to Castro's plans. This scenario never came up during training: no one could have possibly surmised its outcome.

Castro left him standing on the beach alone with his thoughts, which he was having a hard time pulling together. He heard static in his ear and a voice started to speak. "What was that all about, Commander?"

It took a moment for Xavier to realize that he was being contacted by one of his men. He stood straight up and placed his hand to his ear. "Repeat your transmission."

Guzman sighed. "It seems to me the commander has gotten in a lot deeper than he expected."

"Expect the unexpected." Xavier mouthed the words, but found them impossible to believe. "What's the latest on Santiago?"

"So you did hear that transmission yesterday." Guzman happily delivered the news. "He's planning to lead a coup attempt against Castro. That could make our job easier."

"Have you forgotten what DeCana said? Santiago would only use the U.S. until he's achieved what he wants. Then bloodshed will be required to get rid of him. That's not part of our mission. Neither is Santiago, but that could change. Follow through with your plans. Come to Castro's villa to inform me of Santiago's plans. I'll take care of the rest."

"You're the boss," Guzman answered. "So, what does she look like?"

"That's not important! I expect to see you within the hour."

¤¤¤¤

Fifteen minutes later, there was a commotion at the front gates of Castro's compound.   "What's going on?" Xavier asked Demetria.

"Some man is attempting to enter the grounds," she answered. "No one knows who he is. The guards will take care of it."

"Senor Ciefuentes," one of the guards yelled. "There's a man at the gate. Manuel Guzman. He says he knows you and has an important message for you." The guard waited for a reply.

"Please, show him in." Xavier waved towards the guard. "He's one of the men who returned to Cuba with me. He means us no harm."

The guard searched Guzman from head to toe before escorting him in. At first, one of the guards insisted on staying with the two men as they talked, since Demetria was in the area. Castro waved him on so that Xavier could speak privately with his guest.

Guzman leaned close to Xavier. "I see what's gotten into you. She's beautiful. Have you had the opportunity to…?"

Xavier cut him off. "Don't even think about saying that, Guzman. Why must you always show your lack of refinement? I'd hate to let the guards have their way with you."

Guzman whispered, "So, boss, what's the plan?"

"I'll arrange it so that you're at the party tonight in case Santiago decides to try anything there. We'll just have to wait him out. DeCana will have to give us advanced warning. Come with me. I want you to meet Castro so that he's comfortable with you."

"I don't want to meet that Commie bastard!" Guzman started to turn.

"It's part of the mission." Xavier smiled. "Besides, I insist. You'll be fine."

Guzman stood at attention. "Yes, sir. Should I salute you?"

Xavier grabbed Guzman's arm. "You do and I'll tear your fucking arm clean from its socket."

They walked over to Castro. The guards closed in to provide protection. "This is Manuel Guzman, sir. He is one of the loyal men who returned home with me. He's brought important news."

Xavier sat with Castro as Guzman explained Santiago's plans.

For the first time since being with him, Xavier saw Castro's rage. "I'll have them all killed for this."

Xavier's voice rose, forgetting his place because of concern for Demetria and DeCana. "No, pardon me, sir, but I think we should handle it somewhat differently. Santiago will be here tonight. He won't attempt anything at an event like this, as he knows your men are loyal. Let's wait him out. We'll catch him before he has a chance to do any real damage. Guzman's cousin is one of the men inside his operation. He's an intelligence gatherer for Santiago, and is pretending to go along with him, while compiling information that he'll share with Guzman." Xavier curled his hand into a fist. "He's all we need to defeat Santiago."

"Very well. For now I'll listen to you." Castro shook his finger at Xavier. "If one mistake is made I'll have their heads, all their heads, including your friend's here."

Xavier suggested it would be a good idea if Guzman attended the party tonight, just in case. Castro agreed, since he knew Santiago and his men were unpredictable. He walked Guzman back to the gate, along with Xavier, and reminded him what would happen if he aided Santiago.

"Make sure you touch base with DeCana. Keep me informed." Xavier touched his ear. "I'll see you tonight. Be ready."

Chapter 39

The president jumped from his chair with so much force that it slammed into the wall behind him.

"What?" he shouted.

The loud noise alarmed the Secret Service agents. They rushed in to make sure everything was okay. Alex waved his hand indicating that all was fine. The agents retreated to their post.

"Castro plans on installing Benderis as President of Cuba? Has he lost his fucking mind?" The expression on Alex's face was one of pure bewilderment. "Where did this information come from?"

Secretary Mackenzie sat on the edge of his desk examining his freshly filed fingernails as he spoke. "NSA heard the entire conversation."

"You have got to be kidding!" Alex said.

"That's not the best part, sir. Castro plans on announcing the engagement of his niece to, get this, Commander Benderis, tonight." Secretary Mackenzie enjoyed giving the president the information, especially since he was so powerless to stop it.

"This was supposed to be a simple operation. Go in, remove Castro from power, and get the hell out! We're supposed to select Castro's replacement at a later date. I think it's high time I limit who has access to this info. I'll get back to you."

"Fine, sir." Mackenzie smirked with a look of satisfaction when he hung up the phone.

Alex looked up at Dee, who sat across from his desk. She arrived just as the call came from Mackenzie. "Dee, you won't believe what Castro has done now."

"I think I can. That's what I came here to tell you, sir. I see Ian got the jump on me."

"Did he know you were on your way to tell me about the situation in Cuba?" Alex asked.

"Yes, sir. I left his office to come here." Dee handed him her notes.

Alex relit his cigar, taking a moment to reflect before speaking. "Dee, it's time to throw a smoke grenade in the foxhole and see what, or who, comes crawling out."

"I couldn't agree more, sir. What's your plan?"

"The first thing we need to do is limit the number of people who have anything to do with the mission in Cuba. I want you to handpick a team from the NSA that will monitor Cuba twenty-four, seven." Alex sat her notes on the desk. "Then, move the monitoring location to Camp David. Other than the team you pick, only tell Mackenzie what we're doing. You go with the NSA team, and I'll join you there later. I want to talk to Commander Benderis myself and find out what the hell he thinks about all this."

"Yes sir, I will have it done right away." She left the room to formalize the move to Camp David.

"Annie," Alex yelled. "Arrange a four day vacation for me to Camp David. Contact Press Secretary Tynes so that he can let everyone know. On second thought, have him come in here for a minute. I want to cover a few other things."

Coleman Tynes came to the president's office and took a seat on one of the leather couches perpendicular to his desk. Alex moved from around his desk and sat directly across from Tynes on an identical couch. "Coleman, I want to get your opinion of Schaffer O'Grady. He's been somewhat of a thorn in my side for some time now. But I wanted to get your take on him as a reporter."

"Well, sir, he's a very capable reporter. He cares about the everyday citizen, and has little use for big government bureaucracies, as he sees them. That's quite an about-face from his days in the Secret Service. Now, he feels it's his duty to report on anything that affects the people as a whole, not just the viewpoint of how anyone in particular would like to see things. He's also really good at playing devil's advocate. He claims it gives him the upper hand and throws off his opponents, allowing him to find out the real story, probably a technique from his days with the Secret Service."

"Do you think he's well respected by his peers?" Alex asked, peering into Tynes' eyes. "Is he enough of a team player to be a part of our team?"

"I wouldn't classify him as a team player. In fact, just the opposite. A lone wolf, so to speak. What did you have in mind?" Tynes knitted his fingers and let them fall to his lap.

"I'm not sure yet." Alex tapped Dee's notes with his knuckles. "We could really use him on our side for a change. Contact his editor at the *Post* and arrange a meeting. I'd like to talk with him. I'll be at Camp David for a four-day vacation. If you can reach him in time, invite him there." Alex knew very well that Schaffer would not be available to meet. "Maybe knowing that the President of the United States wants to chat with him would get the *Post* off my back."

"I'll let you know what I find out as soon as possible, sir." Tynes started to leave the room. "Mr. President, isn't O'Grady a personal friend of yours?"

"Indeed he is."

Tynes' brow furrowed, perplexed by his thoughts. "Then, why wouldn't he go out of his way to help you?"

"Why don't we ask him when we find him?" Alex looked at Tynes dismissively and waited for the door to close. He pressed the intercom. "Annie, get Director Caprelotti on the line for me."

Seconds later, the intercom buzzed. "Mr. President, Director Caprelotti for you."

"Thanks Annie, put him through." Alex impatiently tapped his cigar against the ashtray while waiting for the Caprelotti's call to go through. The second the phone rang, Alex answered. "Anthony, what have you found out about O'Grady?"

"Sir, he's been asking around bars in Havana, but not about an invasion. He's looking for Ciefuentes, or, rather, Commander Benderis. We were fortunate that Guzman was in the bar when he started nosing around. I think it may be time to prevent any further inquires."

"Just hold on. I'm not finished with him just yet. He may still be a service to his country." Alex hung up the phone and began to plot his next move. He folded his hands and brought them near his face. A fresh Opus X protruded from his fingers.

Dee stepped back into the Oval Office. From the look on the president's face, she knew that he was about to speak. "Dee, word of Castro's plans to replace himself with Xavier will soon be public. If Xavier were to put forth his ideas to reform Cuba, O'Grady would paint it as a new revolution for Cuba. And if the United States were to support this new government as one that they could work with, I'd be viewed as the man who broke Castro's back. We could walk in and take what we really need to get the economy moving."

Dee announced that she had formalized plans for Camp David and left the office to contact Schaffer.

He began speaking as soon as he heard the beep. "I heard the whole thing," Schaffer said. "That old man still knows how to shake up a party."

"The president wasn't amused. Xavier is a SEAL, not the leader of a country." Dee's voice took on a serious tone.

"Why would Alex care? This could play right into his hands. He should count his blessings," Schaffer said.

"There's more to it."

"Yeah, like what?" Schaffer felt his eyebrows jump.

"Not now. I'll tell you when I see you. By the way, I arranged for you to have an invitation to Xavier's reception tonight. It's waiting at the hotel, you need to be there."

"How'd you swing that one?"

"Never mind, just be there." She disconnected their call before Schaffer asked any further questions.

Chapter 40

Initially, Schaffer had not given much thought to the reception.

The desk clerk at his hotel handed him the invitation to the evening's festivities, and he felt like a pawn again, expendable. Worse, he wasn't sure what the rules of the game were. Setting aside his uneasiness, he decided to use the reception as a way to meet Xavier, since he'd come to Cuba with that in mind.

At the reception, Schaffer tried to remain as inconspicuous as possible by avoiding conversation. This proved to be easy, since no one there knew him. Instead, his focus was squarely on Xavier and Castro.

A festive mood engulfed most of the people in attendance. Castro's oceanside villa was decorated with lights. Tropical flowers adorned the top of each table. Draped from the trestle leading to the patio, exotic flowers cascaded like waterfalls onto the lawn of grass and sand. At predetermined locations on the patio, tethered macaws, green parrots, and doves squawked, whistled and chirped at anyone who passed their stands. Guests arrived at the party by bus and on foot. Because of a nationwide gasoline shortage, no one was allowed to independently drive to the soiree.

Castro smiled, appearing relieved. He squeezed Xavier's arm and whispered in his ear, "I'm looking forward to retirement. Of course, this means I'll have to give up power over my beloved country. Still, I feel good, because my country will be in the hands of someone I trust."

Castro always followed his convictions, right or wrong, regardless of what the rest of the world thought. He followed his political agenda to the letter, and insisted that his people do the same.

Castro surveyed the room, noting all who'd turned out for the evening. His smile greeted each of them as he joyously grasped their hands, shaking and thanking each of them for attending. Looking over at the door, he saw Santiago enter the room. His face reddened and his smile dropped. Those around him felt his coldness instantly radiate outwards. Many walked away when they saw him place his hand on the butt of his pistol, and speak his muffled words. "By all accounts, Santiago should be dead now. I don't tolerate any disloyalty in my country, even from my brother. If I did, every fool here would try to take over." A clear path now existed between the two men. Castro's fingers were so tight on the gun butt that they drained of blood.

Santiago approached Castro without fear. "President. What a lovely night for a party."

Castro did not respond. Instead, he turned his attention to other guests.

Santiago backed away, incensed by Castro's refusal to acknowledge him properly. He turned and walked across the room. *You will not be so aloof in the near future, Mr. President!* he thought.

Santiago wore an earpiece so that he could monitor Castro's men as well as his own. At the prescribed time, he and his men would switch to another channel to keep their conversations private. His chest was decorated with military ribbons and commendations he received over his forty years of service in Castro's army. One medal, in particular, stood out among the rest. A deep purple ribbon held the oval-shaped medal in place. A hollow star was in the middle of the medal. Behind it was a microphone.

Castro noticed the unusual medal, but paid no attention because he knew how much Santiago liked to draw attention.

Santiago moved away from the crowd and spoke into the medal. "Testing."

"You are coming in loud and clear," Juan Pablo responded.

Several guests ventured to the patio for fresh air. Outside, they began to question each other. "What is the purpose of tonight's event?" No one knew the answer, which made them all the more curious. Virtually unnoticed, the guest of honor arrived with his beautiful escort. When the attendees saw Demetria, they attempted to move closer to get a better view of the stunning couple. Everyone knew her, but the man who held her arm remained a mystery to most.

"Isn't that Castro's niece? Who has he allowed to escort her?" they asked each other.

Heads bobbed up and down, from side to side, looking in the couple's direction. In the meantime, Castro moved to a platform positioned against the back wall of the room and stood in front of a microphone. "May I have your attention please?"

A hush crept over the room as everyone focused on their president.

"It is my pleasure to have all of you here tonight. We have been brought together by good fortune. This is a night you'll not forget for the rest of your lives." He whetted their appetite for more information, but allowed their anticipation to build before satisfying their curiosity. "For now, enjoy the food and refreshments. I'll address you later this evening." Castro stepped from the microphone.

Cheers went up for their leader. Everyone applauded, except one. "This is a night *you* will not forget for the rest of your life," Santiago mumbled.

Santiago was less than two feet from Schaffer, staring at Castro's back. Schaffer remembered what Santiago's men said earlier, but he knew even the general wouldn't be crazy enough to try something surrounded by so many of Castro's army.

Castro left the stand and took Xavier by the arm, telling him, "I have a few people you need to meet." Xavier and Demetria followed behind Castro. He introduced them to his most loyal party members, some who had been with him since the revolution.

The guests were wide-eyed, giving Xavier their full attention by putting down their food and drinks. An occasional gasp could be heard as he explained the details of his daring escape from the Americans at Guantanamo. Xavier was forced to recount the story at almost every table at which he and Castro stopped.

Xavier spotted Ensign Guzman. Armed guards, loyal to Castro, surrounded the room. Nothing could possibly go wrong tonight. The event was too well guarded. Castro personally hashed out the protection plans over and over with his security team, rehearsing all possible alternatives, should anything go wrong.

Xavier's eyes roamed the room. He had been on guard ever since Guzman informed him of Santiago's plans. At one point, he broke away from Castro's side long enough to speak privately with Guzman. "I find it hard to believe that Santiago will try anything tonight. Even he can see that Castro has beefed up security. He can't be that stupid."

"Remember your own words and expect the unexpected. This guy is unpredictable. Hell, he's crazy." Guzman looked at Santiago. "We can't take him too lightly."

Castro moved to the platform a second time. "Comrades, tonight, as promised, I have a special announcement." He looked out sensing their anticipation, yet waited a few seconds before continuing. "I've been made proud today. This is one of my happiest moments." He paused, torturing the crowd. "My niece, Demetria, is getting married."

Everyone in the room clapped and cheered. Rumbling started as people made comments to each other. The noise grew to a roar as they competed to be heard.

Castro lifted his hands in the air to calm them. "You've not even heard who she plans to marry." He smiled, and waited, keeping them in suspense. The room was completely silent waiting for his response. "She will marry our new hero, Xavier Ciefuentes. The wedding will take place next week here. You all are invited."

Everyone rushed over to congratulate the couple. Xavier's mouth was as dry as the sand that lay on either side of the patio. He wasn't expecting Castro to push for the wedding so soon.

Guzman watched the crowd move around the couple. He used the opportunity to speak to Xavier, through their communication device. Xavier heard a crackle in his ear, as did Schaffer.

"How in God's name are you going to pull off a wedding, execute the bride's uncle, and not break her pretty little heart?"

Xavier was helpless to answer, but the question made him uncomfortable all evening.

Demetria beamed with pride after her uncle made the announcement. She loved Xavier from the first moment she'd laid eyes on him. Now they could be together for a lifetime.

Schaffer couldn't believe what he just heard. Thoughts wildly filled his mind. *Execute her uncle? Oh my God, that's Alex's plan? It sounds more and more like Alex should be my prime suspect in Harold's murder as well as the attempt on my life.* Dee's attempts to reassure him started to crumble. He wondered why Xavier wanted to find him. The possibility exist that he was ordered to take control of Castro's fate as well as Schaffer's.

Schaffer began walking across the lawn towards the car where Guillermo was waiting. He had to contact Dee: it was time for the games to end. Half way to the car, Schaffer turned back. He fought moments of anger-induced paranoia that left him unsure of what to do next. The only alternative was to see what else the evening would produce.

A few minutes after Schaffer returned, Castro tapped the microphone. The gathering turned in his direction. Once again, they noticed that the corners of Castro's mouth turned down and his brow furrowed. The jovial aura that surrounded him most of the evening was gone and his seriousness weighted them down. His hands rose, commanding their attention. Then slowly, he pulled them to his chest, pointing his fingers towards his heart. "For forty years I have lead this country. Together we have made her second to none. Of course, we've seen both good and bad times. Now is one of our more challenging times. As you know, our major trading partner and benefactor has long passed. They no longer have the resources to provide us with basic necessities. We must go out and find new sources to return our country to greatness. We have many resources to offer those in need — sugar, nickel, tobacco, and the most beautiful islands in the world."

There wasn't a sound in the motionless room. "To accomplish our goals we'll need vitality, strength, and the willingness to move in unexplored directions. I'm now in my seventies. I still have the willingness to lead. Youth, and strength have begun to escape me. I will, however, still challenge any of you to a race." He gave a quick laugh, then stopped and looked at his people who silently returned his gaze with utter disbelief. A lump formed in his throat that prevented him from continuing. He made taut his lips and tried to swallow, but the ever-strong Castro couldn't swallow the tears that filled his eyes.

Tears also filled the eyes of many in the room, including Demetria, who clung to Xavier for support. She was not prepared for what would come next.

"I have decided to step down as your president." Castro looked at the floor and then at the people.

Men and women openly wept, already feeling their loss. Only one person in the room smiled. Santiago appeared to receive the news as if it were a long lost friend. He felt it time to fulfill his destiny. Amidst the sobs, he started a slow drawn-out chant, "Fie-dell, Fie-dell," which flowed over the crowd as a wave rising and crashing into a beach.

Everyone attending joined in with Santiago. Their chanting quickly resembled a similar moment during Castro's rise to power. On the day he rode into Havana to accept his destiny, the same chant erupted among his loyal followers. Just as before, he was helpless to calm their chorus. All he could do was watch and listen.

When they began to quiet, he raised his hands and again a hush came over the room. "Of course, I would never leave without having someone to take my place."

Santiago stepped forward moving towards the front of the platform.

Castro continued. "I have decided to name…" He paused, and looked over to Santiago, who was approaching him. "I have decided to name," he repeated, "Xavier Ciefuentes as Cuba's new leader. He's the one person in all of Cuba who possesses the character and youth necessary to move Cuba to a new day." His eyes never left his dejected half brother as he spoke.

"You fool," Santiago screamed, stamping the floor. His face flushed crimson, and his fists clenched at his sides. He looked as if ready to pounce on Castro.

Castro ignored Santiago's outburst. "I'll stay on until our new president is comfortable with his duties. We must maintain Socialism or die! Capitalism must never come to our shores as long as there is one person alive who believes in Marxism-Leninism. To change would mean the end of our social programs. I'll not abandon our goals, even in death."

Castro walked past Santiago, down the stairs, and embraced Xavier. The crowd swarmed around them. Well wishes and praises were offered as those faithful to the party jockeyed for position within the ranks of the newly formed administration.

Demetria was overcome watching people pull and tug at Xavier. Sadly, the image of Castro never being home flashed through her mind. She had witnessed the demands this position placed on her uncle. Now, she would have to give up the second man that she really loved, losing him before she ever officially had him.

An ever-growing sea of people now separated Demetria and Xavier. She looked over and mouthed. "I am going out for some air."

"Wait, I'll go with you," Xavier answered.

"I'll be fine, you're needed here." She looked down. "I'll have one of the guards walk with me."

Xavier could see the despair in her eyes, and wanted to be with her, yet he was powerless to stop her. By now, he could not even reach her. He could only watch as she left. He longed to comfort her in his arms.

Schaffer moved around the crowd nearer to Santiago, who watched Demetria leave the room.

Santiago's eyes radiated hatred for his brother. Turning his back on the incoherent crowd, he spoke into one of the medals on his chest, "Demetria is on her way outside. She's just the protection we need. Take her to our base! She'll be my guest until Castro comes to his senses."

Schaffer tried to move towards the door to stop Demetria from leaving, but the wave of well-wishers cut him off.

Demetria approached one of the guards on the beach. Astonished by all the events of the evening, she didn't notice the trail of blood and the trail left in the sand. It was too late by the time she realized the guard she was talking with was not her uncle's.

Schaffer reached the door and saw a guard hit her in the face with a spinning back-fist, knocking her to the sand. The guard jumped on her, clasping her throat with his hand to prevent her from screaming. Still dazed, she looked into the eyes of Juan Pablo. He thrust a rubber ball in her mouth and secured it with tape. He then wrapped her hands behind her back and taped them together before taping her feet together. Upon completion, he radioed that the prisoner was secured and that they were on the way to the compound.

Two other men ran over. They carried Demetria to a waiting jeep, and drove off. A second jeep remained behind to transport General Santiago to the compound after he gave his list of demands to Castro.

Even with the skills Schaffer learned in his Recon unit and the Secret Service, he was no match for their firepower. He hurried back into the ballroom to get Xavier. Reaching him was impossible.

General Santiago walked to the microphone. Tilting it so that it screeched, he gained everyone's attention. "Thank you for being so patient. I'm afraid there's been a change in your plans, my dear brother."

Castro's eyes shot fire across the room. "What the hell do you think you're doing?"

"Correction. What am I, Raul Santiago, *the predestined President of Cuba*, doing?"

Xavier repeated the general's full name to himself. As if a light just came on, he remembered where he'd heard *Raul Santiago* spoken before. His mother spoke of a Lieutenant Raul Santiago. She called him an evil man who killed his own people who were defenseless to stop him. "Shark bait," was the term Santiago used referring to people attempting to leave the country after Castro gained power.

Castro waved to his guards, who already had their guns pointed at Santiago.

"I wouldn't do that if I were you," Santiago warned. "Right now, my men have our precious niece in their custody. I don't hold the same attachment to sentimentality that you do, but I am sure you wouldn't want anything to happen to her, would you?"

Xavier's fists hung at his sides. His jaw muscles twitched, keeping control over his mouth until the words burst from his lips. "If you touch her, or hurt her in any way, I'll personally rip open your chest and tear your heart out with my bare hands."

"Now I'm terrified." Santiago shook animatedly. "Sorry about your plans, Ciefuentes. Maybe you'll get to marry her after my men and I are finished with her, if there's anything left. As long as you two presidents do as I say, everything will go smoothly. Try anything stupid, and I'll kill her. First of all, I'm not about to let a man who is hardly known by anyone in this room come in and take what is mine! Castro, you were right, this country needs strength. My strength. I will lead Cuba to a new tomorrow. You're a fool! How have you fallen under the spell of this snake charmer?" Santiago tossed his head. "I'll contact you tomorrow with your instructions. If you attempt to follow me or harm any of my men, you'll never see your niece again. Do I make my self clear?" Santiago appeared crazed, his eyes were wild, and saliva dotted his beard.

"Yes." Castro glared intently at Santiago.

Santiago dropped the mike on the floor, creating a loud, obnoxious screech as it rolled across the platform. He laughed when he saw the people grab for their ears. Turning and laughing harder, he left the room.

Schaffer darted out the back across the patio en route to Guillermo. On the way, he pushed the button on his pocket computer and Dee picked up immediately.

"What just happened there?" she demanded.

"You heard the same thing I did. Tell Alex he's got some explaining to do."

"About what?"

"Castro's assassination! Who's next on the list, everyone that knows what he's doing?"

"Schaffer, it's not what you think," Dee pleaded.

"Okay, then you can tell me about it later. I think I know where they're taking Demetria." Before Dee could say another word, Schaffer disconnected the line and opened the car door.

"Guillermo, let's go!" he shouted.

"What's going on inside the house?" Guillermo asked.

"I'll tell you on the way."

"Where are we going?" Guillermo started the car.

Schaffer pointed forward. "To Mariel."

Chapter
41

The president's helicopter arrived at Camp David.

During the flight, Alex changed into jeans, a polo and hiking boots. He hurried from the chopper with Secretary of State Ian Mackenzie and General Dee Roseboro in tow.

The NSA set up a listening post on a screened porch attached to the president's quarters, and Director Pete Rogers had been monitoring the situation all afternoon. Alex plopped down in the chair in front of the control panel.

"Bring me up to speed, Pete."

"Early this evening, Castro was informed of Santiago's planned attempt to overthrow him. During Castro's party, Santiago began to make good on his threat and kidnapped his niece. For that matter, she's Santiago's niece too, or half niece." Pete shrugged his shoulders. "So far, he is only using her as insurance, although I'm sure she'll be used as a bargaining chip eventually. Even though Santiago is her uncle, they have never been close, which is quite contrary to her relationship with Castro, who has been a father figure to her. I contacted the CIA to see what they had. In the past, all conversation between Santiago and Demetria has been strictly formal. Castro made sure of that, as he didn't want to share her with anyone, especially someone he doesn't completely trust."

Alex tapped the monitor with his index finger. "Where was the commander during all of this?"

"Right there, sir. There was nothing he could do. According to Ensign Guzman, who was attending the party also, he was surrounded by a horde of people." Pete flipped through the transcripts. "The girl said something to Benderis, but we need to clean up the tape before we can determine what it was. We know that by the time Santiago made his move, the girl had already been captured. Lieutenant DeCana is at Santiago's camp. We'll have to concentrate on his broadcast for any new information."

Alex took a draw from a freshly lit cigar, holding the smoke only long enough for the flavor to cover his tongue. "Are we certain no one but our team can hear our transmissions?"

Several members of the NSA team smiled. Pete was the first to speak up. "Of course, sir. Our digital technology has several security measures built in. It's so advanced, Bill Gates couldn't break into the system."

"Good, then set it up so I can talk to Benderis." Alex turned to Dee. "Dee, get Admiral Gregory on the horn. Tell him to have a group of SEALs standing by. Retrieve Petty Officers Willow and Suarez from Gitmo. Fly them to the ship. The rest of the team will be waiting there. Set a rendezvous point away from the general population where they can meet. Get them in the air ASAP! I don't want any more people than necessary to have any information about this exercise." Alex turned his attention to the equipment in front of him. "Okay, how does this damn thing work?"

"Put these head phones on, sir. The green button allows you to establish communications. If you press it once, you can hear them. Press it twice, and they'll be able to hear you as well." Alex pushed the button twice. "That's it, now you're live, anything you say now they can hear."

Alex moved the microphone nearer to his face, leaving just enough room for his ever-present cigar. "Commander Benderis, this is President Alexander Nicholas. I'm aware of the kidnapping this evening. This may slow your progress, but the mission must continue. General Santiago is an unacceptable liability. He must be dealt with swiftly. I've arranged to bring in six more members of your team to assist in freeing the girl. We'll need to know where you'd like to arrange a drop off point for the other SEALs. They should be in the air in minutes."

Before Xavier had a chance to speak, he was interrupted. "Mr. President." DeCana said softly. "We're in three abandoned warehouses near Mariel just west of Havana. Come to the sugar-shipping port, on Pier 4. There you will find the three buildings. Santiago's men are in all of them. The main operation center is in the middle. Approximately one hundred and seventy men are here all together. Most will be in the west warehouse, which is the sleeping quarters. The east warehouse is a weapons station. Guards are stationed in front of the east and west warehouses, and the center is left unguarded so that it'll appear unoccupied."

"What's your exact location now, son?"

"I've got the overnight shift in the control center monitoring communications. My desk is on the loft in the back of the center warehouse.

I'm the only one up here all night, so you'll be clear to come in with force if necessary."

Guzman broke in: "Sir, if you'll have the team brought right here to the beach outside of Castro's villa —"

The president cut him off. "Won't that be too dangerous?"

"Mr. President, Ensign Guzman is right." Xavier had already mapped out a plan while DeCana was talking. "Have an HH60H fly within a mile of the villa. The entire area between here and the foot of the mountains is off limits to the locals. The HH60H is equipped with an infrared jamming system that'll allow it to come in undetected. Also, the night vision capabilities will eliminate the need for lights. Finally, if, God forbid, there's a need for firepower, this aircraft is well equipped to handle any situation it may encounter. Guzman and I will meet the team on the beach. We'll set out one of our homing beacons to guide you in as quickly as possible. Then we'll fly over water to reach Mariel. There, we'll enter the water about one mile out and swim into their camp. DeCana can keep us apprised of any changes until we hit the water."

"Good thinking, Benderis," Alex said. "I'll dispatch a chopper immediately." Alex pointed to Dee, who was already calling in the order.

"Estimated time of arrival is fifty minutes, sir," she informed him.

Alex repeated the arrival time to Xavier. "Son, I know my timing stinks, but I need to know how the men Castro is holding are doing. Have you seen them yet?"

"Sorry, sir, I haven't. Castro did mention them in passing, once, but there was no opportunity to delve any further into it at the time. I got the feeling even he doesn't know where they are."

"That's strange, sir," Guzman interjected. "When we were brought to the prison at the naval base in Havana, there was absolutely no talk about Americans being held there. I've even alluded to the possibility since being released, but no one has heard anything."

DeCana added, "I concur, sir. I've monitored intelligence since before Xavier left Gitmo. No one in this area has spoken anything about prisoners. Santiago would use them as a bargaining chip if he knew they existed. It's as if someone has secretly stashed the agents to avoid their detection."

Alex puffed his cigar in long, contemplative draws. "Gentlemen, we've got to locate these men. We've had no further contact from Havana about their status. Castro's making me nervous. He's up to something."

Alex rocked the cigar against his teeth. "Let's get the girl home. Then we can find my agents. God go with you, men. Stay safe."

Xavier and Guzman waited for a moment to make sure the president was done. After several seconds, Xavier turned to Guzman. "First, I must let Castro know that I'll have Demetria back by morning. He's too angry to think clearly right now. I'm afraid he'll rush in like a bull, which could get Demetria killed. We're better equipped to handle her rescue than a bunch of trigger-happy commandos."

"Sir, don't you think you're a little too involved emotionally to aid us on this mission?"

"Guzman, above all else, I'm a SEAL. Duty to my country comes before everything."

¤¤¤¤

Castro's salt-and-pepper beard flowed from side to side as he shouted orders to his commandos reading for their rescue attempt. He stood erect, veins bulging from his reddened face. The first finger on his right hand was tightly laced around the trigger of his pistol, which he waved each time he shouted. His men ducked each time he pointed the gun in their direction. Xavier entered the room, approaching Castro from behind to avoid his pistol. He placed his hand on Castro's shoulder, startling him. Castro jumped, tightening his muscles and firing the pistol, striking one of his officers in the leg. Bodies flew to the ground, rolling to avoid the waving muzzle.

"May I have a word with you, sir?" Xavier said, taking the pistol from Castro's hand.

Castro never stopped giving orders. He took a second to apologetically acknowledge his wounded officer. "We can't wait for that lunatic to give us demands. We must go in, rescue Demetria and crush this rebellion."

"Of course you're right." Xavier nodded and then held up one finger. "Nevertheless, I have a plan that will work, and at the same time prove your strength to any one who'd attempt anything like this again. The last thing either of us wants is for Demetria to be hurt. I promise you, I'll have Demetria home safely by morning. No member of the resistance will ever attempt this again."

Castro stroked his beard. "I've said before, you're a man I can trust. You've proven yourself, but this is my blood we're talking about."

Castro paused to consider Xavier's proposal. "I'll give you until the sun rises, then I'll do it my way."

Xavier reunited with Guzman to further map out their plans. He pointed to the ocean. "The chopper will have to come in just above the water to prevent radar detection, and remain just above the ocean during the trip to Mariel."

They jogged along the beach and placed a small homing beacon less than fifty yards from the mountains in the sand, to guide the helicopter to them. The two men sat on the beach waiting for the chopper. Nearly an hour later, the helicopter had not yet arrived. Turning towards the house, they watched for any activity. Through their binoculars, they could see that nothing had changed. Suddenly, the HH60H chopper flew up to them as silently as any helicopter could. Wind escaping the chopper blades blew bits of sand into the air. Xavier and Guzman squinted to prevent the sand from entering their eyes.

Guzman attempted to ease the moment. "These damned things are getting more hi-tech all the time. I didn't even hear a damn thing!"

Deadly silence surrounded Xavier. He focused on one task: saving Demetria's life. "Thank God DeCana is there in case she needs help." He looked up at the chopper. "When I see that son of a bitch Santiago, I'll kill him. I haven't decided how yet, but it'll be slow." Xavier's frown changed to a look of enlightenment. "Raul Santiago, Lieutenant Raul Santiago. My mother spoke his name over and over in her nightmares. She told me that Santiago was responsible for my father's death. I'll bet he's all but forgotten. Tonight I'll make sure he remembers."

Though Xavier was speaking quietly, Guzman listened carefully. "Well, I guess you've got a good reason to kill him." Guzman didn't ask Xavier any other questions about what he remembered about Santiago, there would be time for that later.

Two knotted lines were hurled from the helicopter. The two men grabbed hold and crawled up using only the strength of their arms. Their climb was so effortless that it seemed child's play. As they climbed, the chopper moved back out towards the sea in the direction of Mariel.

Chapter
42

Xavier and Guzman covered every inch of exposed flesh with a black camie stick.

Dressed head to toe in black, they also put in special contact lenses, designed to darken the whites of their eyes, making them practically invisible in the dark.

During the flight, the SEALs gathered their weapons. They inserted Chinese darts into the back of their diving gloves. They also slid blowguns and poisoned-tipped darts into their belts. On impact, the sharp metal tip of the dart would pierce its rubber covering and enter its target, releasing a poison more lethal than an asp bite. Within five seconds of striking its target, the poison on the tip of the darts would shut down the central nervous system of the victim, and he would die from suffocation. The SEALs strapped on the last pieces of gear: K-bars, Glock side arms, and Uzis. Finally, they packed three bags containing wire cutters, C-4 plastic explosives, grenades, gas mask, and several metal canisters containing cyanide. The SEALs would swim loaded down with forty-five pound packs on their backs.

"Five minutes till drop off," the pilot yelled.

At 11:45 p.m., the HH60H silently hovered one mile from a pier at Mariel. Xavier stood with his gear in place. The black diving cap made him look like a heavily armed Ninja.

"Our objective here is not to take prisoners. Santiago and his men are a threat to our mission. Our job is to eliminate that threat. Three of the people inside are to come out alive: one you all know, Lieutenant DeCana; a young woman, Demetria Castro, is the second. And General Santiago, who belongs to me, is the third. It's imperative that we use silent weapons to eliminate as many of the hostiles as possible. We don't want to attract attention to ourselves. Once we leave the chopper, I want total silence. Our only method of communication will be hand signals." Xavier pulled his glove making it taut. "According to DeCana, there are five men guarding the perimeter, and two in front of each warehouse. Each of you has your assignment. We'll have one hour to complete this mission and rendezvous with the chopper. Any questions?" Xavier waited a moment and no one spoke. Motioning to the door, he was the first to walk over and grab a rope. "Then it's time to take a dip in the drink."

The SEALs rappelled down the ropes, and silently entered the ocean. The warm water made their swim much easier and faster. Although they were heavily weighted down with gear, the one-mile swim took less than thirteen minutes.

As the SEALs approached the dock, they could see five guards walking on the pier. Without a sound, Xavier pointed to five of the SEALs. They obediently retrieved their blowguns, slid a dart into the chamber of each, and raised them into position. The SEALs maintained a steady position in the ocean by treading water without the use of their hands, and waited for further instructions.

Xavier touched his watch, then his chest, and finally held up three fingers. The SEAL team knew this meant *on my mark, in three*. One finger went down, then two. Finally, Xavier's last finger went down, leaving his fist in the air. Simultaneously the five SEALs blew their darts into their assigned man on the pier. The sting of the dart paralyzed each man. They dropped to the ground, and frantically twitched to their deaths.

The SEAL team swam to the pier, reached over, and slowly pulled the dead men into the water. Silently, they moved from water to pier and split into two groups of four. They were ordered to go to the warehouses, four to the east and four to the west. There they would eliminate the occupants, and meet in the back of the center warehouse.

The team saw the two men outside the east and west warehouses guarding the doors. Two pairs of SEALs moved from the back of each warehouse, sliding against the inner and outer walls of both east and west warehouses. Along the sides, the four men slid a thin wire from their belts and twirled it around each hand. Moving precisely at one foot per second, the men reached their targets at the same time. They leapt from the sides of the building. At the same moment, the SEALs spun around, turning their backs to their victims. Reaching above their heads, they crisscrossed their hands in the air, and slid the wire down, snagging the necks of the unsuspecting victims. With one smooth jerk, the wire severed each guard's necks, from Adam's apple to spinal cord. The dead men never had a chance to make a sound.

Blood gushed from their open wounds with pulsing regularity of each heartbeat. Four more men lay dead near the gulf.

Once the guards were eliminated, each team utilized a small high-speed drill to quietly and quickly bore holes into the back walls of the two warehouses. They inserted small infrared fiber-optic scopes into the holes to determine the number and positions of men in each warehouse. In the east warehouse, five men guarded several troop carriers and weapons.

The west warehouse was the sleeping quarters. Guzman counted approximately one hundred and fifty men inside. The west team retrieved gas masks from their packs. Each man had a canister with a small nozzle on top. The team fitted each nozzle with an eight-inch plastic tube.

The SEALs took turns drilling holes in the four sides of the west building. The plastic tubes extending from each canister were placed in each of the four holes and the canisters turned on. Within minutes, the deadly nerve gas filled the room, asphyxiating the occupants. The team patiently waited and, if necessary, would move in and mop up anyone who wasn't already dead. However, tonight, this wasn't a concern.

The five guards of the weapons warehouse stood wide-awake near the front door. The SEAL team positioned itself at the back of the warehouse. Making their entrance from the rear would allow them to catch the occupants off guard. One of the SEAL's grasped his K-bar and dug a two-foot square into the lower back panel of the wall. He lined the square with a flash wire. Three of the men unfolded and draped a heavy black piece of cloth over the work area to block the light from the flash. The other ignited the wire. A quick flare jumped from the square, easily blowing through the wood. One man placed a K-bar into the middle of the square to pull the wood from the wall. By the time the men inside smelled the burning wood, it would be too late. The SEALs deftly moved into position with their blowguns ready.

One of the Cubans realized what was happening, and scurried for the door. Xavier stood, hurling his K-bar. Whistling the air, it severed the man's spine. The other four men dropped to the floor, clutching the spots where the darts had dug into their bodies. Forty-five minutes had elapsed since the SEALs hit the water. One hundred and sixty-four men were already dead, and not a shot had been fired. Moreover, Santiago knew nothing of their arrival.

Both teams met at the back of the center warehouse. They repeated the drilling and fiber optic scope search. Xavier could see DeCana at a communications post. Ten other men stood scattered, attending to their duties. Then he spotted her. Santiago had bound her wrists and hung her from an overhead rafter. Her feet struggled to touch the floor, barely out of reach. Her clothing had been ripped. Santiago sharked her, riding crop in hand, circling her breasts, stroking her hips. Xavier tossed the scope to the ground and bolted around to the front of the building.

Two of his men realized that he'd lost control, something that they had never seen in him before, and pulled him to the ground. "Not this way, sir," one of the men said. "We're going to go in, but as a team. Are you up for it, sir?"

Xavier nodded and his men released their grasp. "Sorry, boys. I'm okay now, but I'm going to kill that son of a bitch when I get in there. Let's get back and make sure we're ready."

"We'll get to know each other very well," Santiago taunted, as he attempted to lift what was left of Demetria's dress.

Demetria spat in Santiago's face. He stung a sharp blow across the back of her thighs with the riding crop. Wincing in pain, she refused to cry out. She would remain defiant, even if he killed her.

Xavier observed Santiago's lips moving in order to determine what he was saying. He trembled with anger, cursed and again vowed to take Santiago's life for all the pain he inflicted on Demetria and his parents. He instructed two of his men to set off a small charge of C-4 to create a diversion.

The east team placed a charge on a jeep's gas tank to cause a larger explosion. The SEALs met in front of the center warehouse. They slid Chinese darts from the back of their gloves, held them ready, and placed the K-bars between their teeth before moving into final position. Xavier dropped his finger and the charge exploded blowing the jeep into the air, lighting up the night sky.

The doors to the center warehouse flew open. Several men came rushing to investigate. The Chinese darts hit the men right between their eyes. Two of the men were still living, but retreated, only to fall over the dead bodies of their fellow rebels. The SEALs moved in, slit the throats of the wounded men with their K-bars, and snapped their necks. Either action was enough to kill any man, but the SEALs took no chances. They were thorough killers.

DeCana stood up and moved towards Santiago, who now held a gun to Demetria's head. DeCana inched closer, giving the appearance of being in shock.

Without moving the gun and barely peeking from around Demetria's head, Santiago looked around at the carnage. He raised one eyebrow in amazement at the destruction. Turning his attention to DeCana, he asked, "Why have they not killed you?"

DeCana didn't have a chance to respond. Santiago pointed the gun at DeCana's chest and squeezed the trigger. The bullet tore into DeCana, knocking him to the floor. The warm blood quickly formed a bright red stain on DeCana's fatigues, draining the color from his face.

The instant Xavier saw the flash of the gun muzzle, he launched his K-bar in the direction of Santiago's outstretched arm. The knife hit its mark in the center of Santiago's wrist, nearly separating it from his arm. The gun fell to the floor. Santiago released Demetria and clutched his wrist tightly in an attempt to help lessen the pain.

Demetria screamed. The SEAL team moved in and grabbed Santiago before he could react further.

"Wait!" Xavier shouted. "He belongs to me." He approached Santiago, looking at him with a stern glazed stare. "You have come to the end of your reign of persecution." Xavier glanced quickly at Demetria when he realized what he'd done.

Demetria had never heard Xavier speak English before. Hearing his words, her body shuddered. She looked at him quizzically, her mouth remaining open as if she wanted to speak. Slowly, she mouthed, "What took you so long?" Even though the words had been perfectly formed, no sound came forth.

Xavier saw the question roll over her lips. He lowered his eyes and moved closer to cut the ropes, relieving Demetria for the first time in hours. Tears streamed from her eyes as she fell into his arms. She longed for his comfort. Unnerved by the ordeal, she held him tentatively. He held her, stroked her hair, and kissed her on the forehead. "We have a lot to talk about." He turned to his communication officer. "Radio the chopper, and tell him we have a man down so get here on the double."

Santiago stood motionless, clutching his wrist watching it bleed. Xavier turned and sharply kicked him in the kidneys. Santiago doubled over, coughing in pain. Xavier pulled out duct tape, and jerked Santiago's legs from the floor.

Santiago fell forward, trying to brace his fall with his one good hand. His effort was futile. His jaw smacked the concrete floor, and blood ran from his mouth. Xavier bound Santiago's hands and legs with the tape but left his mouth free.

"Go to hell," Santiago shouted.

"Fuck you!" Xavier grabbed the back of Santiago's hair, jerking him backwards and delivered a blow to the middle of his chest.

Santiago groaned. He coughed and gagged, struggling desperately against the bile that rose closer to his mouth with each sputter. Regaining control over his stomach, Santiago wiped sweat from his forehead using his shoulder. He struggled to his knees and looked defiantly at Xavier. "What are you going to do to me?"

Xavier ignored him and turned his attention to DeCana and Demetria. The team's hospital corpsman, assisted by two other SEALs, tended to DeCana, who was bleeding badly. His lips were blue and his body shook violently.

Santiago turned his attention to Demetria. "Your visions are worthless. I never believed in them. Does my brother know you've delivered him into the hands of the enemy? You've sold out your country. You're nothing more than a whore like your mother."

Xavier kicked Santiago in the mouth, knocking him backwards to the floor. Several of his teeth fell next to him and the pain silenced his slurs.

Xavier placed a blanket around Demetria. In spite of all she had been through, Demetria held her body erect, determined to show her strength. However, her vision of strength was only in defiance to Santiago. Occasionally, she pulled the blanket closer to her neck and leaned on Xavier for support.

When the helicopter arrived at the warehouse, Xavier carried Demetria aboard. The other SEALs carried DeCana. His bleeding had slowed and a little color returned to his face. The corpsman placed an I-V in DeCana's arm to help stabilize him. After calling for the chopper, the communications officer called the ship and had a surgical team standing by for their return. The corpsman checked DeCana's blood type and enlisted the other team members that were suitable donors to help replace the blood DeCana'd lost.

The rest of the team dragged Santiago and their supplies to the chopper. Once they reached the aircraft, they roughly threw Santiago to the floor and placed a life preserver tightly around his head. "We wouldn't want you to drown if the chopper goes down," Guzman explained as he further tightened the life preserver around Santiago's neck, allowing just enough blood to flow to his head to keep him conscience.

Xavier signaled two of his men to hold Santiago. "I have plans for you once we're in the air. But first let me stop your bleeding. I don't want you to die just yet." While two of his men held Santiago's arm and hand, Xavier used his lighter to cauterize the wrist wound.

Santiago screamed.

The chopper climbed instantly to their cruising altitude. When they were out over the ocean and could no longer see land, Xavier opened the door of the chopper and peered out.

He turned to Santiago. "I'm going to give you the opportunity to live."

Demetria looked at him as if he had lost his mind.

Just as she was about to question him, Xavier slid out his K-bar and dragged the blade down Santiago's arm. The skin on his forearm parted like a zipper as it touched the razor sharp blade. Blood ran down his arms onto the floor. Xavier repeated his torturing ritual on each of Santiago's thighs.

Santiago screamed louder each time the knife separated his skin.

At the age of six, Xavier had been told about Santiago's involvement in his father's death, he swore revenge, now he would fulfill his oath. "My mother used to cry out the name of Lieutenant Raul Santiago in the night. You see, he was in love with her. She on the other hand, loved and married another man." Xavier moved to the open chopper door. "When Castro rose to power, my mother and father decided to leave Cuba. They swam out into the sea with many others in search of American ships." Xavier paused, looking out over the moonlit ocean.

"Lieutenant Raul Santiago decided that if he could not have this young woman, no one could. So, he sped out in his boat and began shooting the swimmers. He didn't shoot to kill. Oh, no. He only wanted to draw blood. And sharks." Xavier spun in rage. He grabbed Santiago's hair and jerked his head backwards. He put his K-bar against Santiago's cheek and slid it down, leaving a gash opposite the one his mother had left over forty years ago.

Santiago screamed out.

Xavier shoved Santiago's head forward in disgust. Then he continued his story. "Twenty people died in the water that day. One of them was my father. Although my mother didn't die that day, your ruthlessness killed her also. You don't deserve to live!"

Santiago cried, pleaded for his life.

Demetria felt repulsed by what she'd just heard. She put her foot on Santiago's chest and held onto her seat. She lunged her foot forward as hard as she could, sending Santiago backwards.

Santiago had no way to grab the sides of the chopper. He screamed as he fell, hitting the water only seconds after being launched from the chopper. The blood flowing from Santiago's open lacerations summoned the same predators he once called upon to do his dirty work.

The moon cast a peculiar glow over the dark waters surrounding Santiago. He saw the fins of the hungry sharks circling him. He kicked his feet and tried to get the tape from his hands in a futile attempt to swim. Spewing from his open wounds, his blood and constant splashing gave the sharks an easy trail to follow. The fins arrived one at a time, popping from below the surface of the water. For a moment, he remained perfectly still. But from behind, he felt a bump of a shark. Terrified, he kicked harder. The sharks grew excited at Santiago's motion in the water. Within seconds, they were in a feeding frenzy. The life preserver held his head above water as the sharks tore his flesh from his bones. Death, although slow in coming, was a welcomed relief.

Demetria looked into the dark water. "I hope he goes straight to hell!" She spat in the water, punctuating her feelings. She fell asleep in Xavier's arms.

For the rest of the flight, no one spoke. Several SEALs laid their heads back and closed their eyes, although they remained in a state of high alert. Xavier held Demetria close and looked over at DeCana, who was clinging to life.

In thirty minutes, they landed at Castro's villa. None of the guards seemed alarmed at the helicopter's descent. Guzman, Xavier and Demetria leapt from the chopper to the ground. The chopper ascended and disappeared into the dawning sky, with the same silent aura that accompanied its appearance at the beginning of the mission.

As promised, Xavier had Demetria safely back home before sunrise.

Chapter
43

Guillermo and Schaffer traveled as fast as Guillermo's car could carry them across the pothole-pocked roads leading to Mariel.

They had about a fifty-five minute head start on the SEAL team. Schaffer told Guillermo everything that had happened during the reception.

Hearing the story, Guillermo grew quieter, angrier, more determined. He pressed harder on the gas pedal, straining his 1958 Bel-Air, ignoring the pothole-infested road. Without seatbelts, they bounced about the open space of the car, occasionally bumping their heads on the roof of the old vehicle. Guillermo had the advantage of holding on to the steering wheel, which helped to cushion his blows. Schaffer, though, was helpless to prevent himself from repeatedly bouncing hard against the roof. After several hard blows, Schaffer extended his arms and pressed hard against the roof of the car.

They found out earlier, from Santiago's drunken men at the bar, that the general's base was located in Mariel. Monitoring DeCana's transmissions to Xavier, Schaffer had pinpointed the exact location. Schaffer knew they would not be able to drive right up to Santiago's location undetected, so for the last half mile they'd have to walk.

Schaffer could feel the adrenalin kicking in. "Guillermo, do you know where Pier 4 is in Mariel?"

"Yes."

"That's our destination." He turned and looked out the window. "I don't think it's wise to drive all the way in. Stop about a half a kilometer out and we'll cover the remaining distance on foot."

"We can't waste time on foot!" Guillermo shouted.

"Yes, we can. Santiago's men are heavily armed. We don't have any weapons, unless you are harboring something you haven't told me about." Schaffer looked around the car. "We should assess the situation and inform Castro so that he can mount a rescue. We're no good to anyone dead." Guillermo's stone cold expression remained in place for the balance of the trip.

Schaffer and Guillermo arrived in Mariel and parked the car a half mile from the warehouses. Setting out on foot, they jogged on dirt roads away from the normal routes. Schaffer didn't want to run into any of Santiago's men on the main roads. The landscape, covered with tall weeds and trees, they used for cover since the full moon lit everything. When they saw the warehouses, both men crouched to hands and knees, inching closer to Santiago's makeshift base.

The warehouses had been abandoned for a long time. The neglect was evident. Paint loosely clung in one or two spots, and the windows were heavily stained with dirt and grime. Tall weeds, in various stages of growth, surrounded the road leading to the pier. Schaffer and Guillermo hid in the tallest bunch of weeds, fifty meters from the warehouses. From there, they witnessed the movements of soldiers in and out of the warehouses. Guillermo raised his binoculars to get a count of Santiago's men.

An hour passed. Guillermo and Schaffer remained crouched behind the weeds waiting for any significant action. Schaffer moved around as much as possible to keep his legs loose. Pulling his Nikon F5 from his backpack, Schaffer dropped a roll of 1600 speed film into the camera and took several pictures of the soldiers' movements. The film was so sensitive to light that he could take pictures with very little illumination; the moon would be more than enough.

Guillermo kept vigil with binoculars. He heard an approaching jeep and turned in its direction to see its occupants. Several rebels pulled a woman, bound and gagged, from the jeep.

Guillermo's gasp made Schaffer turn just in time to see him attempt to stand. "I've got to save her," he said a little too loudly.

"No," Schaffer demanded in hushed tones. "There're too many of them for us to handle." He tackled Guillermo to keep him from lunging forward and revealing their position. "Let's watch and see what they do. Then we can report it to Castro. I told you before we can't do her any good if we're dead."

Guillermo sat up and placed his head in his hands. "I guess you're right." After a moment, he lifted his head and put the binoculars to his eyes to continue watching the scene. His face contorted, showing his elevated level of helpless anger.

¤¤¤¤

Half an hour later, Guillermo and Schaffer witnessed the execution of one hundred and seventy men at the hands of a few skillfully trained commandos. The helicopter arrived and waited for fifteen minutes for the men to wrap up. At the warehouses, the men stalked around like a group of Ninjas, effortlessly performing their duty.

Schaffer whispered to Guillermo. "The efficiency with which those men killed was no mistake. They've trained for this type of mission at length." Guillermo didn't seem to be paying attention to what Schaffer was saying, so he tapped Guillermo's shoulder. "Has Castro ever dispatched a hostage recovery team in the past?"

Guillermo shook his head. He could see that Demetria was now safe, yet he still looked unsettled. As a government guide, Guillermo was also a sworn spy, who was required to selflessly give his life to save a head of State, or anyone deemed worthy. Demetria was at the top of that list. He had failed by not trying to save her before these men did. "How can I tell Castro what happened here tonight after not mounting her rescue?"

"Easy," Schaffer laughed. "You just tell him I kicked your ass and wouldn't let you go." Schaffer's attempt at humor was lost on Guillermo. He looked at Schaffer without the slightest bit of amusement on his face. Schaffer was beginning to think that Guillermo had been born without a sense of humor. Hard times had a way of making many in Cuba serious about far too many situations.

The chopper blades struck a musical note, whose pitch rose as they spun faster. In a matter of seconds, the HH60H climbed skyward laden with the extra passengers. Fear for their personal safety kept Schaffer and Guillermo in place until the chopper was out of sight. There was no mistaking the GCAL-50 machine guns that protruded from either side of the chopper. Schaffer had sat behind such guns on past missions. He knew they were used to mop-up anyone left on the ground.

When Schaffer and Guillermo could no longer hear or see any sign of the chopper, they rose and walked over to the warehouses in order to view the destruction. Blood and bodies were everywhere. Crabs, attracted by the smell of death, rushed ashore to help clear the dead. Guillermo and Schaffer stared at the scene for several minutes, unable to speak.

Guillermo was about to open the front door to the west warehouse. Schaffer grabbed his arm. "Hold on a second. Can't you smell almonds?"

Guillermo sniffed the air. "Yes, that's strange."

"No, it's cyanide." Schaffer gripped him tightly. "If you open that door, you die in ten seconds."

"Who were those men?" Guillermo asked.

Schaffer didn't attempt to answer. Instead, he turned and spoke nearly under his breath. "Those were the good guys." He then spun to face Guillermo. "How soon can we get in touch with President Castro?"

"Immediately."

"I think we should inform him of what we've seen." Schaffer turned and started walking in the direction of the car.

Guillermo picked up a large rock and threw it, smashing a window on the west warehouse. "We best air it out before the president's men get here." He moved to catch up. "Don't you think he was the one who sent these men to free his niece?"

"I wouldn't be so sure." Looking towards the sky, Schaffer knew the American military chopper would need Castro's help to get into Cuba untouched. He couldn't understand how Alex convinced Castro to let him in. "There's more to this story than we can see. And damnit, I intend to find out what it is."

They climbed into the car and drove towards Havana.

Within forty-five minutes, they arrived at the entrance to Castro's villa. There was a buzz of activity at the villa, none of which involved outsiders. As Schaffer and Guillermo pulled up to the front gates, at least twenty heavily armed guards were there to meet them.

Six of the guards locked their AK-47's, chambering a round, and pointed them at Guillermo and Schaffer. One of the guards yelled. "Get out of the car!"

Schaffer and Guillermo stepped out of the car with their hands raised. It was obvious that the guards were in no mood for discussion. "What is your business here?"

"I'm Guillermo Leon. He is a tourist from Mexico. We've just witnessed the resistance being crushed, and Miss Demetria being rescued. We're here to inform President Castro of what we've seen and to offer our assistance."

"Miss Demetria is safe inside. She's not left the compound all night. Get back in your car and go home."

"Wait." The voice rose from behind the guards. They moved to let the man through. The guards lowered their guns, but remained ready in the event they were needed. Castro emerged smoking a cigar, something no one in Cuba had seen him do in years. Xavier was by his side doing the same.

In his haste to clean up after the rescue, Xavier had missed a small streak of black camouflage behind his left ear. He stepped forward and asked, "Who are these men, and what do they want?"

"I am Guillermo Leon. He is a Mexican tourist. Earlier, at a bar we overheard men talking of overthrowing your government." He yelled and tiptoed, trying to see around the guards blocking his view. "We followed them to their headquarters to investigate. We've seen everything that's happened there since dusk."

Xavier locked eyes with Schaffer. Without speaking a word they nodded towards each other. Neither of them was who they pretended to be, and they both knew it.

Schaffer could tell something was wrong by the look in Xavier's eyes. Xavier looked at Schaffer as if he were surprised to see him. If Alex had ordered Schaffer's execution there was nothing to prevent Xavier from carrying it out right now.

Castro turned to his guards. "Go and bring us coffee around back." He motioned Schaffer and Guillermo in. He offered each of them a cigar. Schaffer felt it was a gesture designed to put them more at ease so that they would speak without fear. He declined.

The four men moved to the back of the house. There, Guillermo recounted their earlier observations.

Castro looked in wonder as he told the story. "I've never heard of such killing efficiency. I can use this information. Once news of this story is disseminated throughout Cuba, no one will dare try to rise against my position."

"I was surprised you'd attempt a rescue on a night with a moon full, sir. That must have put your men at greater risk." Schaffer couldn't resist acting as a reporter. "Tell me, Mr. Ciefuentes, where did you obtain your training?"

"Training for what?" Xavier asked.

"For tonight's mission."

"I was not on any mission Mr. ...?"

"Gonzales. The name is Gonzales. You must have been. All the men were dressed in black. Even their faces were black. Some of your facial covering still remains." Schaffer touched his face along his jaw line just under his ear to show Xavier where he'd left the makeup.

Xavier wiped behind his ear. "You notice a lot Mr. Gonzales. How long do you plan to stay on our island?"

"I haven't decided yet. This trip has proven to be most interesting."

"Please let me know if I may be of further service to you while you're here. I would enjoy showing you more of the island."

"Thank you, I'll do that." Schaffer held out his hands palm side up, then placed his right hand over his heart and bowed his head. He hoped Xavier understood he was offering his loyalty. Another attempt on his life could prove fatal, given the skill level of Xavier and his men. Schaffer looked over at Castro, who was speaking to Guillermo. He turned back to Xavier and very softly said. "Ooh-Rah."

Xavier was unable to prevent the smile from creeping across his face.

The men talked for a while longer. Demetria's doctor came out to inform Castro and Xavier that she was fine. "I gave her something to help her sleep. She's been through a lot."

Schaffer looked out over the water. The sun was in the middle of the azure horizon. There was not a cloud anywhere, the winds were calm, and the humidity was low. There was nothing to indicate a storm was brewing in the northwest, just off the American shoreline. By the time it hit, Castro would be helpless to prevent it from coming ashore.

Chapter 44

Secretary of State Ian Mackenzie finished his second cup of coffee when his phone rang.

Calls this early were usually from the White House, or from Cordell. The number that appeared above the word 'MARYLAND' was one that he did not recognize. He set the phone back on the table and continued to read the paper.

After two more rings, Mackenzie lifted the phone and pressed the button to answer his call. "Yes?"

"Secretary Mackenzie?" the voice called gently.

"Yes?" Mackenzie answered again.

"I have something that I think you would love to have in your possession."

"And who are you?" Mackenzie asked with mild curiosity.

"Names aren't important." The caller paused, unable to hide his nervousness. "I work at the White House in the president's chief of staff's office."

Mackenzie began to listen with a bit more interest. "Then you are aware the president currently doesn't have a chief of staff. So why are you calling me?"

"Yes, sir, I realize the chief of staff is deceased. That however, does not stop mail from coming into his office." The caller sounded more confident. "Actually, the item I have was returned to his office. You may have heard about the incident in D.C. where several mailmen were dumping mail rather that delivering it. This envelope was returned to the Chief of Staff Cosby's office since the intended address label peeled off."

"How does that involve me?" Mackenzie now sounded a bit concerned.

"In the envelope was a memo from the president, and a letter. One may infer the chief of staff suggests you might have had something to do with his early departure from this earth. The memo from the president suggests that the U.S. is indeed invading Cuba." The caller began his negotiations. "The press would pay a fortune for something like this, especially since the note inside was addressed to Schaffer O'Grady."

Mackenzie maintained his cool. "So why are you calling me if you plan to sell it to the press?"

"I thought you would rather have it. Going to the press can get too messy."

"What did you have in mind?" Mackenzie dialed Cordell's number on his cell phone and punched in a code to begin a trace on his personal line.

The caller decided to roll the dice. "A half a million shouldn't be too much to ask, considering the sensitive nature of the contents."

Mackenzie lifted a pen and wrote down the number on his caller ID. "What's going to assure me that you won't attempt to sell this to the press after I give you what you ask for?"

"I have no axe to grind with you." The caller tried to sound friendly and sincere. "I just want to retire early. I'm tired of the day to day."

"I see," Mackenzie said. "And I'm your ship coming into port?"

"I guess you could say that," the man answered apologetically. "By the way, I'm sure you're going to cross-reference the number you see with those on file at the White House. Don't bother. This phone was carelessly left on the seat on the subway this morning. It's going in the Potomac river as soon as we hang up."

"Then how do you expect me to contact you after I have the money together?" Mackenzie waited for a response.

"I've already taken care of those details. Meet me tonight at The Rib Bone near Howard University at 7:00 p.m. Bring a cashier's check and your cell phone number. Once I'm safe, I'll call you on your cell phone and tell you where you can find the envelope. You come alone, I know what you look like so don't try anything that could jeopardize our relationship."

"You have been very exact," Mackenzie flattered him. "I have no reason to doubt your resolve. I will be at The Rib Bone at 7:00 p.m." He heard the phone hit the water and the line go dead. The grip he had on his coffee cup was so tight that the cup smashed, sending coffee spilling over his table and floor.

He hung up his line and immediately reconnected, calling Cordell. Mackenzie didn't even give Cordell a chance to say hello. "What the fuck are you doing? Are you trying to stab me in the back?"

Cordell sounded puzzled. "What the hell are you talking about?"

"I just got a call from some punk that said he has the envelope you took off of Harold Cosby." Mackenzie took a second to catch his breath.

"That's impossible. It's right here in my safe, just where you told me to keep it."

"That's just great." Mackenzie grew angrier by the second. "We've got a run to make tonight at 7:00. Bring that damn envelope with you. After we finish with this little fucker, who ever he is, I want that envelope destroyed before my eyes. Goddamnit, all this shit should have died with Harold. How many more of these little incidents will pop up?"

Cordell attempted to answer. "I have no —"

"I'm not asking you for a fucking answer. It was a rhetorical question," Mackenzie spat. "Am I the only one who's not a complete imbecile in this city? I'll see you at 7:00. Bring a van." He wanted to slam the phone, but he had the portable, so he had to settle for disconnecting it by pushing the button then slamming it against the wall.

¤¤¤¤

At 6:55 p.m., Secretary Mackenzie sat in The Rib Bone sipping iced tea that was too sweet and trying to pretend he was enjoying the greasy ribs. Exactly at 7:00 p.m., a man left the bar to join him in his booth.

"Damn good ribs, aren't they?" the man said, looking around.

Mackenzie didn't even bother to look up. "There's enough grease here to clog every artery in China. I'm only eating them to prevent myself from looking like a fool sitting in a booth waiting for something."

The man drummed his fingers on the tabletop. "I take it you have what I need?"

Mackenzie pushed the letter-sized envelope to the man. "It's all there. Now when will I get what I need?"

The man tucked the envelope into his jacket. "If you continue to follow my instructions you should be back at home safe in less than two hours."

Mackenzie looked up for the first time, staring the man directly in his eyes. "You can take this any way you want to." He wiped his mouth and pointed with the dirty napkin. "If you fuck me over, you will want to go to hell to escape the torture I'll put you through."

"Take it easy. No wonder you need to avoid fatty foods, you're wound too tight. I've got what I want and you'll have what you want. Now, here are my instructions. Enjoy the rest of your meal for at least another fifteen minutes. Don't turn around when I leave. I'll disappear and so will your problems. Can you handle that?"

"Goodbye." Mackenzie looked at his plate. "Don't ever let me see your face again!"

The man jumped up and headed out the door. Ten seconds after the door closed, Mackenzie followed. He stepped outside just as Cordell was escorting the man to a waiting van at gunpoint. Calmly, Mackenzie got into the van just behind them. Cordell handcuffed him to a hook on the floor of the van and moved into the driver's seat.

Mackenzie sat in the only seat in the back of the van. "Let's go." The van pulled off and the man handcuffed to the floor wet his pants.

"I...I...If you hurt me you'll never find out where that envelope is," the man whimpered.

Mackenzie slapped him hard across the face with a section of rubber hose. "That's the least of my worries, boy. Now we're going to have a discussion. If I'm satisfied with the results I'll let you live. Cordell, drive to the construction site near the landing strips at National Airport."

Cordell pressed the accelerator and the van sped off towards Virginia.

Mackenzie looked at the man. "I've read extensively on methods of torture. Let's see how many of my favorites it will take to get you to talk tonight."

The man sputtered, "My name is —"

Mackenzie smacked him across the face again. "I don't want to know your name, dumbass. And if you try to tell me again, I'll cut out a piece of your tongue. Humanizing yourself won't work, because I don't give a fuck about you. I don't care how many kids you have or what their names are. What I do care about is that envelope. Now, where is it?"

"Let me go first."

Mackenzie held up a glass vial. "This is sulfuric acid. One drop could burn a hole through the floor of this van." He filled the dropper and held it over the man, who squirmed to get out of the way.

"What the fuck —" the man panicked.

Mackenzie released one drop of the acid on the man's crotch area. The acid instantly burned through the man's pants and hit him in the groin area.

The man violently kicked. He screamed in pain. "Okay, okay. I'll tell you! Stop!"

Mackenzie raised the dropper again.

"My chest. It's taped to my chest!" the man screamed. Tears poured from his face, and mucous ran from his nose. "Stop the burning!"

Mackenzie lifted a water bottle. "Now, wasn't that easy?" He took a drink of the water.

"Water!" the man shouted.

Mackenzie held up the bottle. "This water?"

"Please." He writhed. "God!"

"God? God, God," Mackenzie whimpered, mocking the man's plea. "God can't do anything for you. I'm in charge here."

"Yes," he blubbered. "You're in charge." He bowed his head.

"Much better." Mackenzie dumped the bottle onto the man's crotch.

"Thank you." He sobbed more intensely. "I'm sorry. I'll never say a word. Lemme go."

Mackenzie reached down and pulled a saber out of its sheath. "That all depends on how strong you are."

"What do you mean?" the man asked, looking at the saber.

"I told you. I know torture." Mackenzie laughed. "One method the Indians would use on cavalrymen was to bind their hands and feet. Then they would use a small piece of rope to attach the hands to the feet. They'd leave the cavalryman in the hot sun balanced on his saber, tilting backwards. If his legs were strong enough to support him until more troops arrived, they could save their fellow cavalryman. If not, he would become too fatigued and fall on the saber." Mackenzie slid two fingers down either side of the saber. "Of course, we don't have the benefit of the hot sun. But if you can last until the construction workers arrive in nine hours, you may live."

The man began to scream.

Cordell parked the van. He shoved a tennis ball into the man's mouth, and duct taped it closed.

Mackenzie arranged the man on the saber, and gave him final instructions: "As I'm sure you've figured out by now, there's not a fraction of an inch of play in these ropes. Don't make any sudden movement, or it will be your last. If you can't hold out until morning, I've positioned the saber right behind your heart. Death will come quickly. Good luck."

Cordell and Mackenzie closed the door to the van. Cordell asked, "How long do you think he will last?"

"If he's lucky, about an hour." Mackenzie changed the subject. "Did you plant the explosives?"

Cordell slid out a remote detonation device and showed it to Mackenzie.

"Very good. Wait until he falls on the saber, and then detonate it. Make sure that both these envelopes burn with him."

Cordell felt so shocked at this violence, he couldn't speak. Instead, he saluted Mackenzie and walked to his motorcycle.

¤¤¤¤

Thirty minutes later, Cordell arrived back at the van on his motorcycle. He looked in the window. Blood was all over the floor. He jumped back on the bike and drove off. After he was a safe distance away, he pushed the detonation button and a fireball lit up the pre-dawn sky.

Chapter
45

Xavier tiptoed into Demetria's room.

She was still groggy from the drugs given to her earlier, but managed to sit after he walked in.

"How are you feeling today?"

Demetria looked as if she had been in a bad car accident. Her lip was split, and there were large blue bruises on her face, wrist, and legs.

"Better, I guess. What time is it?" she asked.

"It's four in the afternoon. You've been out for a couple of days." Xavier stroked her hair. "The doctors thought it would help your recovery if you slept. Maybe your pain would be less, and maybe you wouldn't remember as much."

"If this pain is better, I'm glad they kept me out. However, there's nothing wrong with my memory." Demetria looked at him intensely. "I think you have some explaining to do."

"You're absolutely correct. I'll explain later." Xavier spun and looked at the door. "For now you'll have to trust me. I know that I ask a lot, but for now it's best."

Demetria almost screamed. "Who gave you the right to decide what's best for me?" She clutched at her head as the pain radiated.

Xavier cradled her head in his arms. She didn't have the strength to push him away. Quietly, she began to cry.

A tear slipped from the corner of Xavier's eye. "I promise I'll never lie to you. Please trust me. Anything I keep from you is for the best and because I have to." He gently kissed the top of Demetria's head, rocking her before he tucked her into the bed. He turned and walked out of the room.

Tears ran down her cheeks. The past few days had been a nightmare from which she desperately wanted to wake.

Unsuspected, Castro had witnessed their exchange from an adjoining room in her suite. After he heard the door softly close, he revealed himself from behind the archway leading to her bedroom. "I can see that you're in tremendous pain, both physical and mental." Gently, he sat on the side of her bed and touched her face. "You know that I have always felt your pain and you know that talking about it helps to ease the burden you feel. Will you allow me to help ease your concerns?"

"You don't understand, Uncle. Something happened that night in Mariel that made me feel I don't know Xavier at all." Demetria turned and looked at the closed door.

"What could be so terrible to shake your belief in him? Didn't he jeopardize his life to save you?" Castro asked.

"Yes, but —"

"What greater love could a man show than to risk his life for the one he loves?" Castro lightly swept the hair from her eyes.

She looked at him with childlike eyes. "Could it be, Uncle, that he's someone other than he claims to be?"

Castro sat silently for a moment, as if in deep thought. "Aren't we all? However, if he was lying, I would know. You must trust your visions, no matter what happened during your capture. He's a good man. No matter what happens now, you must trust your visions. Trust what they have told you." Castro pulled the girl close and held her, as he looked off into the distance. "This moment reminds me of when you were a little girl just coming to live with me. I would hold you and rock you, and tell you everything would be all right. Some nights it would take longer than others would, but eventually you drifted off to sleep. Always." Lost in thoughts of the past, he chanted over and over, "No matter what happens, trust your vision, no matter what happens, trust your vision." He rocked Demetria until she fell asleep. Castro placed her head on the pillow, and tiptoed to the door.

Xavier heard the sound of voices when he left Demetria's room and waited just outside of the door to take in what he could of their conversation.

Castro emerged from the room, quietly closing the door. "She's asleep. We have to complete our plans since we leave in the morning to begin our tour of the country. I'll introduce you at each of our stops, where you'll make a speech." Castro rested his hand on Xavier's shoulder and looked deep into his eyes. "It's your responsibility to gain the trust and respect of all the people in this country. That's the only way for Cuba to survive."

"I'll do my best." Xavier acknowledged the enormous task that lay before him. "You are the only ruler Cuba has known for over four decades. I will convince the people of Cuba that I am the leader for their future." He recalled the whispers of rumors surfacing about a new revolution designed to relieve the economic stress plaguing Cuba.

Castro pointed his finger at Xavier, shaking it feverishly. "It is imperative that you be so convincing that there's no civil unrest in any part of the country. You have to come across as a strong, yet, compassionate leader who believes in his people and his country."

Xavier shook his head, affirming Castro's statements. He turned and walked down the hall, feeling the weight of the task that lay in front of him. It was a lot to ask of any man, but especially difficult for someone who gained a country by adoption.

¤¤¤¤

Schaffer heard the now familiar beep enter his ear. He let it continue for some time. Schaffer was convinced that Dee knew when he was alone. Finally, he gave in and pushed the button.

"It's about time you answered," she snapped.

"You have quite a knack for contacting me when I'm alone." Schaffer held the device, looking at it in different angles. "Does this thing let you in on that, too?"

Dee sounded defensive. "What difference does it make?"

"It makes a hell of a lot to me." Schaffer stood and walked to the hotel window peaking through the blinds. "Shit, you probably know every move I make."

Dee tried to put him at ease. "Somebody's got to make sure you're safe, sugar."

"Whatever you say," Schaffer said sarcastically.

"I say you're safe. So stop winning." Dee showed no sympathy, but enjoyed the banter.

Schaffer did a one-eighty, redirecting their conversation. "Answer a question for me. How in the hell did Alex get our choppers into Cuba?"

She felt her body stiffen even though she had been waiting for the question. "Schaffer, that's not important right now. What is important is that Xavier completes this mission."

"What you're asking me to do is sit by while Alex has someone assassinated. I'm not sure I can —"

Dee cut him off. "The president has not had anyone killed and I didn't say that's what he planned."

"Why are you being so defensive? Did you forget that it was Guzman who suggested Castro was to be killed? Not me." Schaffer expected the accusation to make Dee more defensive.

"Schaffer, you've got to trust me on this."

Schaffer grunted. "Like I have a lot of choices."

"I will personally fill you in as soon as I can about everything." Dee kept her voice level to protect her honesty.

"Are you going to tell me who killed Harold?"

She sighed. "I wish I knew."

"That's really what I should be investigating." Schaffer looked out over the water. "But I can't do that from here."

"If you come home you will not be able to complete the story you're working on there. We both know you can't walk away from something this big. Harold's murder is in some way tied to what's unfolding in Cuba. Stay there. You'll get your man soon enough."

"You say that as if you've got foreknowledge."

Dee spoke quickly to prevent his rising suspicion. "Not in the least. What I have is confidence in you. You're not about to let anyone get away with Harold's murder. That possibility ended the moment you were involved in this mess."

"I've got to warn you, I've grown inpatient standing in the dark. You'd better enlighten me soon." Schaffer disconnected the pocket computer and lifted a phone to call Guillermo. He wanted to get to Mariel before Castro's entourage.

Chapter
46

Schaffer and Guillermo arrived in Mariel early in the morning with plenty of time to stake out where they would be along the procession.

Unlike their last visit, the streets were alive with people discussing the raid.

News of General Santiago's failed coup attempt spread rapidly throughout the country. There were reports that Castro sent five hundred of his top commandos to crush the resistance. The evidence of such an altercation was clear. Bodies littered the three warehouses in Mariel. The smell of death and decay lingered heavy in the air. Flies, maggots, crabs, and an occasional banana rat feasted on the decaying flesh of bodies left in place to make a point. The buzzing noise made by thousands of flies drowned out the sound of the waves that rolled towards the warehouses.

¤¤¤¤

Castro proceeded on his tour, making a show of force along the route. He and Xavier first stopped just outside of Mariel. There, Castro and Xavier left the comfort of their armored limousine and entered two tanks leading the procession. Xavier was now dressed in the familiar olive drab uniform worn by Castro. On his head, he wore a red beret for emphasis, reminding Schaffer of Castro forty years earlier when he first entered Havana after leading the successful revolution. Xavier and Castro pulled into town accompanied by a full battalion of tanks leading the way. The tanks stopped just short of the warehouses.

Guillermo and Schaffer had waited along the parade route since the early morning. They left the parade route and drove into town just ahead of the tanks. Luckily, they had enough time to position themselves in the middle of the crowd before Castro disembarked from his tank.

Two armed guards escorted Castro from his tank and walked him to the microphone in the center of the platform. The townspeople quieted, anticipating his message. As expected, he began with what'd happened three nights before.

"I will never tolerate any type of insurrection in Cuba! We shall remain Marxist-Leninist, even if we're the only country left on the face of the earth to do so." He pointed to what was left of several men lying on the ground. "These dead men are an example of what awaits those who wish to rule my country through force. They should be left to the rats and insects to devour their flesh, leaving their bones for the dogs! They have no place in a society such as ours. Look around." He paused. "Do you have food to eat, clothing to wear? When you're sick, are you taken care of at no expense to any of you?"

Accusingly, he looked across the gathering. Shouting with one hand raised in the air, he asked, "Then why are there some who wish to change this? There are many who flee to the United States where there are no such benefits. Do you think they're better off?"

For the first time since he began speaking, muted cheers rose from the crowd. "Here in Cuba is where we belong! Here where we are respectful of one another and treated as equals." The cries grew in strength and persistence. "There are some who say that the time for new leadership has come. I say they are right!"

Many people gasped and looked at each other in disbelief. All cheering ceased, and the crowd grew silent. Although Havana is only twenty-five miles from Mariel, word had not gotten to all its residents concerning Castro's decision to step down.

Castro looked over the hushed crowd. He had their full attention. He spoke to them with no sign of doubt in his voice. "I've selected the only man who can lead this country into the future. He's already proven himself by leading his countrymen home from their captors in Guantanamo." Instantly, they knew of whom he spoke. Xavier's status had already grown to a legend throughout Cuba, and cheers slowly rumbled over the crowd until it was a low roar. "Good people of Cuba, I give you Xavier Ciefuentes!"

The roar grew louder. A deafening chant flowed over the crowd, "Xa-v-ier."

Castro looked on, forcing a smile. He rewound the memory of his rise to power. What he was witnessing as Xavier moved to the microphone paralleled his assent the moment he reached Revolutionary Square. People lay in ruins along the path he'd traveled to reach Havana. Just as the dead in Mariel, the fodder along the streets forty years ago had opposed him.

Change in Cuba always came with a heavy human price tag. The cries filling his ears, just as before, represented the expression of triumph and loss.

On stage, Xavier looked left and panned right. He chose not to remove his sunglasses before speaking. They gave him a more mysterious aura, and in the event this moment was ever televised internationally, they would help to protect his identity.

"Cuba will today embark upon a new journey. We'll enter a time when there is no cause for concern in this country. Our people will not want to leave. All will want to come here in increasing numbers."

The people started to murmur approval. As his confidence grew he spoke more openly. "We'll enter a time of plenty, a time when our women do not walk the streets to earn a living. A time when everyone earns a good living and everyone has plenty to eat. We will make the Cuban peso a force throughout the world."

The crowd grew warmer and louder with each of his passing words. Xavier let the people cheer and shout his praises before going on. "Our resources are needed all over the world. There're countries willing to pay top dollar for our sugar, coffee, and tobacco. Our scientists will develop new methods to increase production of these crops. Better processing facilities will be built to increase efficiency and decrease cost. We'll do these things together, and together we'll rule Cuba!"

The crowd roared. It took nearly three minutes to calm everyone. Xavier scanned the gathering.

Schaffer saw Xavier focus on the center of the crowd where he stood fiercely taking notes. He wondered whether Xavier had rehearsed the speech, if he'd discussed it with Castro. Schaffer didn't want to use his pocket recorder since it might raise questions from Guillermo, who Schaffer now knew was a member of the party faithful.

Momentarily, Xavier's eyes met Schaffer's. He knew that Xavier would confront him soon, one-on-one. Schaffer knew Xavier viewed him as a complication. Nothing had been settled the first time that he and Xavier met at Castro's villa after Demetria's rescue. Except, they both knew that they held a common bond, the United States.

A hush came over the gathering and Xavier spoke again. "If someone wants to buy our cigars, we'll require them to buy sugar as well. If they want sugar, we'll also require them to buy coffee. In turn, we'll have them set up companies to package our products and sell them all over the world, including the United States. This way, everyone receives something out of the deal. They get the product they want, and we get new markets for our products." Castro looked at Xavier. His eyebrows were raised and his mouth was slightly open. He appeared truly amazed at the cunning ideas that Xavier came up with, and his bold, confident delivery.

"We will immediately renegotiate our contracts with the buyers of our goods. People will be put back to work, and warehouses such as these will not be left vacant, to be taken into custody by rogues for perverse deeds. Instead, they'll be filled with our products and people bustling to fill the ships that will be waiting on these docks."

Schaffer looked on in awe. As he struggled to write, listen, and watch the people's reaction, English words slipped from his lips. "This is going to make one hell of a story." Everyone around Schaffer was too wrapped up in the moment to concern themselves with his comments. They continued to cheer their new leader.

Schaffer stopped writing and slowly looked up. Several thoughts coursed through his brain, drowning out everyone in the cheering crowd. This event seemed to be too well planned to be a coincidence. Since Castro was handing his country to Xavier, why would Xavier need to assassinate him?

Chapter 47

President Alexander Nicholas and Chairwoman of the Joint Chiefs of Staff General Dee Roseboro reviewed the transcripts from an earlier broadcast in which Xavier spoke to the Cuban people.

His ease of delivery and comfort with the subject matter made him seem a natural.

"Wow, who came up with this stuff?" Alex asked. "You must have prepared him for every situation. It's not that easy to stand before a group, for the first time, and instantly win them over."

"I'm afraid, sir, it's strictly ad-lib at this point. It wasn't part of our agenda for Commander Benderis to become Castro's replacement. Castro came up with that one on his own. We suspect that the commander is wearing his earpiece since he's transmitting." She paused. "Would you like us to feed him lines to use during his speeches?"

"No, he's doing just fine." Alex smiled. "He's doing just fine."

Alex and Dee left his study to join the cabinet in the Oval Office.

Alex tossed the transcripts on his desk, addressing the assembly. "So where do we go from here? Castro threw a monkey wrench into our plans." He lit an Opus X and shoved both his hands into his pants pockets. "We didn't plan for Commander Benderis to become Cuba's new leader. At this point, we're helpless to stop it."

Dee was the first to speak. "I think we have to let it play itself out, sir. Commander Benderis is not a rookie on his first assignment. We've spent years training him for this mission. Although we didn't prepare him to become the leader of Cuba, he seems to know just what he should do. If I know Xavier, he's probably five steps ahead of us anyway."

"Point well taken, General Roseboro. However, you said yourself his training didn't included running a country." He paused and turned his gaze towards Director Caprelotti. "Anthony, what are your thoughts on this? Have you received any reports from your men in Cuba?"

"Well, sir, I think we need to get Castro out as soon as possible. We have a couple of men in place who can handle the job. Then we can deal with Commander Benderis afterwards."

"That's a bit hasty." Alex pulled the cigar from his lips. "We sent the SEALs in to do the job. They're not in any immediate danger. Besides, that could backfire since these people may not like Commander Benderis without Castro's influence. Then what? I think unless someone can come up with something better, we'll have to accept General Roseboro's suggestion. We'll let this play itself out." He returned the cigar to his mouth and blew out several puffs of smoke. "In the meantime, if any of you come up with something else, or there is a material change in Cuba, let me know. That's all for now."

Chapter 48

Schaffer's op-ed piece appeared on the front page of the *Post*:

Cuban President Under Attack. U.S. Involvement?
Earlier this week, Cuban President Castro fell prey to accusations that he was an unfit leader. The accusations led to an attempt by General Raul Santiago and a small faction of his men to overthrow the current regime. Santiago, Castro's half-brother, had his plans end in death after he and his men kidnapped Castro's niece. She was the bait to garner Castro's attention and force him to resign. Eight highly trained men came in and destroyed over one hundred and seventy men without making a sound. As quickly as they had come, a helicopter that appeared to be an American chopper arrived and evacuated the commandos and the hostage, leaving behind only carnage.

The dead were left to rot in the hot Cuban sun where they had fallen. Castro went to Mariel three days later to use these men as an example, lest anyone else was thinking of plotting a second attempt on his presidency.

It is difficult to believe that Castro would send a team of men in to destroy his enemy and leave. He would want everyone to know he was responsible for their deaths, and he would leave his men around to emphasize his strength. This act was too unusual even for the unpredictable Castro. It wasn't until he arrived in Mariel that he claimed responsibility for thwarting the uprising.

Next, there's the question of the helicopter, which was brand new. Cuba hasn't had the money needed to purchase a used helicopter, much less a new one. Where did this state of the art helicopter come from? Could it be that a new savior has come to Cuba's aid?

In addition to these confusing facts, Castro named a successor to his presidency, Xavier Ciefuentes. Until a few weeks ago, no one in the Havana area knew him. Then in one remarkable day, he was transformed to a national hero. He led a group of men from the U.S. Naval base at Guantanamo across a field of landmines to a Cuban military base. There he met with and since has been in the company of Castro. In this short time, he has not only been able to gain the presidency, but has also gained the hand of Castro's niece. What kind of magic does this man wield? It would seem Castro has great plans for this hero. Since he's unknown, the world will have to wait to find out the direction that he chooses to lead his country. It is unlikely Castro would choose any successor who didn't believe in Communism.

In his first speech in front of the warehouses in Mariel, Mr. Ciefuentes sounded more like a Capitalist than a Communist. Not once has he pledged loyalty to a party, yet he talks of change that would put Cuba back on the right track to have the United States return and serve as benefactor. If he continues in this vein, he'll build the support of his fellow Cubans who have suffered since the fall of Soviet Union. All the party loyalists are waiting for Castro to demand Ciefuentes profess his loyalty to the party. After all, Castro is the last of the hard line Communists in the Western Hemisphere, vowing to continue the fight even if there only remains one loyal to the party.

Could it be that we've seen the invasion of Cuba, an invasion of one? This man has managed to rise to a power position in a matter of a few short weeks. If this is a plan manufactured by the President of the United States, it's a masterful one. At the rate Mr. Ciefuentes is moving, Cuba could have the U.S. back on its shores before the next election, ending the embargo the States has maintained for over forty years, and sealing the election for the current administration.

Chapter 49

The president read over Schaffer's piece and sipped a cup of coffee.

He found it hard to contain his elation. The op-ed article confirmed Xavier's progress towards completion of the operation.

The story also had a downside, as it would undoubtedly raise eyebrows at the opposite end of Pennsylvania Avenue. Especially with the Speaker of the House Davis, who hoped to unseat Alex in the next election.

An investigation or hearing could prove detrimental to the ultimate goal of the mission. Alex quickly formulated his next move to thwart any unwelcome inquisition.

Mackenzie excitedly burst into the Oval Office. He hadn't knocked. He aggressively waved his copy of the *Post*. "This is great news Mr. President."

Alex sat his paper down. "For the most part I guess you're right. Now, however, we have to — or I should say Xavier has to — pull this thing off. If not it could prove to be very damaging."

"Don't worry, Mr. President," Dee offered, raising her coffee cup in Alex's direction, "he'll get it done."

Mackenzie looked dejected. "I see you've already discussed this." In truth, he was pleased it appeared Castro was on his way out. But his overt enthusiasm was a ploy to keep the president off balance. He wanted Castro out of power and he needed a way to cause Alex the identical fate, eager as he was to take control of the country himself. "This seems to be the perfect time to have Commander Benderis pull the trigger. He can then use his newfound power to get us in the door.

Alex looked at Dee. "What's your take? It would allow us to proceed at a much faster pace."

Reflectively, Dee took a drink from her coffee. "To be honest, sir, I believe that's a call the commander needs to make. He's just been introduced as Cuba's future leader, the man the world believed would succeed Castro was killed in a failed coup attempt. If all of a sudden Castro dies, it may raise far too much suspicion." She stood and lifted the paper from Alex's desk. "After reading this, it would stand to reason that we would be suspected."

"You're quite right. Tell Tynes I'll need to see him at 10:30. We'll have to deny all these allegations of U.S. involvement with the raid in Mariel. I'd like to get ahead of the pack on this one."

¤¤¤¤

By 11:00 a.m. Press Secretary Coleman Tynes was on every the major network.

"The President of the United States wishes to inform you that, at this time, the United States Government has no involvement in Cuba. Furthermore, we've neither aided nor assisted the Cuban government in any type of mission to stop aggression against Castro. This government wishes to see Castro removed from power. We feel that with him gone, we may be able to initiate talks designed at normalizing relationships with Cuba. As long as Castro's in power, there's absolutely nothing to talk about."

Hands shot up when Tynes finished reading his statement. "Mr. Secretary, has any effort been made to authenticate Mr. O'Grady's story?"

"We have no ties to Cuba. There would be no way to find out any more than what you have read. As I've said, we have no involvement there. Maybe you should question the *Washington Post* for clarification." Tynes' eyes twitched when he told his obvious lie.

"What does the United States know about the man Castro named as his replacement?"

"We've not had a chance to investigate his background. We'll be getting back to you when we have more information."

Armed with a leak from Senator Hernandez's office, another reporter stood with his question. "Mr. Secretary, what can you tell us about this 'Operation Smokeout?'

Tynes lost some of the color in his face. Usually he did not show any emotion, always cool under pressure; this however, caught him off guard. "I'm sorry I don't know anything about any Operation Smokeout." Tynes shifted his weight from leg to leg several times trying to get comfortable. "Therefore, I have no comment."

After the press conference, news agencies were contacting their foreign desk to book flights to Cuba. The race was on to find out the validity of the reported story. Schaffer O'Grady had a reputation among his fellow reporters as someone who didn't report a story unless he had first-hand knowledge. It was time now for them to share the task of gathering information. It was obvious to them that Schaffer was already there, well ahead of the game.

Chapter 50

On his third day of the speaking tour, Xavier decided it was time to confront Schaffer, since he'd seen him at every gathering.

While waiting for the group to quiet down, Xavier turned to one of his guards. "That man out there with the Panama hat, taking notes. I'll need to talk to him. Don't create a scene. Take him to a quiet place so the two of us can talk."

The guard left the side of the stage and circled around to the back to meet a second guard. They walked on opposite sides of the crowd, finally meeting at Schaffer's side. "You'll have to come with us."

"Where're we going?" Schaffer demanded.

"Your presence is required. That's all you need to know."

Schaffer knew better than to argue with two men holding AK-47s, so he complied. The guards took him to a small grass hut on the edge of town. There, Schaffer was left with another soldier.

"Shoot him if he tries to leave." The guard leaned close to his associate and whispered. "In the leg. Don't kill him."

Thirty minutes later, Xavier arrived. He insisted that everyone leave the hut, and reluctantly they obeyed. "You have a keen interest in my speeches Mr. Gonzales. You've not missed one yet. Why is that?"

Schaffer looked at Xavier accusingly. "Why don't you speak English? We both know that you aren't from Cuba, at least not originally."

"It seems I may have underestimated you, Mr. O'Grady. Knowing your reputation, I should expect your intuitiveness."

Schaffer didn't know what to expect, so he played along. "How'd you know my name?"

"So you still haven't figured it out yet? Has it been that long?" Xavier smiled. "Then again maybe it's the last name. It's actually Benderis, Dr. O'Grady."

"Damn, I didn't recognize you," Schaffer laughed. He thought his acting was getting better. "Where's the beard and long hair?"

"This is the new me," Xavier answered, continuing to look at him sternly.

"Last time we talked, you were in my journalism class at Georgetown." Schaffer placed two fingers over his lips and then pointed to Xavier. "As I remember it, you wanted to become a priest. How'd you end up in Cuba?"

"I go where my boss tells me to go." Xavier sat across from Schaffer, still not yielding.

"Boss?" Schaffer looked surprised

"Yes. The president." Xavier whispered. "I'm a SEAL now."

"I'll be damned! I knew the U.S. government was involved."

"You always said a good journalists would get close to a story no matter how dangerous the situation." Xavier raised one eyebrow. "Does he calculate the risk before deciding to take an assignment?"

"Surely you don't assume that I am the only representative here from the news media." Schaffer crossed his legs and relaxed.

"Let's just say that no one else has been as close to the inside as you have. Over the course of your stay, you have managed to be near any action that's cropped up. You're either exceptionally lucky, or exceptionally dangerous." Xavier worked hard to keep from sounding threatening. He stood. "I'm not about to let anyone prevent my mission here. If you're not on board, stay the hell out of my way."

"I wouldn't dream of interfering with you unless —" Schaffer stood and walked in front of Xavier, meeting his eyes.

"Unless what?" Xavier challenged.

"One of your associates suggested you were here to assassinate Castro. We both know that's against international law. I won't stand by and be party to an illegal act."

Xavier looked surprised. "How could you possibly have information like that?"

Schaffer continued to stare without responding.

Xavier lifted two fingers. "You know I could snap these and my men would come in here and end my problems?"

Schaffer didn't blink. "You haven't been under Castro's tutelage a month yet and already you're threatening anyone who disagrees with you. Oppression always breeds rebellion. Brush up on your history, Commander."

Xavier turned away from Schaffer, embarrassed by his actions. "Yes, well, I think we can help each other."

"You do? What'd you have in mind?" Schaffer asked.

"Dr. O'Grady —"

"Schaffer, please."

"Very well," Xavier nodded. "Schaffer. You have a knack for writing stories that incite people, such as the one you wrote in the *Post* yesterday."

Schaffer smiled, proud of the recognition of his work. Xavier's knowledge of the article confirmed that he had spoken with someone in the United States, a conversation Schaffer hadn't heard over his device. When Schaffer sent the story to his editor, he gave explicit instructions not to put the story out on the Associated Press wires to prevent a firestorm of global speculation. It was only printed in the *Washington Post*. It would be released to other news agencies today after the president had had a chance to respond and other news agencies could digest both sides.

"I need the people of Cuba to accept their destiny. They must be ready for democracy." Xavier looked into Schaffer's eyes. "You can get this message out to them, making the process easier."

"Earth to El-Presidente. The papers here are government owned and controlled, in case you haven't noticed. And right now, Castro is still the government." Schaffer touched his notes. "There's no way for me to get a story of that type in these papers."

Xavier's gaze never waned. "I am the government for all practical purposes. But, that doesn't matter because we're not using the paper. We're using leaflets."

"Of course you have a plan to get these leaflets printed and distributed." Schaffer's interest piqued.

"Of course, Dr. O'Grady. A friend of mine, Mr. Guzman, will meet you at the warehouses in Mariel tomorrow at 5:00 p.m. I believe you've had the occasion to visit previously." Xavier turned and looked at the door of the hut. "Everything you'll need will be there by tomorrow. Don't worry, I've had the bodies removed and the location sanitized. Other help will soon follow. I'll provide you with a list of the party faithful, so that you can avoid them. Guzman will give you the drop-off points. Most of them will coincide with the speeches that I'm making. These leaflets will be distributed after I'm gone. They'll serve to reinforce my message of change. The people will do the rest."

"Okay, so that's how I'm supposed to help you. I'm not saying I will." Schaffer crossed his arms. "First, I want to know how you figure to help me."

"First of all I can assure your safety. Let's face it, after your story in the *Post*, many news agencies will be contacting their foreign desk to send investigators. I can see to it that they are swamped with paperwork and kept off course by their party-appointed guides. They'll not be able to get any current information. I'll also make sure that Castro and I will not grant any interviews. Thus, you'll have an exclusive story. In addition, your guide, Guillermo, will be reassigned, leaving you free to operate as you wish. Do we have a deal?" Xavier put out his hand.

Schaffer studied Xavier as he spoke. "If I agree I'll need a show of good faith from you."

"What'd you have in mind?" He pulled his hand back.

Schaffer uncrossed his arms and sat back in his chair. "There are two things I'll need from you. First, there were four men taken into custody before you arrived. I have it from a reliable source that they are CIA. Where are they now?"

Xavier sighed, releasing most of the air in his lungs. "I haven't found them yet. They are not in the main prison and Castro hasn't mentioned them to me."

"Do you think he's harmed them?"

"Not likely," Xavier answered confidently. "Castro likes to show any force he wields, especially if it is against the United States. I'll see what I can find out."

Schaffer's expression grew in intensity. "As soon as you find them, I'll need to talk to them."

Xavier appeared surprised. "The source you referred to earlier sent word that I should cooperate with you. But, as I informed the president, there's no telling where they are. Castro will eventually say something. Until then, we're fucked."

"One of the men captured, Tito Valencia, served with my unit in the Corps. He's one of my closest friends."

"I wish I could help." Xavier sighed. "You said there were two things, what's the other?"

"Tell me about Xavier Ciefuentes, the man. There's more driving you here than orders from the president. You act as if it's personal."

Xavier looked down, breaking eye contact for the first time, and again sighed. He seemed to be drifting and mumbled something about his childhood. Collecting his thoughts, he began to tell Schaffer his story.

"My mother and father fled Cuba in 1961. Castro was just gaining his stronghold on this country, forcing out all those who'd been loyal to the Batista Government. As you know, there was a mass exodus to the United States. People left by any means. They did whatever was necessary to gain their freedom. Many risked their lives and swam for miles in hopes that the Americans would see them and pick them up."

Xavier paced the room. "My mother and father were included in that lot. She was pregnant with me at the time. On that particular day there must have been a hundred people swimming to freedom. Some men loyal to Castro, led by then Lieutenant Raul Santiago, came out in boats to harass the swimmers. They began to shoot at the people in the water, hitting a few. They meant to draw sharks, thinking that none of the swimmers would be rescued."

He pulled his beret off and ran his fingers through his hair. "Luckily for most of the people in the water, the Americans, sent by President Kennedy, were already on their way to aid the swimmers. They didn't get there soon enough to save all of them. The sharks did come, and they did kill. My mother was one of the people hit by the spray of bullets. My father, attempting to keep the sharks away from my mother, was killed by one of the beasts. In reality, Santiago was in love with my mother. She rejected him to marry my father. Santiago's act on that day was an act of jealousy. In all, thirty people lost their lives."

Xavier took a seat facing Schaffer, but his eyes were miles away. "My mother was rescued. When the Coast Guard pulled her from the water, she was still holding my father's hand, but the shark that had him in his jaws was too strong. It was the last time she ever saw him. I wasn't due for another month, but my mother went into labor shortly after they'd pulled her aboard. She was determined not to deliver until she reached American soil. The doctors aboard ship were swamped with the wounded. They never knew that she was in labor, there was so much confusion. One of the Coast Guard guys tended to her leg as best he could, considering the circumstances. She was in labor all day."

Schaffer thought he saw Xavier try to wipe his eye.

"That evening, the ship arrived in Miami. Medical crews were waiting to transport the injured to the hospital. When she was en route to the hospital, she asked if she was in America, and received a positive response. She let out a short scream and I arrived. We were taken to Our Lady Queen of Peace hospital in Miami, since most of us were Catholic, and because the Coast Guard knew we wouldn't be turned away. It also helped that the nuns at the hospital spoke Spanish. My mother never fully recovered from the distress of losing my father. She hung on for six years. I think she died of heartbreak."

Xavier stood and walked to a window. "She left me in the care of a group of Jesuits. There she felt I would be properly cared for. The last thing she told me was to help bring peace to my homeland. She took her last breath, and her hand fell from my face. That was the moment I realized I was alone, and that I had to fulfill her request, although I didn't fully understand what she meant at the time."

Xavier turned and looked at Schaffer. Slowly, he walked back to the table. "I was raised in a very loving environment. Of course, I attended Catholic schools. Living with the Jesuits influenced my decision to enter the priesthood. A young priest, Father Sanchez, who also came from Cuba, convinced me to attend college before making the decision to enter the priesthood. I was then sent to Georgetown University in 1986 and decided to major in international studies. To help pay for college, I entered the Navy ROTC. And, as they say, the rest is history. Or destiny, as the case may be."

Schaffer sat motionless and listened. He was genuinely amazed at Xavier's story. In all the stories he'd covered, he never met anyone like Xavier. Here was a man working side by side with the man who ultimately caused the deaths of his parents. Schaffer couldn't resist any longer. "How can you stand to be this close to Castro day in and day out and not seek revenge for the deaths of you parents?"

"That's very simple, Mr. O'Grady. I'm fulfilling a promise made to my mother almost thirty years ago. I intend to bring peace and prosperity to Cuba."

"You believe your mother's last words to you were… some sort of premonition?"

"Even God's words allow for seers. I was set on becoming a priest and yet, here I am in Cuba, seeking to end tyranny and bring freedom to my people." Xavier tilted his head towards Schaffer. "She must have seen something."

"Which brings me to another point. How can a guy who was studying for the priesthood and who outwardly condemns the death penalty be out here doing this type of work? There was nothing compassionate about what you did in those warehouses."

Xavier tensed, but not to a point of confrontation. "There are two absolutes this job has taught me. One is that there is evil in the world and two, the chance for world peace gets a little closer to reality every time I eliminate some of the world's evil."

"When did you get a promotion to God?"

"I'm not trying to be God," Xavier snapped. "I am a soldier trying to make the world a better place. Let's face it, some people just need killing."

Schaffer raised his eyebrows. "I see."

Xavier jutted his hand at Schaffer. "You've seen the people here! They are suffering because of a lack of economic stimulus. If the United States returns, they'll bring money and jobs with them. That is enough to bring peace to my homeland and fulfill the promise I made to my mother."

"So, you're here to bring this stimulus from the United States?" Schaffer continued to pry.

"In a manner of speaking, you might say that. Like it or not, Dr. O'Grady, you're a part of this now." Xavier tossed his beret on the table. "The world will know that you're here, if they don't already. Why not use your talent to help?"

"Before coming to Cuba, Alex — I mean the president — told me about a U.S. plan to overthrow Cuba called 'Operation Smokeout.'" Schaffer put his hand on his note pad. "Are you implementing this objective?"

"You've got friends in high places." Xavier observed Schaffer wryly. "I'm the leader of the mission. But then, you already knew that too."

Schaffer slightly nodded. "What's your stated objective?"

"That, Dr. O'Grady, is classified. I'm surprised you don't already know. You seem to be ahead of everyone else on this mission."

"Your answer could determine if I decide to help or not."

Xavier looked at Schaffer. "You place me in an awkward position."

"That's what I do. I'm a reporter. You were saying...?"

Xavier tried to steer him in a different direction. "There're only a handful of people who know my mission here. I'm afraid telling you will place the mission in extreme danger."

"I'm not asking you this as a reporter. You have my word, as an American citizen loyal to America, that nothing you tell me now will be printed in any paper in the United States, or any other paper." Schaffer stood, looking much more serious and pointed to Xavier. "I came here to find my friend and the truth about this mission. A man gave his life because he felt more people in the U.S. should know about it. Don't let his death be in vain!"

Xavier looked puzzled. "Who are you talking about? I haven't heard of anyone dieing that was connected to this mission."

"His name was Harold Cosby. You may recall he was the president's chief of staff." Schaffer's face flushed. "He called me to meet him one night. By the time I arrived, I found his brains on Lincoln's feet at the memorial in D.C. Even though someone killed him, the story still leaked. A few weeks later, I came to Gitmo to investigate how a group of men could leave over our mine fields and not be killed. I cut my trip short to return home. Once I reached Orlando, someone posing as a Marine tried to kill me. I guess he thought I knew too much already. I immediately boarded a plane to Mexico, and eventually came to Cuba, to find the man who led the refugees from Gitmo." He touched Xavier. "You weren't hard to find. You're all the talk around Havana."

"I won't let anything jeopardize my mission, especially the media." Xavier put his beret back on.

"If my plans were to jeopardize your mission, this conversation would be too late to stop it. I told you, I came here to find Tito and the truth." Schaffer bristled feeling impatient with the discourse. "You've already stated that you need help. Obviously you feel I can do more than just print leaflets."

Xavier tried to avoid Schaffer's last comment. "When the time is right I'll let you know what else I need. But first, do we have a deal?" Xavier held his hand out.

Schaffer crossed his arms. "You haven't answered my question yet."

"You are one persistent fucker. My mission here is to remove Castro from power, but you already knew that too didn't you?"

Schaffer looked at Xavier dumbfounded. "But he named you as his successor… why physically remove him from power?"

"It does seem a bit odd, doesn't it?" Xavier adjusted his beret. "Nonetheless, Castro has made my job easier. I have orders to follow and they are to remove him from power, that's what I intend to do."

Schaffer knitted his brow and formed a question. After a long pause, he ran his hand across his head several times. "From what I have been able to gather in the streets, the people of Cuba don't dislike Castro. The U.S. would have us believe the opposite is true. They do, however, dislike the economic hardship they're suffering. If they find out you had something to do with removing Castro, they may turn against you. And what about Demetria? Won't she consider you evil?"

"Because of the economic hardship," Xavier answered, "opportunity has been born. We're just here to exploit it. I'm not concerned about anyone finding out I was involved in removing Castro from power. If they do, you told them." Xavier stood and offered his hand again. "Do we have a deal Dr. O'Grady?"

Schaffer knew he'd have to assist Xavier. The last attempt on his life was still fresh in his mind, and the consequences of not helping weren't at all appealing. Schaffer shook Xavier's hand and pledged his confidence, at least until after the mission. Stuck in his gut was the unconfirmed knowledge that something else was in play with this mission. Alex hadn't alluded to anything else, and Xavier had been very forthcoming. And yet, Schaffer knew it was there.

Chapter
51

Xavier left the hut.

Schaffer flipped his device back to the U.S. just as Dee informed Alex about his conversation with Xavier. He still had his portable listening device, and heard the entire conversation between them.

"I'll be damned." The president looked at Ian Mackenzie and General Roseboro. "Benderis has recruited O'Grady. Now that son of a bitch should push out positive stories." His comments were designed for the NSA crew, and to a lesser extent for Mackenzie. "We should glide into the finish line from here. Ian, would you excuse us for a few moments? General Roseboro and I have a few items to cover."

Mackenzie didn't like feeling left out. "Are you sure you won't need me here to clarify a few points?"

Alex assured him, "We'll be fine, thanks."

Hesitantly, Mackenzie left the room.

Alex showed Dee the transcript of the conversation between Xavier and Schaffer. He'd circled the line where Schaffer said that someone tried to kill him while on the Marine base in Orlando. "Dee, what the hell is going on? I didn't authorize anyone to kill O'Grady."

"I'm not sure, sir. This is the first I've heard about it. I'll call down to Orlando." Dee lifted the phone and placed her call. She strained to maintain control during the conversation. After a few minutes, she hung up. Although she already knew everything about the earlier attempt on Schaffer, she hadn't yet informed the president.

Schaffer listened to their conversation and was convinced that Dee had his best interest at heart.

Dee used the incident as if someone had lobbed a grenade in the room and she was looking to see who was still standing. Like Schaffer, she needed to be convinced further by observing the president's reaction to the information.

Alex waited silently with his hands folded in front of his face. Slowly, Dee looked up. "Sir, two Marines detained the would-be assassin until the C.O. arrived. Schaffer was long gone by the time the Marines subdued the man, so they never got his side of the story. He presented CIA identification and explained that he was on a secret mission for this office." Her face now held an accusatory look directed at Alex.

"I gave no such order!" Alex slammed both hands on his desk and stood up. "Goddamnit, get Caprelotti on the phone! I want him here immediately!"

Dee placed the call. The room grew cold, as ice seemed to form around the two friends who waited as motionless and quiet as stone statues.

Dee had just thrown Alex to the lions in as attempt to call his bluff. Schaffer wasn't sure if she was trying to prove his innocence or trying to get him to break. From what Schaffer could tell, though, Alex seemed genuinely surprised. He did know that further conversations with her would have to wait until another time.

Chapter 52

Joe DeApuzzo felt more stressed than usual these days.

So much so, that his other reporters avoided coming within twenty feet of his office whenever possible. He considered Schaffer a star reporter, but more importantly a good friend. But Schaffer hadn't contacted him or anyone at the paper for weeks. Joe continued his search hoping to turn up something on Schaffer's whereabouts. He'd already called several other news agencies searching for any information that they might have. Unfortunately, his efforts proved futile. His only alternative now was to wait and pray that he heard from Schaffer soon, before he sent someone looking for him.

Schaffer had been so involved in helping Xavier's cause that he had not been conscious of the amount of time that had elapsed since his last story. Many of the meetings he held to distribute leaflets were with priests in towns and villages across Cuba. He'd grown very fond of one priest, Father Jose, who for years prayed to have someone sent to his land to free its people from tyranny. To Father Jose, Xavier was his answer. He looked forward to sharing the good news with his Cuban friends in the United States.

Years ago, the parishioners of St. Carmen's erected an antenna and covered it with creeping plants to conceal it. This, along with a short wave radio, supplied by the CIA, was their emergency link with the free world. It had been a good source for keeping in touch with the politics outside Cuba. Over the years, when the United States and Cuba had their more intense spats, it proved to be the only link with the U.S.

Their main contact in the United States was Father Sanchez, of the Jesuit monastery in Miami. He left Cuba in 1961 after the Bay of Pigs invasion. His bishop felt that a young priest whose father was an American solider would not be well received by Castro. Since Father Sanchez's arrival, Father Jose had been the main link to the United States. Maintaining a list of thousands of former Cubans now living in the States, he kept them up to date with news that seldom crossed the borders of the island.

Schaffer found out about this radio on his last visit with Father Jose. Since rumors of a U.S. invasion coursed Cuba, all calls leaving Cuba were to be monitored, preventing Schaffer from conveying any additional news stories. Schaffer went to St. Carmen's to see Father Jose with a request to send a message to the United States on his behalf. It was late in the evening, as this was the time when clear airwaves permitted better transmissions.

Schaffer walked into the church just as Father Jose was finishing his evening prayers. "Father Jose, how good it is to see you again," Schaffer said, then quickly dispensed with the pleasantries. "I need to request a favor."

"What can I do for you?" the priest answered.

"I must get a message to my editor at the *Washington Post*." Schaffer handed Joe's information to Father Jose. "Please tell him that I'm safe and will be in touch as soon as I can."

"Come with me." Father Jose motioned to Schaffer. "We can call my friend Father Sanchez now. The airwaves should be free. Castro doesn't try to jam our signal at night."

They walked into the basement of the church. The floor was dirt, as were the walls. A musty smell lingered in the basement because of the humidity and lack of circulating air. Looking closely, one could see an occasional lizard dart across the floor in search of its next meal.

Father Jose walked to a corner of the room and swept an area about four and a half feet tall and three feet wide. This revealed a small door, which had been covered in dried mud to match the dirt of the basement. Locating the rope handle, he opened the door and lit a lantern. They walked down three dirt stairs to a small room. The room was only big enough for two or three men, but there, in the corner was a short wave radio.

"We've kept this radio here to avoid detection from anyone who might snoop. The mud-covered door has never failed to protect us when Castro's soldiers have subjected the church to inspections." Father Jose pointed to the crude looking door. "Families have used the radio to keep in touch with their loved ones, who made it out of Cuba before Castro closed our borders. Help yourself, my friend. You have more than earned the right."

Father Jose turned the radio on and began to place his call. After his second attempt, Father Sanchez answered.

"Father Sanchez, I have a young man here who is in need of your help. Perhaps you have heard of Schaffer O'Grady of the *Washington Post*?" Father Jose smiled showing his pride at being able to call out Schaffer's name as he would the name of a saintly man.

"Yes, yes, I have," Sanchez responded. "He's the young man who reported on what's going on inside Cuba. How is it that he happens to be your guest?"

"He's been sent by the Lord to deliver us to a better world," Father Jose explained.

"No, Father Sanchez, I don't have that kind of power." Schaffer held up one of his leaflets. "Xavier Ciefuentes is the man who'll deliver this country to a new tomorrow. I do, however, have a favor to request. Would you please contact my editor, Joe DeApuzzo? You can reach him at (202) 555-2463. Just tell him that I've been very busy, and that I'll be in touch again soon. As a matter of fact, ask him to come down to Florida so that I can talk to him in person, so to speak. I'll call back in a week." Schaffer looked at Father Jose for his approval. "That should give Joe plenty of time to get to Miami."

Chapter 53

At 7:30 p.m. in Washington, Joe was still in his office trying to finish his day.

Some days were better than others, but Joe was getting better at working through the distractions of Schaffer's lack of contact. When his phone rang, he almost jumped from his chair. Not many people had the direct number to his office and tonight the ringing phone made his heart pound against the walls of his chest. After the second ring, he lifted the receiver. "Joe DeApuzzo."

"Mr. DeApuzzo," the man spoke with a heavy Spanish accent.

Joe now felt his heart in his throat. "Yes." He waited.

"I have a message for you from Schaffer O'Grady—"

"It's about damn time his sorry ass got in touch." Joe's voice was filled with relief.

"You sound like a worried parent," the man answered. "Schaffer wants you to know that he's safe, and will contact you next week here in Miami at the church."

Joe rubbed his eyes. "Hell, I wasn't worried. I was just about to take him off the payroll." Joe looked at the caller ID. "I'm sorry. I forgot to ask your name."

"My name is Father Sanchez, from Miami, via Cuba."

"How'd you hear from Schaffer?" Joe's face twisted with confusion.

"We maintain contact with Cuba as best we can," Father Sanchez explained. "Castro has not found a way to own or control the air waves."

"That's amazing." This intrigued Joe. "How'd you two manage to avoid detection by the Cuban Government?"

"We have a higher power on our side." Father Sanchez looked to the sky and laughed. "Mr. O'Grady would like you to be here one week from today to receive his call."

Relief crept over Joe's face. "Father Sanchez, thank you for getting in touch with me. We've been worried sick about Schaffer. You've helped to ease my day, in more ways than one. I do have your number on my caller ID." Joe read off the number. "I'd love to have your address as well."

Father Sanchez gave Joe the address.

The two men continued to talk for a short time. With his dry sense of humor, Father Sanchez made the conversation light. Joe exhaled as if a hundred tons had just been lifted from his chest.

"If you ever get tired of your day job," Joe told Father Sanchez, "you could make a killing as a comedian."

"Thanks, but I already have a loyal audience and they get to see the show for free. You should come down to see it yourself when you're here."

After hanging up the phone, Joe pulled out his checkbook and wrote out a check for five hundred dollars. He addressed the envelope and jotted a note: "Thanks for the help. I'm sure you'll put this to good use."

Joe lifted the phone and called home. "Nina, start packing, we're heading to Miami."

"Joe, I don't know if I can get away from the hospital so quickly."

"Do what you can. A priest from there just called. Schaffer wants me there in the next few days. I'm leaving tomorrow." He sat back in his chair with his hands behind his head. "Nina and I could use the break."

Joe called his travel agent. They'd leave tomorrow for a short vacation and to talk to Schaffer.

Chapter 54

The president awoke at 4 a.m. and retrieved his copy of the *Washington Post*.

He found it waiting on his desk on top of other papers from across the United States and around the world. Lifting the *Post*, he scanned it for news stories from Cuba, but did not find any. However, one particular story caught his eye. It was not what he wanted to see. His face contorted, scowling as he read the headline:

President in dead heat with both Democratic and Republican contenders

"When the hell will Benderis wind this thing up?" he asked aloud. His mood had deteriorated with each day that no new news surfaced from Cuba. In forty-five minutes, he would be in his morning meeting with his cabinet. New strategies would have to be arranged if his administration intended to regain their lead in the polls.

Alex heard movement in the corner of his office near a window. Dee turned the high back leather chair she sat in from the window. She'd been staring out into the darkness. "You're in early this morning." She stood and walked over to his desk.

The buzz in Schaffer's ear instantly woke him up. He reached over to the nightstand and pushed the button so that Dee could transmit. "What's up?" There was no response, just voices in the background.

"I wanted to get through most of these papers before our meeting," the president was saying.

"Sir, about the other day. I didn't mean to be so aloof." Dee apologetically hung her head. "The attempt on Schaffer caught me by surprise."

Alex looked directly into Dee's eyes. "Yeah, me too. I was more stressed out after Director Caprelotti denied having anything to do with it. He's never lied to me."

"So, who do you suspect?" Dee sat on the sofa. "I think it may have been an inside job."

"That's what we have to find out. And we have to do it before anything else happens." Alex sat behind his desk. "Did you have a chance to talk with Schaffer?"

"Yes, and he is quite uneasy with us right now." Dee stood. "We're having composites drawn up now from the information we gathered at Orlando and Gitmo. We should have them soon."

"How is he otherwise?" Alex looked at Dee. "When does he plan to get me additional information?"

"As I said, he's not feeling a lot of trust for us right now. He did say that when he had something to add, we would see it in the paper." Dee knew nothing new had been published. "I take it you didn't find anything in your papers on Cuba."

"No." Alex looked dejected. "No new developments."

"Mr. President, allow me to be blunt, your meetings have become futile. It's the same thing over and over. You are obsessed with how things are coming in Cuba, and how long it will be before the mission will come to a close. Most of your meetings center on this topic, with little time left over for the other matters of state." Dee leaned on Alex's desk, moving closer to his face. "You have become too preoccupied with this mission. Let's move on."

"I hope you told Schaffer I had nothing to do with the attempt on his life. I want the son of a bitch as badly as he does." Alex sat back and looked into space. "I don't blame him for not trusting us right now. It doesn't look good for our side."

"No sir, it doesn't. I'm just thankful that he's still communicating with us. I'm not sure I would be doing that." She paused to think. "Mr. President, I'll give you odds that the same person who killed Cosby tried to kill Schaffer." Dee felt certain of his answer, but felt Schaffer would benefit from the president's reinforcement. "Were you involved, in any way, with Harold's death or the attempt on Schaffer?"

The president didn't hesitate. "Damnit, Dee! I thought I made that clear. Hell no! You know me better than that. How many times do I have to tell you and Schaffer that before you believe me? If I lose your vote of confidence, this whole thing could turn to shit." Alex calmed and spoke more slowly, "There are four men being held somewhere in Cuba who are counting on this mission to succeed. Everyone has forgotten about them, instead focusing on getting Castro out of office. Do you have any idea how terrible I feel allowing them to be captured?"

Dee crossed her arms and fell back in her seat. "You had no choice, sir."

"Sure I did. I could have sent Special Ops in with enough fire power to level the island. Then we could already be in Cuba rebuilding the island and explaining to the world it was the only humane thing to do. Forget the casualties on both sides. We're all better off."

"Sir, you've done everything correctly. Charging in is exactly what Harold wanted to avoid. Your plan avoided senseless deaths on both sides."

Alex looked at Dee. His eyes were filled with sadness. "I haven't done everything correctly. If we'd received a positive response about what we expect the agents to find, maybe Harold would still be alive. Did you ever stop to consider the fact that they've found nothing? If that happens to be true, this whole exercise is a sham."

"Don't second guess yourself, sir. We both know that greed is more dangerous than your decision to stay quiet about their findings. Findings, I might add, that you still have not been able to confirm. The decision you made will allow you to maintain control and benefit both countries. You honor Harold by sticking to your conviction to help others."

The president closed his eyes and laid his head back in his chair while Dee continued looking into his face. Neither spoke for the next few minutes.

Alex was the first to break the silence. "Deidre, why haven't we ever gotten together? You're very good for me."

"I don't think the country is ready for the chairwoman of the Joint Chiefs of Staff to be involved with the president. Remember the criticism Kennedy got after appointing his brother to the position of attorney general? We don't need the hassle."

"You sure it's not our obvious differences?"

"I'm sure I don't know what you mean." She did, however, notice the contrasts between the brownness of her hand and the paleness of his face. "Maybe another time, another place and most definitely different jobs."

"When I think about it," Alex mused. "You're the first African-American woman to rise to your position. You saved men trapped behind enemy lines, earned a Medal of Honor. Worked for the Pentagon."

"Sir. I know all this. You don't have to list my credentials."

"Quite impressive," Alex continued. "White House Fellow, Mid-East intelligencer, Desert Storm rescue missions, National Security Advisor."

"Sir," Dee cut him off.

"I know," Alex said. "Forgive me. It was just a fleeting thought."

Alex's emphatic response to General Roseboro's earlier question helped to alleviate some of Schaffer's anxiety. He knew that Dee could hear him even if she couldn't answer him at the moment. Schaffer spoke quietly into the palm device. "Thanks, Dee. And that is quite an impressive record."

Dee smiled.

¤¤¤¤

The cabinet members in the room had grown weary of the president's line of questioning as it related to Cuba. NSA had presented no new information.

Thankfully, the intercom buzzed before Alex started the meeting.

"Mr. President, I have NSA on the line."

Everyone held their breath. Some even crossed their fingers in hopes that this call brought good news from Cuba.

"Put him through, Annie," Alex said. "This is President Nicholas, you're on the speaker. Go ahead."

"There's been a break in Cuba."

The entire room let out an audible sigh.

"Just three minutes ago Castro told Xavier that he had set the end of August for a formal transfer of power."

No one spoke.

"Is there anything else?" The president looked at the members of his cabinet.

"It's still coming across now, sir. Castro wants to hold the ceremony at the villa where Xavier's introduction party was held."

"Thanks for the information. Keep me informed of any further developments." Alex hung up the phone.

As the cabinet members cheered, Director Caprelotti entered the room. "Sorry I'm late, but I'm glad you all are so happy to see me."

The president shared the news with the Director.

"Then you may also be glad to know," Caprelotti said, "that Mr. O'Grady has been in touch with one of our operatives, Father Raphael Jose. We also found out that he was assisting Commander Benderis throughout his tour of Cuba. He and Guzman were responsible for distributing the leaflets with our offer for aid to the Cuban people. It's only a matter of time now before we can wrap this thing up."

"Did he happen to say whether any other stories were forthcoming?" The president looked like a child waiting for a gift.

"Nothing has been confirmed to me, sir."

"For the most part, today we've had good news. Let's hope the worst is past. That'll be all for now." People rose from their seats. The president reminded them, "We'll begin tomorrow half an hour earlier." He wanted to take time to savor the moment. He took out an Opus X and walked out of the room with his cabinet behind him. Five Secret Service agents escorted him to his favorite window above the Rose Garden, on the Truman balcony. He inhaled deeply, enjoying the fresh air before lighting his cigar.

Chapter 55

Schaffer had been away from the U.S. for five months.

For the past four or so he freely moved around Cuba interacting with the people. He returned to Havana just ahead of Xavier and Castro, who completed their whirlwind tour of the country. Near the middle of August, there was a transformation in the streets of Cuba. People were moving more freely through the towns and villages. They openly discussed life under Xavier's regime. He'd returned optimism to the majority of Cuba's people. Many church leaders spoke to packed congregations of a new dawn, a time of healing, a time of rebuilding. They proved ready to move Cuba forward, forgetting the past to ensure a better tomorrow.

Those faithful to Castro, however, were quite uneasy. If Cuba's current political structure collapsed, their power would evaporate as well. Castro was their salvation. As long as he remained in power, they were assured a place in the hierarchy of Cuba's government. Castro confirmed their place during several speeches given in their homeland. He promised to continue the battle. He would not let them down. Communism would be saved. In the event Castro had underestimated the general population, the Communist Party members sent representatives to squelch suspected rebellion wherever they found signs of a renewed feeling of freedom.

The information Guzman and Schaffer distributed just minutes after Xavier and Castro had left each town generated much of that feeling of hope.

Over Cuban radio and in live performances all over the land, music took on a renewed political tone. Several stations played a song, *Freedom's Return*, without apprehension. Salsa bands and radio stations led the charge announcing. "Music has always led the movement of change. It shall be no different here in Cuba. We sing for a new day."

This caught many of the hard liners by surprise, since their younger citizens had known only Castro as their leader. Fearing massive insurrections, government officials sent the police and military to shut down stations that played this type of music. If a band even alluded to political reform, their performance was immediately halted. So far, Castro's politicos met with no resistance. However, it was just a matter of time before idealism was a more powerful influence.

The people as a whole grew unsettled. Like bubbles forming on the bottom of a pot just before it boils, their rumbling could be heard, even though the water had not yet roiled.

Father Jose could wait no longer for his people to take a stand. He could feel their unrest as well as their apprehension. Something needed to be done to set their restlessness in motion. After observing men from the Communist Party frequent his church over the past several weeks, he resolved to push just a little harder.

"There is a wave rolling over our land. It is a wave that refuses to be stopped and one that no man can resist. It is much too strong. Listen to its roar!" He put his hand to his ear and paused for what seemed to be an eternity. "It shall come crashing down, drowning all who would seek to stop its progress." His fist slammed down hard on the wooden pulpit. Then, very quietly, he whispered. "Listen, listen, you can hear it in the streets. You can hear it in the music. And if you listen to your heart you can hear it there." He put both his hands over his heart. Then his voice rose abruptly. "What is the name that is given to this wave?" He paused as if expecting a response, then immediately proclaimed. "This wave, my brothers and sisters, is called freedom!"

Four men in back of the church shuffled as if they would stand when Father Jose spoke, but when he quieted, they settled in their seats. Two men sat in one pew and two in another on opposite sides of the aisle, with no one sitting anywhere near them. Their olive drab uniforms were worn as an intimidation factor since everyone present already knew who they were: muscle sent by the Communist faithful.

Father Jose surveyed the room from his worn pulpit. No one made a sound. It was obvious to him that his congregation was fearful because they knew the men from the government would make notes of everyone present. Father Jose's expression softened. "All it takes, my people, is for just one of you to take a stand. When the government ends a performance because of content, stand up and say 'No, let them play'. If they try to beat you down because of the words you use, stand tall and speak them anyway. Cry louder each time and you will be heard. Has He taught us nothing?" Father Jose pointed to a crucifix. "Everywhere that the people have chosen to cry for freedom, they have been heard. East Germany, Poland, Yugoslavia, and of course, Russia. Is there a cost for this freedom?" He pounded the pulpit and stood straight. "Yes, most definitely. Some will even pay the ultimate price, but we can't let that deter us. There are forces standing by, waiting to help." He looked at Schaffer, who was sitting among the congregation. "They must first know that we wish their help. We must take a stand and we will be freed."

The four men got up and walked towards Father Jose.

Seeing them move closer he looked directly into their eyes and continued. "Nothing can stop the wave!"

Schaffer moved to intervene, but Father Jose's stern look, coupled with an earlier discussion — *the Cuban people must be moved into action. You can't be the first to respond. It must be my people* —- reluctantly made him settle back in his seat.

The congregation was too frightened to move. They didn't want to loose their jobs, houses, possibly their lives. The government men pulled Father Jose from his pulpit and dragged him by his vestments down the aisle out of the church.

He chanted, "Nothing can stop the wave! Freedom shall prevail. Nothing can stop the wave! Freedom shall prevail."

A young girl about six years old yanked herself free of her mother's grasp and ran to the aisle. She pointed to the men dragging the priest. "Don't you hurt Father Jose. If you do, very bad things will happen to you."

The girl's mother ran out and grabbed her daughter. She kept her head bowed, too afraid to make eye contact with the men, and too ashamed to look at Father Jose. "Why won't you help him?" the girl cried.

Her mother put her hand over the girl's mouth, whereupon the girl bit her mother to free herself. Again, she ran to the aisle, this time kicking one of the men.

Receiving the sharp kick to his shin, the solider winced in pain. He turned and slapped the girl to the floor.

Father Jose tensed. "She has placed a hex on you. Your slap sealed your fate. You will not escape His wrath." Although he knew that these men were not religious, he did know that they were very superstitious. Father Jose began reciting a Santeria hex, which shocked his parishioners and frightened his captors. Santeria was as much a part of their heritage as was the Spanish language. Father Jose knew the hex would burn at that man all day.

Even with Father Joe's warning, Schaffer couldn't sit by and do nothing. He burst from his seat and gave chase. Forgetting momentarily that he was not in the States, Schaffer defiantly walked up to the soldiers. "What in the hell is going on here?"

The four men continued moving as if they didn't hear him. Schaffer moved forward, blocking their way. The two men in front lowered their AK-47s.

Father Jose looked at him and gently waved his hand. Schaffer understood not to get involved. Human rights meant nothing to these men. If he pressed too hard, the soldiers wouldn't hesitate to use their guns. The men tossed Father Jose in the back of a jeep and drove away, littering the air with dust from their tires.

Schaffer slammed the doors of the church so hard they sounded like a shot ringing out when they struck the walls. "What the hell is wrong with you people?" He moved from pew to pew in search of an answer from the lifeless, terrified group of parishioners. Most refused to meet his eye.

A little girl was the only person to speak up. "They tried to hurt Father Jose. I tried to stop them but no one would help me."

The people seated in the church realized that the little girl was the only one who believed in what Father Jose said about getting involved. Some even began to cry, embarrassed by their lack of action. Father Jose had always been there for them. He provided them with a link to their relatives in the U.S. Whenever they wanted to use the radio in the basement, Father Jose provided it for them. If a call came in, it was he who informed them that a relative was sick or had died in America. And they did nothing to help him. They sank deeper into their pews, hoping to become invisible to Schaffer's probing stares.

Schaffer wanted to rip them from their seats and thrust them into action. But at this point, it was hopeless. Father Jose told him earlier, *Patience and time is required for transformation. Once freedom eases its way into the veins of the people, nothing will hold back their change.*

Still, Schaffer looked on in disbelief of their apathy. He walked over to the girl. "I'll help you." He wiped the remaining blood from her lip. "I'll do all I can for Father Jose. Don't worry, he'll be okay."

Schaffer stood and walked to the pulpit. From his work with Father Jose distributing leaflets, he recognized most of those seated in the church despite their attempts to disappear. "It is time you decided to help yourselves. The United States is waiting to assist you the moment this government has changed. They have the money and manpower to change this country, but first you must take charge. What are you afraid of? Death is not near as bad as your inaction." Schaffer went on for nearly ten minutes. Most of the people sat lifeless in the pews. From their appearance, he'd failed to rouse them. Years of living under a dictator had paralyzed their free will. Schaffer felt as if he were speaking to the deaf. Disgusted, he hurriedly walked from the church.

Chapter 56

The soldiers took Father Jose to a small shack where he was interrogated and beaten.

"Where is this propaganda coming from?" One of the men held a leaflet in front of Father Jose.

"I don't know what you mean. All I see in your hand is a message of truth." Again he was struck. He doubled over in pain.

"Who is the leader of this group?" The solider tightly held Father Jose's clothing.

"A movement like this needs no leader," Father Jose preached as blood gushed from his mouth. "Justice is the leader. Freedom is the leader. Truth is the leader!"

They beat him furiously.

After several hours, he still did not tell them anything they wanted to know. The men had specific orders not to kill the priest, so they dumped Father Jose onto the dirt path leading to the church. He lay in the street, moaning with pain and praying that someone would come help him.

Guzman, who was looking for Schaffer, almost didn't see Father Jose on the dirt road. He swerved his jeep just in time, missing Father Jose by inches. His tires kicked more dirt on the priest as they skidded to a stop. Startled by the near miss, Guzman jumped from the jeep. "Father Jose, what happened? Who did this to you?"

Barely able to speak, Father Jose looked up. "Four men came to the church today. Rumor has it that they didn't like my homily."

Schaffer ran from the church to help Guzman get the priest inside. "What have they done?" Schaffer asked when he saw Father Jose's condition.

In his usual fashion, Guzman responded. "Isn't that obvious? They kicked the shit… Sorry, Father. They beat him up. I'm going to tell Xavier about this. Someone needs to stop these rogues from running around attacking citizens."

Father Jose sat upright. "It's part of the process," he explained. "There's nothing that can be done."

"I would still feel more comfortable if I let him know." Guzman pulled out his pen and spoke into it. "Come in, Commander."

Schaffer heard the entire conversation in his earpiece. To determine if anyone else present knew he had the ability to monitor conversations, he said, "Man, that looks like something from a James Bond movie."

Guzman ignored Schaffer's comment, turned his back, and repeated his call. In about a minute, he saw Guzman put his finger to his ear and listen intently. Schaffer listened as well.

"You should see the priest, he's in pretty bad shape." Guzman looked at Father Jose.

"Anyone else hurt?" Xavier asked.

"I don't think so. Schaffer was here when they were pulling Father Jose out of the church. He didn't notice that anyone else was injured."

"Wait a minute." Schaffer interrupted and leaned over Guzman. "I saw a six-year-old girl, who attempted to stand up to the men dragging Father Jose out. She was slapped across the mouth. It didn't appear too serious, but she was bleeding. I couldn't believe they would attack a child."

"I'll look into the situation." Xavier wondered where the orders originated. He had not left Castro's side. "We'll take care of it."

Schaffer reached down to help the priest. "Father Jose, do you think you can help me get in touch with Father Sanchez? I think another story in the *Post* might help speed things up on the American end."

Father Jose, assisted by Guzman and Schaffer, led the way to the underground radio base.

On the way down, Schaffer leaned towards Guzman. "I'd like to know more about your technology."

Guzman continued walking without responding.

When they arrived, Father Jose made the necessary adjustments, turning the knobs to the correct channel. The radio lit up.

Schaffer sat in front of the microphone. "Cuba base calling Father Sanchez, come in please."

"Mr. O'Grady," Sanchez answered. "Good to hear your voice again."

"Father, I need a huge favor. Did Joe DeApuzzo arrive yet?" Schaffer began crafting the story as he spoke.

"Yes," Father Sanchez said. "As a matter a fact, he is here now."

"Joe?" Schaffer said, somewhat surprised, because Joe was early. "When did you get to Miami?"

"God, Schaffer it's good to hear your voice," Joe answered.

"Yours too. I don't mean to be rude, but I have very little time."
Schaffer looked at Father Jose, who nodded in and out of consciousness.
"Grab a pen and a sheet of paper. I've got another op-ed piece for you."

"I've got my lap-top right here, hang on a second." Joe paused
briefly as he turned on the computer and positioned himself to type. "Okay,
shoot."

Schaffer organized his thoughts then dictated the story to Joe:

For the past several weeks, there has been a rising tide of
unrest brewing in Cuba. The newly named President Xavier
Ciefuentes has crossed the country spreading a message of
change that hovers on the horizon of this small island. His
speeches prophesy a return to a better time. He has promised
new trading partners, stronger and better endowed than the
former Soviet Union.

In every town and village where he has spoken,
there have been mysterious distributions of leaflets
suggesting that the United States stands ready to assist the
people of Cuba when and if their help is requested. This,
coupled with the uplifting speeches delivered by Ciefuentes,
has moved the people of Cuba to begin taking action. A
festive people, music predominates their lives. Thus, music
has been the first form of action to address a return to
freedom. These songs are heard on the radio and at live
performances. The current government has shut down
stations playing this music, and confiscated the tapes. Live
performances are terminated when these songs are sung.
Nevertheless, the seed has been planted, and like many a
forest, nothing can stop its growth. All attempts to do so
will only serve to make the people more resistant, thrusting
their roots even deeper.

Unlike her current leader, Cuba is a religious
country, and one that is overwhelmingly Catholic. This
past Sunday, priests began to speak out against the current
regime. Because of their influence, the government has
chosen to treat them much more radically. One priest, telling
his congregation to take a stand against oppression, was
dragged from his pulpit, taken away, and beaten. A six-

year-old girl, in fact the only one to hear and understand this message, attempted to stop these men from taking her priest. One of the men slapped her to the floor, drawing blood, and no one was brave enough to lift a hand to help her. These people are frozen by years of fear fueled by ruthless acts of an insecure dictator.

It is very clear that the government intends to continue using force to prevent change in this country. The United States must take a stand. Demand that our trading partners cease all contact with Cuba until the will of her people has been met. FREEDOM!

"That's some pretty powerful stuff." Joe DeApuzzo looked over the words that Schaffer had just given him. "Can I take credit for this story?"

"I'll give you the byline, maybe."

They both laughed.

"I'll run it in the morning edition. I think I can just make the cut-off for a front page column." Joe read over the article. "Schaffer, please stay as far away from these people as possible. Now they're desperate. You can never predict actions of a desperate group of people when their power structure has been challenged."

"Would I be Schaffer O'Grady if I backed off?" Schaffer laughed. "Don't worry, Joe, I've got some really good people on my side."

Joe wasn't ready to let him off the phone. "I've got one more question before you go. You're really high on this Ciefuentes guy. What's up?"

"I have it from a very reliable source that he's got backing from a very powerful benefactor." Schaffer looked at Guzman, who turned away. "And he's still doing the right thing. He cares about his people and has their best interest at heart."

"Enough said. Be careful." Joe hung up.

Chapter 57

The president proudly held up Schaffer's article from the *Post*.

"This should just about do it. Now we have to get to the rest of the media on this and let the world know that we stand ready to help the people of Cuba, if they request our assistance."

Secretary Coleman Tynes sat listening to Alex. After a brief pause, he looked up. "How will we get a message to the Cuban people? Since we want Castro out, we sure as hell can't call his office."

"That really won't be a problem." Alex held up the paper. "You can bet that foreign news crews, after reading this story, are preparing to board planes for Cuba. They'll help spread the word. Also, keep in mind that Xavier is scheduled to take power next week. We're home free."

Vice President Gillespie spoke up. "Let me play devil's advocate. What if Castro prevents these news agencies from entering Cuba? Even if he does let them in, they'll have government-sponsored escorts. That's going to make it a bit more difficult to spread the word."

Alex took the cigar from his mouth. "You underestimate Commander Benderis. He'll have a say as to who gets in the country. It'll benefit him to have outsiders covering this type of story."

"That's true," Gillespie said. "I'll be a lot more comfortable after Castro is gone. He's just too unpredictable." He stood and walked to the open window and looked out.

The president and secretary of state stared each other.

Dee Roseboro took the floor. "He won't be a concern much longer. Commander Benderis will take all matters under his control any day now."

✿✿✿✿

Later that evening, Xavier and Castro had a heated exchange.

Castro yelled and waved his hands. "The people of Cuba are not ready for what a democracy will bring. They're not ready for choices. There'll be too many mistakes made."

Xavier pleaded his case: "There're mistakes made all the time, no matter what type of ruling party is in power. Democracy is the only way to move this country where it needs to be. Everything else has been tried, and all of it failed. We will not throw out the positive things that you've brought to the country, that much I promise. We just need to raise money, and there is no country out there with enough money willing to give any to a Communist dictatorship. We must begin to change. Consider what minor changes have done for China. They are reaping benefits because of compromise and we stand behind a locked fence, content to starve because of pride."

"My people don't know anything else. Batista almost ruined this country. I brought them their pride, and parity as well. How will they cope with what democracy will bring to them? It's too soon, they're simply not ready!" Castro's face reddened. A vein in the center of his head rose, and looked as if it would burst.

Xavier backed off and changed his approach. Castro was like a parent suffering from the "empty nest" syndrome. He could not bear the thought of losing his children. "Every parent finds it hard to let go of their children at first. They know, however, that ultimately, it's the best thing for them. Despite our need to hold on, the children continue to forge their own way. They'll learn from any mistakes they make. It's part of life. It must be better than watching our people leave the shores in droves. What does that say about us to the rest of the world?"

Castro thought about his own daughter fleeing to the United States. He'd been furious upon learning this, until he realized that she needed something more than he could provide. Still, it was not easy. "I'll have to think harder about this. Maybe after I've had the chance to sleep on it I'll feel differently." But sleep was the last thing Castro would get right now.

Xavier left the room and headed towards the beach. He walked near the water's edge and sat on a rock to listen to the waves rolling in. It was a beautiful night. Outside everything was peaceful. A steady wind was blowing, tumbling the waves, and crashing them along the beaches. His thoughts turned from troubles of running a country to the trouble in his relationship with Demetria. Sooner rather than later he would have to tell her the truth. He could not marry her with this burden hanging over his head.

The decisive moment came earlier than he had planned. Demetria was crossing the sand. Her white linen outfit flowed with the gentle breeze and was as white as the smile that grew broader the closer she came to him. Xavier could see that her smile was strained, and sensed her fear. The last time they were together on the beach, he killed several dozen men to free her. After her rescue, he and his men spoke to each other in perfect English, which seemed to cause Demetria confusion and distress.

Three feet from him she stopped. "What brings you out tonight?"

Xavier felt a flash of weakness run through his heart to his legs. Slowly, he opened his arms. "I was just thinking of you." He smiled, stood up, and took her hands. She wrapped her arms around him, hugging him tightly. His heart melted in her grasp. "We need to talk."

"Yes, we do. I believe that's where we left off two months ago. You were about to explain that night in Mariel." Demetria looked into Xavier's eyes.

"Let's take a walk." He rose from the rock without releasing her hands.

They walked. Xavier searched for the right words. He wanted this conversation to be just between the two of them, so he eased his pen from his pocket, depressed the plunger and gave it a counter-clockwise turn. For the first time since Demetria's rescue, Xavier broke radio contact with the U.S.

"I promised you two months ago that I wouldn't lie to you and I have not. However, it's with great difficulty that I talk with you tonight." Xavier kicked the sand as they walked. "Some things I tell you may be taken the wrong way. I don't want to upset you. I just don't know where to begin."

Demetria looked at Xavier, his face lit by the moonlight. She could see his anxiety. "Whatever it may be, nothing could be greater that the love we have for each other."

"I hope that's true." He looked up to the moon. "Remember that night in Mariel? You heard me speaking English to my men. I'll never forget the look on your face when you heard me. It was a combination of fear and disbelief. By the time I realized what I had done, it was too late to reverse the situation."

"Yes," she admitted, "I was more than just a little stunned." She gripped his hand tightly. "I've also had a couple of months to think about that night. I'm sure that there's a good explanation for what happened."

"There is an explanation, but I'm not sure how good it is." He stopped walking and turned to Demetria. He wanted to see her face when he told her about his mission. He looked deep into her eyes and then spoke: "I'm a commander in the United States Navy, here on a secret mission. My unit is part of an elite group known as the SEALs. We intend no harm to you, your uncle, or your people. If we had, we would not be standing here having this conversation. You've seen what we're capable of when you were in Mariel. When death is our intent, we are extremely efficient."

Demetria was not surprised at what she had just heard. She waited to hear more of what Xavier had to say before passing judgment. "What's your mission here, Commander?"

Xavier took a deep breath and let out a sigh. "Before I tell you my mission, I must tell you what it is not. My mission was not to come here and fall in love with you. But I've never met anyone like you before. From the first moment I saw you, my heart has belonged to you. I've never let myself love before, it just never seemed right. Then you walked into my life and all the rules changed. I only hope that you'll find it in your heart to continue to love me."

"Why wouldn't I?" Demetria's heart began to beat faster and more forcefully as she awaited his answer.

Xavier tried to look into her eyes, but the burden of what he had to say made it difficult. "My mission here is to remove your uncle from power so that a favorable government may be established."

Demetria jerked her hand free. "Favorable to whom?"

"To the United States," he answered.

Demetria was obviously offended by what she heard. Her uncle had been her life since losing her parents. Xavier's words stabbed her heart. For the next few minutes, she walked with her arms crossed in total silence.

Xavier felt his heart sink further with every passing moment. He knew that he couldn't be the first to speak, though he desperately wanted to. After nearly ten minutes, Demetria eased his pain. She uncrossed her arms and slid her hand into his. Air rushed back to Xavier's lungs, helping him to relax. Slowly the blood eased back into his face, returning it to its normal color. He'd never let things get so out of control before. But he was helpless to stop it this time.

"My uncle is a very good judge of character." She remembered the word that Castro said to her after her rescue. "He trusts you, so I'll trust you as well. He's grown weary of his presidency and the people here are exhausted waiting for the economy to return to normal. I don't think they could have waited much longer, if you hadn't come with a message of change."

Demetria felt it necessary to defended Castro's position. "My uncle was heartbroken when his daughter fled to the United States in search of a better life. She was spoiled here living as an elitist. When Uncle demanded that everyone sacrifice, she could only hold on for a short time before bailing out. How do you think her leaving looked to the rest of the country?"

Xavier nodded, understanding her point. "I see what you mean. Why should anyone else suffer if Castro's daughter did not have to?"

"You do understand. You should also be thankful that my uncle has made your job easier by appointing you as president." Demetria reached for his other hand. "He chose you to lead this country, and establish its greatness. Will you fulfill your destiny, or will you simply complete your mission and go home?"

Xavier waited before answering. "I don't see any other choice in this matter, I'll have to stay. At least I'll have you at my side. I'll need all the help I can get."

"Will your government allow you to continue in this position?" she asked.

Past the puzzled look on his face, Xavier answered confidently, "They don't have a choice in the matter. To maintain peace they can't risk installing anyone else right now."

"In my heart I've known your purpose here. Though it does sting to hear you actually speak the words." Demetria looked down. "My uncle has no idea that I too wish to see Democracy come to Cuba. I think it's our only option if we're to survive. I've never tasted the fruits of freedom that you enjoy, but I have seen it on the faces of many who have." She looked over the ocean. "When my uncle went to speak at the United Nations, he asked me to come along. He didn't allow me to venture freely into your world. However, I did go out into New York. I had to see for myself how the people of your country lived. Before I boarded our plane for home, I breathed deeply in an attempt to take a little freedom back with me. It must be a powerful force, or the party wouldn't guard us against it so fervently. As sweet as it was, you must know that I would never speak out publicly against my uncle. I don't think his heart could take it, and I know mine couldn't."

Xavier nodded. He stopped and leaned on a big rock, remembering the words to the song in the square. *Two hearts united in the same cause.* Demetria backed into his arms, and he encircled her waist. She leaned her head back to look at him.

"I was thinking about the words to that song we heard in the square," Xavier said. "You saw my coming before I arrived. You had to know my mission as well. Why did hearing me speak English upset you so?"

Demetria hugged herself tightly and looked out over the water. Her spirit drifted over the waves. "I wasn't totally honest about my vision of your arrival with my uncle." She shuddered thinking about her lie. She had never lied to Castro before. "Because he believes in my visions, he trusted you before you ever arrived. I told him that you would be the person who would save our homeland."

"So the vision isn't true? Then how did you know that I was coming?"

"Father Jose asked me to stay after church one day a few months ago. He took me to the back of the church, where three other people were waiting. They told me that they were aware that my uncle wanted to retire. They also knew that he wouldn't as long as he could not leave and save face with the people as well as save the country. These people were aware of my gift of sight. After I agreed to work with them, the vision of you was born."

Xavier sucked in air filling his chest. Suddenly it came clear. "I knew this was the easiest mission I've ever undertaken. I'm surprised you would agree to work with them. I've never seen anyone as loyal as you are to your uncle."

"Loyalty is the very reason I agreed to help. My uncle has never done anything but serve his people. He's tired. He deserves an easier life, which is exactly what they promised for him in return for my help." Demetria laughed and looked down at her foot playing in the sand. "Who would have thought a life-long enemy would be that which offered my uncle what he needs most?"

"Are you speaking of the United States?"

"Of course. It was the CIA I met with in the church. I hope their word is as good as mine."

Xavier pulled Demetria closer, holding her in his arms. "I'll personally see to it that they keep their word. Your uncle has nothing to worry about."

"You have that type of power, Commander?" Reaching up, Demetria grabbed the back of Xavier's head, bringing his lips to hers. They kissed a long, passionate kiss, drawing each other deep into themselves. Demetria's arms were around Xavier's neck, his around her waist. He kissed her neck, moving his tongue down its length.

Demetria writhed with pleasure. Her fingers tugged at his hair each time he crossed the sensitive area on her neck. Xavier moved his fingers lightly across the open back of her top.

Their bodies heaved as if they would explode.

Xavier stopped, cuddled her head, and pulled her to his chest.

"Don't worry, we're alone here," she said to him.

"There's nothing I want more. However, I'm still a little too old-fashioned. We'll be married in two weeks. I want to hold on to this moment until then."

Demetria held her head still against his chest. She smiled warmly. He'd just passed her final test. In the face of temptation, he chose to wait. Her mother and grandmother repeatedly tried to teach her this lesson. All traces of doubt retreated. Even though her mother was not the woman she had once been, Demetria knew she would be pleased.

Xavier re-engaged his pen and heard an immediate crackle in his ear. "Is everything okay, Commander?"

He knew that he would have to respond soon, but was grateful the NSA hadn't overheard his conversation with Demetria. She would have been considered an unacceptable liability and he would have received orders to terminate her immediately; something he knew he would never do.

Hugging Demetria tightly, he leaned near the pen. "Everything is just fine."

Chapter
58

Schaffer lay in bed motionless with his eyes open and his mind racing.

Helping Xavier as he'd been doing for the past couple of months had diverted his attention from his initial agenda.

He felt certain that Xavier's mission was the reason Harold had been killed. Yet, it didn't make sense; there had been no invasion and no one else had been killed. Except for Santiago and his men.

More troubling was the fact that he had not found Tito and the other three agents. He had looked, not only throughout Havana, but also in the towns and villages he visited distributing leaflets.

Schaffer raised his arm and looked at his watch, which glowed in a luminescent green: 1:00. To hell with the early hour, he had to talk to Dee. He sat on the edge of the bed and grabbed the communications device. His thumb waved back and forth over the contact button hesitantly. Finally pressing it, he waited for Dee to answer.

Dee's device beeped repeatedly before she pulled it from her nightstand into the bed with her. She put in her earpiece and activated it, closing her eyes at the same time. "Damn, Schaffer, it's one o'clock in the morning. There can't be anything going on at this ungodly hour."

"Sorry, Dee, but I'm afraid there is."

Dee sat up, wiping the sleep from her eyes. "Okay, I'm awake. What's up?"

"I've been sitting here unable to sleep, or get Tito off my mind."

Dee rubbed the side of her head. "I knew this was coming. I wish there was something I could offer to put you at ease."

Schaffer put his elbows on his knees making hand gestures as he spoke. "Castro threatened to kill them right after he captured them. Has he said anything else about them since taking them into custody?"

Dee took a drink of water from a glass on her nightstand. "Not one word."

"They didn't just disappear!" Schaffer was on his feet now. "Hasn't he mentioned them to Xavier? Since Castro named Xavier his successor, he'd have to tell him something."

"Haven't you been monitoring Xavier's transmissions?"

"Sure I have, but I don't have the luxury to review transcripts. I could have missed something. Xavier sure as hell couldn't have mentioned them by name without raising suspicion." Schaffer plopped back to the side of the bed.

Dee yawned, still feeling the effect of her interrupted sleep. "He couldn't bring them up at all. As far as we can tell, Castro has kept the entire incident to himself. Our CIA operatives haven't been able to find out anything."

Schaffer's anger rose. "What about the damn satellites? Shit, we've used them to pinpoint hostages plenty of times before."

Dee paused, not sure what she wanted to reveal. "Of course we've used them —"

"And?" Schaffer aggressively rubbed the stubble on his chin.

"Well, we know that they were originally taken to Castro's villa just like Commander Benderis."

"Shit, they've been there the whole time?"

Dee ran her fingers through her hair. "Xavier was brought there a couple of days after the agents. He's been all through the place, and there's no trace of them there."

Schaffer's mind raced faster. Staring into the darkness, he tried to piece possibilities together. "If they're not there — Xavier checked after he arrived — then they were moved. But you couldn't confirm that by using the satellites, is that correct?"

"We haven't seen any thing on any of the photos from space. Believe me, the president wants to find them as badly as you do."

Schaffer bounced one leg rapidly up and down. "We have to assume they were moved before Xavier got there. Castro must have given the order before he arrived with Xavier from Gitmo."

A frown crossed Dee's face as she flashed back to the time between the CIA agents' capture and Xavier's arrival at the villa. "Schaffer, I'm fairly certain Castro never gave any such order."

Schaffer's leg stopped bouncing. "What makes you say that?"

Dee knew that she was about to tread on thin ice, but she'd already ventured out too far to turn back. "Schaffer, what I'm about to say is extremely sensitive. Please don't question me further after I've tell you this. I've already gone too far. A CIA op was with Castro during the time in question. We would have known if he'd given the order to have them moved."

"Who?" The question left his lips as quickly as his feet hit the floor.

"I asked you not to do that. I can't say."

"What happened to your full disclosure, or did you just forget about that?"

"I'm sorry. This issue is not open for any further discussion." Dee knew she had to give him something else. She didn't want to risk deflating his trust. "What I can tell you is they must have been moved when Castro left for Gitmo, not when he was returning from there."

Schaffer froze in place. "You think the op had them moved. Haven't you talked with them since?"

"Unfortunately, no. I don't think we will either, they've gone in deep."

Schaffer moved to his window and looked out on the quiet city. "This person has to be someone Castro trusts. Why isn't he looking for them?"

Dee peeked at the clock. She was fully awake and moving from the bed. "I can't say."

"You won't say, or you don't know?" Schaffer snapped. "Which is it?"

"I don't have a clue."

Schaffer nervously tapped his arm. "Okay, Dee, we both know Tito could escape from most any situations. If Castro didn't have them moved, who else would have the power to have them constantly guarded?"

Dee stopped just outside her bathroom door. "Maybe they don't feel threatened and are just waiting for a chance to make contact. Our CIA ops haven't turned anything up. If there had been a real problem, the agents would have tried to make contact."

"I want a list of possible locations you all have plotted. I'll check them out myself."

Dee held onto the doorjamb. "They've been checked and rechecked. There's no sign of the men. The only place we haven't accessed is the naval base where Tito and the other men were spotted before they were captured at the hotel."

Schaffer spun and walked over to turn on the lamp beside his bed. "Where's it located?"

"On the beach less than three miles from Castro's villa." She moved into the bathroom and turned on the light. "It's crawling with Castro's men and has been ever since they took our men into custody. If you go near it, you're going to get yourself killed. They're jumpy, and it's not a good time."

"I'll take that into account."

¤¤¤¤

Schaffer left the hotel wearing shorts, a tee shirt, sandals, and carrying a backpack. When he was far enough out on the beach, he pulled the black clothing from the backpack and put it on.

At a steady jog, he reached the naval compound in less than thirty minutes. Reaching into the backpack, Schaffer took out his Nikon F5 and attached a 500 mm lens with infrared capability.

He noticed very little movement around the base, so he moved in for a closer look. He snapped off several shots while planning how he would gain entry to the facility.

Schaffer froze and lowered the camera as he felt the unmistakable presence of cold metal pressing against his skin where his spine met his skull. He listened intently, trying to gauge if more than one person was behind him. If it were just one, he had a better than an even chance at turning things in his favor.

"Don't even consider moving," the man standing behind him said. "This trigger is so sensitive a mosquito could set it off."

Schaffer didn't think. He swung one leg at a forty-five degree angle while tucking the other, readying to fire it into his assailant's face. His leg caught the would-be assailant hard in the side of his head, knocking him to the sand.

The man rolled over twice to avoid any other blows and as quickly, came to his feet.

Schaffer lunged to his feet and towards the man. He threw a block to knock away the gun, but the attacker was just as quick, and looped his arm. Dodging the block, he thrust the muzzle of his gun at the center of Schaffer's forehead. Schaffer raised his hands in surrender.

The man reached his left hand to the bottom of his mask and pulled it over his head. "What the hell are you doing out here? I almost sent your brains for a walk in the sand."

Schaffer lowered his hands, and shoved the gun from his forehead. "I've had enough guns pointed at me for four lifetimes. Don't ever do that again."

"From where I'm standing, it's SEALs one, Marine Recon zero."

Schaffer laughed. "Then you'd better look in the mirror. That mouse swelling on the side of your head is going to look real good at the ceremony tomorrow."

Guzman reached up to feel the rapidly swelling knot. "Goddamnit, Schaffer, I should pop this cap off in your sorry ass for GP."

"Don't flatter yourself. I'd have your ass in the sand before you could raise that gun three inches."

Guzman flinched.

Schaffer hit him, dislodging the gun before dropping to one knee and flipping Guzman over his head.

Guzman slammed down into the sand. He grunted. "Where the hell did you learn that? It surely wasn't Recon. You guys aren't that good."

Schaffer held out his hand and helped Guzman up. "Thanks for the complement. Mom enrolled me in Kempo at age five. She said I needed to work off my excess energy. I've studied it and several other forms of martial arts ever since."

"I might have to get you to teach me a couple of moves. I've never had anyone flip me by grabbing my leg." Guzman brushed the sand from his clothes and retrieved his gun.

"Not to change the subject, but what the hell are you doing out here?"

Guzman nodded towards the naval complex. "Somebody had to save your sorry ass. You were thinking about going in there, right?"

Schaffer's expression turned deadly serious. "I've got to find Tito."

"He's not in there and that's for damn sure." Guzman picked up Schaffer's camera and backpack.

Schaffer took them and slung the backpack over one shoulder. "How do you know that?"

"The commander was here earlier to tour the place. I stayed behind in case these numb nuts decided to bring anyone in after he left. There's been no such luck."

Schaffer placed the camera in the backpack. "How long are you going to stay out here?"

Guzman looked out over the ocean. "Probably until sun up. But you should be getting back."

"One question first. Where were you hiding? I didn't see you."

A huge smile ran across Guzman's face. "I'm a SEAL. We blend in with our surroundings."

Chapter 59

The evening of the formal transfer of power arrived with little fanfare.

Schaffer was there, along with small gathering of the Communist Party faithful, as well as Castro, Demetria and Guzman. With little exception, there were no non-party citizens in attendance, as far as Schaffer could tell. It seemed to him that Castro wanted to make Xavier appear to be a puppet under his control, especially to his Communist followers. From what he'd seen coming from Xavier, Schaffer knew nothing could have been further from the truth. Xavier was already making plans to move his new country forward. In some small way, Schaffer felt that he'd made a contribution to the cause. Schaffer moved in closer when he saw Demetria walk to Xavier's side.

"I'm very proud of you." She placed her hands on Xavier's shoulders and tiptoed to kiss him on the cheek. "You'll serve this country well."

"We'll serve Cuba together," Xavier said. "I only wish more of the people could have been part of the ceremony. I'll serve all of them, not just a few select of his party." Xavier pointed to Castro. "It's time this country started looking forward, remembering the good of the past but tossing out the bad."

Xavier's disappointment in the ceremony was as obvious to Demetria as it was to Schaffer, who stepped forward to offer his support. "Soon they'll be involved, Mr. President. You're a strong leader who's offered to share power with the people. It's only a matter of time before they learn and accept their responsibility."

"Yes, but this type of event sends the wrong message," Xavier said. "It makes my promises seem shallow and devoid of substance."

Xavier walked further away from where Castro gathered his followers. Schaffer decided to leave him alone for the evening, but Demetria was close behind him.

Castro avoided contact with Cuba's new leader, clinging fast to his last few remaining minutes of presidential power. Instead, he concentrated on the members of his party, reassuring them of their future with Cuba's new leader.

The people questioned Castro. "Why hasn't he formally joined the party? How could you make him the leader of Cuba without first joining the official Communist Party? Are we going to end up regretting your decision?"

"He'll join after the wedding," Castro assured them. "I've planned a grand service to introduce him into the party. You all will be invited to attend." This pacified them for the moment.

Demetria continued to try to take Xavier's mind off the lack of popular participation. "What'll be your first act as the new president?"

"Reestablishing ties to stimulate our economy and maybe hold a public hanging for the people that put us in such dire straights. What do you think?"

Demetria could see Xavier was in no mood to be soothed. Silently, she stood by his side, hoping he would not act rashly.

Chapter 60

Secretary of State Ian Mackenzie walked up to the president. "It feels like fall will arrive early this year, Mr. President."

"That it does, Ian," Alex said. "We have a huge lead in the polls. In the next two weeks we'll be back in Cuba." He pointed his cigar in Mackenzie's direction. "That should seal the election."

"The election is already sealed, if you ask me," Mackenzie replied.

"It doesn't hurt to have an insurance policy." He turned his attention to General Roseboro. "What's the latest on Benderis? Will his wedding be held this week as planned?"

"As far as we know, sir." Dee moved closer to Alex and leaned near him. "What'll you have him do after Castro steps down tonight?"

"I guess we'll have to leave him in power. He's gained the trust and respect of the country. It'd be a mistake to force him to step down too soon." The president looked down at his papers. "Ultimately, we'll have to send in someone new. Benderis is a SEAL, not a politician. We don't want to repeat another forty year standoff, so we'll have to choose his replacement wisely."

Mackenzie jumped in. "We won't have to worry about that, sir. Our tenure in office will be long over."

"That's the problem this country has now," Alex said. "The first presidential term is spent looking for ways to get re-elected. The second, no one gives a damn about because they can't repeat another term."

"I'm sorry, Mr. President, I didn't mean to sound as if I didn't care," Mackenzie said offhandedly.

¤¤¤¤

In three days, Xavier and Demetria would be married. Xavier had many things to get done, not the least of which was to contact Admiral Gregory.

The rest of the SEAL team needed to be in place and ready to move the moment he implemented the last stage of the mission.

Castro and Demetria were in town picking up a few last minute items for the wedding. Xavier decided to use this opportunity to contact the Admiral. "Admiral Gregory, come in. This is Commander Benderis." Xavier waited for a response. In thirty-second increments, he repeated his broadcast.

Aboard the USS Enterprise, an intelligence officer monitored the line and sent for the Admiral after the first transmission. Communication with Xavier was forbidden with anyone except the Admiral, so the officer received each of Xavier's transmissions without responding. General Roseboro, who was also monitoring the line, immediately placed a call to the Admiral as well.

"Commander Benderis, this is Admiral Gregory," the admiral finally responded to Xavier. "Please proceed with your transmission."

"The time has come to launch the final stage of the mission," Xavier said. "You'll be contacted on a secure line four minutes after this transmission ends. The details of this portion of the operation will be made clear then. The only communication you will have, from this point on, will be on the secure line. This ends the transmission. Benderis over and out."

The line went dead.

Admiral Gregory fought his uneasy feelings since meeting with President Nicholas. To him, the president was being unnecessarily cautious with information. Everything came in bits and pieces, as if he was trying to protect a track record by only releasing information after being assured of its success. The president was a former military officer, and knew that additional input could be invaluable. The admiral also knew that he wouldn't be asked for his input.

Admiral Gregory went to his quarters to wait for further contact. His entire body tensed, thinking what the final stages of the mission held. No mistakes could be tolerated from this point on.

A special digital radio device was installed in the admiral's quarters before leaving shore. Seconds after he entered the room, a red light came on the headset, indicating a call was coming in. Quickly, Gregory placed the earphones on and pressed the prescribed button.

Silence was broken with the president's carefully chosen words spoken by Xavier: "Opus X."

Admiral Gregory responded rolling his eyes wondering if there was some type of unwritten code that required mission authentication responses to be obtuse. "As good as anything Castro has to offer."

"Welcome, Admiral Gregory," Xavier said, "to the last and final stages of Operation Smokeout. Sit on your bunk and run your fingers along the bottom edge. There you'll feel a notch about three-quarters of the way down."

He fumbled a moment beneath the bed. "Yes, I have it."

"Good. Push the shorter quarter towards the back of the bed. It should reveal a small silver button."

He felt for the button. "Here it is."

"Push the button," Xavier said.

He pushed the button and a small plastic capsule popped out from the bottom of his bunk.

"Break the capsule. In it, you will find the names of ten members of your crew. They are not currently using these names, so you won't recognize any of them. These men are part of the president's SEAL team. In addition to the names, you should have a ribbon for your uniform. Only these men will recognize its meaning. Call for general inspections in the areas where they are assigned, and you can see each area they work in next to their names. When they see the ribbon, they'll know it's time to move into action. They'll meet you in briefing room Alpha, at zero hundred hours. Carry your headset with you. Instructions will be delivered at that time."

Before Admiral Gregory had the chance to ask anything further, Xavier's voice was gone.

He radioed his First Officer. "I want to inspect the flight deck and kitchen right away. Have all medical personnel meet me at the kitchen."

"Aye, aye, sir."

The admiral's orders to assemble were given. The sailors scurried to get into position for inspection. The admiral stood and moved to a mirror to adjust his new ribbon. He then began his inspections. Having no idea what these men or women looked like, he tried to read the expressions on each of their faces, but to no avail. He looked at his watch. It read eighteen hundred hours. He would have to wait another six hours before finding out who these men were and the details of their duties.

He left the flight deck en route to the kitchen. Again, he tried to read the men. Again, he failed. All he could do was wait.

¤¤¤¤

Guzman, now a common face to all at Castro's compound, delivered a package to Xavier. After receiving the package, Xavier took it to his room. He removed the wrappings and opened the box. From it, he pulled out a small mold that looked as if it were used to make sewing needles. Next, he removed a bottle of clear liquid. From his lunch tray, he gathered a teaspoon of sugar and placed it into a shallow bowl. He pushed the rubber on top of dropper, allowing it to fill with the clear liquid. Careful not to spill any, he placed ten drops in with the sugar, and stirred with a toothpick. This made a thick paste, which he placed into the mold.

While the darts were setting, he looked for something inconspicuous to deliver them to their target. Since he would use them during the wedding reception, he would have to find something that they would fit in and not break. He walked around the compound, investigating. Whatever he used would have to be small enough to fit between his lips and remain hidden from everyone. It would also have to be digestible, since he would have to swallow it after delivering the dart to its intended target.

Just outside the house, he leaned on a rail and watched the waves creeping onto the sand. One of Castro's men, Jorge, walked over to Xavier. He was assigned to comply with the needs of the guest in the compound.

"May I get you something, Xavier?" Jorge asked.

Slowly, Xavier turned his head. He moved as if he were coming out of a trance. "Yes, Jorge. I'd like one of the drinks Castro's so fond of."

Jorge left to prepare the drink. He put crushed ice into a chilled glass. Then into a mixing container he poured dark rum, papaya juice, and pineapple juice. He put a top on the container and shook fiercely. Then he poured this mixture over the ice and placed a papaya blossom into the glass.

Jorge delivered it to Xavier. "Here is your drink, sir."

"Thanks, Jorge." Xavier pulled the blossom out, and like Castro, separated the blossom from the stem to squeeze the nectar from the flower into his drink. Using the stem, he stirred. Instinctively, he lifted the stem to his mouth and sucked the remaining juice from it. As he anticipated, the stem was hollow. In his hands, he held his delivery system. This would carry the dart of sugar and curare to its mark. Briskly, he walked back to his room to see if the darts had set.

Xavier practiced shooting the darts into a banana sitting on his dresser. He inhaled a little too deeply, and swallowed the first dart. Ingested, curare has no effect on the body, but given intramuscularly it would shut down the neuromuscular system, just not as fast as it would if he hit his intended target, the carotid artery on the right side of Castro's neck. He needed to test the darts on a human to make sure that the dose of curare in the dart would be effective yet not lethal. Getting the proper quantitative mixture was tricky since he had to guess at the weight and general health of any target. He gathered five of the darts, inserted them into five three-millimeter pieces of the papaya stem, and went out to the beachfront. There he'd have his choice of guards to experiment on. Ideally, he had to find someone who had just finished doing some type of strenuous activity, which made the carotid artery stand out as the blood rushed through it.

Xavier stopped at least twenty-five yards from the closest guard. He signaled for the man to come to him.

"Is that boat coming towards the compound?" Xavier motioned out over the water.

The guard placed his rifle on his shoulder and raised his binoculars to his eyes. He turned to watch the boats. Xavier slid the loaded papaya stem between his lips and concentrated on the right side of guard's neck, watching his carotid artery pound. Xavier was more careful and did not inhale quite as deeply this time. With one quick puff, the dart was on its way. It cut through the air, striking its mark. The guard slapped the side of his neck and examined his hand for the remains of the bug he thought he'd crushed.

The guard turned to Xavier. "It's just a few children playing. I don't think we'll have to worry about them. I'll keep them under surveillance just to make sure."

"I don't mean to seem paranoid. I just don't want a repeat of what happened at the last party held here a couple of months ago," Xavier explained.

"We lost a lot of good men that night, sir. I'll make sure that nothing will go wrong at your wedding."

"Thank you. I'll remember your effort." Xavier touched the guard's shoulder and gave him a warm smile. He watched the man for any changes in appearance. He was about to send the man back to his post when he began to look lifeless. The guard attempted to reach out for Xavier, but his arms would not move. He fell to his knees, then to his back. Xavier watched closely. There was no movement in the man's body.

Twenty minutes passed. Xavier looked at his watch, noting it was about time for a replacement guard to come on duty, so he radioed for help.

The extra guards arrived with their weapons drawn, searching for any sign of trouble.

"What has happened here, sir?"

"We were talking and he passed out. I listened for a heartbeat, but I heard none. We need to get him to a doctor right away." With a move of his hand, Xavier dispatched his men to get transportation. Based on the guard's estimated weight, Xavier realized he should wake soon. He injected two more darts into the side of the fallen man's neck. It was risky to double the dose, but he had to know if his mixture was safe.

By the time they reached the doctor's office in the village, an hour and ten minutes had elapsed. The near-lifeless guard was carried into the office and placed on an examining table.

The doctor listened to the guard's chest. "This man is dead." Again, Xavier explained what had happened. The doctor examined the dead patient's body for signs of anything unusual. He found nothing.

The sight of their friend lying there troubled the guards. "Someone will have to tell his wife."

"Let's get him out of here for now. I'll tell her later." Xavier turned to walk from the room. Again he inspected his watch. Almost two hours passed. The dose of curare that he used should only have paralyzed the guard's muscles and made his breathing and heartbeat undetectable. Xavier began to wonder if he had mortally wounded an innocent man.

"Where shall we take him?" the soldiers asked.

"Take him back to the compound. We'll have someone come there to care for his body." Xavier was attempting to stall, hoping for the man's recovery.

The truck pulled back into the compound and stopped.

"I saw his finger move!" one of the guards shouted. He jumped from the truck and reached into his pocket. He retrieved a pouch that contained magic dust given to him by a Santeria priest to ward off evil spirits. He sprinkled himself with the dust and recited an incantation the priest told him to use.

Xavier glanced at his watch, which revealed two hours and forty-five minutes passed since the he'd shot the last dart. Two of the guards attempted to see if the man's heart was beating.

"Let me see." Xavier placed his ear to the man's chest. "Quiet, I'm trying to hear." All of his men leaned forward in a vain attempt to hear. "There! His heart is beating. It is just very slow. Give me a mirror or a piece of glass." Xavier held the mirror under the reincarnated guard's nose. Still, his breathing was so shallow no fog appeared on the mirror. Thirty more minutes passed, three hours and fifteen minutes all together. Xavier and the guards kept vigil. A short groan emitted from the unconscious man. By the time he regained full consciousness, three hours thirty minutes had elapsed.

Xavier went back to his room and recounted the events of the afternoon.

Demetria and her uncle returned from a day of shopping for the wedding. Things had still not calmed down on the grounds of the compound. The sight of a group of guards standing in a circle looking down caused Demetria to fear the worst. The car hardly came to a stop before Demetria jumped from the moving vehicle, and ran over the group of men. "What is going on?"

The guards stood apart to let Demetria in.

"This man passed out while talking to President Ciefuentes. The doctor said he was dead. Yet, as you can see, he's made a miraculous recovery."

She grabbed the man, shaking him. "Do you remember what happened to you?"

Still groggy, his speech was slow. "I was looking through my binoculars and an insect bit me. After that, everything is blurry. That is, until now." He grabbed his pounding head and lay back down.

Relived that she had not found Xavier lying there, Demetria set out to find him. Together, they would put the finishing touches on their wedding plans.

ＸＸＸＸ

General Pete Rogers called the president. "Sir, Xavier just completed his testing of the curare darts. All has gone as planned."

"Very well. Then the final step is a short time away." Alex rose and moved to his humidor. He selected his favorite Cuban cigar. "Very soon now I'll not have to hide when I want to smoke one of these." He lit his cigar and moved to the Truman balcony over the Rose Garden to survey his beloved kingdom.

A few minutes later, Annie walked down the hall to where the president stood. She watched him looking out over Washington. For several minutes, she just stood there, watching the man who bore the weight of the world on his shoulders. "Is there anything I can do to help ease your burden?"

Alex looked over to his secretary. "I wish there were, Annie. Time will take care of everything. Thanks for asking."

Chapter 61

The morning of the wedding greeted Havana with dark, ominous clouds. The sun struggled to appear on several occasions, only to be beaten back by the more formidable cumulonimbus.

"This isn't a good sign," Demetria said, watching out the window. "I can feel something disturbing in the air."

"Calm yourself, Demetria." Castro sat back with a glass of sherry in hand. "Some say rain on the morning of your wedding is good luck."

She continued looking out the window, fearing what her senses told her, even though she had not truly had a vision.

¤¤¤¤

To his own surprise, Xavier was extremely calm. Much of that he attributed to the fact that he concentrated so much energy on the other matter at hand. Today he would eliminate Castro from Cuba. Paramount in his mind was to make sure no one detected him. He went over the plans in his head a thousand times, which left him little time to worry about his wedding. After the ceremony, there would be the customary father-daughter dance. Unlike typical American weddings, the dance would be faster. Exertion on Castro's part would enable Xavier to locate Castro's carotid artery easily. Shortly thereafter, it would all be over, and Castro would be gone.

Xavier began his morning transmissions. "Archangels, this is Father Time, come in."

The SEAL team, already aboard the submarine, responded: "We read you, Father Time."

"The sub should be en route to Havana by sixteen hundred hours. At eighteen hundred hours your lost soul will be ready for his journey."

"Roger, Father Time. The Archangels will be standing by to escort the package. By the way, congratulations on your upcoming nuptial. It couldn't happen to a nicer guy."

Xavier could hear laughter in the background. "Thanks. Thanks a lot. Father Time out."

¤¤¤¤

The information Schaffer had gathered over the past days was sketchy at best. Xavier's last comments, using the handle 'Father Time,' suggested that Castro's time had come. He needed to contact Dee to get her to fill in the blanks.

General Rogers of NSA placed a call to the president. "Mr. President, we have just received a transmission from Commander Benderis. At eighteen hundred hours the SEAL team will meet Castro's body."

"Very well," Alex responded. "Inform me of any new developments the minute you receive them today, Pete."

"Yes, sir."

"Well Dee," Alex said. "It looks like everything has come together after all. In a few hours, Castro will permanently leave Cuba and be a nuisance to no one."

Schaffer found no comfort in Alex's words and shouted in Dee's ear. "Dee, talk to me! There's no reason for Alex to have Castro killed! Damnit, answer me!"

She ignored his protest and continued talking to Alex. "Remember, sir that you said O'Grady was to have full disclosure from this office? When do you plan to tell him what's really going on with this operation?"

"He's not doing anything to disrupt the plan is he?" The president lifted his head slowly. Fear began to ease onto his face. He knew Schaffer wouldn't sit quietly and allow anyone to be assassinated, even Castro.

"No, Mr. President. However, the plan to terminate Castro is not sitting well with him."

"You and I are the only two who know the entire plan. We can't risk telling anyone else. Too many things have already gone wrong. After everything cools down and the transition is complete, maybe then I'll tell him. For the time being, make sure he doesn't interfere with my SEALs. God knows, I don't want him getting hurt. They won't be stopped. Recon or not, he's no match for a group of trained killers."

"I'll take care of it, sir. But you are going to have to give him something." She shook her head. "You know he won't stand by for too long without a good reason."

✿✿✿✿

In Cuba, this would be the closest thing to a royal wedding ever. Xavier insisted that Castro let many commoners attend the wedding. He held a lottery to determine who would be allowed in. The drawing was held in the middle of Havana for all of Cuba to see. The winners rushed home to prepare their finest outfits for the occasion. The attendees would be the envy of all who did not win.

Xavier decided against wearing his new military uniform. Instead, he chose the more formal clothing Demetria bought for him before the introduction party.

The Havana symphony filled the villa with music. It wasn't long before the prelude ended and the march began, indicating the time had come to stand for the bride's entrance. Xavier stood in front of the room, waiting for his bride to enter from the ballroom. Strangely, he was not nervous, as most grooms would be. Everyone attending saw a man full of pride and determination.

For her entrance song, Demetria selected *Canon in D Minor* by Pachelbel. The drone of the string bass hummed below four intermittent thumps from the cellos. Together, they called to the violins, which slowly sang above the horizon set by the lower strings. Each instrument grew in intensity, giving Xavier the feeling of the sun rising. He anxiously looked for Demetria and felt his anticipation rise with the crescendo of the music. The musicians reached their crest, and the notes of violins gamboled above the fray. Demetria stepped into view and the music warmed even more, sending her forward.

Her gown was simple and elegant, appealing to Xavier. Time seemed to stand still as he reviewed every inch of the most beautiful woman that he had ever seen. Her breasts protruded from the lace holding them. The gown was close fitting at the top, blossoming as it reached the top of her thighs, and then generously caressed the floor. Ten children, also selected by lottery, held her train on either side. Castro proudly stood by her, ready to walk her to her husband.

Demetria floated towards the front of the room. Xavier could wait no longer, so he left the altar and walked to meet his bride about half way down the aisle. "I will always meet you at least half way. If you need me, I will come all the way to be by your side."

Those in attendance rewarded his comments with their audible approval. Xavier turned to Castro and hugged him. He thought how easy it would be to plant the dart into Castro's neck while holding him. There was no discord in the music and there would be none during the ceremony.

Xavier placed his hand on Demetria's back and turned to walk to the front of the room. His hand revealed Demetria's bare back. She remembered how he enjoyed her opened back outfit on the beach, so she'd left the gown open. Xavier could hardly contain his enthusiasm at the discovery. His thoughts turned to a time when the two of them would be able to explore each other without hesitation. At this moment, no one but the two of them existed. There were no sides to take, no one to remove from power, or to put in power. There was only the harmony of their union.

Castro stood still and watched his niece and Xavier walk to the front of the room. Even after they arrived in front of the altar, he couldn't get his feet to leave their place. He knew his reign as Cuba's leader was now over. All that was left of his life was to wait for the inevitable. His life passed before his eyes, arriving at the present moment, which should have been a time of joy. However, he could only feel sadness. Demetria was the bright spot in his life and now she too was leaving him.

The music stopped and Father Jose motioned for Castro to take his seat. He didn't acknowledge this gesture. Demetria and Xavier turned to see what was going on.

"It's okay, Uncle. You can sit down now."

Castro spoke as if coming out of a fog. "Yes, yes, of course. I was just reminiscing on our time together."

Everyone present smiled at his words and could also sense the bittersweet moment for Castro. Xavier saw something deeper in the old man's eyes, a restlessness like that of a wandering soul. He wondered if Castro sensed his destiny. Xavier alone knew that Castro's life in Cuba was rapidly coming to an end.

Father Jose continued with the ceremony. "We have been brought together today by this couple. They have asked us to witness their union, as it is their wish to enter into a life of love as one."

He was careful with his words. The congregation, with the exception of Demetria, Xavier, Guzman, Schaffer, and most of those selected by lottery, were Communist Party members. Time would tell if Father Jose would be successful at not offending them. Schaffer knew Father Jose well, and expected him to shake things up a little.

Though her uncle had taken her in at a young age, Demetria never gave up the religion of her mother, Catholicism. Often she went to mass at noon during the week and on Sundays. No one chose to mention this, especially to Castro, at least not since he'd set a group of his loyal party members straight, after one of them complained about it. None of them dared to speak of it again.

"What is your intention here today?" Father Jose asked.

"To be married," they answered as one.

Father Jose turned to those in attendance. "As witnesses, is it your contention that this couple has come here of their own free will?"

Castro looked across his shoulder at the people. His silent intimidation was as effective as ever and, they promptly answered, "It is."

Father Jose completed the ceremony. Xavier and Demetria knelt before him. "I bless this union, in the name of the Father, the Son, and the Holy Spirit."

At that moment, the church was so quiet it seemed no one breathed. It was the only time that Father Jose made any reference to God. What was more amazing was Castro signing himself as Father Jose spoke these words. The loyal Catholics joined him. Castro didn't realize what he did until he felt his friends staring at him strangely. They were not sure what to do, being unaccustomed to the tradition. Castro ignored them as he walked to the front of the room and kissed his niece and Xavier. He turned to the Orchestra and moved his arms as a conductor would. Purcell's *Trumpet Tune and Air* broke the silence and led the couple to the ballroom.

The reception began immediately after the service. Everyone helped themselves to the abundant food and drink. The newly married couple moved through the gathering to address each of the attendees.

Castro rose, reached to the side of his glass, pulled out the papaya blossom, and crushed it to send forth the nectar. Then he stirred the mixture and raised his glass skyward. "Let's toast our newly married president and his lovely wife. You've been blessed with one of Cuba's most beautiful flowers. May you always cradle her close to you, and protect her from all harm." Castro looked directly into Xavier's eyes. His words seemed as much a threat as they were a toast.

Xavier raised his glass and turned to his new uncle. "Don't worry. I'll always protect her, just as I will our beloved country. Nothing can prevent Cuba's destiny that's been set forth for all today."

The room was silent with a tension thick as jelly. Xavier smiled and walked towards Castro to embrace him. Initially, Castro stepped back. He was on edge, and reached down to the pistol on his side. He looked like a paranoid old man expecting someone to jump him at any moment. Castro's fingers continued to dance across the butt of his gun as Xavier embraced him.

Guzman and Schaffer tried to enjoy the reception as much as possible, but they were on high alert. Even with General Santiago and his men dead, they still felt uneasy. Any number of the Communist Party members in this room could pose a threat, especially since they'd openly criticized the direction their new president seemed to be taking the country.

Xavier was too busy with the next step of his mission to worry about who might want to end his short reign.

Guzman and Schaffer did the worrying for him.

Chapter 62

Silently a submarine inched its way through the murky waters of the Atlantic. It was headed towards Cuba and Admiral Gregory was in command. Only a handful of the men on board knew what their mission would entail.

In the lower portion of the sub, a surgical room was set up with the SEAL team standing by. The surgeon, also a member of the SEAL team, assisted with the construction of the room. The half of the floor where the SEALs worked was inaccessible to the rest of the crew. Two Marine sentries were stationed in front of the door with instructions to shoot anyone who tried to enter the room.

On an area of the wall, the surgeon taped the left, front, and right views of two different men side by side. The first picture the SEALs recognized as Castro, the second no one knew. She studied them with intensity. "This will be our new creation, gentleman," she said pointing to the second picture. "Everything must go according to plan so that we will be able to deliver the package to the president in two days."

All of the team members gathered around to finalize plans for the evening. Dr. Hunter gave all her final instructions. "At eighteen hundred hours Ensign Guzman will lead a burning pyre out to sea. Keys, Harkless, and Tisdale, you'll go out to meet the pyre."

"What the fuck? Did Castro join some type of Viking cult or something? A burning pyre is bizarre even for his standards."

The surgeon turned away from the projected picture to challenge the surprised SEAL. "Do you mind if I continue?" She pressed a button, advancing the picture. "The pyre is the easiest way for us to get Castro out of Cuba without public interference."

She turned back to the picture on the screen. "On the bottom of the vessel, you will find four screws. Guzman will enter the water and help you remove them so that the body will slide out into the water. An oxygen mask should be in place with a mini tank on it. Turn it on by twisting the knob on the tank counterclockwise. You'll then have ten minutes to return to the sub before the tank runs out. Enclosed in plastic, with the body, will be several pouches. They contain five hundred of the finest cigars from Cuba. They're a gift for the president from Castro. Successfully retrieving this pouch will net a box for us to spilt, so graciously awarded to us by the president."

The SEALs laughed. "Generous bastard, isn't he?"

"Yeah, we get to keep a whopping two and a half percent of the booty."

"Okay, cut the shit." Dr. Hunter tapped the operation table. "Once you have returned with the body, I'll need each of you to assist me in this operation. We'll help Castro turn over a new leaf by giving him a new identity. President Nicholas will take it from there."

"You'll also have to carry an extra tank for Guzman, as well as a little C-4 to destroy his boat. The apparent accident will explain his not returning to the mainland. If there're no questions, let's get over to the gear for inspection."

The SEALs moved to their gear and inspected it once more. Satisfied that everything was in order, they went over their plans in detail, right down to smoking the cigars on their return.

Isolated from the rest of the crew on the sub, the SEALs climbed into their bunks in the operating room to rest before the night's mission.

Chapter 63

The reception was in full swing. The fortunate invitees consumed food and rum in large quantities.

Castro, however, grew increasingly more irritable and drunk as the afternoon progressed.

Xavier felt uneasy at the prospects of dealing with Castro inebriated. He looked at his watch. Fifteen hundred hours. It would not be long now before his mission was complete.

Schaffer was quite nervous, mentally examining the possible outcomes of the day. Xavier had said that the body would be ready for transport. Castro was his only possible victim. But, if he killed him in front of all these people, there would be many panicky guests. And there was no way to predict how the soldiers would react. Then there was the toll killing Castro would take on Demetria. What disturbed Schaffer most was the fact that there was no need to kill this man. He'd already given Xavier everything.

Demetria took her place in the middle of the floor. The band played a salsa tune. Castro was beckoned to come by her side. A wide smile crossed his face. For the first time in hours, he seemed happy. Castro grabbed a flower and placed it between his teeth. He slid forth, placing one hand in the air and the other behind his back, snapping his fingers as he approached his niece, drawing laughter from the guest. Castro took a step towards Xavier. He pulled the flower from his teeth and slapped it across Xavier's chest. "Hold this while I teach you a thing or two about dancing."

Xavier smiled and bowed, yielding to Castro's self-proclaimed prominence on the dance floor. He then slid his hand into his coat pocket and fingered the contents. He selected a papaya stem loaded with a curare dart, and slowly brought it to his lips as if he were slipping a mint. Carefully, he watched Castro's every move. As the sweat ran down Castro's face, his carotid artery pumped intensely. When the song ended, Xavier applauded and crossed the room to embrace his new uncle. Castro turned to look at his niece, revealing the pulsing artery. Less than a foot away, Xavier let out the silent puff, sending aloft the dart. He swallowed, and the papaya stem was gone. The dart, invisible to all, struck its mark. Castro slapped at his neck as the stinging dart dug its way into his artery. His eyes never left his niece until he raised his hand to examine it for the remains of the crushed bug.

In a few seconds, everyone at the reception would see the effects of the dart. Castro embraced his new nephew and placed Demetria's hand in his so that they, too, could dance. Castro left to get the drink already prepared at his table. As the couple danced, Castro began to feel the effects of the curare. He started to wiggle his toes, which felt numb as he took a drink from his glass. "I must have danced a little aggressively. My toes feel numb."

One of his friends responded to his statement, but to Castro everything sounded as if it were traveling down a tunnel in slow motion. He reached for his neck, which by now also felt numb. The drink he was holding slid from his hand and crashed to the floor. Realizing that his legs had no feeling and couldn't support his weight, he started to fall. Two of his friends helped him to his chair. He tried to communicate with them, but he could not make his lips form words. Saliva drooled from the side of his mouth, forming a string connected to the table. His head collapsed, crashing to the tabletop. One of the women screamed loudly, stopping the music and gathering everyone's attention.

Xavier and Demetria stopped dancing and turned in the direction of the scream. A crowd gathered around the table, blocking their view. Castro's personal physician was in the middle of the people begging them to quiet down. Xavier and Demetria moved slowly to the table. As they came closer, Demetria moved a little faster. She could see Castro's upper body slumped across the table. Tears filled her eyes and gradually slid down her cheeks.

The doctor stood with a baffled look on his face. "He's dead."

"No!" Demetria screamed, and fled to her uncle's side.

Xavier moved in for support. "What happened?"

Schaffer had not been more than a few feet from Xavier since the reception began. He wanted to avoid witnessing any more death. While the attention was focused on Castro, Schaffer used a napkin to soak up some of the drink Castro had dropped on the floor. He wanted to know if the liquid contained any poison. If this was an execution, he intended to tell the world.

The doctor looked at the corpse. "The dance must have been too much for his heart."

Xavier angrily turned to the doctor. "Has he been having heart problems?"

The doctor looked puzzled and answered. "Nothing serious, age will cause the minor changes we've noticed. I'll have to perform an autopsy to determine the actual cause of his death."

Xavier moved to Castro's side. "No! There will be no autopsy! He wouldn't have wanted it. He expressed to me emphatically that he never wanted to be embalmed, and there would be no mutilation. We'll hold the funeral at sundown. He entered the presidency in a blaze of glory and he'll leave the same way."

"What do you mean?" The doctor showed no respect for his new president or his decision. "The people will want to know what happened here."

"They have seen what has happened. That's all they need to know," Xavier insisted.

"You are being unreasonable!"

"Not at all." Xavier touched Castro's limp body. "I am just carrying out the wishes he expressed to me earlier this week. It's as if he anticipated death."

"The people will not stand for this! I'll see that an investigation is launched immediately!" the doctor yelled, and stormed from the room.

"That's not in your best interest," Xavier shouted after him. He turned to his men. "We'll set a pyre ablaze and send him off to glory. Castro always had an affinity for flair. He wouldn't want us to send him off any other way." Xavier reached down to offer comfort to his wife who was sobbing. "Give us some time. Would you all please leave the room?"

Hesitantly, they obeyed at the insistence of the guards. One by one, they looked back to get just one more glance of their fallen leader. Twenty minutes passed. Xavier knew that he had about thirty minutes before the effects of the curare wore off. He would have to give Castro another dose soon. Demetria was almost in shock and didn't even acknowledge Xavier's presence. He slid his hand to his pocket, grabbed another papaya stem, and repeated the procedure. Accuracy was not as important since Castro was already under the influence of the curare.

"We need to go, Demetria. Let's prepare for this evening." Xavier signaled for help when he got Demetria to the door. "Take her to our room," he told two of his guards. "I'll be along soon." Xavier called Guzman over. "I'll keep everyone out of here. Start preparations for his trip."

Over the next hour, servants brought Castro's best dress uniform to the room where the two men were arranging the body. Guzman inserted a needle, attached to a bag containing a four-hour supply of curare, into Castro's femoral artery. It was time released, much like an IV, which would prevent distributing a lethal dose of the muscle relaxant.

"I must go and get ready," Xavier said. "Take him down to the water. Everything you need is there. I had some of the guards set the pyre on the old boat Castro kept behind the villa. They'll keep everyone but you off after the body is placed on board."

"I'll gladly get this Commie bastard out of here." Guzman grinned. "Maybe I should increase his dosage. No one will miss his ass."

"We have our orders. I trust you'll follow them to the letter," Xavier said without any trace of humor.

"Yes sir, Commander, President Ciefuentes, sir."

Xavier flipped Guzman the bird. "Fuck you! Just get it done." He turned and left the room.

The room was empty except for a handful of soldiers who would serve as the Honor Guard to Castro.

Xavier entered his room and found Demetria completely distraught. She was still in her wedding dress, lying across the bed, sobbing bitterly. He sat beside her, placed his arm around her, and pulled her head to his chest. "Everything is not as it seems. You feel you've lost your uncle. Actually he's gained his freedom."

Through her tears, he could clearly see the accusation on her face. "How could you say such a thing? He spent a lifetime caring for me. You treat his death far too lightly." Demetria pulled away, falling back to the bed.

"Demetria, I'm not making light of what's happened here this evening. Keep in mind what I told you. You'll see your uncle again soon. We'll visit him together." Xavier stood and walked to his dressing room to prepare for the funeral.

Demetria's weeping eased while she tried to comprehend what Xavier'd just said. Her mind raced with the possibilities of his statement. She stood and joined Xavier in the dressing room. "How is it that we'll visit a man who has died? Are we going to die too?"

"No." Xavier shook his head. "We're not going to die. Not just yet. That's all I can tell you for the time being."

"Did you have something to do with his death?" Demetria folded her arms across her chest waiting for the answer.

"You'll have to trust me. We must change and get down to the pier. I'm sure it's filled with people waiting to see Castro off to his final resting-place. They'll be deceived by what they see. Our job is to make sure that they believe everything that they see."

Demetria didn't fully understand all that she was hearing. Her uncle's words ran through her mind. *No matter what happens, you must trust your visions.* "Xavier, I need you to tell me the truth. What really happened to my uncle tonight?"

Xavier looked up at the ceiling and blew all the air from his lungs. He sat down next to Demetria and started to hold her, but thought better of it, and put his hands in his lap. "Castro is not dead." The words quietly left his lips. "He will soon be on his way to the United States."

"Why? What are they going to do to him?" Demetria asked frantically.

"I don't know. And that's the truth." Xavier placed both palms on his chest. "I do know that they don't want him dead, because if they did, he would be."

Demetria bristled. "What do you mean by that?"

"If they had wanted him dead I would have been required to kill him. Right now, he's just under the influence of drugs. And we must make the people believe he is dead. If we don't, we're all dead, starting with your uncle." Xavier answered sternly. "I can only assume this is what the CIA planned after talking with you."

The couple left the room and joined the guards in the main quarters waiting to escort them to the waterfront. Demetria sobbed at the sight of her uncle lying on top of the pyre at the pier. She was so confused at the moment that she didn't know what to believe. Try as she might, no visions came forth to ease her confusion.

Xavier raised his hands to quiet the crowd. Heavily armed guards stood all around him. They were there to ward off any attempts on their new president and to squelch any attempts to get closer to Castro's body. After a few moments, they were quiet, and Xavier began to speak.

"Today I've been blessed, and I've suffered a great loss. I gained a wife, and lost a mentor. It's the latter that brings us here tonight. As you are watching the sun set on our country, you also will witness the return of our former leader to the heavens. Castro came to rule this country in a blaze of gunfire, which signaled the birth of a new Cuba. He shall leave tonight in a blaze of glory, which too will signal the birth of a new Cuba. Join me in singing our national anthem as we return our leader to his maker."

The people sang, and Guzman started his boat pulling the pyre off shore before lighting it. In the water, already black with nightfall, three SEALs observed the events on the shore. Five hundred meters further sat an American sub. Inside, Admiral Gregory also witnessed the unfolding events through his periscope.

Once Guzman reached a distance of seven hundred meters from shore, he stopped the boat. He lowered his anchor to prevent the boat and pyre from drifting back. He lifted an unlit torch, soaked in kerosene, and moved to the back of the boat. The pyre also was soaked in kerosene to ensure a quick start and a brilliant fire. Guzman grabbed the towline and pulled the pyre to the rear. He had not carefully checked the boat before leaving and didn't notice a leak in the fuel line that fed the engine. Pulling a Zippo lighter from his pocket, he flicked his thumb to start the flame needed to light the torch. Trustworthy as ever, the lighter lit on his first effort. He placed it on the side of the torch, which caught immediately. Guzman waved the torch towards the pyre. The fumes from the leaking fuel line ignited and the boat's engine exploded. A fireball engulfed the boat sending bits of teak into the air.

Xavier's heart stopped when he saw the explosion. Looking out over the water, he saw two separate burning objects in the ocean. "Oh my God." The words left his lips as if he were speaking a prayer. No one, except Demetria, realized that he said this in English. The explosion was too overwhelming, and that held their attention.

In the water, the SEALs went to work. Guzman, who was scheduled to return with them tonight, was blown ten meters from the boat, which went unnoticed by his fellow SEALs. The fire on the pyre was burning much faster than anticipated, causing the SEALs to work at a frantic pace. Their orders were to recover Castro and return to the sub. The explosion left them one man short, and because of the rapidly burning fire, they had less time to perform the job.

The SEALs moved to the underside of the pyre. Using an underwater drill, they removed the screws holding the plate, which would free Castro's body. Half way through their procedure, they noticed another rapidly approaching obstacle in the water.

With his digital radio mask, Keys spoke to the other SEALs. "The explosion must have injured Guzman. Sharks are moving into the area. We'll have to hurry if we have any chance of rescuing Guzman." He knew Guzman shouldn't be too hard to find. The sharks would lead them to him.

They worked at a furious pace to free the plate. The last bolt was almost out when it stuck under of the weight of the off-centered metal. The three men grabbed the plate and jerked until it fell free. Castro's body crashed into the water. Instantly, one of the SEALs retrieved a mask, placed it over Castro's mouth and nose, and turned the knob, freeing the mixture of oxygen and nitrogen. It only contained enough for ten minutes, which, under normal circumstances, would have been enough to make the return trip to the sub. Now, however, they had to find Guzman as well as an alternative meal for the sharks if they wanted to get him out in one piece.

The SEALs swam around, trying to find Guzman among the sharks. Two minutes elapsed. They also were careful not to place themselves on the shark's menu. There was no moon out tonight, making it impossible to use their lights in the water for fear that someone might detect them. One of the SEALs located Guzman and alerted the others. Two sharks made a pass, bumping into him, trying to get some type of reaction. Luckily, he'd been knocked unconscious by the blast. Quickly, one of the SEALs pulled a spear gun from his leg and shot one of the two passing sharks. The wounded shark twitched trying to free itself from the spear's barb embedded in its side. Blood spewed from its side, which was enough to take the attention from Guzman. Other sharks quickly moved in on their wounded companion.

The SEAL who had first spotted Guzman swam to the surface. Smoke still rose from Guzman's badly burnt flesh. Carefully, he placed the extra mask and tank on Guzman who for the first time twitched and grunted in pain. At least he was alive. The team took Castro and Guzman and swam rapidly towards the waiting sub. Four and a half minutes had elapsed and they were still about three minutes from the sub. They were careful not to attract any unwanted attention from the sharks. Using a section of the plastic that covered the president's cigars, they wrapped Guzman's wounds as they swam. The biggest shark in the group was now in pursuit of the swimmers, attracted by the noise and trail of blood. Other than knives, the last useful weapon they had was a bang stick, which held a twelve-gauge 00 buckshot shell in the tip.

The leader of the SEAL group yelled. "Everyone stop! I'll have only one attempt at this sucker coming at us. We can't out-swim the bastard, so if I miss I'll try to hold him off while you get to the ship."

"Don't you think it'll be difficult to hold off a fish that weighs a thousand pounds per foot?" He pointed in the direction of the oncoming shark. "And that's one big motherfucker!"

"I'll do what I can. You all make sure you don't move until I hit him. We don't want him to go into a feeding frenzy."

No one moved a muscle. The shark was closing in very fast. The SEAL raised the stick, ready to bring it down right on the shark's nose. If he didn't hit the shark directly on the nose, he couldn't kill the animal. Timing would be the key to success, since he had no way to reload. The shark reached him, but veered. Thrusting the stick downward, the SEAL missed the shark entirely. The shot didn't explode. He raised the bang stick for another try. The shark circled the team, stopping just before the SEAL holding the stick. Precious time slipped by. Nine minutes and fifteen seconds had elapsed. Without any warning, the shark turned and swam away.

"You all go on. I'm going to wait a second or two to make sure Jaws don't try to come back."

They swam to the sub. The SEAL pulling Castro tried to determine whether he was still alive by looking for condensation in his mask but it was futile under these conditions. Thirty seconds later, the third SEAL caught up to the others. The sub was in sight and everyone swam faster. They all wanted this night to be over as soon as possible.

They reached the sub and pushed Castro through the hatch first, followed by one of the SEALs. The second SEAL turned to get a better grasp on Guzman and to push him into the hatch. He turned and screamed, "Look out, the shark!"

The SEAL carrying the bang stick spun.

The shark closed quickly.

Without thinking, he thrust the stick forward. The charge went off as it hit the shark's nose, but the momentum propelled the fifteen hundred-pound shark forward, and it slammed into the SEAL, knocking him backward into the side of sub. Bubbles rapidly escaped his mask. He floated limp and motionless. The shark's lifeless body slowly drifted to the ocean floor. The stick had done its job.

The injured SEAL struggled to get to the hatch. The force of the shark had knocked the breath from his lungs, leaving him only momentarily unconscious. Four of his ribs had broken. In intense pain, he swam for the hatch.

The first SEAL entered the hatch and pulled Castro and Guzman's limp bodies in behind him. The second team member waited until the injured team leader arrived. They swam in together.

The two uninjured SEALs hurried from the pool to get gurneys for Guzman and Castro. Guzman had second and third degree burns over most of his body. When they got him on the gurney, he attempted to speak. "Did… did we make it?"

They looked down on him. "Yeah, we all made it."

Mercifully, Guzman slipped into unconsciousness.

Chapter
64

On the Cuban shore, men moved frantically to get to boats. Xavier demanded that someone take him to investigate the explosion. Three boats arrived at the pier simultaneously. Schaffer jumped in just before Xavier and steadied the boat by pulling the tie line around a pylon.

Demetria watched in near panic as Xavier boarded. "You aren't going to leave me here by myself!"

"It may not be safe for you out there." As hard as he tried to implore, he could see that she was in no mood to be deterred.

"I've lost one man who was very close to me today," she said. "If the other is to die, then I'll go with him."

"On second thought, you should come along." He held out his hand. He wanted her to see that there was no trace of Castro's body in the water.

She stepped towards the boat and Xavier helped her in.

When the boats pulled out, the loud creaking planks of the pyre rose above the roar of the boat engines. The sea swallowed the burning heap. Xavier sighed with relief at the sight of the capsizing pyre. No one would see any remnants, so no one would know Castro's body was absent.

The men on the boats shined lanterns onto the water. The light could not penetrate the water in the dark of night. The sea reflected the distorted images of the horde searching for the sunken tomb.

One of the men holding a lantern raised it above his head. "This is the spot. See, oil remains on the surface."

"Yes," Xavier said. "It would also appear that Guzman is lost as well. He's had some unwanted company." Xavier pointed to a tattered and burned shirt floating near a group of sharks looking for a feast. They swam around the sunken pyre. Xavier wondered if this was how things were for mother and father when they swam from Cuba.

One of his men used a gaff to pull the shirt from the water. "What shall we do now, sir?"

"There is nothing anyone can do except pray for their souls."

Xavier took a flashlight from one of the men and shined it a little further out to sea. Schaffer looked towards the shining light. They both saw the gentle swirl of the water, indicating the sub's departure from the area.

For a long time Xavier looked out onto the sea. Ambivalence coursed through him as he realized he'd just completed his last mission as a Navy SEAL. The realization left him with the unsettling duty of having to lead Cuba out of the darkness.

He turned to the man piloting the boat. "Let's return to shore. There's a lot that I must do before morning."

Demetria moved to the fore of the boat where Xavier stood. Gently she placed her arms around his waist, and laid her head on his back. No words needed to be spoken to convey her love and compassion for him. Momentarily ignoring her grief, she wanted to ease his pain. She knew that tonight her husband lost two friends.

When they reached the shore, Father Jose was the first to greet them. "I understand there's been another tragedy tonight. Why don't the two of you return to your home? You need the rest."

"Padré, I must finish here first. These people will expect their leader to explain the events of the evening before going in for the night. I can't let them down. Would you kindly grace us with a blessing for those who've died tonight?"

Father Jose stretched out his hands and began to speak of restless souls. The strong wind stirring the sea intensified his words. He made the sign of the cross over the water. The people in attendance signed themselves, and the wind halted, which they took as a sign that restlessness in their country had also come to an end, and that peace would now prevail.

Chapter 65

The front page of the *Washington Post* held pictures of Castro on one side and Xavier Ciefuentes on the other. A full color picture of the burning pyre sat beneath their photos. The headline read:

CASTRO DEAD. CIEFUENTES TAKES OVER. SENDS CASTRO OFF IN A BLAZE.

Yesterday, during the wedding of his niece, Demetria Castro to Xavier Ciefuentes, the newly appointed President of Cuba, Castro suffered a fatal heart attack. Ciefuentes decided that Castro should return to his maker in the same fashion in which he took over Cuba, in a blaze of glory.

The funeral was held on the ocean, in what is more typical of a Viking funeral. As evidenced by his actions, Ciefuentes is wasting no time assuming his new role as Cuba's leader. Appointed by Castro, most of the Communist Party faithful of Cuba will expect Ciefuentes to conduct business as usual, but will quickly learn this could not be further from the truth. Ciefuentes covered the countryside, assuring the people that change is blowing into Cuba. Not once in any of his speeches has he professed an allegiance to their party.

Ciefuentes told this reporter that his plans include bringing the United States in to aid the rebuilding of Cuba. However, he said many of the programs that Castro implemented will remain in effect. For instance, all children must graduate from high school, and if they desire, college is free for those who qualify. In addition, medical care is free to all in Cuba. Cuba remains one of the most medically advanced countries in the world. He also stated the U.S. should not return expecting to take over the island. "We're not for sale, but we welcome the United States' assistance."

Ciefuentes plans to open his country to all people. In an interview conducted earlier he said, "We were once known as a playground for the rich. It is easy to see why. We have the most beautiful island in the Caribbean, and we have a festive, loving people waiting to share our riches with the world."

Ciefuentes has also offered the possibility of joint partnerships with the Americans in regards to businesses that were nationalized when Castro took over. One stipulation he set forth is that the Cuban people must remain in their jobs, with a fair wage comparable to their foreign counterparts. In addition, at least half of the management positions will go to the locals. He stated that he will allow no one to come in and take advantage of his people, who have suffered enough.

This is a great opportunity for the President of the United States to show good will towards the Cubans, and solve some of the problems that have existed between the two countries for over forty years. He has a chance to do good in a country plagued by poverty, and, in return, both countries will be enriched. The gesture surely will be viewed favorably by other Latin American countries, such as Venezuela, which should loosen the flow of their oil, relieving the rising inflation the American people have had to bear during President Nicholas' first term in office.

¤¤¤¤

"Annie, call a press conference for 11:00 a.m. We have to get on the air and let the Cubans know that we're ready to move in and help them. After that, call the crew and make sure that they are on time for this morning's meeting. We have a lot of work to do."

"Right away, Mr. President."

The president didn't try to hide his smile. "We've done it!" He shouted and made the short trip to his humidor and picked out a cigar. "This is not one of Castro's any more." He lit the cigar and slipped out of his side door, hurrying across the two hundred yard path to his study. Viewing his kingdom today gave him tremendous pleasure. In a few short months, his plans had come together. Removing Castro from power would allow him to relieve tensions with other Latin American countries. He was ready to plan a celebration to toast their success. Abruptly, the sound of familiar footsteps brought him back to reality.

Annie approached. "Your morning meeting is ready to begin whenever you are, Mr. President. The pressroom will be ready at 11:00. Calls are already coming in, asking questions ranging from who you'll name as Ambassador to Cuba, to how long before you'll send a delegation to Cuba. Have you written a list of questions that you will not respond to during the press conference?" Annie paused. "I would like to have them distributed to the press before you arrive."

Alex felt jovial, free from stress for the first time in months. "I think we'll leave the floor open to all questions today, Annie. Of course we've not contacted the President of Cuba as of yet." He smiled. "Until we do, there're a lot of items that we can only speculate about. Don't worry. I'll be ready for them." He gave Annie a kiss on the cheek and turned to go down the hall to his meeting.

"Congratulations, sir." Annie beamed with pride as he walked away. Soon she hoped to accompany the president on an official visit to Cuba.

Alex bounced as he walked into his office. "Good morning all. I trust you've had a chance to read the good news. So let's get down to the business of Cuba." He moved around his desk and took his seat.

"We need to put together a delegation I can lead to Cuba. We'll go to assess the needs of the country, and to re-establish trading ties with them. As a gesture of good faith, we'll present them with a check for a purchase of sugar, rum and cigars. Of course, we'll have a freighter on its way to pick up what we purchase. Let me hear some of your ideas."

Vice President Gillespie said, "I think our delegation should be comprised of business men and women who can best help the Cubans begin to rebuild their country. Of course, it should include those who Castro threw out when he took over. Any property that was theirs should be returned."

"Your idea to send in businessmen is good." Alex complimented Gillespie. "However, there's no way we should expect former businesses and land to be returned. Too much time has expired. It'll never happen. The CEOs who choose to return to Cuba are shrewd enough to get what they need. Let's leave it at that."

Mackenzie spoke up: "More importantly, we need to go in and establish a sound government. We can't leave such an important task to Commander Benderis. He has no experience."

"What if he has already begun this process on his own?" Director Caprelotti stood ready to move in and eliminate any problem people.

General Roseboro jumped into the discussion. "He has proven himself quite capable, gentlemen. We all agreed that he can't be removed from this position too soon. We should suggest that free elections be held in one year to allow the people to choose whom they would like to run their country. By then Commander Benderis will be ready to come home and we can exert our influence on any candidate that we choose."

"You sound very sure, General Roseboro. He may enjoy the power he has tasted and not be willing to relinquish it," Press Secretary Tynes said, flipping open his pad, jotting down some notes.

Alex stood, asserting his will. "All of you are forgetting that this man works for my office. He is a dedicated SEAL who'll obey orders from his commander in chief. Let's not worry about him and move on."

The meeting went on for another forty-five minutes. Alex and his cabinet concentrated on the press conference, emphasizing aid to Cuba and reestablishing diplomatic ties.

The hour for the press conference rapidly approached. Alex stood to leave. Annie beeped the intercom. "Mr. President, I have President Ciefuentes on the line for you."

Everyone in the room turned and looked at the president. Alex looked at each of his cabinet members. "Put him through, Annie."

Slowly Alex took his seat. "This is President Nicholas."

"Hello, Mr. President. This is President Xavier Ciefuentes of Cuba. We, the Cuban people, would like to request a meeting with the United States. It's time to dispel the disdain that's kept our countries apart."

"I couldn't agree more." Alex muted the speaker. "He's playing the part really well, don't you think?"

"It doesn't sound like he is playing, if you ask me," Director Caprelotti offered.

"How do you suggest we precede, President Ciefuentes?" Alex sat back in his chair and bounced an Opus X between his fingers.

"As a show of goodwill and to express our sincere desire to work with the United States, we will place the four men detained here on a flight home." Xavier gave Alex a moment to consider his gesture. "Our country needs money to build and create a better working environment. Your country needs our products. We'd be willing to discuss allowing businesses from your country to re-enter Cuba. I must caution you, though. Any businesses that come here must continue to employ Cubans, at a comparable wage to any American workers. In addition, at least fifty percent of the managerial positions, in these plants must remain with my people. The opportunity also exists for minority ownership of some of our companies. No foreign company however, will be allowed to purchase more than fifteen percent of our existing companies. New industry will be welcomed as long as they meet the aforementioned stipulations. There can be no negotiation on these points."

"I congratulate you for taking the first step and freeing our men. We graciously accept your gesture of good will. I'm sure that everything else can be worked out in a meeting between our respective governments." The president frowned and again, muted the speaker. *Who does he think he is, making these demands?* Alex wondered, baffled at Xavier's words, his tone. *He works for me.*

Director Caprelotti offered his opinion: "From the beginning of this conversation he's sounded much too official. He's supposed to be your SEAL, not your contemporary. Would you like me to prepare my team for an extraction?"

"Sit tight, Anthony. Let's not jump to any conclusions." Turning his attention back to his phone call, Alex reengaged the speaker. "When would you suggest we begin our talks?"

"I'm sure you have a team ready to move. Tomorrow is Tuesday. I think we shouldn't wait too long. Bring your team to Cuba Friday. We can begin then."

Alex sat back in his chair trying to collect his thoughts. "Will you have a negotiating team in place that soon?"

"They're currently preparing the conference room for our meeting. We look forward to meeting with you and your team on Friday."

Confident that the United States was prepared, Alex tapped his hand against his desk. "Then it's set. America shall officially return to Cuban soil on Friday."

"Very well." Almost under his breath, Xavier redirected the conversation. "Did Guzman make it?"

"We're still waiting for the final reports, but they made it to the sub alive. Guzman was severely injured. I'll have more information for you on Friday."

"Sir, I look forward to seeing you again." Without another word, Xavier hung up the phone.

The president sat listening to the buzzing phone line. The look on his face was one of concern and disbelief. It took a moment for him to lift his head. Was he to treat this man as his equal? Xavier worked for him, for God's sake...

Chapter
66

The Shipjack class submarine cut through the Atlantic at thirty knots.

The teardrop shaped hull of the sub made it to appear to be a giant nuclear-powered mahi-mahi cruising the ocean. On board Dr. Hunter worked frantically through the night to stabilize Guzman. She did the best she could with her unskilled assistants and limited supplies aboard ship. Guzman needed an advanced burn unit as quickly as possible.

"We'll have to air-vac him out as soon as we can get to any port." Dr. Hunter informed the balance of her team. By zero three hundred hours, she turned her attention to Castro. "Time to get a new face, Mr. Castro."

The team assisted, gauging a proper anesthesia and amount, and administering it to Castro. Within minutes, they were ready to begin. The first item of business was to shave Castro's head and face. Next, subcutaneous incisions were made behind his ears, beside the nose and chin. A metal probe was inserted into each incision and used to separate the skin from the skull. Once loosened, the surgeon broke Castro's nose, removed bones, and re-shaped it into a new form. Dr. Hunter reshaped cheeks and chin with silicone, held in place with small titanium screws. Dr. Hunter sutured the incisions and began winding gauze around Castro's head.

"He looks like Frankenstein," one member of her team suggested.

"Frankenstein was the doctor, not the monster," someone explained. "Dumbass."

"I hope he doesn't look that bad," Dr. Hunter said. "I've tried to do a little better than a hack job."

They all laughed.

She completed applying bandages to his entire head. The next time Castro looked in the mirror, he wouldn't recognize the person he saw. He was clean-shaven and Dr. Hunter had shaven off several years from his face as well.

In a few days, if everything went as planned, they would deliver Castro to the president's team. From that point on, no member of the SEAL team would know where the former President of Cuba was. As far as they were concerned, he died, just as the Cuban people believed.

Castro remained under heavy sedation for almost two days. The entire SEAL team stayed in the isolated area of the sub with him. They took turns watching over him, seeing to his needs.

They received word from the naval burn unit that Guzman was doing better and would live. He still faced a long recovery and would need extensive skin grafts and plastic surgery to repair the damage he had suffered. He'd be in the hospital for several months at a minimum. The other SEALs decided to save their cigars until Guzman could enjoy one with the rest of the team.

A low moan rose from behind the bandages. The current watchman moved closer to investigate. Groggily, Castro addressed him, asking, "What happened to me?" He attempted to touch his face, but could only feel bandages. He wanted to sit up, but the influence of the drugs would not allow him to rise.

"You are on a United States Naval Submarine en route to Norfolk Virginia," the SEAL answered in perfect Spanish.

"How long have I been here? Where is my niece? Where is Xavier?" Castro's eyes widened despite the drugs and appeared as if he may be in a panic.

"Take it easy, sir. We are here to help you. In a day or so, you will meet with the President of the United States. There, I'm sure, you'll find out everything you need to know."

Castro settled back into his pillow and tried to compose his thoughts. He could tell that he was in no immediate danger, though he didn't remember what had happened. He did know that he wouldn't see Cuba again. For that matter, he wasn't likely to see Demetria, Xavier, or anyone else he knew. His tears burned as they ran onto his freshly stitched face. He understood this was how things had to be. Even so, his acquiescence did nothing to ease his pain, mental or physical.

Chapter 67

At first light, Schaffer stood on the pier where Castro's funeral pyre had been launched.

He was carrying scuba equipment that he'd rented for the day. Schaffer tossed everything into a boat that he also rented for the morning. After making sure everything worked properly, he climbed aboard and started the engine. He wanted to be the first person out that day because he knew others would soon fill the water looking for souvenirs from their fallen leader.

Schaffer looked at his Breitling's stopwatch function. Last night, when Guzman pulled the pyre out to sea, he started the stopwatch, and stopped it when Guzman reached his destination. In about ninety seconds, he was in the general area where the pyre went down. The waters were crystal clear, which made it easier to locate the downed vessels in the first light of dawn.

He threw the anchor over the side of the boat and waited for it to settle. He sat to pull on the scuba gear. He checked the gear for the third time, slid it in place and flopped backwards, plunging into the water. Clear waters are deceptively deep. It took him a while to reach what was left of the two sunken vessels. Schaffer swam around the pyre and boat looking for any sign of former life. He found it strange to find no bits of clothing or any sign of anything human on the bottom near the burnt out boats. About fifty yards from the boat, he discovered the remains of a shark's dorsal fin that appeared as if ripped from a shark's body. Schaffer reached out to retrieve it and his hand hit another object. He brushed away the sand exposing a machine bolt, bent so severely it nearly formed a 'J'. Swimming over to the pyre, he found the hull completely burnt out. He ventured in, and after a few seconds realized the pyre was lying on its side and that the bottom was gone. Strange, because the water should have prevented too much damage on the bottom. As he swam from the port side of the pyre, he saw the sun reflect off something on the bottom. Schaffer moved in for a closer inspection. It was a large metal object that he couldn't lift by himself. When he brushed away the sand, he saw a hole in the corner. Schaffer took the bolt from a pouch on his side and placed it into the hole. It was a prefect fit.

Looking back to the bottom of the pyre, he realized that the plate of metal came from the bottom of it. *Why would anyone remove…*before he could finish his thought, Schaffer had the answer: someone had removed Castro's body! But why, and more importantly, who?

It was time to get back to shore and question Xavier as to what was going on. First, he wanted to make one last pass by Guzman's shack to look for other clues. Since Guzman apparently died in the explosion, his house should be intact. It wouldn't be long before the Cubans would be investigating this site themselves. Then the questions would surely start. As Schaffer drew nearer to the surface, he could see the boats beginning to arrive.

This was only the second time Schaffer went to Guzman's apartment. It was a little two-room shack just outside Havana. Inside stood a bed, one chair and a small table. Schaffer walked in, not sure what he was looking for. With what he'd already seen off shore, he wasn't surprised when he didn't find any of Guzman's personal belongings. It seemed as if Guzman never planned to return to this place.

Schaffer sat in the chair, exhaled, and remained completely quiet. The only alternative he could reach was that Guzman had faked his death. The bottom was removed from the pyre and no traces of either of the two men remained. He wondered why it was so important to remove Castro's body. Rather than struggling with speculation or indulging his imagination, he contacted Dee.

"I just got out of a meeting, sugar," Dee said. "How are you feeling today?"

"After I get home, you owe me dinner so we can discuss this 'sugar' thing."

"It'll be my pleasure." She smiled.

"So, it's a date. Until then, how about a little of your full disclosure? What the hell have you all done with Castro's body?" Schaffer said, bluntly reaching the point.

Dee's jovial tone was gone. "Schaffer, we can't discuss anything else about Operation Smokeout until we're face to face. At that time I'll tell you everything."

"I've busted my ass for you and Alex." Schaffer slammed his fist against the side of Guzman's bed. "The least you can do is fill me in."

"Not over this thing." Dee looked at her device.

"Why, is someone else listening?" Schaffer looked over his shoulder.

"I've told you that we are the only two to have these instruments. That does not preclude anyone from using conventional means to intercept one side of our conversation." Dee was with a team of Secret Servicemen sweeping her office for bugs. They had already detected several that had been placed there since the morning sweep. Under normal conditions, once a day was sufficient to sweep for bugs; but lately she had the Secret Service check several times a day and never at the same intervals. She jotted a note for the men to leave one of the bugs and go to sweep the president's office again.

"Sugar, see the red plate near the top of your transmitter?"

Schaffer looked at it carefully. "Yeah, what's it for?"

"Place your right thumb across it."

Schaffer did as she asked and a screen rolled from the top of the transmitter. Across the screen, a message read: *"I alone can hear you but someone wants to hear what I say to you. The Secret Service just found four bugs in my office. I left one in place to throw my intruder off."*

"Damn, Dee. You'd better watch out. Looks like our killer may be back at work."

"My thought exactly," she said in response.

He looked at the screen as another message scrolled across.

"I sent the Secret Service back to the president's office. They'll sweep it every time anyone comes or goes."

"Good idea. We've made someone nervous again. Make sure you keep several good men around you at all times. You know, of course, that it has to be someone on the inside who can come and go as he pleases."

"I'll be in touch soon. Bye, sugar."

Schaffer hurriedly left the shack in search of Xavier. When he reached the compound, the guards prevented him from entering.

"We have orders not to allow anyone passage to the compound. You will have to go," an irritated guard insisted.

"I don't give a damn what your orders are, you get on that radio and let the president know that I'm here to see him." Schaffer demanded.

"I'm sorry sir, we —"

Schaffer snatched the guard's rifle from him, placed it under his head and moved behind him in one swift motion. "Do I have your fucking attention now? I've had a bad day and you're not helping to make it better."

Immediately, Schaffer drew the attention of several other guards. The commander of the guard recognized him and told the other guards to lower their weapons. "Is there a problem here?"

"You bet your ass there is. I politely asked this bastard to let the president know I was here. As you can see, he refused. Now what do you think we can do about that?"

"If you will lower the weapon, I'm sure we can work something out."

"Not a chance." Schaffer was careful to keep all the soldiers in sight. "Get on that fucking radio now! I'm in no mood for games."

Demetria, coming back from her afternoon walk, noticed the problem at the front gate. She walked over to lend her assistance. "Mr. Gonzales, this seems to be a bit extreme."

"I tried to be reasonable, but no one will listen." Schaffer told Demetria and kept the gun in place. "I need to speak with Xavier."

"That's a reasonable request. If you would be so kind to release this man I'll escort you to the house." Demetria shot a stern look at the guards and waited for Schaffer to join her.

"Thank you very much." Schaffer pushed the man to his knees and held on to his rifle until he was with Demetria. "These men could use more training. I was able to take over too quickly."

"Indeed." She looked harshly at the commander of the guard. "Come this way, we'll find my husband."

"Ah, Dr. O'Grady how nice of you to visit." Xavier sat in a large leather chair smoking a Cohiba robusto. "Can I offer you one?"

Still irritated, Schaffer looked at Xavier. "I've never smoked a cigar, but today seems like a good time to start."

Xavier pulled one from his humidor. "Be sure not to inhale the smoke. It is just for taste, and in your case, relaxation."

Schaffer took the cigar. Following Xavier's instructions, he lit the end before bringing it to his mouth. He drew deeply from the cigar, allowing the thick blue smoke to escape his lips. "That's got some kick. I think I understand what all the fuss is about." He took another draw from the cigar. He felt relaxation spreading over his body. After another puff or two, Schaffer mellowed, and could feel the beginnings of a slight buzz.

"You wanted to talk to me, I understand." Xavier puffed his cigar.

Schaffer glanced around the room. "Are we alone?"

Xavier never moved. "Yes, I believe we are."

"Turn off your transmitter." Schaffer pointed to Xavier's pen.

"What?" Xavier pulled the cigar from his mouth shocked by what Schaffer said.

Schaffer pointed to his device and earpiece.

Xavier pulled the pen from his pocket and sat it down.

"Good," Schaffer said. "What's going on here?"

"What do you mean, Dr. O'Grady?" Xavier asked innocently.

"I went out to the site where the pyre went down last night and there's no trace of any corpse." Schaffer reached in his pocket feeling for the bolt. "There's not the slightest sign that anyone was on either of those boats."

"My dear Dr. O'Grady, I should have known that you would go out to investigate." Xavier drew deeply from his cigar and let the smoke slowly escape his mouth. "Of course, there's no information that I can share with you at this time."

"You owe me that much!" Schaffer pounded Xavier's desk.

"I owe you more than that. However, there's nothing that I can tell you because, I don't know anything."

"You'd better get ready to answer questions from your people. The water is full of boats where the pyre went down." Schaffer's face softened. "At least tell me if Guzman is okay. He could really get under your skin, but he was my friend."

Xavier looked more serious. "I only know that he made it. There's no other report at this time."

"How about Castro, did he make it also?"

Xavier laughed. "You overestimate my knowledge. What makes you think that I have any more information than you do? You saw with your own eyes that Castro died at the wedding."

"Did he really? Or is that what we were made to believe? If he died, why is there no trace of a corpse? And why was this removed from the bottom of the pyre along with a large metal plate?" Schaffer tossed Xavier the bolt he found on the ocean floor. "You don't expect me to believe sharks took this bolt out too?"

Xavier picked up the bolt and examined it. "I have no idea."

They continued smoking their cigars in silence.

Demetria walked in. "Can I bring either of you a drink?"

"That would be nice," they answered in unison.

"Will port be okay?"

"Certainly," Xavier answered.

She left to fill their request.

"Look Xavier," Schaffer said, "I know you told Demetria that Castro wasn't dead and that he was on his way to the United States."

Xavier rocked in his chair. "How could you have possibly have heard that?"

Schaffer slid out his transmitter and earpiece. "You're transmitting now. Why don't I turn it off for a minute?" He turned off the receiver. "I've been working with the president to try and solve Chief of Staff Harold Cosby's murder. When someone decided that I should join Cosby in the grave, I hopped on a plane and headed here to see for myself what you were doing. This thing continued to work so I guess the president decided having me here was to his benefit. I've monitored you, your men, and certain places at the White House since before I arrived here in Havana. You should be careful what you say when you are transmitting, because the NSA can hear you as well. They may not like what you have told Demetria about Castro. They won't risk letting that information become public. Cosby died trying to tell me about this operation." Schaffer stopped abruptly. "I've got to ask you a question. Was your assignment to become President of Cuba and send Castro to the U.S.?"

"I was sent here to eliminate Castro's reign. I was just as surprised as you when he named me to fill his post." Xavier puffed on the cigar. "Now that it has happened, I can't let my people down."

"I'm glad to hear you say that." Schaffer edged forward in his seat. "In that case, you'd better prepare yourself for what will come next. The president and his team will be hard hitting trying to force their will."

"They've grossly underestimated us. We're ready." Xavier looked towards the door.

Demetria returned with the filled glasses. They took the glasses, and Xavier spoke. "The President of the United States will be here Friday. He asked if you were still in the country. He also wanted to thank you for the stories coming from Cuba. It seems they'll help to get him re-elected. He also would like for you to join the American delegation during the negotiations."

"Yeah, I heard. He asked my editor if I'd be interested in the Press Secretary position." Schaffer sighed. "I hate politics, especially re-election politics."

"That may be the way for you to get answers to your questions," Xavier suggested and sipped his wine.

"I hadn't thought of it that way. Maybe I'll be able to stomach it for a while."

"Then I'll see you Friday?"

"That sounds like a good idea." A frown crossed Schaffer's face. "By the way, would you please make sure that your goons know that I'll be expected? I'd hate to have to take matters into my hands again."

"Consider it done."

Schaffer drained his glass and stood to leave the room. "I'll see you on Friday. Until then, might I suggest you rethink transmitting your every move. If you're content to stay on as the president of this country, your people will need a leader, not a puppet controlled by the States. I'm sure that's not what your mother had in mind."

Chapter
68

Schaffer turned and walked back to the front of Xavier's desk.

"There's another reason I came here."

Xavier lowered his cigar to an ashtray. "Mr. Valencia."

"Exactly."

Xavier knitted his fingers and brought them to his face. "I'm supposed to keep them isolated until we get them home."

Schaffer sat back down. "Under whose orders? You're not subject to orders from anyone. You're the President of Cuba now. Tito hasn't been in contact with his family for months, none of them have. You said you didn't know where they were… they could be rotting away in some prison for all we know."

"They've not been rotting away." Xavier lifted the cigar and took a puff. "This may really surprise you. Then again, maybe not. You seem to be ahead of everyone else on just about everything. I just found the men myself. They've been very well cared for. Demetria…"

The door to the office opened and Demetria walked in. "Can I get you anything else?"

Xavier held out his hand. "We were just talking about you."

She walked over and took his hand. "What were you saying?"

Xavier nodded towards Schaffer. "Dr. O'Grady here was inquiring about four men that have been under your care."

Demetria looked at Schaffer suspiciously. "When did you stop using Gonzales? Am I to believe now that you're Irish?"

Schaffer snickered. "I get that a lot. O'Grady is the name my great-great grandfather chose when his father set him free from slavery."

"What is your interest in the men?"

Schaffer appeared more serious. "One of the men, Tito Valencia, is my best friend. No one from home has heard from him in months. He said if I didn't find him that he was dead. There was also something about a setup."

Demetria smiled. "Mr. Valencia is quite charming." Her smile dropped. "From what I've seen of his record, he's also quite dangerous. I'm surprised he never tried to escape, but then again that would not have made much sense."

Schaffer worked to think his way past his confusion. "There's something I'm missing here. How do you know that Tito is charming and why wouldn't escape make sense?"

"Dr. O'Grady, I have met often with the men. They were as confused as you are about their capture. They insisted that they were here on a diplomatic mission. It wasn't until your government's CIA representatives met with them that their fear subsided. Since then, only a few soldiers and I have known where they are. My uncle didn't even want to know."

Schaffer's surprise was audible. "You've held them all this time? What could they possibly have that you want? When can I see them?"

"They have nothing that I want, Dr. O'Grady," Demetria said forcefully before relaxing her expression. She sat beside Schaffer. "I understand your eagerness to see them. Maybe we can help each other."

Schaffer sat forward, leaning to give Demetria his full attention. "I'll do whatever I can."

Demetria touched Schaffer's knee. "My husband says that you are a man of your word. Once we hand the men over to the United States, you are the only hope I have." She swallowed hard and brought her hands to her face as if praying. "My uncle put me in charge of the four men and told me that they could prove invaluable. I didn't understand, but I did as he asked. Since he wouldn't allow me to tell him where I planned to take them, I hid them at his mountain home."

"Castle is more like it," Xavier chimed in. "I was there earlier. That's where we'll hold the meeting on Friday."

Schaffer shot Xavier a stern look. "You've seen the men. Is Tito okay?"

"Everybody is fine. They have not suffered in the least."

"Dr. O'Grady, I doubt anything you've witnessed here in Cuba was a mistake. I don't know why those men were captured, but I know my uncle wanted me to take care of them. Now, they are my only hope of finding out anything about my uncle. Will you help?"

Schaffer dropped back in his chair and put both hands on top of his head. "You think they are connected to your uncle?"

"I'm certain of it! I just don't know how."

"I want to know as badly as you do. When can I see Tito?"

¤¤¤¤

The car wound its way around the mountainous roads. Soon Schaffer saw the castle, and his heart raced with anticipation. He looked forward to the reunion.

Demetria and Xavier sat opposite Schaffer in the limo. Their conversation remained focused between them until crossing through the gates guarding the castle. Demetria addressed Schaffer. "I'm sure Mr. Valencia will be happy to see you. I know he misses home."

"I'm not sure who'll be the happiest," Schaffer said. "I stood up for him at his wedding. All I've been able to think about during the ride was Judy and the kids."

Demetria offered a warm smile. The car pulled to a stop and she reached for Schaffer's hand. "Let's go see you friend."

They entered the house and walked down a hall. Two guards stood beside two very large doors. Seeing Xavier and Demetria, the guards saluted and opened the doors. Inside the four CIA agents worked hand-in-hand with the delegation that was preparing the room for President Nicholas' visit.

Schaffer stood behind Xavier and Demetria with his head slightly bowed to give him the element of surprise. The first voice he heard came from Tito.

"It's my angel. I see you've brought friends."

Demetria put her hand on Xavier's shoulder. "This is my husband, Xavier Ciefuentes, President of Cuba."

Tito walked forward with his hand extended. "Your wife, sir has been a blessing these past few months." The next sound caused Tito to freeze in his tracks.

"Ooh-rah, devil dogs — fighting for the Corps even if we die." Schaffer stepped between Xavier and Demetria. He lunged forward and threw both arms around Tito. He was helpless to prevent the tears that freely flowed down his face. "I was worried I'd lost you."

The two men held on to each other rocking back and forth. Xavier watched them. "There's a bond we don't see often enough in the world." He ordered his men to bring refreshments to celebrate the reunion.

Schaffer sat down with the four agents. Tito slapped him on the back. "What took you so long?"

Schaffer's confusion returned. "Getting to Cuba was easy, but finding you guys was nearly impossible. What can you tell me about what happened?"

Tito looked at Xavier and Demetria, who were sitting just across the table.

Schaffer sensed his concern. "It's okay. Ciefuentes, until recently, was a Navy SEAL."

Tito did a double take. "But she introduced him as President of Cuba."

Schaffer nodded. "He is. Trust me, it's a long story, I'll fill you in." He explained as the four men listened. "So, now that you know what's been going on, why do you think you've been held so long?"

Tito and the other men had listened patiently. By the time Schaffer asked his question, Tito's puzzlement became a dumbfounded expression. "If the president sent you here to look for us, how come he didn't tell you that he had the assistant director of the CIA come here to meet with us and ask us to stay put until he sent for us?" Tito pointed to Demetria. "Angel here allowed us to call home once a week so our families wouldn't be worried."

Schaffer looked accusingly at Xavier. "Did you know any of this?"

Demetria answered. "I didn't tell Xavier, or my uncle. These men were given to me to protect. I didn't feel it was right for them to be cut off from their families, I let them call home on my own." Her eyes filled with tears and she looked at Schaffer. "Can any of you return the favor and let me talk to my uncle?"

Chapter
69

Reporters crammed into the East Room of the White House waiting for President Nicholas to arrive.

The networks also had reporters stationed on the White House lawn broadcasting live, explaining, with their usual clairvoyance, what those inside would hear during the press conference.

Alex strolled down the hall to the East Room accompanied by a host of Secret Service agents and several CEOs who would travel with him to Cuba.

A hush came over the room when Press Secretary Tynes took the podium. After several seconds, he looked up. "Ladies and gentlemen, the President of the United States."

Alex took the floor, welcomed his guests, and proceeded to tell them the United States would return to Cuba. Although the story had been leaked hours ago, the reporters welcomed the news with jubilation. The president went on to tell them that his delegation would leave Friday morning for Havana. After questions, he ended by introducing a few of the CEOs he'd personally asked to come along on the trade mission.

Just a few blocks from the White House, the Willard Hotel had ballrooms waiting for several press conferences being held by the CEOs making the trip to Cuba. After the president dismissed his conference, teams of reporters scurried to the hotel to continue coverage of the breaking news of Cuba. They also knew that a lavish reception awaited them after the press conferences. Deadlines be damned until they ate and drank on the companies' tabs.

John Cordell sat at home, eagerly anticipating USA Tobacco's press conference, which CNBC broadcast.

Robert Whittaker, President and CEO of USA Tobacco, conducted the conference. "We have been asked by the President of the United States to accompany him on a trade mission to Cuba. The new President of Cuba invited the U.S., and I anticipate that all former privately held companies, confiscated by Castro, will be returned to their rightful owners at this meeting. Thus, we'll gain the U.S. rights to ninety percent of all the Cuban cigar labels." Robert could not hide the smile that crept across his face.

Nor could he have been more wrong.

"Today my office has been flooded with calls from cigar shops around the U.S. requesting a supply of our newest cigars. It's my belief that this acquisition will have a profound effect on our company's earnings, providing us with greater profitability for years to come. We look forward to returning to Cuba, and providing them with new technology that will benefit both our interests. We'll increase the employment of the Cuban people, helping to deliver them from impoverishment. We also intend to maintain their management teams, adding advisors from our country. Let's face it. They've done an excellent job with the cigars they've produced. We only hope to aid the quantity of their production to make these cigars available to meet the increased demand."

Cordell raised his phone as the conference ended. He dialed Gus Stewart. By his calculations, he had $1.5 million in USA Tobacco stock when the market closed last night. The market was open for an hour and a half this morning, and the news relating to Cuba was disseminating quickly.

"Gus Stewart."

"Gus, it's —"

"Mr. O'Grady, I know," Gus interrupted.

"Dinner is on me tonight," Cordell said.

"Well I guess you're one happy person right about now."

"I guess you could say that. Where's the stock now?" Cordell asked eagerly.

"Since the announcement, it's already doubled in price, and is still climbing. With the popularity of cigars, there's no telling how high this thing can go. What would you like me to do?"

"I'd like you to pick out any restaurant in D.C., and tonight I'm taking you to dinner."

"Well, that's mighty nice of you."

"Come on, Gus. I told you everything would be okay," Cordell reassured him. "We didn't do anything illegal. There's nothing that the government can do to us."

Gus still felt uneasy. "That may be true, but you cost me ten years off my too-short life. Besides, my boss wouldn't let me buy any of the stock."

"You've got to be kidding? You mean to tell me you didn't get even one share?" Cordell shook his head.

"I didn't say that." Gus laughed. "My ex-wife's sister in California picked it up for me. I only bought $50,000 worth though."

"That does help to ease the pain then doesn't it?"

Both men laughed. They went on to discuss what they would do with the extra money. Cordell could retire, but Gus still had a few more years to put in before he could cash in. "The first thing I'm going to do is take a long overdue vacation." Gus lifted a brochure from his desk. "I need to get away from clients like you that drive me crazy."

"Where're you going Gus?" Cordell asked.

"Do you honestly think I'd tell you? Hell, I'm trying to get away from you."

"In that case, I'll see you tonight. Then you're free to go." Cordell quickly retracted his offer to be at dinner. "On second thought, send me the bill. I'll take care of everything, including the drinks. I'll see you another time."

Chapter 70

Descending to Havana International, the president's pilot slowed Air Force One to a crawl, giving it just enough power to hang in the air.

When the tires squealed along the asphalt, the pilot threw on the reverse thrusters, lurching the passengers forward. Havana's airport seldom saw a plane the size of the president's Boeing 747, and the pilot wasn't sure the runway was long enough to allow the plane to slow. As the plane taxied down the runway, the president reminisced about the gray fall skies he left behind in Washington. The brilliant Cuban sun made everyone on board the plane feel festive and excited as they prepared to disembark. The United States' return to Cuba would be a grand one.

At the edge of the runway, lights whirled on the tops of police cars, keeping the Cubans at bay as they cheered, happy to see officials of the United States on their soil. With a benefactor, the Cubans would be able to earn enough money to support their families. Many in the crowd waved homemade American flags, many of which were not cosmetically correct. Nonetheless, all the Americans leaving the plane were gracious in acknowledging their effort. Cheers rose to the sky when President Nicholas stepped to the top stair of the ramp to wave to the crowd.

At the bottom of the stairs, Xavier waited to greet the president. "It is good to see you agai…uh, sir. Welcome to Cuba."

"President Ciefuentes, the pleasure is all mine," Alex said with a wide smile on his face.

The two men entered Xavier's waiting limo. The other members of the delegation boarded a waiting bus. They would now take the twenty minute ride to Xavier's compound near Havana, in the hills. All of Alex's delegation strained their necks to take in the countryside. The land was more beautiful than many imagined or others remembered. For the members of Brothers for Freedom accompanying the delegation, this was a triumphant homecoming.

The vehicles pulled into the heavily guarded compound, and the ten-foot gates closed behind them. Onlookers lined the streets leading to Xavier's compound, curious to see the Americans. So many people were there, it appeared the entire country had taken a holiday.

"Welcome to my home," Xavier said enthusiastically.

"Thank you for the invitation," Alex answered.

They pulled to a stop in front of a magnificent mansion. The two presidents were the first to enter the house, followed by the others in the delegation.

Demetria waited in the front of the entrance foyer. "This is my wife, Demetria Ciefuentes." Xavier loved introducing her as his wife. He was proud of her contribution to his life.

Demetria slightly bowed and shook the hands of everyone who entered the house. She led them down a long hallway through two enormous doors that Xavier tugged open. Behind the doors lay a breathtaking room. Antiques and heirlooms from Batista's regime filled the room. Castro, who never used the room or its contents, viewed these antiques as too pompous. Tapestries hung on the walls. Pieces of silver and gold were tastefully placed throughout the room, which was now converted into a conference room.

Xavier's negotiators waited for their counterparts in the room. To the surprise of the American team, many of those in attendance appeared to be commoners. Xavier insisted that they dress this way to cause them to be underestimated.

"Don't be surprised, ladies and gentlemen. Despite their relaxed appearance, they're skillful negotiators."

Many of the Americans salivated at the opportunity to sit down with their counterparts. For their part, the Cubans were prepared to be underestimated, which they realized gave them the upper hand.

Scanning the room, the president's eyes fell upon Schaffer, standing in a corner. "Excuse me for a minute, I see someone that I need to speak with." Alex moved to Schaffer's side. "Did you get word of my offer?"

Schaffer nodded. "Yes, Mr. President, I did."

"What have you decided?"

"I find your offer to become the press secretary interesting."

"Then you'll take it?" Alex extended his hand.

"With conditions." Schaffer would hold out until the last possible moment.

"Let's hear what you have in mind."

Schaffer openly listed his demands: "First, you must be completely honest with me at all times. I can't function if I only get part of a story. Not to mention that I shouldn't have to work to get information from you. Second, I'll need unencumbered access to information that involves your office. In particular, what has happened here in Cuba. In return, you'll have my undying loyalty. At any time, if I feel any of these conditions are not met, I'll resign."

"Then I suggest you start today." Alex shook his hand. "I'll have Tynes fill you in. He'll be glad to know that he can now move into his new position. Let's get back to the table and down to business."

The session began at noon and went late into the night. Xavier had food brought in so that they wouldn't have to leave the room during their negotiations. Just before they broke for dinner, Alex and Xavier left the group and moved to Xavier's private office.

"Mr. President, there's something that's bothered me about this mission since I arrived in Havana. First of all, it was just too easy. Everything worked like clockwork. I've never seen a mission so involved that work so well." Xavier locked stares with Alex. "What's the reality behind it? There's no way you gave me all the details."

"I'm not sure I follow you, Commander."

Xavier reiterated. "You told me before I began this mission that you gave me all the known details. We both know that's not true."

"You know how these things are, everything is given on a need to know basis." Alex tried to put aside Xavier's concerns. "The ease with which you carried off your mission is a testament to your skill. It was not part of the plan for you to fall in love with and marry Castro's niece. Nor was he to appoint you the new President of Cuba. I don't know what made him think of doing that. Then again, he has always been unpredictable. Castro and I agreed that I would send someone in who would take care of his people. We'll just have to live with what he's done for now. Since we smuggled Castro's body from Cuba and changed his identity, we are in the process of giving him a new place to live."

"Where is he?" Xavier grabbed Alex's arm. "I'll need to take Demetria to visit him. His death has devastated her."

"That information is not now, nor will it ever be, available to anyone." Alex looked at Xavier's hand on his arm. "At Castro's request, I might add. You'll just have to let your bride believe what she currently does."

"Sir, you don't understand." Xavier looked desperate. "This man was her whole life. After her father was killed her mother lost her mind, Castro took her in and raised her. He is love to her."

"I'm sorry, son. You'll have to fill that void in her life now." The president patted Xavier on the shoulder and returned to the conference room with the other members of his team.

✿✿✿✿

When Xavier and Alex left the conference room, Schaffer moved over to Dee's side and grabbed her arm. "Let's take a walk. I want to show you something."

Mackenzie watched them leaving. "Hey, wait up. I'll go with you."

Schaffer looked at him sternly. "Sorry, Secretary Mackenzie, not this time. We'll be right back. The general and I have to take care of a private matter."

Mackenzie snarled in contempt, "Sure you do. Hurry back. I wouldn't want you two to miss the beginning of our meeting." As they passed him, Mackenzie hissed, "Sugar…"

Dee looked at Schaffer abruptly, but he kept his eyes on Mackenzie. She tugged at his arm. "Come on, Schaffer, let's go."

They left the room and went to a balcony that overlooked the mountains. Schaffer turned to Dee. "I hate that bastard. He's the one who had to be bugging your office. Calling me 'sugar' was his way of letting us know."

"I've reviewed some of the recordings from the computer," Schaffer said. "I've been so involved here that I've neglected things at home. What I do know is that Mackenzie contacted Cordell quite a few times."

She shook her finger vigorously at Schaffer. "John Cordell doesn't exist, at least on paper. Director Caprelotti may know something, but the president wanted me to wait until you were back. Anyone in as deep as Cordell would disappear if we tipped our hand."

"From what I heard, I've amassed quite a large amount of stock in USA Tobacco. That was an attempt to discredit me and have the SEC investigate me for insider trading. They must think I'm stupid." Schaffer leaned both hands against the railing and looked out over the mountains. "This whole thing started with Harold. The only other piece of conversation I heard between Mackenzie and Cordell was about an envelope Harold had for me. Apparently, there were two of them — one Harold carried, the other he'd mailed. The mailed one was returned to his office. An aide called Mackenzie and offered him the envelope in exchange for half a million dollars. I want you to contact Harold's office and see if any aides have turned up missing."

"Obviously you think that someone's missing," Dee concluded. "What if you're right?"

"There's no doubt in my mind. But it will confirm that Mackenzie's our man. Now I want to know why."

"He makes my skin crawl." Dee rubbed her arms to ward off the chill-bumps. "We should tell the president right away."

"No, let's wait. He'll show his hand soon enough and then we'll have all the proof we need. Besides, I'd be willing to bet you that Cordell did his dirty work, and that he'll show up soon, too." Schaffer stood from the railing and crossed his arms.

Dee nodded. "So, you want to catch them both with the same net?"

"It will make life easier if we can flush them both out at the same time." Schaffer spun facing her. "Right now I want you to tell me everything that's happened surrounding this mission."

Dee was somewhat reluctant, but started with her explanation. "Most of it you already know. What you haven't heard is this. Three years ago, Castro came to the United States to address the United Nations. The president attended to hear what he had to say. He wanted to know if any possibility existed for our two countries to hold further discussions on trade. From Castro's speech, the president found no hope. Castro continued spewing the same rhetoric and disdain as always, insulting us out of one side of his mouth while asking for help out of the other side. As his speech was ending, the president left to go to the restroom." Dee turned leaning her back against the rail. She paid close attention to Schaffer's expression.

"The United Nations, as you know, is a sovereign nation, and is governed by independent laws. One of those laws is that only heads of state are allowed in the executive restrooms. From your time as a Secret Service agent, you know that our security teams are not allowed past the guarded doors. As luck would have it, Castro also came to the restroom while the president was there. Then the most amazing thing happened. Castro spoke to Alex as he was about to leave. He asked the president to stay. They moved into the lounge area, where they shared a cigar." Dee let her hands fall to the railing and her head drifted towards the ground.

"Castro told the president that he'd grown tired of ruling Cuba. For all his adult life, it was all he'd done. He came back to Cuba after being exiled, took control of the government, and spent a lifetime defending their right to be Communists." She flashed a fleeting, contemptuous expression. "Or at least what he thought passed for Communism. He said he was ready for something different. But of course, he couldn't step down, because it would open the doors for the United States to come in and gain control. Not to mention the fact that he didn't trust anyone in Cuba to take over his position, especially not his brother Raul, who headed the military. Castro didn't want us to ruin the social programs that he established, and he didn't want anyone he left in power to cave in to strong demands from the United States."

Dee turned and looked towards the mountains, breathing deeply. She knew that the secrecy surrounding her next comments affected Harold's death. "We needed a plan that would allow both countries to save face and get what we both wanted. Thus, they came up with the plan to send in a small SEAL team, one of whom was to gain the trust of, and then eliminate, Castro. Then he would be free to relax anonymously for the first time since taking control of Cuba."

Dee's story surprised Schaffer. "Other than you and Alex, who else knows what's really happened to Castro?"

"Only the SEALs who were involved. Both presidents wanted it that way."

Schaffer's face gathered into a frown. "Wait a minute. Castro knew Xavier was coming, which explains why he trusted him so readily. But I thought Demetria was the reason Castro felt he had nothing to fear from Xavier?"

"Demetria was insurance. We knew about her propensity for having these so-called visions. Using that information, along with Castro's desire for retirement, she was an easy recruit. Castro had no idea the vision was a fabrication. We thought that would help put him at ease with his decision. He bought it, which is probably why he named Xavier as his successor. That wasn't supposed to happen."

Schaffer stepped closer to Dee and waited for her to look at him. "That still doesn't explain why Harold and Mackenzie fought over this plan. Harold was worried about the agents, but it seems to me that everyone got what they wanted."

Dee looked away. "Harold and Mackenzie only knew about the men being held. They didn't know that that was also part of the plan. Why do you think Castro never harmed our agents? We never told Harold or

Mackenzie that we also planned to bring Castro out alive." Dee couldn't hold her head up against the weight of guilt about keeping secrets that cost Harold his life. "The president only mentioned getting Castro to see their reaction. Mackenzie clearly viewed it as an opportunity, and insisted we take him out."

"That explains the fight they had." Schaffer let his eyes wander from Dee. Thoughts pulsed through his head, settling on Harold's death. "Now the question is why did Mackenzie want Castro dead so bad that he was willing to kill to ensure it?"

"That also explains why he wanted you dead." Dee's fingers tightened around the railing. "If you broke the story that we were about to assassinate Castro, the mission would have been scrubbed and we'd be left to defend ourselves against the accusations."

"Exactly." Schaffer paused. "There still has to be something else, we're missing it, I can feel it."

Dee wanted to say no, but she realized that Schaffer wouldn't stop until he was completely comfortable that he knew everything. "Your sixth sense is too strong for your own good. I can see why the president wanted you involved. He did offer you full disclosure from his office. However, only six people know anything about this. After I tell you, there will be seven, and I don't expect to hear it from anyone else until we're ready. Do we have a deal?"

Schaffer looked at Dee. "Do I have a choice?"

"None at all. I mean it. I must have your complete assurance." She watched his eyes.

"I'm reluctant. But if that's the only way you'll tell me, so be it." Schaffer leaned back.

"The four men captured at the naval base in Havana were not exclusively CIA. They're also geologists. I don't think you even knew that about Tito."

Schaffer raised his eyebrows.

"We have suspected for some time that there was oil in or around Cuba. But the Russians never found much and they were experts in oil exploration."

Schaffer's eyes lit up. "The gulf is full of oil. Mexico and the U.S. both successfully drilled in that area, so why not Cuba? It sounds completely logical, once you think about it."

"Yes. And our geologists, your friend Tito included, have found what they believe to be one of the largest deposits of oil in this hemisphere, just off the cost of Havana."

Schaffer's cynicism started to rise. "The president wants a favorable government in place so that the U.S. can take advantage of this oil deposit?"

Dee stepped back and crossed her arms. "God knows we need it. We don't want to see inflation like we saw in the seventies or eighties. Besides, retrieving this oil will not only alleviate our inflation, it will help to make Cuba a wealthy country."

"So, that's your justification." Schaffer stiffened incredulously. "Harold lost his life for an oil deposit he didn't know anything about."

"No!" Dee insisted. "Harold lost his life because of Mackenzie."

"Does he know about the oil?" Schaffer crossed his arms.

"Not a clue. There has never been anything written down about the oil. The president handpicked the geologists and gave them strict instructions only to communicate with him. We didn't even have confirmation about the oil until these men got home on Thursday."

Schaffer relaxed and looked out over the mountains. "I'll let you in on a secret. That's not the 'something else' I was talking about. If Harold and Mackenzie had known about the oil, I could begin to understand. Greed is a powerful master. Regardless, Mackenzie has to pay for what he did."

"I agree." Dee pressed her nails into the skin on her arms. "So how do you plan to expose him?"

"I have a trick or two up my sleeve. As soon as we get back home, I'll be able to complete my investigation. There's bound to be something else waiting on the computer in my wall."

¤¤¤¤

Heading back to the meeting room, they were intercepted by a Cuban guard escorting Mackenzie. "I was just coming to find you two. The president should be ready to get started very soon."

"We're on the way. Relax." Dee put her arm in Schaffer's and they entered the room together. Alex and Xavier weren't in the room and didn't return until after Dee and Schaffer.

Schaffer saw Xavier at the door speaking with Demetria. He walked over and excused himself. "Xavier, may I speak with you?" They moved to an area that was free of people. "I'll do everything I can to find out the location of Castro. When I do, I'll contact you. All I know right now is that he's in the States."

"Let me know if I can do anything to help." Xavier grabbed Schaffer's hand and shook. "I'll forever be in your debt."

Schaffer looked into Xavier's eyes. "There's one thing you can do for me. Stay on as President of Cuba. Lead your people to a new and prosperous tomorrow. You know what's best for these people. Give it to them. You've already brought a strengthening economy to Cuba. I'm sure your mother and father are smiling down on you. You've kept your promise to their memory. Watch who you bring into your cabinet and stay as close to your enemy as possible. That way you'll always know what he's up to. My last piece of advice is just because Cuba has the intention of being an ally of the U.S. that doesn't mean you can forgo the responsibility of your country and let them take advantage of you. That must come before all other loyalties and your country is Cuba."

Chapter 71

The fifth day of negotiations and touring found the American and Cuban delegations standing outside both their mine fields at Guantanamo.

A team of one hundred and fifty soldiers, composed of men from both sides, combed the fields, dismantling and discarding the deadly mines. For years, the fields had claimed the lives of countless numbers of people trying to get into and out of Cuba.

Press agencies from all over the world filmed the progress of the soldiers in the fields. Their reports would serve as testimony that Cuba welcomed the entire world to her shores. Schaffer felt proud that in some small way he had contributed to their progress.

As the sun began to set, Schaffer joined the American delegation. They boarded Air Force One at the American airstrip at Gitmo to return home. Already, ships were heading to Cuba to load the goods the Americans had purchased earlier in the week. The Cubans were in possession of a five hundred million dollar check securing the purchase, officially opening the doors of trade with the small island nation.

Robert Whittaker returned with ten cases of Cuban cigars bearing the labels of companies that he gained the U.S. rights to. Seven of them he would auction off as the first Cuban cigars to legally come into America in over forty years. One case had already been given to the president. Another case would be shared with his team who made the purchase possible, and the last case would end up in his private walk-in humidor, to be savored on special occasions. By the time Robert got off the plane, he learned that USA Tobacco's stock price had quadrupled since his announcement the week before. His wealth now exceeded nine figures. After stock options and bonuses, he would be one of the wealthiest CEOs in America.

¤¤¤¤

Schaffer's first assignment as the new White House Press Secretary was to coordinate a press conference scheduled for the day after they landed. He suggested that it be held at 6:30 p.m., right when most Americans were having dinner, maximizing viewership.

"I knew I liked this guy for a reason. He thinks like a winner," Alex said, easing his first legal Cuban cigar into his mouth. He handed one to Schaffer.

During the press conference, Alex pronounced Cuba's doors once again open to America. He also urged the U.S. Congress to grant most favored nation status to Cuba, as well as approve a ten billion dollar aid package to be implemented over the next seven years. Americans everywhere began packing their bags to head to Fantasy Island. Cuba was once again destined to become the playground of the rich and not so rich. The American government developed and paid to have commercials run on networks across the country promoting Cuba as a great vacation destination.

Bringing democracy to Cuba was a tremendous coup for the president. He was re-elected by a landslide in November, carrying all fifty states. Early in the evening after the election, the Republican and Democratic contenders yielded to the newly re-elected Independent, Alexander Z. Nicholas. By his side, at his acceptance speech was his secretary, Annie, as well as Vice President Ross Gillespie, General Dee Roseboro, Secretary Ian Mackenzie, Chief of Staff Coleman Tynes, and Press Secretary Schaffer O'Grady.

¤¤¤¤

Xavier Ciefuentes, eager to allow the Cuban people to freely vote, held elections in December. One old Communist hard-liner ran against him, and in total received one hundred and ten votes. Xavier easily won the election and began his new life as the first freely elected President of Cuba. No one in Cuba knew much about his past. Only a handful of people had ever seen him before Castro made him known. Only Demetria knew his true identity and past, a secret she planned to take to her grave.

Cuba was again blossoming with the help of their newfound benefactor, the United States. American tourists were flocking to Cuba in record numbers. The hotels were booked solid for five months. All of this brought new life and construction to Cuba's shores. New businesses were opening faster than could be counted. Disney entered Cuba to build Caribbean Disney. Although close to Disney World in Florida, they expected it would attract even more people because of the island flavor. In addition,

Cuba gave them a new cruise destination for their ships. "Spend three days in Disney World, Florida. And cruise to Caribbean Disney for the vacation of a lifetime," quickly became one of their advertisement slogans.

With all her newfound fame, Cuba was increasingly an attraction for potential tourists. For their citizens, education and free medical care for all remained a priority. As promised, Xavier kept all of Castro's successful programs while rebuilding the country. Cuba was a model of achievement made possible when countries worked together.

Chapter 72

Schaffer walked into his house just as the shadows of evening began to cast eastward. Following closely behind him were two Secret Service agents, who immediately began sweeping the house for electronic surveillance devices.

Schaffer watched the agents methodically move over each room. Forty five minutes later, they were gone. He took his Sig Sauer .357 down from the shelf, dropped it into a side holster, and moved to the closet in his foyer. If Mackenzie or any of his goons came into the house, Schaffer was ready with a surprise of his own.

Removing tape that blended with the walls, he opened the panel concealing the servers and began to download the recordings onto the jump drives. After recovering all the data, Schaffer sat at his dinning room table and began listening to the conversations. It wasn't long before he heard Senator Hector Hernandez talking with the Speaker of the House Bill Davis and Secretary of State Ian Mackenzie.

"Bill?"

"I'm here."

"Ian?"

"How many times do I have to tell you never to use names over the phone? You know, Senator, sometimes you act like a goddamned idiot. It's amazing that you continue to get reelected."

"You damn well better hope I continue to get reelected — your plans depend on it." Schaffer heard Hernandez clear his throat at this point. *"What the hell would you like to be called?"*

"Attila."

"Attila? You're a sick bastard. I see why Harold and you used to lock horns before you had him popped."

"You're treading on thin ice, asshole. Continue blabbing on an open line — you may prove to be necessarily expendable."

Schaffer identified this voice as the speaker chiming in. *"Gentlemen, none of us can get anywhere behaving like this. We've got to work together if this is going to work."*

"Fine!" Schaffer noted Hernandez speaking again. *"Then you can call me Pedro."*

"And I'll be Emperor." The speaker said this. *"Now that our problem is resolved, we've got to make sure things proceed."*

"The main problem has been eliminated." Mackenzie said this calmly, too calmly for Schaffer's taste. *"O'Grady could still be a liability, however. My assistant is taking action to discredit him. I'm hoping he'll prove to be enough of a problem for the president that he'll have to deal with him."*

"Excellent! So, what's our next move?"

Schaffer isolated the conversation in a separate file and continued to dredge through the recordings. A conversation between Mackenzie and Cordell shortly after the attempt on his life left Schaffer shaken. He paused the recordings and used the break to contact Dee.

"Hey, sugar. How's the research coming?"

"You know, Dee, I never cease to be amazed by the depths to which people are willing to sink for power. Harold's dead because he cared about people and chose to defend their right to live."

Dee sat in an over-sized chair and pulled her feet under her. She didn't want to sound overly excited anticipating good news from Schaffer. "It didn't have anything to do with our operation in Cuba?"

Schaffer balled his face into a tight frown, unable to prevent the anger in his voice. "It had everything to do with Cuba! That and trusting people with hidden agendas."

"There's no way you're talking about the president?"

"I haven't finished with everything yet, but I'm fairly sure he's in the clear."

Dee felt heat rising from her head and inhaled sharply. "Thank God! I don't think I could take it if he were involved."

Schaffer looked back at the computer and let the silence linger a while longer. "I don't think he was. At least I don't think so yet. There's no need to speculate. I'll have everything together in a week or so." He knew Mackenzie was responsible, even if he had not pulled the trigger, but he refrained from saying anything more to Dee.

"There's no need to rush things," Dee concluded. "It's better if we're completely certain before taking people into custody."

"You'll be the first to know when I'm ready. I want to finish the recordings first in case there are any other surprises."

"What kind of surprises?"

"I guess it's not fair to mention that without giving you more to go on, but I'm afraid it's going to have to do for now." Schaffer could hear protests forming in Dee's throat. "I'm sorry, Dee. Until I have everything in place, I'm not saying anything to anyone." He smiled to think this was exactly what she'd done to him.

"I hope you're finished with this thing soon. The waiting is driving me crazy, despite what I said a minute ago."

"I'll be in touch soon." Schaffer hung up. He placed a call to Ralph.

"I've been expecting your call," Ralph said anxiously. "What took you so long?"

"Things took a little longer than I expected to wrap up this afternoon." Schaffer glanced at the name he'd written on a note pad. "What did you find out about Hernandez and House Speaker Davis?"

"You're playing on a dangerous playground. These guys want to rule the world. Do you ever do things the easy way?" Ralph whistled through his teeth. "They're willing to do whatever it takes to have that privilege. They couldn't stop Nicholas in the last election, so they're making plans for the next one. I wouldn't be surprised if the speaker hatched a plan to eliminate the president and the vice president since he's third in line."

"Nothing would surprise me about those three."

"Unfortunately, everyone's been quiet since the election and I haven't heard anything new. Hernandez has been putting the screws to Gato since November. I heard he told Gato it was time to make good and deliver the votes. But Gato is spending all his time in Cuba trying to make headway there." Ralph sighed. "I'm sorry, I wish there was more."

"That's plenty. Add to it what I already have and we shouldn't have to worry about seeing any of them in office again. Thanks, Ralph. I'll talk

with you later."

Chapter
73

From the White House lawn, the president, his cabinet, and the staff watched fireworks bring in the New Year.

This New Year's party was especially lively because of the earlier election victory. It lasted well into the early hours of the morning.

For four months, Schaffer had looked through government documents attempting to locate Castro or any information that would point to his direction. He came up empty on every occasion.

In eighteen days, President Nicholas would again be sworn in as the leader of the most powerful country in the world. Seeing to it that Alex was reelected and celebrating the election overshadowed Schaffer's mission of finding Harold's murderer.

Schaffer's passion didn't include working for the government. Just considering four more years was akin to asking if he wanted to spend four years in prison. He needed to be free to wander the streets in search of new and exciting stories. He needed to talk to Joe. He glanced down at his watch. It was 2:00 p.m. He knew that Joe would be in his office, so Schaffer picked up the phone and dialed the number.

On the third ring, Joe answered. "Joe DeApuzzo."

"Hey Joe, it sure is good hear your voice." Schaffer nervously played with papers on his desk.

Joe needled him. "What's wrong? You tired of your ho-hum job at the White House?"

"You're dammed right I am!" Schaffer answered abruptly.

"Whoa buddy, don't sound so emphatic."

"I can't help it Joe." Schaffer looked around his office. "We both know this isn't me."

"Sure, I know it. I just figured you were trying to uncover some other secret information that you weren't ready to share with anyone just yet. You've never been the political black tie type." Joe let his feet drop to the floor and then he looked at the clock. "So what's up with you?"

"I'm prepared to hand in my resignation one week before the inauguration, if you'll have me back." Schaffer didn't expect any difficulty, but waited for Joe's response.

"Well I don't know…" Joe's voice climbed to what his reporters liked to call 'his Brooklyn voice.' "Whad'ya mean askin' me somethin' like dat?" Joe let the question hang in the air and then cleared his throat. "Who's yo' daddy?"

Schaffer was puzzled. "What?"

"Should I rephrase? Who's my bitch?"

Schaffer dropped his head and laughed. "Okay, you win. I'm your bitch."

They both laughed.

"I do love a humble reporter. By the way, I never let them clean out your office. We'd be excited to have you back. And now I know you've heard that you're up for a Pulitzer for your coverage in Cuba. I kept you on the payroll to protect your eligibility. Real gusty stuff, they said." Joe scratched his head. "I told them it was total fucking bullshit."

"Thanks a lot. I always knew I could count on you." Schaffer's voice took on a more serious attitude. "You know, there are things about that story that still bother me."

"Like what?" Joe anxiously waited for the details.

Schaffer looked at his watch. "Why don't you meet me for a cup of coffee? We can talk about it then."

¤¤¤¤

One hour later, they met at The Capitol Grill. It was a cold, gray January day. Two feet of snow from the previous week's storm continued to smother the ground. Inside, the Grill was empty, with the exception of the staff, Joe and Schaffer. No one else cared to be whipped by the wind in order to have afternoon drinks.

Joe never missed a chance to pick on Schaffer. "Your taste in coffee has taken a turn towards gourmet since you have been hanging with your presidential buddies."

"Cut me a little slack, would you? They know me here, and it's a quiet place where we can talk undisturbed." He turned to the manager. "Matt, we'll take that booth in the back. If you would, please leave a pot of coffee on the table. We'll call if we need any thing else."

"Yes, sir, Secretary O'Grady."

"Secretary O'Grady?" Joe raised his brow. "That's a step up for you, not to mention you're on a first name basis with the maitre'd. How much did you slip him on the way in, a C note?"

"Very funny," Schaffer said. "By the way, he's the manager. I take care of him and he takes care of me." Schaffer moved his cup closer and added cream. "Do you want anything to eat?"

"How about some of those fancy little biscuit things, you know, the ones you hold with just two fingers and dunk in your coffee." Joe stuck his pinkie in the air and lifted his coffee cup.

"Matt, would you bring a plate of biscotti." Schaffer turned his attention back to Joe, "I don't want to hear any shit from you. You can dress em up, but you can't take 'em out."

Matt brought the food.

"I promise I'll eat them in little bites so I won't embarrass you." Joe lifted one of the biscotti from the plate and ate half of it in one bite.

"Enough bullshit, lets get down to business." Schaffer pushed aside the coffee so he could use his hands for expression. "When Castro died," he placed his hands in the air and gestured as if he was making quotation marks, "I went out to the site where the pyre sank and dove down to the burnt hull. That's when things got strange. I found a bolt on the ocean floor, which fit perfectly into a sheet of metal that had, at one time, covered the bottom of the pyre. Since the bottom of the pyre had not burned, it was obvious that the sheet of metal had been removed. Later I questioned Xavier about the pyre, why it had a removable bottom, but he wouldn't tell me anything. He said he couldn't. But when the president came to Cuba, I found out the truth. They took Castro out of the country, alive, changed his identity, and now he is supposedly living somewhere here in the States. I've spent the last four months trying to find him, with no luck. I believe only two people — the president and the chairwoman of the Joint Chiefs of Staff — know where he is. My guess is Castro may want some peace, but why didn't he tell Demetria where he would be? It just doesn't fit. He wouldn't leave behind the one person he loved more than anyone else in the world." Schaffer's eyebrows shot up. "Unless he was trying to protect her."

Joe's face knotted. "Demetria?"

"Demetria, Xavier's wife. Castro's niece. She was almost destroyed by Castro's death. The president won't tell Xavier where her uncle is. These people are my friends. I'd like to help them find him."

"A monumental task, buddy." Joe uncrossed his arms and took a drink from his cup. "What do you think they're trying to protect her from?" Joe held his cup of coffee inches from his lips.

"More like from whom. Knowledge of his whereabouts sounds like fatal information to me, or they wouldn't guard it so closely." Schaffer seemed lost in the moment. "That would explain the silence."

"That's one hell of a story." Joe finally took a drink.

"Yeah, but I can't tell it." Schaffer shook his head. "It would disrupt our political system as well as Cuba's. I think Harold Cosby was about to tell me about the planned invasion and Castro's assassination when he got waxed. Then, of course, after I broke the story about the invasion someone tried to kill me. I didn't stick around long enough to find out who it was. Since I've been home, I've compiled concrete evidence of who had Harold killed. There's a lot more to it than I first suspected. When I deliver my report, it's going to bring down a lot of powerful people." Schaffer watched for Joe's reaction.

"You could be in one hell of a pickle if anyone found out that you have that kind of information. So what is it that you want me to do?" Joe sat back and folded his arms across his chest.

Schaffer repeatedly tapped a spoon against the side of his cup. "That's one reason I asked you here. When I resign next week, I'm going to deliver my findings. The heat could be turned up again. If anything happens to me, I want you to have my story printed in the paper. Of course, print it in the *Post*, but also give it to the *New York Times*, the *LA Times*, the *Chicago Tribune*, and any other paper that will run the story. The shit will definitely hit the fan then."

They finished their coffee. Joe left first, in the event someone had followed Schaffer to the restaurant.

Chapter
74

Alex pressed his intercom.

"Annie, would you have O'Grady come here for a minute? I want him to look over some ideas for my speech."

"Right away, sir."

Soon after Annie's call, Schaffer arrived at the president's office.

Alex pointed to a chair. "I'd like for you to at some point take a look over some ideas I have for my inauguration speech."

"Certainly, sir." Schaffer took the speech, left the president's office, and headed to Dee's office. "Hey, you got a minute?" he asked, poking his head through the door.

"Anything for you, sugar." Dee pulled off her reading glasses and gave him her full attention.

"Put your boots and a coat on." Schaffer pointed to her Timberlands in the corner. "We're going to play in the snow for a few minutes."

"That sounds like fun." Dee smiled and grabbed the boots.

They left the White House and walked towards the Washington Monument, the snow crunching beneath their feet. After a few minutes, they were far enough from the White House for Schaffer's comfort. There wasn't another soul anywhere around them. He looked over at Dee. "I'm going to resign next week."

She folded her arms pulling them tightly against her chest. "I'm not surprised. You really don't care for this type of work, do you?"

"No, I really never did." Schaffer looked down at the snow. "I just needed to use the influence of this office while I was in search of the truth."

"So, have you found what you are looking for?" Dee asked and dug her neck deeper into her scarf.

"Almost." He held up one finger. "There's one missing piece to my puzzle."

Dee looked at him and relaxed her arms. "And you think I have it?"

"I know you do." Schaffer's eyes seemed to apologize and plead at the same time. "I have to know where Castro is. I made a promise to Xavier and I intend to keep it."

"Why would he want to know?" Dee shook her head. "Castro has a lot of enemies in this country because of his reputation in Cuba. I'm not sure it's a good idea to part with that information."

Schaffer took a moment allowing the vapor stream to flow from his mouth and nose while gathering his thoughts. "Allow me to get philosophical for a moment. Those who we view as famous or infamous, society has chosen to attach themselves to an act, thought, or invention that stands out as a testament to their belief. This view of men is myopic, for who among us can possess greatness without faults, or infamy without goodness?"

"So, who are you quoting? That doesn't sound like a Schafferism to me."

"The truth is, I don't know. Maybe the Gospel of Luke… judge not least ye be judged. If so, I've paraphrased it."

Dee's eyebrows rose, impressed but not convinced. "You realize I would have to break an oath to divulge that information. And of course if I tell you," she smiled weakly. "I'll have to kill you."

Schaffer reached out holding her arms. "I know what I'm asking you to do. I'd rather you tell me now than for me to bring it up in a group of people next week."

"Next week?"

"At my resignation." Schaffer reached into his pocket. "Here is the list of people I've asked Alex to assemble for my official presentation." He handed the list to Dee.

She read over the list. "Other than the obvious ones, why these people?"

"Each of them was involved in some way with Operation Smokeout. One of them is responsible for Harold's death." He gently closed her hand around the list.

"In that case, I'm not flattered to be on your list." Dee turned and looked at the White House.

Schaffer walked behind her and began to rub her shoulders. "You're going to play a major role. I expect a few of our guests won't be too happy when I make my presentation. That's where you come in. I need you to arrive five minutes late with five Marines fully armed. Don't use anyone here at the White House to pick your men. Do it yourself at Quantico. Give them a signal in case we need them and have them waiting just outside Alex's door when the meeting starts."

"I hope you know what you're doing." Dee looked down, exhaled loudly, and slowly raised her head. "I don't suppose you're willing to share any more information?"

Schaffer stopped rubbing her shoulders. "I can't. I haven't planned everything out yet. You'll have to trust me. Don't worry, this will strengthen Alex's administration."

"I don't know if I'm comfortable fulfilling your request. You haven't told me enough."

"Remember when you insisted I trust you when things got crazy?" Schaffer nodded his head as if encouraging Dee to do the same. Eventually, she did. "I need you to trust me now. It may be an overreaction, but my gut tells me it's not."

"You haven't let me down so far." Dee turned and hugged Schaffer.

"I'm glad you feel that way." Schaffer smiled and gave her an extra squeeze. "So how about supplying my missing puzzle piece?"

Dee stepped back. "Whip out that little device that got you through Cuba. Tonight the address will be on the screen. Please wait a few months before doing anything with it. You're going to stir up a big mess, and I want some of what's going on right now to cool down before you make contact." She put her hand in the center of his chest. "Whatever you do, the president must never know that you have this information. If you share it with Xavier, Alex can never know how you got it."

"I give you my word." They crossed the snow and headed to the White House.

Back in the warmth of the White House, Schaffer read over the president's speech. He looked at his watch. Six o'clock on the dot. It was dark outside. He had been reading for two hours, changing and correcting Alex's inaugural speech. He lifted the phone and called the president's office to make sure Alex hadn't left for dinner. Finding that he was in, Schaffer began the trip down the hall to his office. He felt himself grow increasingly nervous as he got closer. He was about to tell Alex that he would resign Monday at one o'clock. Tuesday was Alex's inauguration, so the president had the weekend if he needed Schaffer. When he arrived, Alex's door was open.

Alex waved. "Come in. Did you have to make a lot of changes?"

"No, Mr. President. You wrote a very good speech." He sat down in front of Alex's desk and handed him the speech. "There are some things we need to discuss."

Alex put the speech face down on his desk. "You have my full attention."

Schaffer's mouth was dry and his heart raced. "Alex, on Monday I'll be handing in my resignation."

"Damn, Schaffer. What brought this on?" Alex's fingers came to a steeple in front of his face.

Schaffer maintained eye contact. "I can't do this any more. I need to be free to come and go as I please. I'm a journalist. I will always be a journalist. It's the only place that I feel free."

Alex's hands moved and he inhaled deeply before speaking. "Is there any way I can talk you out of this?"

"I'm afraid not. I'll be here Monday at one. At that time I'll deliver Harold's murderer to you and explain why he did it."

Alex dropped back in his chair. "You know who killed Harold? Why don't we have him arrested right now?"

Schaffer shook his head. "It goes a lot deeper than I originally thought. This information is going to bring down more than one person on that list."

Alex looked into Schaffer's eyes. "Please make sure you have all the facts straight. I don't want any backlash."

"My evidence is irrefutable," Schaffer said without a hint of doubt.

"I'll see you on Monday." Alex stood and leaned forward with both hands on his desk. "Have a good weekend."

"You too, sir. And don't worry, this information won't hurt your office." Schaffer turned and left Alex's office. At Annie's desk, he pulled an identical list as the one he had handed Dee out of his pocket. "Have these people meet in the president's office at one o'clock Monday afternoon.

Chapter
75

At eleven o'clock Monday morning Schaffer left his house.

    He carried several U.S.B. jump drives, a note with Castro's new address on it, and a letter addressed to Joe DeApuzzo. Inside the letter to Joe was another letter addressed to Xavier and a note for Joe to mail it if he didn't check in within a couple of days.

    He left Georgetown en route to the White House. During the weekend, the temperatures reached the high forties so the snow turned to slush and D.C. was back in full swing.

    Schaffer arrived at the White House and went into his office. He gave his assistant orders not to disturb him. He used the quiet time to pack his office and reflect on what he was about to do.

    Annie had informed Alex of Schaffer's list and request. At precisely 1 p.m., Annie showed Secretary of State Mackenzie, Senator Hernandez, Speaker of the House Davis and FBI Director Daly into the Oval Office.

    "Thanks for coming, gentlemen. We're going to be a moment or two longer. I'm waiting for two more people to arrive." The president let them sit there to wonder why they had been summoned. He wondered as well, but continued to look over some paperwork to pass the time.

    Schaffer left his office at 1:04. Walking down the hall, he was joined by Dee and five impeccably dressed Marines in full battle gear. When they reached the Oval Office, Dee turned to him. "I guess this is your moment of truth. Good luck."

    Schaffer opened the door and followed Dee into the room. When the door closed, the Marines stood in formation, two on either side of the door and one directly in front of it holding their weapons slightly out in front.

    Dee took her place standing beside the president's chair, directly behind the intercom. Schaffer walked in front of Alex's desk, set his briefcase on it, and retrieved the items he needed for the meeting. He then turned and faced the men sitting in the room.

Schaffer took the floor. "I want to thank each of you for coming today. There are several items of business we need to cover before we leave. First of all, Mr. President, I want to thank you for the opportunity to serve in your administration. It is with regret that I give you my resignation, effective immediately." Schaffer handed Alex his letter.

The president accepted it and placed it on his desk. Then he folded his hands in front of his face and continued to listen.

Schaffer turned to the other men in the room. "The past ten months have been very troubling to me. I'm sure you all wonder how that concerns each of you. The answer is simple. Each of you has played a role in the cause of my discomfort." Mackenzie folded his arms across his chest and crossed his legs as Schaffer spoke.

"On March eleventh of last year, a phone call woke me up in the early hours of the morning." Schaffer looked directly at Mackenzie. "When I answered the call I was surprised to hear Chief of Staff Harold Cosby's voice on the other end. He requested a meeting, which ultimately resulted in his assassination about an hour later."

Schaffer had all of their attention. He noticed them squirming. He turned up the heat. "At Harold's funeral, the president requested that I assist him in finding out who murdered Cosby. I agreed to help and he offered his full cooperation. The first thing I had him do was to install a state of the art server into a wall at my house. Then the president authorized me to have each of your phones, home, cellular, and office tapped. Each time you placed a call a signal was sent to the server and your calls were recorded, noting both time and date."

Director Daly jumped to his feet. "Mr. President, most of the calls from my office are highly sensitive. I find this to be very irregular and dangerous to national security."

Schaffer intervened. "Pardon me, Director Daly. Your phones were not tapped. You were, however, an unfortunate and unwilling participant in this game. Give me a moment longer and I think you'll understand." Schaffer pointed to the chair and Director Daly sat down. "My plan was to review your calls each night but an attempt on my life caused me to disappear for longer that I had expected." Schaffer pulled a composite drawing from the top of his papers and held it in front of the men. "This is the man who tried to kill me. Take a good look."

"That's John Cordell," Director Daly blurted out.

Secretary Mackenzie murmured, "Shut up, Daly. O'Grady's on a fishing expedition."

"Ian," Daly said, ashen faced, "you told me Alex wanted John to follow O'Grady. You didn't say anything about killing anybody."

"Daly, shut the fuck up!" Mackenzie's face burned bright red.

Ignoring him, Schaffer turned to Daly. "Where is Mr. Cordell now?"

"He should be at his desk at headquarters," Daly answered, still puzzled where everything was going.

Schaffer handed him a phone. "Why don't you call over there and have a couple of your men arrest him?"

Daly looked at Schaffer as if in shock.

"Go ahead and do it now."

Daly turned to the president.

Alex nodded.

Daly took the cell phone and looked at it for a second. Then he placed his call.

Schaffer waited until he was finished. "After the attempt on my life, I wasn't sure who I could trust. Dee continued to assure me that the president wasn't involved. But, I must admit, at the time I wasn't sure."

Mackenzie looked at Dee. "Bitch!"

"If it makes you feel any better, Ian, you were always my chief suspect." He glared at Mackenzie. "Of course, I couldn't confirm that you were responsible for Harold's death until I got home and reviewed the phone conversations."

"You know what?" Mackenzie said. "Fuck you."

"You are not my type," Schaffer shot back. "What I couldn't figure out was why you wanted Harold dead. The argument you had with him the night you ordered the hit wasn't reason enough. Even for a disgusting snake like you."

"You think you have all the answers, don't you?" Mackenzie said. "You don't know shit."

"I know I have the answers." Schaffer sat on the edge of the president's desk and pointed at Mackenzie. "You want to be President." Schaffer's statement caught all but three of the people in the room off guard.

Alex sat back in his chair and let his hands fall to his lap. He started to speak, but decided he wanted to listen a bit longer before saying anything.

Schaffer turned to Alex. "Mr. President, I know what you were thinking. How can Ian become president if he wasn't born in this country?"

"Damned if you didn't hit that one on the head." The president couldn't wait for an explanation.

"It's easy. He made a deal with the devil. Or in his case, two devils." Schaffer turned in the senator's direction. "Senator Hernandez here is facing re-election in November. For the first time in his career, he's facing some stiff competition. The mistake you made, Mr. President was asking the opinions of your Hispanic senators about the precursor to Operation Smokeout."

"But I received their blessings," the president protested.

"As you should have," Schaffer said, and returned his focus to Hernandez. "What you didn't know is that Harold went straight to Hernandez when he left your meeting. My guess is that he hoped the senator would see his side. Harold terribly misread what Hernandez would do. The senator is an opportunist. He knew, as we all do now, about Ian's aspirations. Couple that with the fact that he held several meetings with Gato Canoso. Brothers for Freedom were about to pull their support from Hernandez unless he pushed harder to return them to a Castro-free Cuba. When Harold told him your plan was to eliminate Castro from Cuba, Ian's option of eliminating Castro was the only viable choice for the senator."

Alex stood, Opus X clenched in his teeth, and looked as if he were about to do battle. "You two are a couple of real sick people."

Schaffer redirected the conversation. "Wait a minute, Mr. President, it gets better. Hernandez called Ian after Harold left. He told the secretary that if he prevailed in convincing you to go forward with getting rid of Castro, he would sponsor a constitutional amendment to allow anyone who has lived in this country continuously for at least fifty years to run for president, no matter their place of birth. Ian came here fifty five years ago at age six months."

"You can't prove any of that," Senator Hernandez said. "There's no way you could have taped what you've just said."

Schaffer shook his head. "Senator, you made the biggest mistakes of all. One day after Ian had Harold killed, you show up to lunch with Gato Canoso. You were so excited about telling him the good news and receiving his endorsement that you were not careful whom you shared it with. And yes, you are right. At that point, it would have been impossible for me to prove anything. Except for the fact that you still had a problem, the promise you made to Ian. The day after your lunch I heard about your meeting, so I had your phones added to those I was tapping."

Alex, Dee and Director Daly hung on to every word Schaffer said. Everyone else in the room knew that their time had come. "Now, Senator, for your grand finale." Schaffer turned to Speaker of the House Davis. "Since you didn't have the clout to get an amendment passed as you had promised, you contacted Davis. Of course, he too wants to be president, so he cut a side deal. If Ian jumped parties and ran with him during the next election, then he would ensure the amendment passes."

House Speaker Davis started to say something, but Schaffer cut him off. "Don't bother trying to deny it. Hernandez wanted to make sure all of you were on the same page, so he put you all on a conference call." He held up one of the jump drives. "I've got it all right here."

"You stupid motherfucker," Mackenzie blurted out.

Schaffer continued after him. "I can't believe you, Ian. Your attempt to have me killed wasn't any smarter."

"Well, I can fix that right now." Mackenzie lunged from his chair, knocking Schaffer to the floor. He clamped his hands around Schaffer's neck, squeezing as hard as he could. "I'm going to kill you my goddamned self!" he screamed.

Dee pushed the intercom. "Get in here now!"

Five Marines burst through the door with their M-16s. One of the president's Secret Servicemen knocked Mackenzie off Schaffer, and the leader of the Marine unit instantly hit him with a stun gun. He fell to the floor twitching helplessly. The other Marines had their guns pointed at each of the other four men in the room.

The president looked to his Secret Servicemen. "Cuff him, and get him out of my office. Make sure no one sees you leave. Take him to Norfolk. I'll have my SEALs ready to take him into custody."

They pulled Mackenzie from the floor. He could barely speak clearly, yet he persisted. "This isn't over, O'Grady. I'll be back and when I return, I'll kill you!"

The president cut him off. "Don't count on coming back, Ian. I'd like to send you to an area of the Amazon Jungle that the Discovery channel hasn't even found yet. But you wouldn't have any trouble surviving. You'd be surrounded by all your slimy relatives."

Alex waved his men out of the room. He turned his attention to Senator Hernandez and Speaker of the House Davis. "I would have no trouble drumming up conspiracy charges, so you two despicable slime have one of two choices. You can join Ian in prison, or you can resign by tomorrow morning. In addition, you can no longer run for any office, including dogcatcher. Let me remind you that there is no statute of limitations on conspiracy against the president. Both of you are accessories to Harold's murder as well. I don't want to subject the country to this scandal right now, but I won't hesitate bringing it up later. So, what's it going to be?" The president waited.

They both agreed to have their resignations to the proper authorities by morning. Alex waited for the room to clear. He pulled Schaffer aside. "Schaffer, your last official act as press secretary will be to deliver the bad news about the crash of the secretary of state's plane."

Schaffer looked confused. "But, Mr. President, I thought you were sending him to a military prison?"

"Prison would mean a trial. That bastard can afford any lawyer in the country, who would twist things where I don't want them to go. Even with all the evidence you've gathered on him, he could still end up in one of the Club Fed facilities. I'm not willing to take that chance."

Schaffer became confrontational. "He has to pay for what he did, Alex!"

Alex put his hand in the air, pausing Schaffer's speech. "And he will. I'd like to put the three of them in a cage together until they were all dead, but right now I've got to try and unite this country, which means sparing them from scandal."

Schaffer's balled his fists at his sides, as if he expected to fight. "You can't let him walk. If you do, Hernandez and Davis get off too. That's just not right!"

Alex took an unlit cigar from his desk. "No, it's not right. That's why I'm implementing plan two." Alex lifted the phone and called the SEAL team waiting in Norfolk. "I need a package dropped off in the Amazon. Yes, the jungle. Make sure the area is remote and the chute is in disrepair. We don't want this package making a return trip."

"So that's it? Hernandez and Davis walk?"

Alex looked at Schaffer through a cloud of cigar smoke. "Not exactly. Dee had a talk with me after your walk in the snow the other day. I took the liberty to put a few other teams in place. I must admit, after seeing your list of people for this meeting, I was a bit concerned. Dee must have figured it out because she had one car pick up both Hernandez and Davis. She's taking care of that right now. I hope you understand."

"I understand, Mr. President." Schaffer answered in a disgusted tone. "Unfortunately, lowlifes like them never seem to get it soon enough."

¤¤¤¤

The Secret Service agents escorted Mackenzie through the caverns of the White House. They loaded him into a jet-black van with heavily tinted windows and drove to Norfolk.

Three hours later, they arrived at Oceana Naval Base. They drove right onto the tarmac and into the belly of a waiting C-130. The plane closed and rolled down the tarmac before lifting into the air. During the flight, the SEALs fitted Ian with a parachute. They left his cuffs on. When they reached the jungles of South America, the bay doors opened. They dragged Mackenzie to the open door. For the first time, one of the SEALs spoke.

"This is the key to your cuffs." He held it in front of Mackenzie's face, then placed it in a pouch on Ian's vest. "This is a military issue K-bar. From now on, this is your weapon. And this is one day's worth of M.R.E.s." He held them in front of Mackenzie's eyes. "Tomorrow you will have to fend for yourself."

As the SEAL was about to put these items in the vest pouch, Mackenzie spat in his face.

The SEAL laughed and one by one tossed both items out the bay door. Then he stood and unhooked the parachute line. He placed the ripcord in Ian's hand. "Pull it or not. I don't give a shit."

The SEAL slapped Ian hard in the chest, knocking him backwards out of the bay door. About ten seconds later, the canopy of the chute opened. The parachute was painted camouflage to match the jungle. The gaping hole in the center caused him to descend at a rate too fast to survive.

"I hear snakes do well down there," the SEAL said, laughing. "Bastard should fit right in." The SEAL closed the door and the plane headed for home.

While en route one of the SEALs pulled a cell phone from his pocket and punched in a number. "Sir, your package has been delivered."

"Very well," Alex said, and started to hang up.

"Also, sir. When we left the office, we noticed that the sedan carrying Senator Hernandez and Speaker of the House Davis had an unfortunate accident with a cement mixer. There were no survivors."

"I just received the news. Sad. I've always heard cement mixers were prone to flip over. See me when you return." The president hung up.

Chapter
76

Two months later, Schaffer was back with the *Washington Post* reporting staff, and loving the freedom it afforded him.

Life was back to normal as far as he could tell. It was an unusually warm spring day in early March considering this was the first month D.C. had not seen snow in the past four months. When Joe asked Schaffer to go to Charlottesville to cover a story about a professor at the University of Virginia who encouraged his students to come to class in the nude, he saw it as an opportunity to let the top down on the 'Vette and get a little fresh air.

Something tugged at him all day long but he hadn't been able to put his finger on the source of his discomfort. Since Schaffer was leaving for Charlottesville in the morning, he decided to head in early. Joe was springing for a hotel room, and he had some minor packing to do. He put on a Charlie Rouche CD to take the edge off the day. The mellow jazz flowed from the speakers, relaxing him. Schaffer ran to the kitchen to grab a glass of Hendry Cab to speed up the relaxing process. When he pulled a glass from the cabinet, his eyes fell on the kitchen calendar. "March 11th. Shit, no wonder something's been tugging at me all day. Tomorrow is the anniversary of Harold Cosby's death." He poured the glass of wine and looked at his watch. It was 7 p.m.

Schaffer grabbed his keys and ran out of the house. Ten minutes later, he pulled up to a florist that was about to close. The lady inside let him in after making him beg a little first. Harold had commented once on how beautiful the tulips were at the White House in the spring, so Schaffer bought a dozen.

His alarm buzzed at 2 a.m. Just as he had one year earlier, he got up and got dressed. A few minutes later, Schaffer was on his way to the Lincoln Memorial. He arrived right on time, 3 a.m. and walked up the stairs this time. About half way up, he stopped and looked around. The sky was clear and it was considerably warmer than last year. When Schaffer reached the top step he instinctively paused, but there was no blood to meet him this time.

He walked over to where he found Harold and laid the tulips over the spot. "You can rest in peace now Harold, we got the bastards." Schaffer's words were sincere, but they still felt hollow to him. Officially, Harold's death was considered unsolved. Harold's wife and family would never know what really happened. Schaffer assumed it would be difficult for them to arrive at any sense of closure. What was worse, the bastards who caused all this would never spend one day in jail, except for Cordell. But Schaffer was able to keep his promise to Harold. He had found out who was responsible.

He went back home and got a few more hours sleep. At 9 a.m., Schaffer left the house. He stopped at Starbucks, grabbed a bran muffin and a double espresso, and then headed out of Washington on Rt. 29. He slid a cigar from his case, pinched off the end and pulled out his lighter. He flicked the lighter several times but it was low on fuel and refused to light. For just such an occasion, he carried a pack of wooden matches in his unused ashtray. Schaffer pulled out the matches and carefully opened the box. Two months ago, he'd stashed Castro's new address in the box. Things were calm enough now that he felt confident there would not be a problem if he made contact.

After lighting his cigar, Schaffer read the mile marker ahead. As he drew closer, he saw that he was ten miles outside of Warrenton. He was an hour and a half ahead of schedule, so he decided to stop. Taking the exit, Schaffer pulled into a gas station. The rumble of his engine invited anyone at the station to turn in the direction of his spotless car. The president had had the 'Vette fully restored when Schaffer became such a prominent public figure, so this time he didn't hesitate to turn the car off before going in.

Inside, he found just what he was looking for, a map of Warrenton. He picked up the map and placed it on the counter.

The attendant's toothy smile warmly greeted Schaffer. "Man, I haven't seen one that beautiful in years. I guess you're not from around here."

Schaffer looked up after pulling money from the pocket of his jeans. His eyes fixed on the attendant's sewn-on name. "Thanks, Bubba," Schaffer said without sarcasm. "I recently had her restored. Today was such a beautiful day that I decided to leave D.C. and go out for a drive."

"Are you looking for someplace in particular? 'Cause I can tell you how to get anywhere in town."

"No thanks, Bubba. I always collect maps from towns I stop in. It gives me something to remember the town by, Bubba." Schaffer couldn't resist saying the name again. He laid the money on the counter and picked up the map. Bubba gave him change, still wearing his gigantic, toothy smile.

✿✿✿✿

For the short time he had been in this country, Castro enjoyed his freedom for the first time in over forty years. He was free to come and go as he pleased without having guards constantly around him. Even with this freedom, it took him several weeks to leave the house. Survival taught him to be suspicious of everything and everybody. Why should he now trust the very host he had spent forty years denouncing? He'd received President Nicholas' word that no one would ever be informed of his true identity, but he remained skeptical. His self-imposed confinement to the house turned Castro into a C-Span addict. Using the computer, provided by the president, allowed him to purchase politically related books from Amazon.com's vast library and eliminated the probable language barrier that would have existed had he gone into a bookstore.

Quickly, he filled his new home with books and other comforts, thanks to the ten thousand dollar a month budget, generously supplied by the taxpayers of the United States. Castro spent his time indoors, reading and watching C-Span, with the exception of the early afternoon when he went out to work in his garden. Once outside, he pretended to be deaf, never speaking to anyone. It was easier than trying to explain where he came from, or how he chose to live in Warrenton. As lonely as his life may have seemed to others, he was happy to have the solitude. It allowed him to begin planning for his next conquest.

✿✿✿✿

Schaffer sat a few minutes more, planning his route, enjoying a cigar. He snapped a 500 mm zoom lens onto his Nikon F-5. The lens would give him a binocular effect in case he needed to locate any unwanted people creeping up on him. He started the car and sped off.

Ten minutes later, he sat across the street from the house whose address was on his paper. Placing the viewfinder to his eye, Schaffer scanned the area. The only person he saw was an old man working in a garden. Carefully, he examined each window in the house, looking for possible guards. He checked every house on the block, both sides of the street, but saw no one. Schaffer hoped no one was inside any of these houses calling the police suggesting that a peeping tom was in the area.

He sat five minutes longer, just in case the police showed up. During that time, he watched the man closely. Finally, he returned the camera to his original target to look for anyone who might have arrived from an area originally hidden from his view. There was a glowing light coming from a desk in one of the rooms. He turned the lens to better focus the camera, allowing himself to get a better look at the glowing computer screen. Unable to read the screen easily, Schaffer reached into his camera bag and got a 2-X tele-converter, which quickly snapped into place. The increased magnification brought the computer screen into clear view.

At the top of the twenty inch monitor, in large bold letters, was,

The New Revolution: Converting America

Schaffer read the first page of the document, which outlined plans to bring Communism to mainstream America. He found the document amusing and had to laugh at Castro's unproductive doggedness concerning his philosophy.

Stepping from the car, he put the camera on the seat, and walked across the street. Cautiously, he approached the man tenaciously pruning herbs in the garden. He thought it was strange that the man never looked up to see who was there. Schaffer's heart raced, trying to decide what to say as he looked down on the man. Taking a chance, he spoke in Spanish, and then in English, "¿El dia hermoso, no es, el Fidel? Beautiful day, isn't it, Fidel?"

Castro looked up and smiled.